ADV[...]FECT

"If you ha[...]*fect*, is the perfect place to start. It's a domestic mystery starring Tabitha Brewer, a suburban housewife who wakes up one morning to find her husband gone and her life changed forever. Tabitha is a wonderfully relatable heroine, and you'll cheer her on, despite the fact she has a few secrets—or maybe because of them! I love this book!"

—Lisa Scottoline, *New York Times* bestselling author

"With humor and elegance, Elizabeth LaBan explores the burden of perfection and the futility of seeking it in *Not Perfect*. Funny and real, poignant and charming, Tabitha is a delight as she falls from grace, from perfect mother and wife to pilfering food and money to keep her family afloat, until she realizes that perfect is overrated. This novel is a gift for anyone who has struggled to wear a mask or keep up an appearance, which is essentially all of us."

—Amulya Malladi, bestselling author of *A House for Happy Mothers* and *The Copenhagen Affair*

"*Not Perfect* is near perfect. Warm, but not cloying. Moral, but not preachy. A beautiful meditation on redemption."

—Kathy Cooperman, bestselling author of *Crimes Against a Book Club*

"*Not Perfect* is a captivating story about keeping up appearances, written with a perfect blend of humor and drama. Tabitha is delightfully human and flawed, and her struggle to preserve the balance of her world in the face of her missing husband (where *is* Stuart, anyway?) is highly relatable. A fun read that manages to also be thought-provoking."

—Kerry Anne King, author of *Closer Home* and *I Wish You Happy*

PRAISE FOR *PRETTY LITTLE WORLD*

"LaBan and DePino pen an engrossing work, rife with real familial and marital issues . . . This duo is one to watch. An excellent choice for fans of Emily Giffin and Jennifer Weiner."

—*Booklist*, Starred Review

"A wonderful commentary on community, family, friendship, and questioning what these values mean in our lives."

—*Library Journal*

"*Pretty Little World* is an intriguing novel about the walls individuals put up around themselves when the physical walls come down. LaBan and DePino navigate through the lives of three families in an engaging and unconventional way, and they are not afraid to hit on hard topics . . . An interesting story that competently tackles the concept of codependency and individuality."

—*RT Book Reviews*

"When the literal walls come down among neighbors in adjoining Philadelphia row houses, three young families have the chance to create their own urban Utopia. But can they pull it off? Elizabeth LaBan and Melissa DePino pack *Pretty Little World* full of gourmet meals, marital scandal, inquisitive neighbors, and friendships whose bonds are sorely tested. The result is a skilled, funny, and highly engaging examination of family, love, and marriage in the City of Brotherly Love. This book is a win."

—Meg Mitchell Moore, author of *The Admissions*

"Do good fences really make good neighbors? That's the question at the heart of LaBan and DePino's intriguing novel. Brimming with astute observations and chock full of surprises until the very last page, *Pretty Little World* offers a fresh, unexpected look at friendship and marriage."

—Camille Pagán, author of *Life and Other Near-Death Experiences*

"Hilarious, relatable, and surprisingly complex, the families in this engaging novel truly touched my heart. I laughed, I cried—I cringed!—but mostly I recognized their longing to feel true community in a world that often makes us feel so alone."

—Loretta Nyhan, author of *All the Good Parts*, *Empire Girls*, and *I'll Be Seeing You*

PRAISE FOR *THE RESTAURANT CRITIC'S WIFE*

"A tender, charming, and deliciously diverting story about love, marriage, and how your restaurant-review sausage gets made. *The Restaurant Critic's Wife* is compulsively readable and richly detailed, a guilt-free treat that will have you devouring every word."

—Jennifer Weiner, #1 *New York Times* bestselling author of *Good in Bed*, *Best Friends Forever*, and *Who Do You Love*

"Elizabeth LaBan's novel *The Restaurant Critic's Wife* stirs in love and intrigue making for a savory delight that pairs perfectly with your armchair. Prepare to be charmed!"

—Elin Hilderbrand, author of *The Rumor*

"A heartfelt and relatable look at a woman navigating the difficulties of marriage and motherhood—while struggling to maintain a sense of self. Written with charm, honesty, and an insider's eye into a usually hidden slice of the restaurant world, it's a winning recipe."

—Sarah Pekkanen, internationally bestselling author of *Things You Won't Say*

"In her debut novel for adults, Elizabeth LaBan cooks up a delectable buffet about motherhood, friendship, ambition, and romance (albeit one in need of a little more spice). She captures the essence of life with small children (smitten with a side of hysteria) and weaves a relatable, charming love story with the flair of an expert baker turning out a flawless lattice crust. LaBan's four-star story has the satisfying effect of a delicious meal shared with friends you can't wait to see again."

—Elisabeth Egan, author of *A Window Opens*

"Two things engage me when it comes to fiction—characters I want to spend more time with, and details, the juicier the better, from a world I'm curious about but not likely to ever experience. Elizabeth LaBan's novel *The Restaurant Critic's Wife* has both . . . The best part? Ms. LaBan really is a restaurant critic's wife. Her husband writes for *The Philadelphia Inquirer*—which means that the wonderful details in the book both ring true and occasionally are."

—New York Times, Motherlode

"Author LaBan (*The Tragedy Paper*), who is married to a restaurant critic, excellently makes the joys and difficulties of young motherhood feel real on the page. Readers who are in the thick of raising a young family will enjoy, as will foodies looking for insight into the restaurant world."

—Library Journal

"The narrative flows effortlessly, and the dialogue is engaging and evocative. Lila and Sam's love and devotion, despite expected bumps along the way, provides a sensitive look at rediscovering yourself and your marriage."

—*Publishers Weekly*

"Thoroughly entertaining."

—*People*

"LaBan's writing . . . is like a dish of smooth custard—straightforward and a treat to take in. The detailed meal descriptions are likely to spark some hunger pangs, and the spicy and sympathetic Lila makes a perfect meal companion."

—Washington Independent Review of Books

Not Perfect

ALSO BY ELIZABETH LABAN

The Restaurant Critic's Wife

Pretty Little World (with Melissa DePino)

Not Perfect

Elizabeth LaBan

This is a work of fiction. Names, characters, organizations, places, events, and incidents are either products of the author's imagination or are used fictitiously. Any resemblance to actual persons, living or dead, or actual events is purely coincidental.

Published by Lake Union Publishing, Seattle

www.apub.com

ISBN-13: 9781542049818 (paperback)
ISBN-10: 1542049814 (paperback)
ISBN-13: 9781477809228 (hardcover)
ISBN-10: 1477809228 (hardcover)

Cover design by Ginger Design

Printed in the United States of America

First Edition

For my mother

CHAPTER ONE

Tabitha Brewer listened for footsteps before pulling the small notebook out of the junk drawer. She leafed through the pages, seeing that each day had a slightly longer list, before she settled on yesterday's page. She hadn't had a chance to finish last night, and she thought doing it now might make her feel better. Something had to. She grabbed a pen that had no cap and wrote at the bottom of the page: *basil, two dollars*. She thought good basil might actually cost more, but that seemed like a fair compromise. *What else, what else?* Oh yeah, when her cousin took her out to lunch yesterday she put a whole roll of toilet paper into her bag. How much did a roll of toilet paper cost? Again, she wrote: *two dollars*. She heard someone coming toward the kitchen, feet padding on the fancy tile in the hall. She hurried to write the places she took the things from in the far-right column, so she could remember whom she owed, then added it up. Between the basil she found around the corner in a flower box, the toilet paper, and that one loaf of bread she took early yesterday morning that was just waiting in a huge brown-paper bag outside D'Angelo's on Twentieth Street, she wrote *seven dollars* at the bottom of the page, underlined it twice, and put the notebook back in the drawer.

"An everything bagel please," Fern said as she came in and took a seat in the kitchen. She was so polite that Tabitha wished she'd found a way to steal one for her.

"No everything bagels today, Fernie Bernie," she said, noticing that Fern's jeans were just slightly too short and had a hole starting in the knee where a teething puppy they had said hello to the other day had taken a bite. How much longer could she wear those?

"Then I'll take an anything bagel," Fern said.

"None of those either, sweetie," Tabitha said, coming over to kiss the top of her head. It was slightly greasy, and she knew she wasn't doing Fern any favors by having her shampoo every three days instead of every other. But what would she do when the shampoo ran out? They were already long out of conditioner. "How about some toast?"

"Okay," Fern sighed and groaned at the same time.

"Where's your brother?"

"Sleeping still," Fern said. "I don't think he wants to go to school today."

"Wait here one second," Tabitha said, sprinting out of the big kitchen, trying not to slip on the tile, and bumping right into Levi heading to the bathroom. She stopped short and took a deep breath, glad Fern was wrong. She didn't want to be late for her interview.

"Morning, Monkey," she said casually. "You okay?"

"Yup," he said. Just before he shut the door her eyes caught the elaborate vanity light over the sink. It was big and bright and cost a fortune. She wondered how many everything bagels she could get with the money they spent on that light fixture. Hundreds and hundreds.

Tabitha went back to the kitchen where Fern waited patiently. She opened the colorful ceramic bread box and pulled out a king-size loaf of Stroehmann white bread that she got for $1.99 at Walgreens yesterday, using change from the bottom of her purse. They ate the D'Angelo's loaf last night for dinner. She'd grilled it on the stove top, then topped it with chopped tomatoes and the stolen basil, the dregs of the fancy olive oil she and Stuart had bought at Zingerman's in Ann Arbor over a year ago, and a few drops of the precious balsamic vinegar they got on that same trip. She had to make that last.

She put two slices of the bland white bread in the toaster and waited. *Butter, shoot, there isn't much.* But then she remembered the pats of butter she took from the diner when she met her cousin. Did she write those down in the notebook? She couldn't remember. That didn't really count as stolen anyway. They were meant for the customers.

When Levi came in she had his toast waiting, so there was no discussion of what he couldn't have, what she was unable to give him. He ate it without a word. She took the plates from the polished granite island and put them in the sink, wondering where she could get some soap to do the dishes. She had run out last night. That was a hard one, people didn't just leave dish soap around. But maybe they did. She'd have to think of an excuse to stop by Rachel's house later. Rachel had extras of everything under that big sink.

"Come on, come on, come on," she said to the kids as she watched them slowly put on their shoes. Tabitha realized Fern's socks were mismatched but she didn't move to get matching ones. She tried to tamp down the anxiety she felt. She had to be across town by nine fifteen. Once she dropped the kids off at school, which was in the opposite direction, she'd have just under an hour to walk thirty-two blocks. *That should be no problem,* she told herself.

They were all quiet in the elevator, which, of course, was still as pristine and well kept as always—as it was the first day they rode in it, going to the seventh floor to see the apartment that she thought would mean they could finally relax, finally feel like they belonged together and were settled into their life.

The door pinged open and Fern ran for Mort, the morning doorman. He heard her coming and turned just in time to lift her by the waist and twirl her around. She smiled and giggled and leaned in for a hug. He was careful not to hug too closely, Tabitha could see, but Fern didn't notice. Really, Tabitha wouldn't mind. She trusted him. And obviously Fern was already starved for an adult male in her life. Levi, on the other hand, barely grumbled, "Good morning." Did that mean he was doing okay? That he wasn't craving something he didn't have?

They stepped out onto the sidewalk and looked across the street to Rittenhouse Square. The air was cool and smelled like fall as it always did in Philadelphia at this time of year, of crushed ginkgo nuts and woodsmoke swirling up one-hundred-and-fifty-year-old chimneys.

"I want to go this way!" Fern said, moving to cross the street and walk through the Square, which was only slightly out of their way.

"No way," Levi said, turning toward Spruce Street. "I don't want to be late."

Again Fern sighed and groaned at the same time, and Tabitha wondered if constantly not getting what she wanted would take a toll on her. She hoped not. They walked down to Spruce and headed west toward school. They saw lots of kids walking to Sutherfield, the neighborhood public school, with uniforms and collared shirts with the school name printed on them. Tabitha tried not to think about it, about the choices she and Stuart made. But that wasn't even the problem. As far as she could tell, school was paid for. At least Stuart did that. Sending the kids to a public school now wouldn't mean a refund of that private-school tuition. Nobody would hand her $50,000.

"What's up for you guys today?" she asked. They were going to the Larchwood School whether she liked it or not, whether she, herself, could afford it or not, so why give it any thought?

"Today is Sarina's birthday so we're having cupcakes," Fern said proudly. Sarina was her best friend. *Shoot.* That would probably mean a party at some point, and a present. *Shoot.*

"That sounds nice," Tabitha said. "What about you, Levi?"

"Nothing," he mumbled.

The difference between a fourth-grader and a seventh-grader seemed much bigger than three years. Tabitha wished she had someone to talk to about that, someone who cared about her kids as much as she did. But there was really only one other person in this whole world who fit into that category, and he was unreachable. Based on recent events, though, she wasn't even sure he fell into that category anymore, and that terrified her. At the gate Fern ran right to Sarina, who was wearing a birthday crown and huge, colorful sunglasses that spelled out **HAPPY BIRTHDAY**, then turned with a quick wave and was gone in the ocean of kids in the yard. Levi slunk off, no wave, no good-bye. Tabitha didn't linger. She turned and walked east on Lombard. At least it wasn't hot out. At least she didn't have to worry about being sweaty when she got there.

~

When Tabitha was two blocks from the building where her interview would be, she pulled her phone out of her pocket: 9:17. *Yikes.* She picked up the pace, not caring anymore about how she'd look, just wanting to not be too late. Who hired someone who was late for the interview? She should have taken a cab halfway. She still had a little credit on her card—though she was trying to save that for emergencies.

She got to the lobby and ran in, out of breath. Then she couldn't remember whom she was there to see; she'd set up so many random interviews lately. She fumbled with her phone, called up the email. Home Comforts. Right. Someone named Kirk Hutchins. She told the person at the front desk, who waved her through. No time for hair fixing or lipstick refreshing. Did it count as refreshing if she hadn't put lipstick on in over a week? She pushed "4" and waited. It was a slow, jumpy elevator, but she was glad to have a few seconds to herself. The doors opened slowly, like they were giving her a chance to change her mind. *"Flee while you still can,"* she imagined them saying to her.

But she didn't listen. She stepped out and looked left, then right, and there she saw a huge sign that read **Home Comforts** with big rocking chairs settled in what looked like a garden bed. She realized she wasn't even sure what service this company provided. Maybe it didn't matter. The ad was for a receptionist, she could do that. She could certainly greet people and answer phones. And whatever they did, she was pretty sure she wouldn't run into people she knew. That was how she picked her interviews—places people in her life wouldn't ever go. She would have gone farther—to the suburbs or the Northeast—but that would have required a commute, which would have required money. Also, she wouldn't want to be too far from the kids in case they needed her, not now that she was the only parent in town.

She pulled open one of the double glass doors and stopped. It was chaos. It sounded like three phones were ringing at once; every seat was taken in the waiting room, mostly, she noticed, by very old people. One man was standing and banging his cane. Another pounded the side of his walker. There didn't seem to be anyone in charge. She wanted to go back into the hall and take some time to research what this place was. A doctor's office? No, she wouldn't have picked that, too many germs. What was it?

She read the sign over the desk. **We Make It Possible for You to Stay Where You Belong—Your Home.** Right, that made sense. They provided in-home care for people who needed it, mostly old people, she guessed. How bad could that be? Obviously they were in desperate need of a receptionist. Maybe she'd actually get the job. So far she had gotten three rejections—a men's clothing store on South Street that catered to tourists, an offbeat movie theater, and a vegan bakery, though that last one had her worried she would run into people she knew. Better that she hadn't gotten it. Maybe this would be the one.

A man with bright blond hair walked quickly out of a back room right toward Tabitha.

"Are you here about the job?" he asked.

"Yes, I'm . . ."

"Thank goodness," he said, interrupting her, and waving a file around just out of her reach. "Everyone has called out today. I don't know who's going to do the interviews, nobody's even answering the phone."

The phone stopped ringing and it was quiet for the first time since Tabitha walked in.

"Do you have time for the interview?" Tabitha asked. "If not, I can come back tomorrow."

"No, no time for the interviews," he said. She wondered why he hadn't introduced himself. She assumed he was Kirk Hutchins. "But I think this is the most pressing." He thrust the file toward her, then looked around the room. "Yep, these people look okay for now. But that woman is home alone and waiting. Her son's called three times already—my cell! I tell them not to call my cell unless it's an emergency. So I guess he thinks it's an emergency. He's out of town."

Tabitha glanced toward the waiting faces, which were all turned in their direction. They were quiet now, too. What was going on here?

"I'm Tabitha Brewer by the way," she said, reaching out her hand for a shake.

He looked at her sternly.

"I know that," he said, half-heartedly shaking her hand. "The address is here, not far, take the bus if you have to, you can expense it, you know how that works. And call me when you get there. You have my cell, right?"

"No, actually, I don't because . . ."

"Let me write it on the file," he said. He leaned over and scribbled the numbers. Tabitha squinted to make sure she could read them. "Okay? Now go, quick, before the son calls again."

Tabitha looked behind the man to see if there might be someone else she could talk to, someone who might be more coherent. But there was no sign of anyone. She thought about calling out, *Hello? Anybody back there?* but she didn't, it wasn't worth it, this place was crazy.

"Listen, I . . ." she tried to say.

"Please, go, she's waiting," he said, pushing the folder into her stomach. She sighed, grabbed it, and walked out, back to the elevator. Should she call the office and reschedule? No, because no one would ever answer her call. She wasn't sure how she had gotten through in the first place. This was not an office she would want to work in, anyway. She would have to keep looking. She walked slowly out of the building and toward the cheap-looking coffee shop she passed on her way in. There were big windows and a counter in a double-U shape with spinning aqua stools. Tabitha could see the coffee in glass pitchers on a hot plate. That had to be cheaper than Starbucks down the street. And she hadn't had any coffee this morning. She hadn't quite decided what to do about that yet. Withdrawal would be hard, but she'd save a ton of money once she was off coffee. But what about the Advil she'd need in the process? She counted last night and there were ten left—that was five headache's worth, fewer if it was a bad headache that required three at once.

"How much for a cup?" she asked when she walked in. It was late, she'd missed the morning rush, so it was quiet. She almost said, *How much for a cuppa?* Maybe if she sounded like a tourist they would take pity on her. The server turned to look.

"Buck fifty," she said after a pause.

"Seventy-five cents for one cup, no refills?' Tabitha tried. She had been telling herself lately that you don't get what you don't ask for.

"Sure," the woman said, surprising Tabitha and going for the pitcher. She placed a cup in front of Tabitha and poured. Tabitha could see it was weak—it would probably taste like tea. But it smelled good.

"Thanks," she said.

"No problem," the server said. "And I'm happy to give you a refill. The place is empty."

"Thanks," Tabitha said again, hoping she had more than the three quarters she knew were in her bag so she could leave a tip, too. She took a sip, let it absorb into her body. Good. Withdrawal was not an option.

There was a newspaper on the counter, and as she reached for it she realized she'd been clutching the manila folder she meant to leave on the desk of the Home Comforts office. She put it down in front of her, opened it up. From the top of the first page the name NORA BARTON jumped out at her. Really, it startled her. Nora was her mother's name. It was a name she had rarely come upon except in relation to her mother. She kept reading. The woman was seventy-nine years old, a widow, lived in an apartment building on JFK Boulevard, not too far from there, actually closer to home for Tabitha. Her list of problems was divided by mental and physical. Mental: memory loss, confusion (frequently believed she was a nineteen-year-old girl), occasional agitation. Under physical it just said headaches. Tabitha looked through the other pages. That was it? Headaches? She probably didn't need any help today. But then in the comment section she read: *Nora needs company. When left alone she sits on the floor, thinking she is still a teenager, and becomes so stiff she sometimes needs paramedics to get her up. She vacillates between being happy and thinking she is at a picnic, and being distraught because she thinks the love of her life just broke up with her and left her in the park alone. Christina (night nurse) said she once found her sobbing, dehydrated, stiff and hungry after being alone for just a few hours. SHE CANNOT BE LEFT ALONE. If we can't provide service, we must call another agency.*

Tabitha picked up her phone and dialed the number scrawled on the folder. He must think she was going so he wouldn't call another agency. She waited while the phone rang, her precious coffee getting cold. It rang and rang. It didn't even go to voicemail. She hung up, looked through the folder again. She thought about going back up to the office to try to find Kirk, but something stopped her. Did this woman's name have to be Nora? She gulped the coffee and looked up to see the server waiting to pour another cup.

"Any chance I can get it to go?" Tabitha asked sheepishly.

The server sighed, then nodded.

"Sure," she said, "that will be seventy-five cents."

Tabitha fished around in her purse. She knew she had the coins in a pocket, and she found them easily, but there must be something else in there. She felt tissues, one tiny stick of gum. Her hand rested on a cufflink—pure gold. She had put it in there for a moment like this. And she realized there were more where that came from at home, in Stuart's still-very-full closet. She put the coins on the counter along with the cufflink. She knew she could keep it and try to sell it, and she planned to do that with some of the other stuff, but right now she did not want to only take, she wanted to try to give, too. So she left it. The server would probably just throw it away, think she was some crazy lady who was a bad tipper. But maybe she wouldn't. Maybe she'd get five or ten dollars for it, or even more from one of those gold-melting places. All Tabitha could do was leave it and hope.

CHAPTER TWO

Walk or cab it? Or wait for a bus? Tabitha was pretty sure she wasn't going to get reimbursed or paid for this—whatever it was. *A job? No, not a job.* She was still going to have to get a job, obviously. She certainly wasn't certified to do this and briefly wondered if she could possibly do more harm than good. She shook that off and decided to walk; she didn't want this detour to *cost* her money. Besides, if she took her time, there was the chance someone else would have arrived by the time she got there. That would be the best-case scenario.

Two blocks away from Nora's building her phone rang. She had that moment of grabbing for her phone, hoping it wasn't about one of the kids, then thinking hopefully it might be Kirk Hutchins calling her back. It was her best friend, Rachel.

"Hey, Rach," she said, slowing down—she hated talking in indoor public places: coffee shops, stores, lobbies—and would rather walk around the block five times instead to complete the conversation.

"I have a good one," Rachel said.

"A good what?"

"Joke!"

"Oh, okay—lay it on me," Tabitha said.

"What do you call a cow that just gave birth?"

"I don't know, what? Happy? Full of milk?"

"No! Decaffeinated!"

Tabitha laughed. "That's pretty funny," she said. "Another one in your cheese-joke arsenal?"

"Well, I have to say something while the customers are tasting and browsing," she said, referring to her job as head cheesemonger at Di Bruno Bros., a gourmet market near Rittenhouse Square.

"No you don't," Tabitha said, walking past the lobby entrance to the building. If she kept going she could be home in ten minutes.

"Well, anyway," Rachel said. "Where were you this morning? I thought you were coming to yoga."

Tabitha stopped walking. She'd completely forgotten. Usually she would text Rachel with an excuse, to avoid any questions. It wasn't like Tabitha to just not show up.

"Oh, sorry, I had a dentist appointment," she said casually. "I started having this awful feeling on the top of one of my bottom teeth, so I wanted to have it looked at."

"What did they say? Did you need X-rays? I know how you always refuse them."

"Oh, well, actually the X-ray machine was down, so now I have to go back. They didn't say much." Tabitha was a terrible liar.

"You missed a great class," Rachel said. "Maybe the best one yet. How about tomorrow?"

"Maybe," Tabitha said. She still had a reserve of six classes already paid for before she had to reenroll. She wanted to save them. But yoga did sound good.

Tabitha was now at the halfway point between Nora's building and her apartment. If she didn't turn back, she'd be home before she knew it, and then she'd never go. She stopped and glanced at the file again, pushed it open, and saw NORA BARTON. She turned around and headed back toward Nora.

"Are you there?" Rachel asked, clearly annoyed. "Did you hear what I said?"

"About yoga?"

"No, about the tasting."

"Oh, a tasting?" Tabitha asked, trying not to sound too excited.

"Yes, I said we're doing a goat tasting tonight at six, bring the kids. We'll have cheese and crackers but also other stuff: goat-cheese crepes, mini goat-cheese sliders. Can you come?"

"We'll be there," Tabitha said, sounding more enthusiastic than she meant to. She was hoping to have a chance to stop by Rachel's apartment to pilfer some dish soap, but a free dinner was better, much better. She didn't want to sound too eager, though, or Rachel was going to really start to wonder about her. "Let me just check with the kids and I'll call you back."

"Sounds good," Rachel said.

~

Tabitha tried not to think about her mother, or those horrible last three days of her mother's life, as she trudged back along the same path she had just walked. Instead, she kept her eyes on the storefronts, always thinking about what might be there for the taking—not shoplifting, of course—but what she was starting to think of as "light stealing." *Not much,* she realized as she got close to the building. It was huge. There must have been at least two hundred apartments, maybe more. She had walked by this place so many times but never had a reason to go inside. She entered the lobby, which reminded her of a shabby hotel. There were people sitting in various places, many of them on the older side, and she wondered if Nora could be here. She wouldn't know Nora if she tripped on her. She walked over to the desk. She was glad Nora didn't have a complicated last name that she would have to pretend to know how to pronounce.

"I'm here to care for Nora Barton," she said when the man smiled at her. She was ready with a million excuses—*Her usual nurse is out sick today. I'm from a different agency. Her son hired me*—but she didn't need any of them.

"You know where she is?" he asked.

Tabitha knew it was listed in the file, so she opened it and looked, not sure if that made her look more official or less, and even more unsure why she cared so much.

"Yes, I see here she's on the second floor, apartment 206."

"Elevator's over there," he said, pointing. "As far as I know, her door is always open."

Huh. That didn't seem safe, but maybe necessary?

"Thanks."

She took the elevator to the second floor and walked out directly toward Nora's apartment. It was right across from the elevator. Now that she was here she wanted to leave. This was crazy. This Nora was not her mother. She was not her responsibility. She was a stranger who would probably die soon anyway. She turned around and hit the "down" button for the elevator. But then she had an idea. Nora probably had dish soap. If she was sitting on the floor thinking she was a teenager having a picnic, it might not be that hard to take. *No,* she told herself. That was the lowest Tabitha had sunk yet. And even if she wrote it on her list to repay one day, Nora might not live long enough to be repaid.

When she turned back and put her hand on the doorknob, she told herself she was curious and wanted to see if there was anything she could do for Nora since she was here anyway, which was all true. The dish soap need was true, too, but she would get it some other way. She knocked lightly before turning the knob.

"Hello?" she called. She opened the door slowly, expecting to find some awful scene, but she was hit with the sweet smell of something baking. "Hello?" she called again.

"In here, dear," a voice called.

"Nora?"

"In here, dear," the voice said again.

Tabitha closed the door behind her, wondering if maybe someone else had gotten here to help since she'd left the Home Comforts office. She followed the smell and came upon a bright kitchen, more from the lights inside than the sun outside, and a woman standing at the stove holding a small muffin pan with six muffins.

"Would you like a cranberry muffin, dear?" the woman asked, not seeming to be at all surprised by the stranger who had just arrived at her apartment.

"Nora?" Tabitha asked slowly.

"You found me!" the woman said. Tabitha couldn't believe Nora was fully dressed, hair in place, baking—not sitting on the floor thinking it was sixty years ago.

"I'm Tabitha," she said. "The agency . . ."

"Yes, yes I know," she said. "They called to say someone new was coming today. What took you so long?"

Tabitha expected someone to come out from behind a door or sweep in from another room and tell her it was all a big joke, some reality-based television show about people who were looking for jobs and how far they were willing to go. Or maybe it was an attempt to catch people at their most desperate. Tabitha would be a good candidate for either of those setups.

"Come in, come in," Nora said, leading her into a big living room. A large table close to the window was beautifully set for two with china, a teapot, and a light-blue tablecloth. Nora seemed quite sturdy on her feet, and Tabitha continued to wonder what the heck was going on. But the muffins smelled so good, and she hadn't had anything yet besides the coffee. So she followed Nora to the table and dutifully sat down. She looked around the room and wondered where Nora sat when she thought there was a picnic going on. The room was tidy and clean. There didn't seem to be a single thing out of place. There were no pill bottles or pillows or even a rumpled throw blanket for that matter.

Nora handed Tabitha a muffin, which she ate in four bites. Then she handed her another one, pouring tea while Tabitha gobbled that one up, too.

"Aren't you going to have one?" Tabitha asked, wiping her mouth with the back of her hand.

"Oh no, I made these for you," she said. "Plus I have a bit of a headache."

Oh, okay, a headache. At least one thing went along with what Tabitha read in Nora's file.

"Can I get you anything?" Tabitha asked. "Maybe some Advil?"

"Yes dear, that would be lovely," Nora said, leaning back and closing her eyes. "On the kitchen counter please. Then we can play a game!" She opened her eyes and smiled.

Tabitha found the Advil just where Nora said it would be. She reached for a glass on an open shelf and saw the oven was still on. She turned it off. At least she was helping in some way. She poured out two Advil into her palm, wondering if she should slip two into her own pocket. That way she would have enough Advil to get through six headaches. But she didn't. Instead, she placed the bottle back on the counter, filled the glass with water from the tap, and went back to find Nora.

A Monopoly game was open and waiting for her. Nora did that quickly. Tabitha didn't particularly like Monopoly, but Nora seemed sweet. She could play for a few minutes. As she got closer, she saw stacks of money that didn't look like the usual Monopoly money—it looked much more real. Did Nora replace the fake money with more realistic fake money? But as she got even closer, it looked very real, so real that Tabitha thought it might be actual money: stacks and stacks of real money next to the Monopoly board. Then she saw five-hundred-dollar bills. *Do they even exist?* she wondered.

"I'll be right back," she said, handing Nora the pills and glass and going into the kitchen to google "$500 bills." She learned they do exist, but haven't been printed since 1945. She went back in and looked again at the game. The money was all still there: ones, fives, tens, twenties, fifties, one-hundred-dollar bills, and five-hundred-dollar bills.

"Can I fill your bank, dear?" Nora asked.

"Fill my bank?" Tabitha asked. She had to get out of there. Nora seemed fine. She was happy, now she'd had her Advil, the oven was off. "I have to go."

"No, dear, please play a little," Nora said, and for the first time Tabitha heard something other than playfulness in her voice. Sadness? Hopelessness? It sounded awfully familiar.

"Okay, just a little," Tabitha said, taking a seat across the board from Nora. It was all set up with the Scottie-dog piece ready to play on the Go space and the rest in a pile waiting for Tabitha to choose. She reached for the thimble. She felt she needed protection of some kind and this seemed like the best choice.

"I'll go first," Nora said, rolling the dice.

Tabitha couldn't stop looking at the money. She knew there should be fifteen-hundred dollars in front of her, if Nora had counted right. She fingered the dollar bills then went to the far left of her stash and picked up a five-hundred-dollar bill. It looked funny to her. Real but unreal. How hard would it be to take it? To drop two bills on the floor and come back up with only one, after pushing the other one into her shoe? Would Nora notice? Five hundred dollars would buy a lot of everything bagels. But then again, was there any way to *spend* a five-hundred-dollar bill today? Was that part of the setup?

"Your turn, dear," Nora said.

"I'm so sorry, but I have to go," Tabitha said quickly, standing up too fast and jostling the board. Nora's dog fell over onto its side.

"Okay, dear," Nora said matter-of-factly, righting the dog. For a very brief second, Tabitha felt slighted that Nora didn't ask her to play for just a little while longer, that she didn't seem to care anymore if Tabitha stayed or went, but then she told herself again that this was not her mother. Her mother was gone.

"Come back soon, dear," Nora called, picking up the dice and rolling. She moved the Scottie forward.

"Thank you," Tabitha said. "Thanks for the muffins."

"Speaking of," Nora said. "Please take the rest. I can't stand cranberries."

Tabitha hesitated, then went back to the table and lifted the muffin pan, which she could see was disposable.

"Take the whole thing," Nora said.

Tabitha hesitated again, even looked over her shoulder, wondering if there were cameras capturing this exchange. *"Will she or won't she take the muffins?"* A television host was whispering into the microphone in a control room somewhere. *"Well, folks, she takes the muffins. That's how desperate she is. But at least she didn't take the money."*

"Thanks again, Nora," she said.

She pulled the door closed and leaned against the wall while she waited for the elevator. She had to get a grip. Offered muffins were one thing, money was an entirely different animal. That could have been bad.

~

"What's for dinner?" Fern asked the minute she saw Tabitha in the schoolyard. *She must be so hungry.* Tabitha presented her with the muffin tin, four big cranberry muffins. Fern's eyes went wide, and kids swarmed around them, as they always did when there was food in a schoolyard. Tabitha had the urge to aggressively push them away. But Fern was parceling out the muffins, and the kids were cheering and skipping off. In the end, Fern had just one muffin to herself, and it took all of Tabitha's energy to not grab them all back.

"So what's for dinner?" Fern asked again in between crumbly bites. Her question didn't sound as urgent as it had a few minutes before.

"All things goat cheese," she answered, pushing Fern's hair out of her eyes.

"At home?" Fern asked.

"No, at Aunt Rachel's store," she said.

"Oh, that reminds me, they need you to bring a snack tomorrow. They want a cheese plate," Fern said. "With some nondairy alternatives."

If that weren't such an impossible request, Tabitha would have laughed. *With some nondairy alternatives? Why do a cheese plate in the first place?*

"I'll be right back," Tabitha said, leaving Fern in the yard.

She went through the school's front door and stepped into the lobby, feeling normal for the first time all day. Here she was just Tabitha Brewer, Fern and Levi's mom. She was not the poor little rich girl she now felt like out in the world or the recently abandoned wife.

"Tabitha!" Julie called to her. Julie was the head of the parents' association, one year into her two-year term. It seemed to Tabitha to be the most thankless job out there. Sure, she was acknowledged at all the meetings and luncheons, but really, she didn't get paid and she spent her days trying to find volunteers to help her with events that most people could live without.

"Julie!" Tabitha said back, hoping she sounded nicer than she felt.

"Did Fern tell you we need a cheese plate for the parent reception tomorrow? It's at lunch, after the string ensemble concert. I don't know how many parents will be present, hopefully a bunch, so make it nice, and make it feel like a meal. Okay? Baguettes are always a good addition, some fruit. Oh, and there has to be something for those who can't tolerate the dairy—hummus maybe?"

Tabitha just stared at her. Last year at this time she would have marched into Di Bruno Bros. and gathered all of that and more, charging whatever it cost—$100? $150?—to her credit card without a thought, telling herself it was a donation to the school. Now it felt like Julie was asking her to go to the moon and collect some moon rocks to bring back in time for lunch tomorrow.

"I'm so sorry—" she said, just as Julie spotted another potential target.

"Judy!" Julie called, even though Tabitha was in midsentence. *Can Judy gather the cheese plate?* Tabitha wondered.

"Thanks," Julie said back to Tabitha, as she walked over to Judy. Tabitha listened while she asked Judy if she could provide breakfast for the teachers during conferences next month, "Preferably something homemade."

Tabitha wandered back toward Fern. She knew almost every single adult she passed. Both Fern and Levi had been going to Larchwood since preschool, and that gave Tabitha great comfort. Of course, no one at the school had any idea what was going on. Would it be so bad to ask for help? She even turned slightly toward Esther, the warm third-grade teacher. Esther would never judge, she would help. If she knew what Tabitha was dealing with, Esther would probably buy her a dozen everything bagels and invite them over for a meal. She would offer them a big pot of beans and rice and tell Tabitha to take the rest home. It would likely be enough to feed them for days. But then Stuart's letter resurfaced in her mind and Tabitha walked away.

"Hey, Fernie Bernie, you ready to go?" Tabitha asked. Fern was sitting with Sarina, their backs against the side of the brick building. Sarina was still wearing her birthday crown, but it was wrinkled and ripped, and she looked tired. "Hi Sarina, happy birthday!"

"Thank you," the little girl said politely.

"Just five more minutes, Mom, please."

Tabitha smiled and pulled out her phone. She walked to the far corner of the yard and called Rachel.

"We're definitely in for the tasting tonight," Tabitha said when she answered. "So we should come hungry?"

"Yes, come very hungry."

"Okay, good," she said. "And I have a strange question. What happens to all the food that is past the sell-by date and you have to pull from the shelf? Cheese and stuff? Hummus?"

"Generally we put it in the staff room for the taking," she said, somewhat suspiciously, Tabitha thought. "Most of it's still totally fine to eat. Why do you ask?"

For the hundredth time since Stuart left, Tabitha thought about telling her the truth. It would be so much easier. She opened her mouth as if she might say something like, *Do you have a minute?* Or, *Can I tell you something?* But she didn't. She just couldn't.

"Fern is studying supermarket safety—how they date stuff, how they sometimes even redate items to give them more time on the shelf, how they determine how long it will be good," Tabitha said, cringing as she continued to lie to her best friend. "So I thought it would be interesting to see, maybe she could take a few things with her tonight that she can bring in tomorrow? Her teacher seems especially interested in food that is still good to eat but deemed not good enough to sell."

"Sure—there's a fridge with all that stuff, but I have to warn you, some of it has probably been there for too long. I'm the one who's supposed to clean it out. Hey, maybe Fern can help me later. Maybe she can bring some of the really moldy stuff in tomorrow. The kids will love to see it! It can turn some surprising colors!"

"Okay, sure, and maybe some not moldy stuff?"

"Tabitha, what is going on with you? I mean really, what is the deal?"

"What? Nothing. It's just this annoying assignment," Tabitha said, feeling a burn behind her eyes. She could hear Fern and Sarina laughing behind her. *Thank goodness for Sarina.*

"Okay, okay," Rachel said, backing off. "Be here by five forty-five. You don't want to miss the best dishes."

"We'll be there," Tabitha said, wondering what she could say to Fern to explain the fridge cleanout. "In fact, maybe we'll be early."

CHAPTER THREE

Tabitha woke up exactly seven minutes before the alarm was set to go off, just as she had done every day since Stuart left—well, really, just as she always did whenever Stuart wasn't at home. She had that brief moment when she realized Stuart wasn't there, had not come back in the middle of the night as he sometimes did from his long trips. Though, she had to admit, after almost two months, that moment was less and less surprising. She sat up, opened the drawer next to her, and pulled out another list. All her stupid lists. She blamed her mother for it. She always used to tell Tabitha that when she was stressed she should write it down and forget about it. Well, she could do the writing-it-down part, the forgetting about it wasn't so easy. And what would her mother have said about the constantly-referring-to-it part?

This wasn't a list of all the things she had stolen; it was a list of clues. Or at least a list of information. She hadn't started it right away. Those first few days she had been so shocked: shocked that Stuart had lied, letting her think he would still be there in the morning to continue the conversation . . . or, rather, the argument. She told the kids he was on a business trip, which he often was, and she waited. He would be back, she was sure of it. He wouldn't dare not be.

When five days had gone by, long enough to have her concerned, she started to consider what might be going on. The night before he left, she'd learned things that she never knew. Really, she saw a completely different side of him that night, one she had never seen during their marriage. Now, despite her efforts to find him, she still had no idea where he was.

She looked at the list.

Item number one: The Note.

The note was mostly the same as they always were, though of course completely different. The other notes, which he left when he embarked on a work trip, began with *My Dearest Tabitha*. The other notes were neatly written, almost like he had written a first draft and subsequently taken a long time to write them perfectly, prettily even. They usually fit nicely on the piece of paper, centered right in the middle. This one, the most recent one, began *Dear Tabby*. He did sometimes call her Tabby, when he was being playful, which was more and more rare as the years went on. Had he even called her Tabby since they had moved into this apartment? It was what he had called her when they first got together and into the beginning of their marriage. Her maiden name was Taylor, so growing up she was Tabby Taylor. Her parents wanted her to have a cute, perky name. When she married Stuart Brewer, they laughed. From a Taylor to a Brewer. The *Tabitha* came when the playfulness left. When had that been, exactly? But now again, with the most recent letter, *Dear Tabby*.

This note was scrawled, so messy that it was hard to read some of the words. It looked like it was written in a hurry, definitely not written and rewritten. She had folded the letter up so she didn't have to look at the last sentence every time she pulled it out along with the list, looking for clues. His other notes certainly didn't end the way this one did.

Item number two: No talking once he left. Cell phone already turned off, and no call from a landline.

The other times she could usually still reach him while he was traveling, before he got to Michigan's Upper Peninsula or whatever other far-flung place he was headed, where his lawyerly skills were needed and his clients resided mostly, it seemed, without cell-phone service. When she woke up and found a note, she would call and he would answer, either still in an airport or in a car. They would talk quickly, he would explain where he was going, real or not real, and she would let herself believe him and tuck it away, get through the next two or three weeks without him. She wanted to believe him, it was so much easier that way.

Item number three: No sex for four months, and then sex the night before he left.

This item was initially just as perplexing, though maybe not quite so now that she knew what she knew. They had never had a great sex life, but it seemed okay. They did it at all the times she thought they should—their wedding night, when they wanted to get pregnant, when too much time had gone by—but they were rarely spontaneous, rarely moved by a true sexual attraction. She had been aware that they hadn't done it in a long time, the longest they had ever gone as a married couple. But then the night before he left he came to her, and they had sex, good sex, or so she thought at the time. But that was when everything started, at least when her true awareness of it all began, and even though it was on her list, she wasn't quite ready to unravel that yet, though she was fairly certain it was one of the keys to where he was now.

Item number four: The last supper.

This item referred to the fact that he had not eaten dinner with them for weeks, months. He always had to work late, and their normal pattern was that Tabitha would eat with the kids and Stuart would eat at the office or on his way home. Only on weekends did they sometimes eat dinner together. The truth was, Tabitha didn't mind. It was easier to eat with just the kids. But the week leading up to what Tabitha was now thinking of as The Disappearance, Stuart came home for dinner every night. Every single night. He just showed up, looking drained and, now that she thought about it, somewhat shell-shocked. He wasn't demanding or even opinionated about what they ate—hot dogs, macaroni and cheese—he just slipped in, took his seat at the big wooden table in the kitchen, and ate with them. There was no discussion about what had changed or if it would continue. In the way she spent much of her marriage, she just didn't know what to expect, didn't know what Stuart was thinking, didn't feel like she knew Stuart well at all. And Tabitha was surprised to see that she liked his being there and looked forward to it. On the last night, a night that she did not, of course, know would be the last night, she began to think of Stuart when she decided what to cook for dinner. That evening she made cherry chicken—chicken rolled in bread crumbs and french-fried onions, topped with a sweet-and-sour dark-cherry sauce. It was Stuart's mother's family recipe from his childhood in Michigan, where cherries were abundant. He had eaten every bite, and when he was finished she thought for a second that she saw tears in his eyes. She still wondered if that was, in some way, what set everything in motion. *No,* she told herself now, *it was already set in motion, wasn't it?* She quickly glanced at the last three items.

Item number five: The fight.

Item number six: Stuart's Michigan T-shirt in the closet.

As she read through each one, she immediately went on to the next one. She just didn't have the energy to dissect these now. Also, there were other items she should put on the list, two in particular. She knew that. But she wasn't ready to yet.

Tabitha looked at the clock and realized it was late, very late, and the kids were going to miss the whistle. Where was Fern? She usually came in to get Tabitha up before getting herself ready. She was such a good girl. But where was she now? Tabitha put the notebook back in the drawer, covered it with random stationery and pencils. She didn't want one of the kids to find it. She went to Fern's bedroom. It was still dark. Tabitha pushed the door open and walked to the bed. Fern was out cold, breathing through her mouth as though congested. She reached out to touch her forehead. It was hot.

"Hey, Fernie Bernie," she said gently.

Fern stirred, then moaned.

"Hey, Fern, it's time to get up for school. Are you feeling okay?"

Tabitha thought about her day, what it would mean if Fern had to stay home sick. Thankfully, she didn't have a job interview, but she had planned to walk through the city to see what there might be for the taking. She had canceled her membership to the gym, which automatically charged her credit card each month. She still had the six yoga classes left, but after that, walking was going to be her only exercise. She might as well combine it with a hunting-and-gathering mission. She was sort of excited about what she might find. She had noticed a robust rosemary bush on Emerson Street.

Fern twisted, so that she was lying on her back, then quickly flipped over and threw up on the floor. It wasn't too much, and Tabitha tried not to be relieved that it might not require many paper towels and instead to be more concerned about what was going on with Fern. Fern retched again, and again, and Tabitha started to worry. She tried to sit her up a little, but Fern resisted, apparently unable to get any relief. Levi stumbled in.

"What's going on?"

"Fern's sick," Tabitha said, just as Fern stopped retching and curled into a ball of misery.

"Too much goat cheese," Levi said a little meanly, or maybe a lot meanly. "Who has just goat cheese for dinner?"

"No, it couldn't have been that. I feel fine. Do you feel fine?"

"I guess."

"So listen, I can't leave her here. Do you think you can call Dash and see if you can walk with him and his parents?"

"I'll be fine," Levi said. "I'm almost thirteen. I can walk to school alone."

Tabitha hesitated. Lately, she was always worried about these small decisions she made on her own without Stuart there to say, *"He'll be fine."* But really, if Stuart were there he would walk Levi to school, and this wouldn't even be a discussion.

"Okay," she said slowly. And for the first time in a long time, Levi smiled.

~

Levi Brewer was aware of the air hitting his face in a way he hadn't been before. Maybe because he was usually ducking his head, waiting for his mother to embarrass him. *Whatever.* He was finally free. He couldn't believe his luck. Well, he was sorry Fern felt bad, of course, but he was very happy to be out here alone. So many things ran through his mind as he stepped onto the sidewalk after nodding to Mort. He could skip school. He could run away. He could go to the train station instead of school and just see where he ended up. He could go looking for his father, who hadn't been home for so long and hadn't even bothered to call. Levi was fairly sure this was not normal. *No,* he told himself, he had to play it cool. If he pretty much did what he was supposed to do, then maybe he could walk alone more often. He should wait to do something crazy. He should take his time and plan it.

He hesitated before deciding to go his usual way, just in case his mother was watching him from the window, which was likely. But as soon as he knew he was out of sight, he turned north again, away from school, and walked up Nineteenth Street toward the Square. By now he would bet his mother had moved away from the window and gone back to Fern. He glanced at his phone. He was a little early, and really, he could be a little late, so he calculated that he had about twenty solid minutes to sit and think. He went to La Colombe, his father's favorite coffee place. He walked in slowly, scanning everyone. Of course he knew his father wasn't going to be here. There was no way he was just waiting two blocks from their apartment. He was supposed to be away, on a business trip. But something didn't seem right, no matter what his mother told him. He chose one of the few empty tables, farthest from the coffee bar, and sat down. He opened his backpack, then unzipped the deep inner pocket. This was where he kept the envelope.

He wondered if he dared pull it out. Everyone around him looked busy, so why not? He brought it out onto the table and held it. Then he lifted the flap, which was getting pretty ratty. He had to be careful. He didn't want it to rip. Inside there were five ten-dollar bills and a note. He could get coffee! He could do anything! But so far he hadn't spent a dollar of it; he hadn't broken a bill. He wanted to keep it just as his father had given it to him. He counted the bills, then let them settle back to the bottom of the envelope. He pulled out the note. It was on plain printer paper, and it looked like it was written quickly.

> *Dear Levi,*
> *I am so proud of you. Everything you're doing, especially for your bar mitzvah, is exactly what I hoped you would do. I have to go away for a while, and you're sleeping now so I don't want to bother you, but I wanted to tell you a few of my ideas. You are going to rock your Torah portion, I just know it, and I'll do whatever I can to help you with that. Also, as far as your community service project goes, I think you should do something to help the hungry. Feeding people is so basic, so important. There is an organization called The Family Meal that my old firm worked with, reach out to Nancy there if you want to. If you have something else in mind, go for it! I love you. I'll be thinking about you.*
> *Dad*

Levi pretty much had it memorized by now, but he read it over and over again, hoping something new would appear or that he would suddenly realize he had missed something, a clue or an extra page. But every time it was the same. Nice enough, but not what he really wanted to know. He wanted to know where his dad was and why he'd been gone so long. He wanted to know why he left this note instead of just calling from wherever he was to talk about it. He put the note back in the envelope, which he slipped into his backpack. He scanned the crowd one more time, and then he left, headed to school, told Rhona at the front desk that he was sorry he was a little late but his sister was sick and they had had a rocky morning. Rhona smiled and nodded. He could probably tell her anything and she would believe him. As he walked to his classroom, he ducked into the bathroom. He knew he was supposed to text his mother, she was probably waiting with her phone in her hand, but it was late, and she'd wonder what took him so long. Better to pretend he forgot. Before he put his phone away for the day, he found the tracking app, the one with orange stick figures, thinking he would turn on the notification part so he could see if his mother tried to track him, and then bust her since she promised she wouldn't do that. But as he was about to do it he had a better idea and turned off the tracking ability altogether. He just blocked it. *Ha.* Really, he could disappear at this point and nobody would know.

~

Tabitha had told Levi to text when he got to school, but he never did. She had already called the school to let them know Fern would be absent, and she didn't want to call the front desk again and draw attention to herself. So now she was going to have to spend the entire day just hoping he made it and would then get home safely. It was only 8:55 in the morning. It was going to be a long day.

She dialed Julie's number.

"Hi! It's Tabitha," she said. "I am so sorry, but Fern is really sick and I can't leave her, so I'm not going to be able to get the cheese plate together or the nondairy alternative." She couldn't resist throwing that back at her. Julie hesitated, then quickly thanked her and said she would go in search of another snack provider.

Tabitha had elaborated on her initial lie last night and told Fern that Rachel wanted to show her the rotting food because she thought it was cool. Rachel made a few references to a school assignment, but Fern just let them go by, looking vaguely confused. Tabitha had banked on the fact that Fern wouldn't correct Rachel, and she had been right. Tabitha was starting to think she was a better liar than she gave herself credit for. Fern had been polite and accepted some old cheese that Rachel offered her after the tasting. Tabitha brought it home and put it in the fridge, but even if it was still good enough to eat it looked awful, smashed and slightly discolored, with the faintest smell of ammonia. Tabitha had briefly thought about plating it nicely and dripping the luscious balsamic vinegar on the really bad spots, but it would have taken too much, the whole rest of the bottle maybe. Besides, she wouldn't dare present that to the school. Or maybe she should, then they would never ask her to bring food in again. But no, she wouldn't do it, despite her seemingly desperate state. She was especially glad now that Fern had eaten only the fresh cheese last night and not any from the possibly rotten pile. Rachel had wanted Fern to taste it, going along, Tabitha knew, with her phantom supermarket project, wanting her to see the different stages of cheese decline. Tabitha had wondered at the time if Rachel was onto her, if that was Rachel's way of pushing her to the point of having to confess there was no assignment, that it was something else. But Tabitha had said, "No, that wouldn't be necessary," and Rachel had let it go.

At noon Fern was still sleeping and Tabitha was going crazy—stuck at home with that stupid notebook demanding her attention and worrying about Levi making it to school. She tried for the tenth time that morning to use her Find My Friends app, but the cursor just spun and spun, never settling on a spot. She pushed on Stuart's face, right next to Levi's—she couldn't resist. And as it always did, as it had since the minute she realized he was gone, she got a big fat Can't be located.

Great, nobody could be located. She returned to her room, made the bed, and pulled the list out again.

Back to item number two—no talking once he left. She tried. It was only 7:00 a.m. when she found the note. And they had been up until just a little after midnight. She had crashed—in fact, now that she thought about it, he had encouraged her to take a Xanax that night, the evening had been so hard. She added that to the list—item number seven: The encouraged Xanax. So when she fell asleep, she was really asleep, and when she woke up she was groggy. Still, how far could he have gotten by then even if he'd left the house as soon as she'd conked out? She imagined he would be at the airport, or maybe on the other end of the flight, renting a car and starting that long drive north, assuming he was going north, which in this case made more sense than ever—though maybe not—there were so many unanswered questions. He could have been going south, or west, or east. Whatever the case, her calls kept going to voicemail, over and over again. Finally that stopped, and it just rang and rang. And of course he didn't call. Maybe he wasn't ever going to call her.

Part of the reason she wanted to reach him so much was the fight. She had thought they were going to be able to sort things out, together, to finally be honest with one another. And if she had been able to reach him that next morning, she would have asked him if he felt the same way. She could see now that he had given her the answer in the most dramatic way possible.

Stuart and Tabitha didn't fight much in their marriage. Did they really fight at all? That one time over the wedding cake—Stuart had wanted plain, plain, plain, and Tabitha had asked for a basket-weave design, something she had always imagined she would have on her wedding cake, ever since she was a little girl. He had finally given in, but he never embraced it. He never seemed to have liked their cake. She had had boyfriends along the way, before Stuart, with whom she had huge yelling fights, sometimes throwing things, blowouts that ended with one or the other storming away. One boyfriend had even left her alone at the movies and never came back. But she and Stuart never did anything like that. She had always thought it was a good thing—a stable home for the kids, and really, who had time to fight like that anyway? Now, though—now she wondered if the not fighting was the bad part. She started to think about the specifics of the fight; she even considered outlining it, but she wasn't ready. Not yet.

Next item on the list—the T-shirt in the closet. His University of Michigan shirt—maize and blue and old and tattered, something he never, ever traveled without. This time he did. It was still folded on the middle shelf in the closet. Why would he leave that? Or a better question might be: Why did he usually feel he had to take it? Well, now she could probably guess, but for years she had wondered about the significance of that shirt. After he left this time, she was shocked when she first saw it there. Now she went into the closet and touched it, as she often did lately. Usually, she didn't want to disturb it, but she pulled it out and looked at it. It was clean and creased where the folds were. She couldn't make any sense if it. Instead of folding it and putting it back in its place on the shelf, she brought it out to the bed with her, pulled back the covers, and shoved it to the bottom on Stuart's side. She was just pulling the comforter back into place when she heard Fern.

She half jogged to her room, a little afraid of what she was going to find. Fern was sitting up, glassy eyed and flushed. Tabitha went to her, felt her head again. It was even hotter. She knew she should call the pediatrician, but she didn't want to deal with the co-pay—the one that must be paid at the time of the visit. She got the thermometer and took Fern's temperature. *At least she isn't throwing up anymore,* Tabitha told herself, *for now.*

"Do you want a cold washcloth?" she asked, as they waited for the thermometer to beep.

Fern nodded. Her skin looked sweaty and her eyes kept shutting.

Finally they heard the beep-beep-beep. It read 103 degrees. Tabitha sighed with some relief. That was high, very high, but not emergency high. She fetched the cold washcloth and put it on Fern's forehead. Then she pulled out her phone and texted Holly, a mother of a girl in Fern's class at school who was an emergency room doctor at the local children's hospital. She was one of the most generous people Tabitha knew, never seeming to mind if anyone with kids contacted her with a question or concern. Even so, they were just becoming friends, and she didn't want to overstep anything. But really, what choice did she have?

Hi! It's Tabitha! I am so sorry to bother you, but Fern has a high fever—103—and I just wondered, is there anything going around right now?

She pressed "send" and waited. If Holly was working, it could be a long time. But right away she saw the bubbles indicating a response.

Oh no! I'm so sorry to hear that. But yes, there's a bug with a high fever, some vomiting. Not much to do but wait it out and keep her cool. A cool bath might help. Text if you need anything or if her fever goes up . . .

Tabitha texted back THANK YOU in all caps, and suddenly didn't feel so alone. She ran a cool bath, making sure it wasn't too cold, and eased Fern into it. She sat with her, reading *When You Reach Me*. They were loving the book, and Tabitha didn't want to waste it when Fern wasn't feeling well, but she perked up and listened. Tabitha heard her phone buzz, and she saw Holly had written again.

Keep her hydrated!

Tabitha nodded, like she was talking to Holly directly. When she got Fern out of the tub, into fresh pajamas, and watching television, she gave her a big glass of ice water, which Fern happily sipped. All was well for about two hours, until Levi didn't come home.

At 3:20 she became aware that it was time for him to be leaving school and decided to wait until 4:00 to text him. At 3:55 she could barely sit still. It took only fifteen, maybe twenty, minutes to get home, so even if she was being generous, he should be home by now. She looked out their window overlooking the Square. She could see down and across but not much to the left, which was where he would most likely be coming from.

What's your plan? she texted when she couldn't stand it anymore. No response. She tried to locate him with the app on her phone again, but still nothing. She looked at Stuart's face next to Levi's but didn't push on it. This, like so many other things, was not going to help her. She went to sit with Fern, who was much happier and much cooler. One crisis averted, another one just beginning. What was it that Rachel always said? That motherhood seemed like a very long game of Whac-A-Mole to her—that crazy game at the arcade where you had to keep whacking the moles to win. You just manage to control one and the next one pops up. Well, this certainly felt like that. She started to make a plan in her head. If he wasn't home by 4:15 she'd start calling around. But really, whom would she call? If he wasn't home by 4:30 she'd go looking for him. At 4:14 a text came in: at 7-11. A strange sound of relief started somewhere in her chest and escaped through her mouth. Fern looked at her but didn't say anything. Then she looked around.

"Where's Levi?" she asked.

"Seven-Eleven," Tabitha said, getting up. She needed a minute to herself. She went into the bedroom and pushed the door closed, stopping just short of clicking it shut. She pulled out the notebook and wrote one of the two things that all along she had not wanted to write, but now felt she had to. It was the easier one to write—there was no question about it. In the end, she thought, it would probably prove to be the most important clue of all.

Item number eight: The threat.

CHAPTER FOUR

With all the commotion of the day, Tabitha forgot about the appointment with the rabbi, which was surprising since she had been dreading it so much. Her iPhone pinged to remind her just as she opened the door to let Levi into the apartment. It was now five o'clock, and the appointment was at five thirty. She was trying so hard to not be mad, to not blow up at him. *How could you forget to text this morning? Didn't you know how worried I would be, literally all day? How could you so casually go to 7-Eleven and not tell me?* It was all simmering under the surface. But she did not plan to say any of it. Levi was suffering, too, she reminded herself. Also, he was okay, he was fine.

"What's that?" he asked in a pleasant-enough tone, as he walked over the threshold and into the apartment. He smelled like the outside, sunshine, and city grit. She realized she hadn't been out all day.

She glanced at her phone. Closed her eyes briefly.

"It's a reminder that we have a meeting with Rabbi Rosen in half an hour," she said through clenched teeth, the same teeth she had just willed to stay unclenched.

"No way," Levi said matter-of-factly. "I'm not going. I have homework."

"You are going," Tabitha said, thinking ahead to what this would mean. Getting the car from the good spot on Pine Street (they used to park in a garage, paying almost $300 a month, but she stopped that weeks ago and got the city parking permit that cost less than $50 a year). She would lose the spot and spend many minutes, possibly an hour, looking for a spot at the exact moment everyone was coming home from work for the night. Levi would beg to be dropped off, she would eventually give in, and by the time she got back the kids would be starving. *Shoot—dinner!* She hadn't even thought about dinner. *And Fern.* She couldn't take Fern. She could, almost, she was so much better. In another lifetime she would bundle her up and they would go together. She would read to her, and they would stop at Square on Square on the way home for the best wonton soup, or Dim Sum Garden for the best dumplings—whatever Fern felt she was up to. But the world didn't work that way anymore. At least their world didn't.

She heard Levi close his bedroom door hard, not quite a slam, but a deliberate close. She looked at Fern on the couch. She was so happy, so much better, watching an old Disney Channel DVD. Making her go out right now was not the right thing. But really, she should have called this morning. What was wrong with her? She hadn't even thought of it. She googled the number for the synagogue and called, but there was no answer. She had the rabbi's cell phone for emergencies. Was this an emergency? She found the contact information on her phone and called.

"Hello?" the rabbi said in his warm voice. Maybe talking to him would be a good thing. Maybe she shouldn't dread it so much.

"Rabbi Rosen, it's Tabitha Brewer," she said quickly. "We were set to come see you today, actually we are supposed to be there in about twenty minutes, but Fern just got sick, as we were walking out the door. And now I just don't think we're going to make it."

She sensed Fern's head turning in her direction. She should have gone into the kitchen to make this call. And, really, lying to a rabbi?

She didn't believe she'd be struck down exactly, but she knew it wasn't the best practice, and certainly, at the very least, it was a bad example.

"Not to worry, not to worry," the rabbi said kindly. "Please give Fern my best. I hope she feels much better soon. Will the same time next Monday work?"

"Yes," Tabitha said, not even checking her calendar. "That would be great. Thank you."

When she hung up, she wrote the appointment on five Post-it notes and placed them around the apartment, then she set a reminder on her phone for the morning of the appointment. There was no getting out of it now. It was the first big meeting with the rabbi to talk about Levi's upcoming bar mitzvah—barely months away at this point. He had been meeting with the cantor, but now they were supposed to talk about his speech, what was that called? Haftorah? D'var Torah? They sounded the same to her. And they were also going to talk about his community service project. She was happy to have him do this, it was always their plan, but without Stuart here, she felt like a fraud. She wasn't raised Jewish, even though her father was technically Jewish. Her mother was a Quaker and, despite the alleged gentleness of that religion, it definitely had the strongest arm and won out in her house growing up. Also, she hadn't told the rabbi, or anyone for that matter, that Stuart was gone. The rabbi expected Stuart to be there. *Please plan to have both parents attend,* the letter said. Well, at least she had another week to come up with an explanation for his absence. Maybe she'd call ahead a few days before and let them know. She'd probably use the same he's-away-on-a-business-trip excuse.

She avoided Fern's questioning looks as she went to Levi's room and knocked lightly.

"What?"

"Can I come in?" she called through the door, trying to sound as unmad as she could.

"I'm not going," he said.

"Can I please come in?" she tried again.

No answer. She took that as a *yes*, and pushed the door open. Levi was sitting at his desk reading a book. She looked closer and saw it was *Lord of the Flies*. His room was neat. For some reason that made her feel bad for him. She took a deep breath.

"Hey, I called the rabbi and moved it to next week," she said. "But we have to go then, okay? No more excuses."

Levi didn't say anything.

"Okay?"

"Will Dad be back by next week?" he asked.

"No," Tabitha said, then, "I don't think so. This time the business has been more intense than usual, you know that. I explained it to you. We'll get started, and Dad should be back well before the big day." *At least I hope so,* she thought, but didn't add. She wasn't even sure she did hope that. She wasn't sure what she hoped.

"I don't want to do it without Dad here," Levi said, still looking at his book.

Tabitha felt so mad she didn't know what to do. Not at Levi, at Stuart. When Levi pretended not to care, it was so much easier.

"Tell you what," Tabitha said. "Let's go meet with the rabbi next week, with or without Dad, and we'll try to figure things out. We have to talk about your speech and your service project."

"I already know what I want to do," Levi said, perking up a little.

"You do?" Tabitha never had a bat mitzvah, and she wasn't sure what the parameters were in choosing this sort of thing.

"I want to volunteer at a place called The Family Meal," he said. "Dad mentioned it a few times and it sounds cool."

"What do they do? What kind of organization is it?" she asked, walking over to his neatly made bed and sitting down.

"Can you just look it up?" Levi said, annoyed. She'd lost him. He didn't want to talk anymore. She never should have sat on his bed, giving the impression she planned to stay and chat.

"Sure," she said.

"I have to read," he said.

"Okay, I'm leaving."

"And what's for dinner?" he asked. "I'm starving."

Dinner. What was for dinner? She glanced at her watch. It was just five thirty now, she had time. And she wasn't even sure what Fern would be up to eating tonight. She left Levi without answering, took her laptop into the living room, and sat on the love seat across from Fern.

"How are you feeling, sweetie?" she asked.

"Much better."

Tabitha reached over to feel her forehead. It was cool.

She logged on to her computer and checked her email. Nothing. Then she went to Stuart's account. Or his old account. She had a feeling he had a new one, or else he'd cut off all ties to electronic mail. She wasn't sure which. About a month ago it occurred to her that she could get into his account. She knew, or thought she knew, some of the passwords he used frequently, and she was right. His Gmail account, which was the only one she knew about, the one he emailed her from when he emailed her, was easy. It took only two tries. The password was GoBlue1990—referring to the University of Michigan and the year he graduated. It was so obvious that once Tabitha was in she looked around for Stuart for a second. She wanted to say, *Really?*

Now she clicked the keys and held her breath as it loaded. There wasn't a single personal email since she last checked. Well, there was one—from a cousin who was just sending a save-the-date notice for a wedding in August. *August!* Who could think that far ahead at this point? She didn't even know what she was going to feed the kids for dinner, not to mention breakfast and lunch tomorrow. She thought, and not for the first time, that it might not have been such a good evolutionary plan to have to eat numerous times a day to stay alive.

An email from Brooks Brothers came up, and Starbucks. And then something from the local University of Michigan Alumni Association. The subject line read "Happy Hour." She clicked on it and saw there was a happy hour that night to "get psyched and sing a rousing round of 'The Victors'" in preparation for the football game on Saturday, when there would be another gathering to watch the game. "Hotdogs, mini burgers, tacos and more!" It went until six thirty. And it was at the Fox & Hound at Fifteenth and Spruce, three blocks away! She pushed her laptop shut.

"Will you guys be okay for a few minutes?" Tabitha asked Fern.

"Uh huh," she answered in a way that made Tabitha think she didn't hear her. Probably better that way, she could slip out and be back before Fern even realized she was gone.

She considered taking a chance and not telling Levi. If he was reading in his room, he might not notice. But that would be bad, completely irresponsible.

She trudged back to his door and knocked.

"What?"

"I'm going to run out for a few minutes," she said. "Will you open your door so you can hear Fern if she needs anything?"

"Is she still puking?" he asked with mild disgust in his voice.

"No, she hasn't for hours. I don't think she's going to anymore."

She heard footsteps, the door opened.

"Where are you going?" he asked.

"To pick up something for dinner," she said.

He looked at her suspiciously, furrowing his brows in a way that made her think of Stuart. She looked beyond him, to the window that overlooked the Square.

"Okay," he said. He sounded tired. "But be back soon. I'm starving. I'm so hungry I feel a little sick."

She went back down the hall and saw Levi's door close, then open again. She headed to her room and looked in the mirror. Did she do any brushing today? She thought not and brushed her hair and used a little baking soda on her teeth. She was saving the toothpaste for the kids. She pulled out her lipstick and gently brushed it over her lips. A little color was better than no color, but she didn't want to use too much. She put the silver tube back in her purse and walked out through the living room to the high-ceilinged foyer. She'd need some sort of container to gather the food. She headed back to the kitchen and looked through the drawers. The big Tupperware was a possibility if she brought a huge bag, but big ziplock bags were probably better. She couldn't find any new ones, but took an opened paper bag of sugar out of one and an opened bag of flour out of another, dumping both plastic bags out over the sink to get them as clean as possible. She pulled tiny pieces of tape off the dispenser and sealed the flour and sugar—she couldn't risk losing it or having the sugar get sticky from water or humidity.

"I'll be right back," she called but no one answered. She knew she looked awful. But who was going to go to a Michigan happy hour on a Tuesday anyway? It would be busy on Saturday, she was sure of it, those Michigan fans were over the top, but today? It didn't matter how she looked.

The air felt so good on her face that she considered not going and just walking around the Square a few times, maybe using a bit of the last of her credit to order that wonton soup. But she knew she shouldn't pass up a chance to get free food, and food that Levi would probably love.

It took just a few minutes to get there. She'd been here before, with Stuart, on a fall Saturday last year when the kids were both busy and she wanted to try to do something he liked, try to connect with him. So they came to the Michigan–Michigan State game. It had been so crowded they didn't even end up sitting together.

She walked in and was happy to see it wasn't full, though there were more people than she would have expected. It was a big place, with lots of young people standing around drinking. It was easy to spot the Michigan group—they were all wearing maize and blue. She could almost hear Stuart's voice in her head. *"They don't call it yellow,"* he would scold her if she ever made that mistake, which she did on purpose just to bug him. She looked down at her ratty red sweater. Ugh. There were holes along the bottom and a small coffee stain to the right side. Worse than that, though, even she knew red was the color of Michigan's arch rival, Ohio State. Well, it was just going to have to do. She wasn't trying to make any friends here, just get some food for her children.

But as she was about to head over to the buffet, a young dark-haired man stood on a chair and demanded their attention. Could she slip over while he was talking? Probably, but she decided not to take the chance. Instead she stood still and tried to cover up as much of her red sweater as she possibly could.

"Okay, so it's a big game on Saturday, and I just want to make sure we'll have a big turnout," he called into the group. "Can I see a show of hands from everyone who plans to be here?"

Everyone raised their hand except for Tabitha. They were really going to think she was in the wrong place, so she raised it. The young man nodded at her, then at the crowd, counting softly to himself.

"That should do it—but tell your friends. I mean, I really think they can feel our energy in Ann Arbor. They need us to gather to support them, so thank you for coming tonight, and please, each of you, bring at least one other person on Saturday, okay?"

Everyone cheered and said, "Yes!"

Tabitha mumbled, "Okay."

She thought it was over and began to inch toward the buffet. She saw pigs in a blanket and mini burgers. She hoped there were tacos. Levi loved tacos.

"Before you guys indulge in the great food provided by the Philadelphia chapter of the U of M Alumni Association, let's join in a rousing round of 'The Victors.' I want them to be able to hear us in New Jersey, okay?"

Tabitha felt like people were looking at her. Why hadn't she grabbed Stuart's abandoned T-shirt before she came over?

"One, two, you know what to do," the enthusiastic chapter leader called off.

Tabitha knew the words. She knew them as well as she knew that you never say *yellow* when talking about Michigan colors. She had no intention of participating, but found herself belting out the words: "Hail to the victors, valiant . . ." She thought at some point she'd lose the thread and forget a word, but she didn't. She managed to sing all the way through: ". . . The champions of the west, Go Blue!" She actually punched her fist up into the air as everyone else did with those last words. When it was over, she was a little sorry. It felt good to sing like that. Maybe she should join a choir or something.

Now she could go get the food, right? She had more than done her duty here—put some positive Michigan spirit out into the world. As she turned, she noticed a man looking at her. He was off to the side and just behind her. He was tall and clean cut, wearing khaki pants, a navy-blue sweatshirt with a big maize *M* on the front over what looked like a dress shirt and tie. He wore glasses, and as she looked at him he smiled at her, a big, warm smile.

"Hi!" she said, without thinking. It was just a reflex. She regretted it right away. She didn't want to talk to anyone.

"Nice sweater," he said, but he said it warmly. He had a very deep voice.

"Oh, yeah, I realized my mistake as soon as I got here," she said. "My daughter is home sick, but I didn't want to miss this, you know, I wanted to put out that good energy. So I ran out of the house, and I didn't change into my usual Michigan gear. I almost left, but, well, I wanted to be here."

"I'm sorry your daughter isn't feeling well." He said it like he cared.

Tabitha looked behind him. He seemed to be alone, unless his companion was in the bathroom. That was likely, in fact, since she realized they were waiting just outside the women's restroom.

"Yeah, thanks," Tabitha said. It was surprisingly nice to talk to a grown-up. "She's much better now. But it was touch and go. I wasn't sure I was going to be able to sneak out. When she was well enough that I could, I just ran, hence the poor choice of clothing. But I should be getting back."

"Oh, sure," he said. "Well I hope she continues to feel better."

"Thanks," she said again. "Me, too. I think she will."

Now Tabitha was stuck. She didn't want to walk out. She needed the food! She nodded awkwardly and ducked into the bathroom just on the other side of the man, hoping his person would come out before she did so he'd move away. But the bathroom was empty. Maybe his partner was in the men's room. Whatever the case, she hoped the man would be long gone when she came out. She checked her phone. It was already 6:12—the food was going to be gone in less than twenty minutes. She waited until 6:18 and went back out. The man was at the buffet, still alone. She took a deep breath and walked over. She picked up one of the tiny plates—why couldn't they have had bigger plates?—and filled it, smiling to the man as she passed him. He was studying the burgers—they all looked the same to Tabitha—and she skipped them as she gathered the pigs in a blanket and fries. She took the plate to a table, set it down, and went back twice more, filling each plate with the tacos she was happy to see there, and finally the burgers. Back at her table, she pulled out one of the bags and filled it, leaving it on her lap and hoping nobody was paying attention. The man was still at the buffet, clearly having a hard time deciding what to choose. She emptied the plates, put the bag in her purse, and decided to go back one more time. She didn't quite have enough, and they had just put out a new tray of something, she wasn't sure what.

The place was mostly cleared out now. If only that man weren't there, she could almost take it all. Why did she have to talk to him? But really, why did she care? She would probably never see him again. She approached the buffet. He had finally decided on one small burger and a handful of sweet potato fries.

"I don't eat a lot of meat," he said when he saw her. She jumped a tiny bit, which was ridiculous. "But this looks so good, I'm just going to do it."

"Good for you," she said, thinking about adding, *You only live once,* but decided against it.

"Mind if I join you?" he asked, turning and pointing toward her table. He saw the empty plates. "Oh, you ate that fast." He must have been paying more attention to what she was doing than she realized, but at least he missed the dumping it into bags and stealing it part.

"Yeah, I guess. I really have to go. I want to get back to my daughter, and my son just texted that he's starving," she lied, "I think I'm going to bring a little of this home for him."

"Good idea," the man said, like it was no big deal at all.

She turned her back to him and loaded another plate. The new tray was full of grilled chicken, which might be just the thing for Fern. It looked plain and juicy. There were also some fresh rolls. When Tabitha turned around again, she saw the man sitting at her table. Who was this guy? She had to walk by the table to reach the exit, and she had to figure out a way to transport the new plate. She couldn't just walk through the streets carrying it. Going to another table would seem strange. She walked over to him but didn't sit. Instead, she pulled the second empty bag out of her purse and put the plate inside.

"You come prepared," he said, but again, his tone was friendly, not accusing.

"I guess I do," she said.

"Will you be here on Saturday?" he asked.

"I don't know," she said, even though of course she had no intention of coming.

"If you think this spread is something, you should see it on game day. They really go all out," he said proudly. She thought back to that day she was here with Stuart. It was a game day. They must have had an incredible spread, but Tabitha hadn't even noticed. She hadn't been hungry, and she certainly hadn't been desperate for food. But she remembered that night for some reason. The plan was to have an early dinner at the steak house on the ground floor of their building, one of the best in the city. Sam Soto, the restaurant critic for *The Record*, gave it three swans, and rumor had it he was considering upping it to four, his highest rating. Stuart wanted to get there before that happened, before it was impossible to get a reservation. But, and now she almost laughed to herself, she remembered that she didn't even want to go. Did they have to have such a big dinner? There was always so much food left on their plates that they would end up taking home and never eating. *If only,* she thought to herself now. She noticed the man waiting patiently for her to respond to what he'd just said.

"Oh, well I will definitely try," she said. She slung her bag over her shoulder, trying not to crush the food already in there, trying not to think about what she wouldn't do to have a refrigerator full of leftovers from the fancy steak house. She held the covered plate in her hand. It was not a paper plate, and she worried someone might say something. "It was nice to meet you," she said.

"Well, we didn't really meet," he said, sitting back and smiling. "I'm Toby."

"Oh, right. I'm Tabitha."

"I graduated from U of M in 1989," he said. "How about you?"

She hesitated. She knew it was a big school, but that was one year before Stuart graduated. It was unlikely, but not impossible, that they could have known each other. She was getting in so much deeper than she meant to. She also graduated from college in 1990, though not from Michigan. She was taking too long to answer.

"I was class of 1994," she said, quickly calculating that he would have already graduated, so there was less likelihood of any potential crossover.

"I loved Ann Arbor," he said wistfully, like he was settling in for a long conversation.

"Oh, I'm so sorry, but I really have to go," she said. "Go Blue!"

"Go Blue!" he said back, smiling.

~

Now she was lying and stealing. But once she was out the door, she felt better. She wasn't really stealing the food—that was meant to be taken—but the plate? She probably shouldn't have taken that. She could bring it back. She'd wash it and bring it back the next time she came to take more food. Okay, now she really felt better. And did it even have to be a Michigan happy hour? It wasn't like anyone asked to see a card or anything, though there was the singing, which luckily she could keep up with, and that awkward conversation with that man. Another school's happy hour might be better. She would be ready with a graduation date next time. She could come up with a whole story. Though finding another one might be complicated. How would she know when they were? She would have to just show up and hope.

She walked by Harry, the evening doorman. He didn't say anything. He didn't even seem to think anything. Nobody would ever suspect that she would steal this food. He probably thought it was from a friend. She smiled and let her shoulders relax a little in the elevator.

That feeling didn't last long. She could hear it before she saw it or smelled it. Why didn't they text her? She ran to the door, losing some of the items on the plate as she jostled it open. Inside she found Levi sitting on the bathroom floor with his head in the toilet, and a sweet, sweet Fern sitting behind him, rubbing his back.

"You'll feel better soon, I promise," she said. "I did."

"Oh my gosh you guys, what happened?" Tabitha asked, trying not to sound panicked and hoping nobody ever found out about this. Talk about the worst mother in the world award! Talk about Whac-A-Mole.

"Well, we were each sitting where you left us—I was watching *Hannah Montana*, which is my favorite show, so I really didn't want to miss it, and Levi was reading in his room. I don't know what book he was reading. I think it was something about flies. Then Levi started to moan, so I went to see what was wrong," Fern explained like she was giving a police report or something where every detail was important. Tabitha eased to the floor and sat back on her heels. "When I went to his room, he was lying on the floor rolling around. He said his stomach hurt. I told him to come to the bathroom with me, because I know how that goes. I picked this bathroom so my bathroom wouldn't get dirty." She smiled for a second, forgetting what brought them to this point, then quickly adjusted back to a serious expression and returned to rubbing Levi's back. He was so quiet, Tabitha wondered if he'd fallen asleep, and just as she moved closer to him to check, he threw up, a big, violent push of vomit that mostly made it into the toilet bowl but also splattered a little onto her.

"Oh, Levi," she said gently, adding her hand to his back. "I'm so sorry you feel so bad."

"What is that smell?" he groaned.

She realized she'd placed her bag full of food, along with the plate, just outside the bathroom. She jumped up and rushed it to the kitchen, where she quickly washed her hands with hot water.

"Fern," she called.

Fern appeared eagerly at her side.

"I picked up some dinner," she said, keeping her voice down. "Do you want anything? How's your appetite?"

Fern chose just a roll, which Tabitha put on a plate, next to a big glass of ice water. She carefully wrapped and froze everything else, even the things that she didn't think would freeze well. She kept one slider out for herself, which she planned to eat later, and she spent the next two hours on the bathroom floor soothing Levi.

CHAPTER FIVE

It took two days to get back to normal. Or at least, it took two days to not be a sick house anymore—normal was a whole other story. Tabitha was so glad that the first day back at school for both kids coincided with another job interview. Fern could have gone back the day before, but it just seemed like too much work, so Tabitha let her stay home and watch television. As everyone felt better and hungrier, Tabitha defrosted portions of the food from the sports bar. Overall, it was pretty relaxing.

Tabitha took her time getting dressed. She settled on a suit that cost hundreds of dollars, shoes that cost almost that, and a designer silk blouse and scarf, which reminded her to check the website of the consignment store on Chestnut Street later. She had taken in a bunch of clothes to sell about a month ago, but so far nobody seemed to want any of her things. Maybe she should consign more.

She chose a necklace studded with colorful semiprecious stones and put on a full mouth of lipstick. It was a different kind of interview today. Instead of going to an office, she was meeting her interviewer for breakfast at the fancy restaurant on the second floor of the Rittenhouse

Hotel, since that was where he was staying. She was trying for a management position at a pest control company that was branching out into new cities, so she was meeting with the son of the company's founder. *It must be a lucrative business for him to stay at such a nice hotel, one of the nicest in the city. Or maybe he has family money.* She shook her head. It really didn't matter either way. Despite the elegance of the setting for the meeting, she knew she was being considered for a job that would basically be answering phones and coordinating appointments, but she didn't mind. It *was* a manager position, and they were offering a whopping eighteen dollars per hour, which seemed like quite a bit to her now. The office, which was still being built, would be on the fifteen-hundred block of South Street. She had walked by it last week. It wasn't impossible that someone she knew would come in there, but she was relying on the likelihood that most people she knew already had their pest control people. This company—unfortunately named "Ratface"—hopefully would appeal to the younger crowd of first-time homeowners.

"Ready?" Fern called into her room. Tabitha glanced at her watch. There was no way she was going to get them to school and be back in time for the meeting. What was she thinking?

"Coming," she called, taking one last look at herself. Nobody, in a million years, would ever think she was broke. She walked toward the door, then came back, pulled off the necklace and scarf. She realized she was dressing more for the restaurant and less for the interview. She didn't want to appear like she didn't need a job, or worse, that she was above it. She quickly pulled off her shoes and chose much less expensive ones. She wished she could start over, but there was no time for that.

Out in the living room she found Levi slumped over on the couch.

"You okay, Monkey man?" she asked gently. He jumped.

"Yeah, fine," he said, sitting up, then standing quickly.

"You sure?"

"Yeah, I'm fine."

"Okay, good, because I need you to do something for me," she said. Levi turned to her and raised his eyebrows. He probably thought she was going to ask him to run something down to the garbage chute. "Can you walk Fern to school today? Just the two of you? I have an interview this morning, and I'm afraid I won't make it in time if I walk you guys all the way to school."

"An interview?" he asked. "For what?"

"I told you, I'm thinking about going back to work," she said slowly, not at all sure that she had mentioned it. "This is just preliminary."

When Levi didn't say anything, she said, "So, do you think you can do that? Get the two of you to school safely?"

"Yeah, I can do that," he said, perking up. Tabitha thought she even saw a tiny smile start at the corners of his mouth. She shut her eyes for the briefest second, hoping she wasn't making a terrible mistake. What if something happened on the way there? What if Levi didn't help guide Fern across the street? *No,* she told herself, he would. She stopped short of asking him to text her when they got there. She knew that would just add to her anxiety, and probably a lot of phone checking during the interview. She watched as Levi helped Fern gather her backpack.

"Bye, Mommy," she said. Fern liked this, too, Tabitha could tell.

"Bye, sweet girl," she said, trying to act like this was perfectly normal. "Bye, Monkey."

When they left, she stood at the window and watched. It took a long time for them to get all the way downstairs and out. Once they were on the sidewalk, she could see there was some discussion about which way to go, and they ended up going slightly out of their way so they could walk through the Square, which she knew Levi was doing for Fern. Tabitha smiled a little as she watched, until she couldn't see them anymore. Now she had a whole twenty minutes to kill. She didn't know what to do with it. She had the time to change her outfit, but she didn't really feel like it anymore. She felt tired. She forced herself to move toward her bedroom, just to consider other clothing options, and as she did her phone rang. She glanced at the number but didn't recognize it.

"Hello?"

"Hello, I'd like to place an order, but not for right now, it's a lunch order."

Tabitha hesitated.

"Is that okay? Are you still doing lunch? I should have asked that first."

"Um," Tabitha said, not sure how much she wanted to say.

"Is this Tabitha's Pantry?" the male voice asked, sounding a little embarrassed. "Your app is glitchy today—it won't let me place an order, so I thought I would call. This is the number I had saved in my phone."

"Yes, it's Tabitha's Pantry," Tabitha said. Her former business had failed on so many levels. She would so much rather put her energy into it than any of these crazy jobs she was going for, but, of course, she couldn't, for too many reasons. "We aren't open."

"Oh, okay. Are you open tomorrow? We were talking about your amazing egg salad, and I wanted to order ten sandwiches. We're having lunch meetings all week. I know you did those boxed meals for dinner, do you do them for lunch, too?"

Tabitha shook her head and started to talk three different times before settling on her answer.

"I'm so sorry," she said. "We're closed for the foreseeable future." And she hung up. She looked at her phone like it was going to ring again, like the man on the other end wasn't going to take no for an answer. He was going to demand ten egg-salad boxed lunches. And she could do it. She would love to do it. She would gently place the eggs in the pot and let the cool water pour over them. She would boil them slowly. Once they were ready, peeled, and grated, she would mix them—her favorite part—with simple Hellmann's mayonnaise, salt, pepper, and dill. Everyone always asked *what* was in that egg salad? Customers were always guessing—*"Was it pickle juice?" "Was it nutmeg?"*

It had to be something magical, something nobody else would think of, but no, sometimes simple was the best thing; sometimes simple was perfection. Once the salad was made, she would build the sandwiches on the grainy bread from Metropolitan Bakery, just south of the Square. She had tried to make her own bread, and it had turned out fine, but there was nothing better than that bread from the bakery. After that, she would put together the boxes. Maybe she would make homemade chips, using her mandoline and small deep fryer, or a pasta salad with peppers and cherry tomatoes, using her favorite cider vinegar (of which there used to be plenty) from a tiny island in Canada, and then add a miniature brownie and chocolate chip cookie to each box as the finishing touch. Or she might make an Asian slaw and peanut butter cookies. At that last thought she leaned against the back of the couch and tried not to think about the worst day, the awful phone call. But was that the worst day? Or was the other terrible day, the one with her mother, actually the worst day? It was hard to know. Without all the information, it was impossible to know. And she didn't have all the information. Maybe she never would. Maybe it was better that way.

She glanced at her watch. She hoped against hope that Levi and Fern made it to school without incident. She thought about texting Levi, but didn't. Better to not text than to text and get no answer. She had to get him to agree to the Find My Friends app or look for another one that didn't require agreement on the part of the person you were trying to find. She sighed and walked out, not changing, not grabbing a sweater, not feeling ready at all.

As soon as she entered the hotel just across the Square, she was glad she hadn't dressed down too much. She walked by the doorman and smiled, feeling like she belonged, and she knew she looked the part. She decided to walk up the one flight instead of taking the elevator. It would give her more time. At the hostess stand she struggled to remember the man's name. Hiffen, that was it.

"I'm meeting Andrew Hiffen," she said.

"Right this way."

The restaurant was nearly empty. She spotted a young man sitting at one of the prime tables near the window, but she dismissed him. Far too young. Sure enough, though, it was her destination.

"What's the scariest thing you have ever seen, or that you could imagine seeing?" he asked, before she had a chance to sit down, before she even had a chance to introduce herself. It was that awkward moment when the hostess was pulling out the chair, and she didn't want to miss the seat. She settled into it and yanked it forward, a little too hard, nodding to the hostess.

"The scariest thing?" she repeated back to him. There were so many things in the running, honestly. But she knew what he wanted. She could play this game.

"The face of a rat," she said.

"Exactly."

How old could he possibly be? Twenty-five? On the one hand she hated that such a young person could have so much control over her fate, and on the other she thought he might be easy enough to please. She could figure out the answers that he hoped to get to his questions.

"I'm thinking of the French toast," he said, surprising her. She hadn't given the menu any thought; she was still gearing up to reach across the table and say, *Hi! I'm Tabitha Brewer.* But that moment had passed, so she let him lead the conversation.

"Good choice," she said warmly, looking at her menu. Maybe if she just supported everything he said, he'd give her the job.

He ordered, and she decided to get the same thing. She loved French toast. Her mouth watered just thinking about it. If only she could take some home for the kids. But she knew that wouldn't be the right thing to do. And she was sort of glad—it meant she could eat it all and not feel bad.

"I got in last night around nine," he said, without any prompting. "Was that the time you expected to get in?"

"More or less," he said.

She waited, but he didn't say anything else, and he certainly didn't ask anything about her career, her hopes and dreams, what she thought she might be able to contribute to the company. She was about to begin offering that information, unsolicited, when the food arrived. Tabitha willed herself to not worry about a single thing while she ate, and she pretty much succeeded. Andrew Hiffen ate only one piece of French toast, then inched his plate toward the middle of the table.

"So good," he said, surprising her again. For a second she had worried he didn't like it.

"Yes, it really is so good," she said.

"Let me just make a quick call," he said, pushing back from the table and getting up.

"Sure."

While he was gone, she slipped the one unopened miniature bottle of maple syrup and one tiny jar of blueberry jam into her purse. She thought for a brief second about eating his French toast, too, what a shame to let it go to waste, but then he was back. She wouldn't have done it anyway.

"So I talked to my father, and he said we still have a few other candidates to meet before we make the final decision," he said, not quite looking her in the eyes. *Shoot.* She thought this was going to be easy. "We hope to have everything in place in the next few weeks or so—a month at the latest."

"That sounds good," she said, trying to remain upbeat. "I would really like this job. I didn't have a chance to tell you, but I am very organized. I like talking to people on the phone. I'm good at creating and implementing schedules, even when things get busy, or I should say, especially when things get busy."

"I'll tell my father," he said. "I really hope it works out. You seem nice."

Nice was okay, she decided. You wanted *nice* when people called to hire you for pest control, right? *Capable* would have been better, probably, but she'd take *nice*.

The check arrived and he grabbed it. If nothing more, she got a good meal and a few things to take home.

"Thank you," she said. "I'll look forward to hearing from you."

She waited, but he didn't get up. He fidgeted a little.

"Should we go?" she asked.

"This is a little awkward, I guess," he said. "I'm meeting someone else after you, another candidate. That's why I ate only one piece of the French toast. I have to do this all over again. I told my father we shouldn't do it this way."

"Oh, that's okay," Tabitha said as she stood. She wanted him to continue to think she was nice. But she wondered once again if she'd ever get a job. "Well, thanks again."

As she walked toward the exit, she saw a young man coming toward them being led by the same hostess who had brought her to the table. As she was almost out of earshot, she heard Andrew ask the man, "What's the scariest thing you've ever seen?"

She shook her head and waited for the elevator with the uneasy feeling that he might not even know who she was after all of that, since she never said her name. Why hadn't she just said it to make sure? If he was going to sit there and meet with person after person, he'd never keep them all straight. She didn't feel like walking through the hotel this time. She pushed the button for the lobby, but when she got in it moved up instead of down. She hated elevators. The minute you put yourself in one, you were completely at its mercy. It could take you up instead of down; it could decide to trap you. She shook her head and breathed deeply as she felt panic beginning in her stomach. She closed her eyes and willed the elevator to arrive somewhere. Finally, it settled on the sixth floor, and even though Tabitha had no business on the sixth floor, she got out. She'd take the stairs. But as she walked down the long, elegant hall, she had an idea. Rooms should be getting cleaned. Housekeeping carts should be in the halls. There wasn't one on this floor, but she started looking, first down to five, then she decided to go up. Maybe they started high and descended. She walked up to the tenth floor. *Yup.* There was an unattended cart right there.

Once again, she was glad she had left most of her nice clothes on. If someone asked, she'd just say she ran out of shampoo. They'd assume she was a guest. But nobody came, and she took and took and took—bottles of shampoo, conditioner, body lotion. She thought about the towels but decided that was silly. She had those, even if they got ratty, they'd still be usable for a long time. She could fit just one roll of toilet paper into her bag on top of all the small bottles and still be able to shut it. She wished she had a bigger bag.

She went back down the steps and breezed outside, her arm over her bulging bag. At home, she distributed the tiny bottles throughout the apartment bathrooms, telling herself they could pretend they were at a hotel. She stored the rest in the linen closet. She was just about to change and go back to scanning the Internet for job openings when her doorbell rang. She froze. It was rare that her doorbell just rang, since usually the doorman called up to let her know who was here. It must be someone she knew well, but who? It must be a neighbor. That was the only thing that made sense. Mr. Wilson probably wanted to borrow an egg or something—and she didn't even have one. She had absolutely nothing extra. She formulated excuses in her head—*I was just about to go food shopping this morning,* or *We stopped eating eggs because we are all doing this strange vegan cleanse*—as she walked to the door and pulled it open. Rachel stood there wearing her yoga clothes, her royal-blue mat rolled up in a bag over her shoulder.

"Where were you?" she demanded, walking in before Tabitha had a chance to invite her.

"Oh shoot, I completely forgot. You know the kids were sick all week. This was their first day back. I just wasn't thinking about yoga."

"Really? Because when we talked two days ago you promised you would meet me there."

Rachel was right. She had promised. Why hadn't she remembered she had an interview and made up an excuse then? She could see Rachel eyeing her suspiciously. Clearly she was dressed for something.

"Have you already been out?" Rachel asked.

"Oh, yeah," Tabitha said. Obviously she couldn't tell her about the job interview. "I met my aunt for breakfast. She wants to start talking about preplanning her funeral." It was official, Tabitha was still the worst liar.

"Oh, that's weird," Rachel said, but Tabitha saw her soften a little. Preplanning a funeral was a touchy subject, since Tabitha's mother hadn't wanted to, then at the very last minute, just weeks before she was completely incapacitated, she did it all without Tabitha's help. She even planned and paid for a luncheon, choosing the menu items in advance. There was some strange tortilla soup and an even stranger butternut squash salad. Tabitha still thought that either the place got it wrong or her mother was trying to give her a message—but what could it have been?

"It is weird, but I guess it's good to get it out of the way, you know . . ."

"Yeah, I know," Rachel said soothingly. "So, what are you doing for the rest of the day? Do you want to have lunch?"

"Oh. Maybe," Tabitha said. The not having any money to pay for anything was getting tricky. "Can I call you in a little while? I just had a huge breakfast."

"Um, okay," Rachel said. "How about yoga tomorrow?"

"Yes, yoga tomorrow should work."

"Promise?"

"Yes, as long as the kids are fine, I promise."

Rachel moved toward the door, then came back and surprised Tabitha by sitting on the bench in the foyer.

"Tab, what is going on with you?"

It would be so easy to tell her everything. But then what would happen if Stuart came back? And what about the threat? She closed her eyes for a second and saw the bottom of the note: *"I'll tell them what you did."* She swayed to the left, feeling dizzy, and when she opened her eyes, Rachel was reaching out for her elbow. Tabitha smiled.

"I'm okay," she said. "Really, I just haven't had enough water today."

"See, it's exactly that sort of thing that makes me wonder about you, Tabitha," Rachel said.

Tabitha shook her head and brushed her hand through the air, as if to say it was nothing. Stuart's words still ran through her head, and she had to work hard to look normal. Would he follow through with it? She just couldn't take the chance. She didn't want anyone to know what she did, or what Stuart thought she did. Her biggest concern at this point was that the kids would hear about one or both of the things—that would be the worst possible outcome. *No,* she reminded herself, not the worst—that may have already happened—but the worst that could happen from this point forward in a long line of possibly terrible things. She'd wait it out. There was no other choice.

"I'm totally fine, I promise. It's just that the kids are each having a hard time—they miss Stuart, and it's always more chaotic when he's away. Things will settle down. I promise."

"Okay, well, I worry about you."

"Thank you. I know you do. But you don't have to."

Rachel stood up and pushed the yoga mat back over her shoulder. She went to the light switch near the door and pushed it up and down. Nothing happened.

"It's so dark in here," she said. "You should really replace the light bulbs."

"I'm working on it."

~

On Saturday morning everyone had someplace to go—Fern to Sarina's and Levi to his friend Butch's to play *Call of Duty* on Butch's PS4—so Tabitha happily made it to the yoga class without any problems, hoping she and Rachel might be able to spend the day together. After, though, Rachel had to get ready to go to work, and Tabitha wasn't sure what to do with herself. She went home and showered. She wasn't there thirty minutes before she couldn't stand being in the quiet apartment. The last thing she needed was time to sit around and think, so she decided to go to the Fox & Hound for the Michigan game. She told herself it was because of the food, but the truth was she was lonely and didn't really know where else to find company, especially with people who didn't know her and wouldn't ask the difficult questions. She pulled Stuart's T-shirt out from under the covers, smoothed out the wrinkles, and put it on over a white long-sleeved T-shirt and jeans. She chose her navy Converse.

It was so crowded when she got there that she thought about leaving. This was a mistake. She might be lonely, but this looked miserable. She was just turning around when she felt a hand on her shoulder.

"Hey, Tabitha!"

It was Henry, Stuart's good friend. They had lived in the same hall freshman year. She didn't know how to respond. What was she thinking, coming here?

"Hey, Henry! It's so nice to see you."

"Here for the big game?"

No, just here to steal some food, she thought. "Yeah, Stu's out of town, as you probably know, so I thought I would hold down the Michigan fort for both of us."

"Huh, that's unlike you," he said, squinting his eyes at her but not necessarily in an unfriendly way. "Doesn't he usually have to drag you here kicking and screaming?"

"Well, I wouldn't say 'kicking and screaming,'" Tabitha said.

"I was actually thinking of calling you," Henry said, and she was glad he was off the topic of why in the world she would come to watch a Michigan game in a sports bar when Stuart was away. Henry was such a slow talker. It bugged Tabitha. It had always bugged her. "I haven't heard from Stu in a while. I was getting a little worried. I've left him a few voicemails and an email. I thought for sure he'd be here for the big game."

"His trip keeps getting extended," she said, smiling and nodding, acting like it was no big deal. "He should be back soon. Those miners' contracts are always so complicated. And I think there was some talk of a strike. You know what that's like—right? The not-so-romantic life of a lawyer? Especially one who singlehandedly runs his own firm." She hoped Henry wouldn't guess that she was completely making stuff up, so she added some facts into the mix. It was true that Stuart started his own firm about seven years ago, after working at huge law firms for years before that. It was also true that he somehow became specialized in mining issues, representing the actual miners' unions in far-flung places around the country, something Tabitha always found a little odd. Whenever she asked Stuart why he chose this niche, he always waved her off, saying someone had to represent them. Now, though, with everything that she had learned before Stuart left, it didn't seem quite so odd. Calculated might be a better way to describe it.

Henry was just about to say something; it took him a long time, moving his head up then down, getting his tongue ready to talk. Why did Stuart like him so much? It took him five minutes to say what it would take someone who talked at a normal pace one minute to say. What a waste of time. She couldn't imagine what it would be like to live with him. As he opened his mouth, she spotted the man from the other night. His name was on the tip of her tongue. What was it? *Oh yeah, Toby.*

"Oh, hey, I see someone I want to say hi to," she said, before Henry got his next word out. "But I'll tell Stu to give you a call the next time I talk to him."

"Okay, but," Henry managed to say, but she was waving over her shoulder and walking toward Toby.

It took about two seconds for her to feel bad. Henry had always been kind to her. She didn't mean to be mean. She was just so afraid he'd catch her in this lie. She turned to him and smiled and waved again. He did the same back to her, looking perfectly happy. Good, at least she hadn't hurt his feelings.

Now she wondered if she could avoid Toby. She didn't really want to talk to him, she just wanted to get away from Henry. What if he asked her more about her time at Michigan? But Toby spotted her, too, and was heading her way.

"How's your daughter feeling?" he asked right away. He talked at a normal speed, which she appreciated more than usual. Also, he looked her right in the eyes, which felt good.

"It's so nice of you to remember. She's fine now, thank you," Tabitha said. "When I got back that night, my son had it. It was awful, but he's okay now, too."

"Did you hold up okay?" Toby asked, like he really cared. The feeling she got reminded her of the time shortly after Levi was born when she had an appointment with the dentist. It was her first time out of the house in weeks, it seemed, and definitely the first time out alone. Stuart was home with the baby. She was so tired, so unprepared for what she had gotten herself into. When the dentist took a seat next to her and asked how she was, like he really meant it, looking right at her and patting her warmly on her hand, she had started to cry. He had been so sincere. She had been starting to wonder if she didn't count anymore, if only the baby counted.

"You didn't get sick, did you?" Toby prompted her, and she hoped she hadn't looked dumb, spacing out.

"Oh, no, I've been fine, luckily," she said. "But thanks for asking."

It hadn't even occurred to her that she might get it. What would the kids have done then? She hadn't been really sick since Stuart left. *Ugh. Something else to worry about.*

"So, are you here with people?" Toby asked tentatively. "Or meeting someone?"

She felt her wedding ring, but not by touching it with her other hand. She sensed the weight of it on her finger. Funny how she could go days, weeks, without noticing it—it was like a part of her body, but now she was so aware of it that it took all her energy to not twist it.

"Nope," she said. "I'm here alone."

"Oh, okay. So am I. Do you want to try to get a seat?" Toby asked. "I see two in that far corner over there. And we'll still be able to see the television."

"Sure," she said. *Why not?*

Toby rushed ahead, hurdling the chairs in his way. He made it to the back corner and put a hand on each of the seats, hard, claiming them. Tabitha laughed.

"It's competitive around here," he said when she reached him. "And I don't mean just the game. You have to fight for your chairs."

"I can see that," she said, still smiling.

He swung a tattered black backpack off his shoulders and pulled two small banners out, which he attached to the tops of the seats. They were navy-blue and said **MICHIGAN**. He went back to his backpack and pulled out a bunch of ribbons and decorated what was still showing of the backs of the chairs. Finally, he yanked out a ziplock bag full of maize-and-blue confetti and threw it into the air around their general area. When he finished, he indicated that the seats were ready to be used. She just stared at him.

"I'm glad to see you're better dressed today," he said, his tone light.

"Oh, yeah, me too. That was a definite lapse in judgment."

"This crowd isn't quite as forgiving as the midweek crowd."

"Also, a little crazier," she said, picking up a tiny navy-blue piece of paper and tossing it at him. "Do you always carry decorations and confetti with you?"

"Oh, I should have explained that," he said. "I have a daughter. She's very into crafts. I'm always trying to come up with projects for her. Oh, that reminds me. I want to take a picture so she can see I appreciate and displayed her work."

Still feeling the weight of her own ring, which she realized was so stupid—she wasn't *doing anything*—she glanced at his left hand while he snapped the photo. No wedding band, but a very clear white line where it once sat while his hand was getting tan—so it couldn't have been that long ago that he took it off. But she guessed it wasn't that morning. She covered her ring with her right hand. She didn't want Toby to see it. She didn't want to have to answer more of his questions.

Toby fiddled with his phone, presumably sending his daughter the photo, then he sat and indicated that Tabitha should also sit. Before she had a chance to ask him anything, the head of the alumni association chapter, the same guy from the other night, stood on a tall table, demanding everyone's attention. Today he was covered from head to toe in maize and blue, with two scarves, one of each color, intertwined meticulously around his neck. Even his face was painted.

"Okay, Wolverines," he called. People were still talking.

"*Okay, Wolverines!*" he tried again, so loudly that a few people jumped.

"Before kickoff, I want to sing a rousing round of 'The Victors,'" he said. "This time I want them to be able to hear us in New York! No, better yet, I want them to be able to hear us in Ann Arbor! One, two, you know what to do . . ."

Once again, Tabitha found herself singing along. She was aware of Toby glancing at her, she assumed to see if she knew the words, to gauge how into it she was.

"Go Blue!" they all shouted at the end, fists in the air. She felt the place reverberate. And once again, she liked being a part of it. She went to a small liberal arts college in Hartford that had no school spirit at all. Well, none that she tapped into, anyway. Why hadn't she been more interested when Stuart was here? Why did she always fight him about this?

All eyes were on the many television sets around their section of the bar. Toby was quiet as he watched the coin toss, which Michigan won, then he groaned when they chose to kick the ball first.

"They should save it for the second half," he mumbled to himself.

Michigan kicked, the other team fumbled, and miraculously Michigan brought the ball to the twelve-yard line. The crowd went crazy. Tabitha felt her phone buzz. It was a text from Sarina's mom.

Hey! I don't want to alarm you but Fern seems a little off. Can you call me?

Tabitha sighed. She could feel her time here winding down. She hadn't even begun to think about how to package up some food. She texted back.

Yes—I'll call in 10! Thank you.

She watched the crowd as Michigan scored the first touchdown. There was another round of "The Victors," then everyone settled back into their seats.

"So what's your story?" Toby said at the exact moment she was about to say she had to go. Her story? *Ha!*

"You know what, I just got a text from my daughter's friend's mom," Tabitha said, holding up her phone as if for proof. "I guess Fern isn't feeling as well as I thought she was. I have to at least call, probably I have to go get her."

"Oh, okay," Toby said, clearly disappointed. "Same time, same place next week?"

She hesitated, and before she could answer, he smacked his forehead with his palm.

"Actually, I think my daughter has a birthday party to go to. I'm taking her, so . . ." he trailed off.

Part of her wanted to ask him what *his* story was, the other part thought it was better to not know. Honestly, wasn't her life complicated enough?

"Okay, well," she said, feeling her phone buzz again. Now Sarina's mom was calling her. "I have to take this."

She wound her way through the crowd, around the maze of chairs, and answered before she reached a quiet place.

"Hold on, hold on," she called into the phone. "Just leaving a noisy restaurant."

She pushed out onto Spruce Street and appreciated the quiet for a second.

"Hi, I'm here," she said.

"I'm so sorry to bother you," Kaye said. "But Fern just isn't herself today. I know you said she had been sick earlier this week. I don't know if it's that, or if she's just tired. She really doesn't seem to want to play, and she says her knee hurts. I don't think she injured it at all, at least not since she's been here, but when I tried to look at it she pulled it away. I thought I better call you."

"Thanks," Tabitha said, glancing at Toby through the window. He kept looking around like he expected her to come back. Or at least that's what she briefly imagined he was doing; he probably hadn't given her a second thought since she walked out. She was not thinking clearly. She took a deep breath. "I'll be right there."

CHAPTER SIX

Tabitha shook her head and closed her eyes as she listened to Fern coming down the hall toward the bathroom, again. She heard the hitch in her gait as Fern tried not to step heavily on her right leg. Tabitha had thought she was really asleep this time. She walked out into the hall.

"Does it still hurt?" Tabitha asked through the mostly closed door.

"Oh, no," Fern said quickly. "I just had to pee."

Tabitha made a face, but there was no one to see her make it. There was no one to widen her eyes at as if to say, *Clearly something is going on, what is her deal not admitting to it?*

"Well, I can hear you limping a little," Tabitha said gently. "It must hurt."

"No, it really doesn't," Fern said. Tabitha just stood and listened while Fern flushed and then ran the water. When she came out, she was standing tall on both legs, but Tabitha thought she saw her grimace.

"Well, will you do me a favor? Will you come sleep in my room tonight?" Tabitha asked. At least then Tabitha would be able to keep an eye on her.

"Okay," Fern said. She walked slowly, but without a limp, into Tabitha's bedroom and sat heavily on the bed.

"Let me see," Tabitha said, patting the place next to her on the bed.

"There's nothing to see," Fern said. "I told you, I think I twisted it a little at Sarina's, but it's much better now."

"Well, I'm glad about that," Tabitha said. "But let me see anyway."

Fern awkwardly brought her leg up so Tabitha could have a look. Really, it looked okay. Tabitha couldn't figure it out. She had given her Advil but she wasn't sure it had helped, and now she couldn't get a straight answer out of her. She'd try a little Tylenol. Maybe that would help her sleep. She knew it was okay to alternate doses of Advil with Tylenol when pain was really bad; sometimes they'd had to do that when Fern was smaller and had earaches. Fern still couldn't swallow pills, so Tabitha hunted for the liquid Children's Tylenol. She looked in her medicine cabinet first, then her travel bag, and finally the medicine cabinet in the bathroom Fern usually used, but she was pretty sure she wouldn't have left it there. And she was right. On her way back to her room, she glanced under Levi's door. His light was out. She felt completely trapped. She couldn't go out and leave them alone, she didn't even have money to buy more Children's Tylenol. Could she give Fern adult Tylenol? She didn't think so, and besides, she would never be able to get it down.

Tabitha walked back into her room empty-handed, wishing someone else could be the grown-up for a while, and saw Fern was fast asleep. She was afraid to move her, even an inch, so she went around to the other side of the bed, Stuart's side, and got in. She lay there with the lights on, hoping Fern wouldn't wake up, hoping her knee would feel better in the morning. She needed to get up to turn out the lights. In one minute, she'd do it.

~

"Get up, it's so late," Levi said, standing over her. She looked around. Fern had curled into a ball, but left her leg straight, and was still sleeping.

"Shhh," she said to Levi, putting her finger to her lips.

"No, she has to get up, too," he said, exasperated. "We're already late for school."

Fern opened her eyes and immediately started to whimper, leaning over her knee, which was probably stiff. As soon as she got her bearings, she was quiet and shook her head a little.

"It's okay," Fern said. "I was just having a bad dream."

It was alarming to Tabitha that even in sleep Fern didn't bend her knee. It must be much worse than she was letting on.

"Levi, you go get ready, I'll call and say you're coming but going to be late," she said. "I have to make sure Fern is okay."

Fern did not seem to be okay. Tabitha was absolutely sure that she was trying not to cry. Tabitha looked at her leg. It looked red in a way it hadn't yesterday. She reached out to see if it felt warm, and it did. She got a cool, wet washcloth, which she handed to Fern, but Fern refused to use it; she just kept saying that she was okay.

"Let me just call school," Tabitha said. "I'll be right back."

"Okay," Fern said. Tabitha was sure she was sniffling a little. Was that from trying not to cry, or did she have a cold? Might she have a virus that settled in her knee? Tabitha thought she'd heard of that happening before. She went to the bathroom, just a few feet away, and slowly closed the door to make her call.

"Larchwood School," a woman's voice said.

"Rhona?" Tabitha asked, hopefully.

"Yes?"

"It's Tabitha. Brewer."

"Oh, Tabitha, I was just about to call you. The kids aren't here yet," she said.

Tabitha pulled the phone away from her ear and glanced at the time. It was almost quarter to ten. She had no idea it was so late.

"Yeah, sorry, we overslept," she said. "Levi is coming—he'll just be late, obviously. I wanted to ask you about Fern. She's having pain in her knee. It looks okay to me, maybe a little red, but she didn't injure it in any obvious way. Can I bring her in to see Monica?"

Tabitha knew the answer. She'd been to enough committee meetings to know using the school nurse this way was out of the question, something that was completely frowned upon. But she'd do anything at this point to have Fern looked at, and avoiding the co-pay at the pediatrician's office would be helpful, too. In fact, she regretted asking. If she had driven Fern to school, she could have pretended it came on suddenly when she got there, and Fern could have gone to the nurse. Too late for that now. Fern would never have agreed to it anyway.

"Hold on," Rhona said, surprising Tabitha. While she waited, she peeked out the door and saw Fern testing putting weight on her leg. Finally, Rhona came back. "Hey, sorry, I just wanted to ask Monica since she was right here, but I'm sorry to say that won't work. Monica suggested a warm bath and also to call your pediatrician. You know how it is, if it happens separate from school, Monica can't look at them. But I really hope Fern feels better soon."

"Thanks for asking," Tabitha said. "It seemed worth a shot. I hate to have Fern miss more school—since she was just out with that stomach bug. Also, I called our pediatrician and they have a wait, so . . ."

"Oh, how long is the wait?" Rhona asked.

"I don't know," Tabitha said. "I'll call back now."

"Good idea," Rhona said. "And I'll keep an eye out for Levi."

After hanging up, Tabitha punched in the numbers for Stuart's cell phone. It connected, the name STUART came right up, and it rang. Once, twice, three times. Now was when it would normally go to voicemail but no, it didn't. It kept ringing, and Tabitha wanted to scream, *Where are you! How could you just disappear like this!* There wasn't even a place to deposit a message that he might listen to later. There was just empty space. Didn't he wonder what was going on with his children?

With her? She pushed the red button to stop the call and went into her messages. She texted him something she had never thought to text him before. If he didn't respond to this, he wouldn't respond to anything. She clenched her teeth, which she knew would give her a headache within the hour, so she unclenched them. She looked at her phone, at the message waiting to be written, and she typed 9-1-1. Then she pushed "send."

Somehow, she thought if she really got desperate, if she couldn't stand it anymore and wrote the worst possible, most frightening message, Stuart would respond. To her, 911 meant something was very wrong, someone could be in serious trouble. It was far worse than a painful knee and being late for school. Still, she felt fine about sending it. But then nothing happened. It looked like it was moving toward being delivered, but there was no confirmation. She shook the phone up and down, waiting for the tiny word of satisfaction—Delivered—to appear below her text, but it didn't. The words *no cell-phone service* ran through her head. She sank to the floor and waited a minute, maybe two. Then she got up and went back to her bedroom.

"Fern, let me just check on Levi, okay?" she said. "You aren't going to school today, so just sit tight. We're going to figure this out."

Tabitha found Levi at the front door, his hand on the knob. She wanted to say, *Really? Were you just gonna leave?* But she didn't. All she wanted was for him to get to school okay.

"I spoke to Rhona," Tabitha said. "She knows you're coming."

"Okay."

"Please be careful," Tabitha said. She had a moment of thinking better of it, calling him back, and taking him in a cab. Somehow, it seemed, he had gone from being walked every day to being totally on his own. Was that what the phrase "he grew up overnight" meant? She hoped not. She walked out into the hall and waited while the elevator made its way to their floor.

"Bye," she called as he got in, and the doors closed.

She went back to Fern without even taking her usual perch by the window to see him leave the building and guess which route he'd take.

Now Fern was sitting up, her back against the head of the bed, a pillow under her knee. Maybe she was the smartest one of all. Tabitha hadn't thought to elevate it. She had the television on, and seemed peaceful enough. Maybe Tabitha should have tried harder to get her to school? No, this was okay.

"It feels even better than before," Fern said sweetly. "But I think a little rest might help."

"It's a good day to rest," Tabitha said, feeling a touch of relief. By tomorrow it would be fine, she was sure. Most things that hurt just needed a little rest.

"You hungry?" she asked.

Fern nodded, mesmerized by the television.

Tabitha went into the kitchen and stood frozen. She wanted to text 911 over and over again to Stuart. *911—our daughter is in pain. 911—we have no food. 911—where the hell are you?* She looked through the cabinets and found crackers. She hoped there might be some cheese. There was—manchego—which she sliced thinly, laid on the crackers, and drizzled with the fancy balsamic (Fern's favorite). There was only about a half inch left in the bottle.

She took the plate in to Fern, who immediately started munching on it. She actually seemed fine.

"Do you want to try to go to school for the afternoon?" If she could get her there before lunch, that would be good. The school provided great lunches, all part of the tuition, so that was already paid for. Tabitha hated to have Fern miss that. Here it would just be more crackers—there wasn't even much cheese left.

"I don't know, maybe," she said, finishing the crackers and using her finger to dab up every last drop of the vinegar. Tabitha had been hoping she would leave a little, but she couldn't blame her. Tabitha could wait until lunch. What she did need was coffee. She'd started using thin, white socks as filters and just a tiny bit of coffee each day, forming her own version of a Melitta drip coffeemaker. It was weak, but enough to get her through. As the hot water soaked through the grinds and cotton and dripped into a mug, her phone beeped. *Stuart?* She rushed to look, but it was just a reminder. The reminder about the meeting with the rabbi. Today. And she hadn't even warned Levi about it. Despite all her Post-it notes, she hadn't remembered. She had gotten so used to seeing them there, she didn't even notice them anymore. She shook her head. They couldn't possibly miss it again.

~

It turned out Fern did not want to go to school in the afternoon. She wanted to eat cheese and crackers with balsamic vinegar—Tabitha was now sorry that she even introduced the balsamic today—and watch movies. After a warm bath, though, her leg seemed much better. Tabitha suspected it was still sore based on the way Fern walked to the bathroom. When Levi came in at a little after four o'clock, Tabitha was almost afraid to tell him.

"We have the meeting with the rabbi today," she said, as casually as she could.

"No way," he said.

"Well, we have to go, we missed last week," she said. *911—our son is having a bar mitzvah soon and it isn't going well!* "The rabbi is expecting us."

"Okay," Levi said.

"Okay?" she asked, surprised by his turnaround.

"Yeah, okay," he said. "Then you can tell Dad about it, and he'll have to come home. If we're working on my bar mitzvah, he has to be here."

"Right," Tabitha said. "That makes sense."

~

Fern agreed to stay home and lie in Tabitha's bed. Tabitha and Levi headed to the car, which was parked on Pine Street in a good spot. She tried not to think about finding another spot when they returned from the meeting as she eased the car out into traffic.

When they got to the synagogue, Tabitha felt like she always did: that this was a nice place, but she didn't really belong. The building was soothing with its art on the walls, carpet on the stairs, and the smell of prayer books in the air. But she worried someone would ask her a question she couldn't answer—like: *"What were the ten plagues?"* or *"Why did Moses part the Red Sea?"* Or ask her to say the Shehecheyanu. They checked in, walked up the two flights to the rabbi's office, and waited outside. The door was closed, and Tabitha thought it was proper etiquette to wait instead of knocking. But five, then ten minutes went by, and nothing happened. Levi was getting restless. Finally, the door opened.

"Oh, you're here," the rabbi said kindly. "I was just going to come looking for you."

So they should have knocked.

"Please, come in," he said.

They followed him into his big office, which was at least as soothing as the rest of the building, and sat around a table.

"Should we wait?" Rabbi Rosen asked.

"Wait?" Tabitha asked.

"For Stuart," he said, pointing toward the one empty seat. For some reason, the image of Toby decorating the chair at the sports bar and throwing confetti around it came to her mind. She took a deep breath.

"He isn't coming," she said. "I am so sorry I didn't let you know sooner. He's on an extended business trip."

"Oh, I see," the rabbi said. Then he looked at Levi. "Do you want to reschedule for another time, when he's back?"

"Sure," Levi said.

Once again, Tabitha felt like she was in quicksand. *911—I can't lie like this anymore!*

"It might be a while," she said quickly. "The miners' unions are having a really hard time."

"Okay then," Rabbi Rosen said, threading his hands together and placing them gently in his lap. "Let's get started, and you guys can fill Stuart in when you talk to him."

Levi shot Tabitha a look, which she caught out of the corner of her eye. She just kept looking at the rabbi, nodding and smiling. He smiled and nodded back. Surely he'd run a meeting with just one parent before. Surely he'd witnessed the fallout from a broken family.

"I want to accomplish three things during this meeting," the rabbi said. He put three fingers into the air. "First, your project, that should be set and you should get going with that right away. Second, and even more important, your D'var Torah, or your speech, talking about your Torah portion, what it means to you, and how your service project fits into it all. That is also the time to thank everyone who has helped you along the way. And finally, three, I want to make sure you're comfortable with your Torah portion itself." As the rabbi listed each item, he pointed to a different finger.

Tabitha sat tensely on the edge of her seat. All those tasks seemed impossible to her. She tried to think of something to say, something that would sound knowledgeable and helpful. When she got home she'd learn the Shehecheyanu.

"I know what I want to do for my service project," Levi said, and Tabitha was hugely relieved that someone else was talking. "I want to volunteer at The Family Meal."

"Ah, that's a great organization," the rabbi said. Tabitha sat back and let their words swim around her. They worked it all out, and it seemed like she almost didn't have to be there. If Stuart were there, how involved would he be? Would he be trading Yiddish words and bits of knowledge with the rabbi? Was this better, letting Levi take the lead? Maybe it wasn't awful. They came up with a plan: how many hours Levi should spend with The Family Meal, what his basic speech would be, and when he should meet with the rabbi again with a complete draft, and they established that, yes, Levi was comfortable with his Torah portion. Tabitha hadn't even heard him practice it, though she wouldn't know what was right and what wasn't anyway.

"You're in great shape, Levi," the rabbi said kindly, reaching across the table to shake Levi's hand. "Your next meeting should be with the cantor. Just call to set that up. Will you just give me a minute with your mom?"

"Sure," Levi said. He jumped up and walked toward the door. Tabitha saw him pull his phone out of his pocket just before the door closed behind him.

"So," the rabbi said, leaning in toward Tabitha. "How is this process working for you?" He stopped short of saying that she was awfully quiet, but she could hear it there, hovering over them.

"It's working," she hesitated. "Well."

"Levi seems to be in great shape," Rabbi Rosen said. "He's right on track. And The Family Meal is a superb place to give his time. I just want to make sure you don't have any questions."

Twenty things ran through her mind. Where was Stuart? How were they going to do this? What was the terrible thing he thought she did? Was there any way to ever get away from it, make amends?

"Not really," she said, not quite meeting the rabbi's eyes. He nodded kindly, patted Tabitha's arm.

"I'm always here if you need me," he said.

When Tabitha met Levi in the hall, he was excited.

"We're going to The Family Meal on Sunday," he said. "I just called. The lady who started it answered. Her name is Nancy. She was so nice. She said they have a new group of families coming in on Sunday, so it's perfect. We have to be there at three. We're going to serve them dinner and help clean up. We have to wear white shirts and black pants. Next time we're going to help cook. We all have to go. You, me, and Fern, and Dad if he's back."

"Great," Tabitha said, meaning it. With all of her stealing, she'd be happy to do something nice for someone.

CHAPTER SEVEN

For the first time since her mother had died, Tabitha wished she could talk to her, and it surprised her. She once saw an article on Facebook about the relationships daughters have with their mothers through the years. She had seen it when her mother was the sickest, the least like her old self. The article listed different ages—age five: can't get enough of your mother; age fifteen: can't stand your mother. It went on to talk about when daughters had kids of their own they would finally understand their mothers and appreciate everything they'd done. Then age sixty—when the mothers were presumably dead and gone—the daughters would do anything to talk to their mothers. At the time Tabitha thought, *No.* She was ready to let go. She was so spent. Her mother was draining so much out of her, and all Tabitha wanted to do was be with Fern and Levi, and in theory Stuart, though now she wondered how much of a factor he really was. When she had read the Facebook post, she thought the article had missed a phase of life, when, around age forty or forty-five, your mother will be sick. You will be stuck in an impossible middle situation: caring for your kids, caring for your mom, and the one person who used to be there for *you* will be an endless fountain of needs herself. Needs that you know you are duty bound to take care of. Needs that you wished you wanted to take care of, only you are just one person, and one person can only do so much. This phase of the relationship would be defined as "the daughters will have a strong desire to be rid of their mothers." But it wasn't in the article. Was Tabitha alone in this? She couldn't be.

But now she wished she could pick up the phone and call her mother. She'd say, *Hi, it's me.* And her mother would say, *"Hi, sweetie pie,"* as she always did, no matter what age Tabitha was. She wasn't even sure what she wanted from her. To ask her for help? Advice? Until her mother had gotten sick, she had always been the person Tabitha went to first. But then her mother had turned into a baby, introducing Tabitha to people as *her* mother, which Tabitha hated more than anything. It hurt her to be around her mother—this wasn't her mother anymore, it was someone else, like a body imposter. And it got so hard to be nice, almost impossible. And she hated that, too.

She thought back to that dinner more than six years ago. It was the exact moment when everything started to change, but it took a while to understand what was going on. They were talking about New York, and Tabitha's mother thought Yonkers was part of the City, not part of Westchester. Tabitha was shocked at the time; her mother had always been so sharp, and she got really frustrated with her. What was wrong with her? She had lived in Westchester County for thirty years before moving to Pennsylvania! Her mother had gotten flustered, suddenly she wasn't sure. Tabitha had no idea it was all a blueprint for everything that was going to unfold over the next few years—her mother's getting more and more confused, Tabitha's getting more and more mean. There was also the emphysema from all those years of smoking, the forgetting to use the oxygen or to turn off the oxygen when she cooked, and the impossibility of keeping track of her medicine. Once, Tabitha's mother had taken double the proper dose of steroids for an entire month before anyone realized. Or worse, the inability to open the top of the pill bottle and never telling anyone, so that after days of not taking her medicine, she would be so sick she would need to be rushed to the ER, and Tabitha would spend endless days at the hospital with her, trying to get her well enough to go home, so they could do it all over again.

"We have to go," Levi said, coming into the dark kitchen, startling her. "Nancy said we should be there by three."

Tabitha stopped herself from saying *Nancy, Nancy, Nancy* in a mean voice, the way Jan had said, *"Marcia, Marcia, Marcia"* on *The Brady Bunch*. All Levi talked about lately was The Family Meal and how Nancy told him how important it was for him to know and use the kids' first names, how that gave them self-esteem. Wow, maybe Tabitha was just mean overall. Mean to her mother, mean to her son, mean to a woman who was trying to feed the hungry. Just mean. Maybe that's why Stuart did the things he did. Maybe that's why he left. But she knew that wasn't true. As more time went by, she feared she had very little to do with why Stuart disappeared. She worried she didn't factor very prominently into many of his choices at all.

"Okay, Monkey man," she said soothingly. "I'm ready."

She looked around for her purse and her phone, checked that she had her car key.

"Fern!" she called.

There was no response.

"Fern!" she called again.

"Come on!" Levi said. "It's for my bar mitzvah!" He made it sound like he was leaving to save the world. Tabitha knew it was because Stuart was always so excited about Levi's bar mitzvah, so into it. If Levi ever uttered the words to Stuart about anything that might someday prepare him for his bar mitzvah, Stuart always gave him his full attention. Tabitha didn't care as much about the actual bar mitzvah, she never really had. But she was relieved to see Levi caring about something. She sighed and went looking for Fern. She found her in her room, sitting with her back against her bed, one leg bent, and the other one, the bad one, as Tabitha had now come to consider it, stretched out and twisted ever so slightly outward.

"Hi sweetie," she said, imagining the ghost of her mother finishing her sentence with *"pie."* "We have to get going for Levi's project."

"Do I have to go?" she asked. "I stayed home that other day. I'm old enough. I just want to stay home."

"Absolutely not," Tabitha said. "That was an exception. Plus, you aren't just coming because I don't want you to be home alone. You're coming because you are part of the project. The whole family is supposed to participate."

"Daddy isn't participating," she said.

"That's true, but he would if he were home," Tabitha said.

Fern sighed and groaned, then moved in a funny way, putting weight on her good leg and swinging the other one around, then leaning heavily on her bed as she stood up.

"Does it still hurt?" Tabitha asked. It had seemed a little better, less inflamed and less sensitive, so she was just hoping it would go away. But now she wasn't so sure. She was ready to take Fern to the doctor, had even called and left a message for the triage nurse, but the second it seemed to be getting better and not worse, she let it go. When the nurse called back, she tried her best to describe what was going on with Fern's leg, but she definitely downplayed it and too easily accepted the nurse's suggestion that it might be a pulled muscle and to just wait a few days and see. She didn't know what it was, but she was pretty sure it wasn't a pulled muscle.

"Not really," Fern answered sweetly. *Okay,* Tabitha thought. She'd keep an eye on it and if it wasn't one hundred percent better by Friday—no, Thursday—she would call and take Fern in before the weekend. She meant it, no matter what Fern said.

They took the elevator down and walked to the car without anyone saying a single thing. Tabitha plugged the address into Waze, and suddenly they weren't alone anymore as the woman's voice gently told them which way to go. They ended up somewhere in Kensington and finally turned into what looked like an abandoned parking lot of what might be, or might have once been, a school. As soon as Tabitha pulled into a spot and put the car in park, Levi opened the door.

"Whoa," Tabitha said. "You have to wait until I turn the car off. You know that."

Levi pulled the door shut again, but not all the way. Tabitha thought about telling him to close it properly but really, she didn't plan to move anymore. She waited five seconds, she wasn't sure why, then turned off the car.

"Okay," she said. "You're good to go."

Levi got out and walked toward a big door that looked like it was anything but open. He pulled, but it didn't budge.

"Are you sure this is the right place?"

"Yes," he said, annoyed. He pulled out his phone and read something, probably an email from Nancy, Nancy, Nancy, before heading around to the other side of the building without a word. They followed him, and sure enough, there was another big metal door, propped open with someone's old flip-flop. Tabitha wasn't at all certain about this, but Levi pushed the door right open, and they found themselves in a big, industrial kitchen. They just stood there as people moved around them, cleaning dozens of green peppers and sautéing something that looked like a mixture of rice and tomatoes in two big pans on the stove. Suddenly, Levi looked like an unsure little kid again, and something snapped in Tabitha.

"Is Nancy here?" she asked the man at the stove.

"That way," he said, pointing toward a door. Now Tabitha led the way, and Levi followed, head down slightly, shuffling. Fern was in the back, extra slow. They walked into the school cafeteria, where the big round tables were covered with tablecloths and the places were set. A woman with short dark hair was placing tiny vases of fresh flowers in the center of each table.

"Nancy?" Tabitha asked.

"That's me!" she said, looking at them, and Tabitha worried briefly that she might not know if they were a family in need or volunteers. Nancy looked at Tabitha's shoes, then at Levi, and walked over, hand out.

"You must be Levi," she said. "I am so happy to meet you."

"Thank you," Levi said, shyly, but he took her hand and looked her in the eyes. "I'm happy to be here."

Then she looked at Fern.

"Are you the little sister? Dragged along I bet," Nancy said in an especially nice way. She really seemed to have a way with people. Fern perked up.

"That's me!" she said in almost the exact same way Nancy had said it a moment before, and Tabitha was surprised by her comic timing. They all laughed a little.

"And I'm Tabitha," she said, reaching out her hand. "Thanks for letting Levi do his bar mitzvah project with you."

"The pleasure is all mine," Nancy said. "Families will be arriving soon. Fern—would you mind continuing to put the flowers on the tables? And there are some more over there that still need to be put in the vases. Levi, I want you to get ready to serve, but I would love it if you would spend time with the kids, so over there I have that list of names next to pictures. As I mentioned, nothing is better for a kid's self-esteem than being called by name by someone they admire. And Tabitha, come with me. There is a lot to do in the kitchen."

"I already know their names," Levi said proudly.

"Wonderful," she said, smiling, allowing a moment to let that sink in. Again, Tabitha was impressed. Then Nancy turned to lead Tabitha back toward the kitchen.

Tabitha looked around, wondering if it was okay to leave the kids, and she decided it was. So she followed Nancy, accepted an apron, and got to work stuffing the peppers with the tomato-rice mixture and topping them with cheese. They looked and smelled so good, Tabitha wondered if volunteers got to eat some, too, but she didn't think so. They were supposed to be done before seven, plenty of time to get their own dinner. *Great.*

The families arrived, and Tabitha was surprised to see how into it Levi was, laughing with the kids, taking his serving duties seriously. Even Fern seemed to enjoy herself, talking to a little girl who was about her age and checking to make sure the flowers still looked good. Nobody looked particularly destitute. Tabitha wondered how each one became involved with the organization. How was it determined that they needed this help? Then each family had a chance to tell their story, with one representative member taking the floor at a time. There were about fifteen families. Tabitha thought, *Really? I have to sit through each one of these sob stories? I can add my own sob story to the bunch.*

As the first woman started talking, Tabitha moved to the back of the room, close to the kitchen, and leaned against the wall. She listened as the woman described her kids and how they were doing so much better in school. When Nancy prompted her to talk about how things were before they came to The Family Meal, Tabitha ducked into the empty kitchen and looked around. Nancy had said they saved the left-over food or let the hungriest families take it home, even though the point of the organization wasn't really to feed people but to teach them how to feed themselves through healthy choices, good budget strategies, and learning to cook. But now she eyed the four cooling stuffed peppers in the pan. Would anyone really miss those? She found a ziplock bag and gently placed one pepper at a time at the bottom of the bag. They fit perfectly. If she got caught, she'd just say she was getting them ready to send home with someone, or she was cleaning up. She heard a loud round of applause from the room next door, and she wondered, briefly, what had been said. She looked around to make sure she was totally alone, pushed the air out of the bag, and placed it in the bottom of her big purse. She took a few deep breaths and waited to make sure nobody had seen it, and then she relaxed. She wandered over to the shelf. Salt, pepper, dried thyme. All of that would be nice, but she could live without it. Salt and pepper were easy to get from really any fast-food restaurant that had the tiny packets. Nothing else on the shelf really grabbed her, and she told herself she never had any intention of actually taking anything, until she saw a full bottle of cinnamon sugar—Fern's favorite. In one motion, she grabbed it and dropped it into her bag, on top of the peppers, which were really starting to smell. She snapped it shut and waited again, but nobody said anything; there was nobody there. She just hoped there weren't any security cameras, and if there were, she hoped there would be no reason anyone would look at them. She thought about opening the refrigerator, or even searching for a few pieces of fruit. A banana would be so nice. But she didn't dare. She went to the door and slipped back into her spot in the cafeteria.

". . . for six days, I think it was," a man said, clearing his throat. Was he crying? "We were just thinking we would have to go to the emergency room and fake something, or not even have to fake anything, since Daniel was really starting to feel bad. His stomach was distended, and he said he thought he might throw up, but we were going to say something worse—something like he fell, or just something so we could settle in for a few hours and hopefully he could get a meal once they figured out he was pretty much okay. Maybe we all could—some hospitals have sandwiches and snacks for the parents when they wait." He said this as though he were saying some hospitals had unicorns and gave out winning lottery tickets. Tabitha really looked at him now. He was tall with dark, neat hair. His yellow shirt had a stain on it, but his jeans looked clean. If she walked by him on the street, she wouldn't think anything of him, she wouldn't think he was starving. "That was the lowest point. Then we got some government assistance and that helped so much. And now this. I think everything is about to turn around for us."

Tabitha felt a moment of terror and regret, all mixed up into one bad feeling. Terror because she wasn't that far away from that moment of not being able to feed everyone, of having to fake an injury to go to a hospital for a meal. *But no, it will never come to that for us,* she told herself. She would ask for help before it came to that, wouldn't she? If it really came down to it, she would ask Rachel for help. And the regret because how was it possible that she was stealing from *these people*? She touched her bag and felt the warmth of the peppers and the hard glass of the jar. She could sneak back in there right now and return everything, but she didn't want to. They'd worked hard, maybe she could think of it like payment, though she knew that minimized their roles as volunteers and do-gooders. She thought of being able to offer Fern cinnamon sugar on her toast tomorrow, and she decided she didn't care. She'd just keep it.

"Hey," Nancy came up next to her, and Tabitha immediately worried she'd smell the peppers. She shifted her bag to her other shoulder, the one farther away from Nancy. "That's one amazing boy you have there. And girl, of course, but Levi is really something. I rarely see teenage boys follow through the way he has with me, or jump in the way he did today."

"He is amazing," Tabitha said, letting a good feeling replace the bad one, even if it was just for one minute. She glanced at Levi. He sat at one of the tables between two boys and laughed as one of the kids poked at him. She scanned the room for Fern and saw her sitting on the floor rubbing her knee. Tabitha shifted her deadline for calling the pediatrician. If it wasn't better by Wednesday, she'd call. She meant it.

They helped clean up and got back to the car. They hadn't eaten anything, and Tabitha felt strange about pulling the peppers out of her bag. Better to put them away at home and serve them like she had made them.

She didn't think the kids would buy it, or forget that they were the exact same peppers they'd helped serve, but at least there'd be some distance. It took an extra minute for Fern to bend her knee and get it inside the car before pulling the door shut, but she didn't say anything or complain about it. Tabitha waited for the kids to say they were starving—they must be, she was—but neither said anything.

"So, I was thinking," Tabitha said. She had been considering offering this since talking to Nancy about what an amazing kid Levi was. He deserved a treat, and she could put a little something on her credit card—just this once. "I was thinking we could go for pizza on the way home."

"Really?" Fern asked.

"Cool," Levi said.

Tabitha planned to find any cheap, corner pizza place where you could probably get a large pie for fifteen dollars. But now she thought, as long as they were doing it, they might as well *really do it*. First, she considered Tacconelli's. She took out her phone, which she'd been worrying about lately. She knew all their plans were on Stuart's credit card, it was an automatic monthly charge, and she hadn't heard anything about the charges not going through, but she worried that at some point service would stop. She held the phone in her hand for a second, then she typed in Tacconelli's. The first picture that came up looked amazing. She was just about to tell the kids when she saw the Cash Only detail at the bottom of the page.

"How about Nomad?" she asked, and the kids cheered in unison. She drove back into Center City and continued south to one of their favorite pizza places, one that took credit cards. And she didn't try to manage them, she just let them order. A movie about animals played on the big screen at the front of the dining room; Tabitha ordered an icy beer. They ate pepperoni pizza and a special pie with creamy sweet corn. Tabitha wished they could stay there forever. The bill was eighty-four dollars after adding a 17 percent tip—15 percent seemed cheap and 20 percent extravagant, so 17 percent it was.

Fern didn't even seem to limp that much as they headed back to the car, drove home, and finally entered the apartment, which was dark and getting darker. The stupid peppers were in her purse that whole time. There was a time when she would never eat something that was left out so long, but the peppers were still slightly warm and smelled good, so she put them in the fridge. She put the cinnamon sugar on the shelf where they used to keep it when they had plenty of it, when it was hard to find room to fit everything. Now there was plenty of room. The kids went to sleep, and she settled into bed thinking it was a good day, maybe the best they'd had in months.

But that night she was restless. She dreamt that she took one thing after another off a shelf, her arms hurt from all the reaching, then put it all back on the shelf—one thing down, one thing back up, over and over again. When she finally woke up for good, seven minutes before the alarm was set to go off, all the contentment from the evening before was gone, and her head pounded. She felt achy and drained. And so mad at herself for the day before—the stealing, of course, but also charging eighty-four dollars! Why had she done that? If only she could get that back. She felt around the bottom of the bed with her feet and latched her toes onto the Michigan T-shirt. When she heard Fern coming down the hall, her gait still slow with a definite hitch, she let the shirt go and sat up. She was the only one in charge, after all. She better act like it.

CHAPTER EIGHT

Once the kids were out for the day—Tabitha hadn't bothered to walk them to school in a week now—she literally didn't know what to do with herself. She knew she should be looking harder for a job—that's what her plan was for the morning—but she couldn't stand the thought of sitting down at the computer. She needed to keep moving, to talk about yesterday, confess her sins, but to whom? And then she knew. It was crazy, but she didn't even care. She got dressed and walked toward the huge apartment building on JFK Boulevard. This time she didn't bother to stop at the desk, and nobody questioned her. She took the elevator to the second floor and knocked. No answer. She waited a few seconds, then knocked again, wondering if she could get into trouble for this. Was it trespassing? Soliciting? No, it was neither of those things. She ran through the worst-case scenarios in her mind. Maybe Nora was inside, sitting on the floor in her bad, altered state. Or maybe another aide was there. What would Tabitha say then? She considered leaving, just going back home, but something tugged at her. She was so desperate to talk to someone, to confess the cinnamon sugar.

She took a deep breath and pushed open the door, which she was counting on being unlocked.

"Hello?" she called. "Nora?"

No answer. She was reluctant to walk deeper into the apartment without permission. It just didn't feel right.

"Nora?"

"Boo!" Nora said, coming around the corner.

Tabitha jumped back, clutching her chest and breathing hard. It took her a second to recover. Nora just stood there, smiling wide.

"It's you!" Nora finally said, and Tabitha wondered if she really remembered; she seemed to.

"Yes, it's me," Tabitha said, trying to mimic Nora's cheerfulness.

"Well, it is perfect timing," Nora said. "My son just left, and he doesn't like me to be alone."

"Oh, okay," Tabitha said, wondering what the plan was then. Was someone else coming? "Why doesn't he want you to be alone?"

"I don't know," she said coyly. "I think he worries I'm gonna have a keg party."

Tabitha laughed.

"Well, are you? Going to have a party?"

"No," Nora said seriously. "I don't like beer, and kegs are too heavy for me to carry these days. But I do have marijuana. Want some?"

Once again, Tabitha had that sensation that she was being watched or filmed. This couldn't be for real, could it? At any second a television host would pop out with a microphone. Maybe they were permanently set up in Nora's apartment, since she was so entertaining. Maybe her bedroom was the control room; Tabitha hadn't seen her bedroom yet. It could be that show where one person is told to say crazy things through a small receiver in her ear. She looked at the side of Nora's head, but didn't see anything, not even a hearing aid. Besides, there was no way they could have known Tabitha was coming.

"Sure," she said.

"Oh fun!" Nora said. "I hate to do marijuana by myself, and my son never wants to."

"Why do you have it?" Tabitha asked, wondering if she was going to roll a joint or bring out a bong. She just couldn't picture it.

"Medical purposes, dear," Nora said. "Follow me."

She followed Nora into the kitchen, where Nora grabbed an old-fashioned-looking tin off the counter. Tabitha looked closely, and there were two ice skaters on the lid, dressed in colorful sweaters, with Christmassy pine trees all around them. Nora lifted the lid to reveal a handful of caramel candies wrapped in wax paper. *Oh,* Tabitha thought, *Nora probably thinks these caramels are edibles,* even though they looked like normal caramels to Tabitha. She leaned in for a closer look. She hadn't actually ever had an edible, and she hadn't smoked pot in years, possibly a decade, though it was one of her favorite things to do in college. *No,* she told herself, *these look like normal candies.*

"Help yourself, dear," Nora said, holding out the tin. "But I suggest only one, or maybe half of one to begin. They can be strong."

"Thanks, Nora," Tabitha said, reaching in to grab one. She could play along. "I'll just take one and eat it slowly."

"Good thinking," Nora said, choosing one after Tabitha. She put her piece of candy on the counter and opened the refrigerator, pulling out a bright-blue bowl covered in plastic wrap. She pulled off the wrap, then reached into a cabinet below the counter and pulled out a small, disposable muffin tin already lined with six bright-pink paper holders.

"Cranberry again, dear?" Nora asked. "I do know how you like cranberry. Today I can also offer you cherry, blueberry, butterscotch, or chocolate chip."

Tabitha looked around. She chose to come here, but what were the chances that an entirely stocked muffin factory would just be waiting for her? It made no sense; there must be a catch. She thought of Fern, who would love chocolate-chip muffins more than anything.

"Chocolate chip?"

"Chocolate chip it is," Nora said. "But first, let me take a bite of the candy. It can take some time to feel anything."

Nora peeled back a small bit of the wax paper and took a bite of the caramel. She closed her eyes and chewed, then swallowed.

"I like to let it sink in," she said, with her eyes still closed.

"Huh, okay," Tabitha said, worrying that she was intruding. "You know what, Nora, you don't have to make muffins for me. I just stopped by to see if there was anything I could do for you. Do you need anything?"

Nora opened her eyes and looked right at Tabitha.

"I need to feel busy and not old," she said. "The muffins help. The marijuana helps. Company helps."

"Well," Tabitha said, wishing she'd been able to think of another place to go to confess her sins, "chocolate-chip muffins would be so nice. My daughter would love them."

"You have a daughter?" Nora asked, wide eyed. She looked like a little kid. "I always wanted a daughter. I have a granddaughter, which is lovely, but it isn't the same as raising a daughter."

Tabitha's mind flashed to the last time she took her mother out to dinner, though of course, they didn't know it would be the last time. How do you ever know it's going to be the last time? Tabitha cringed. Her mother had always been a little obsessed with "last times"—the last time Tabitha nursed each baby, the last time Tabitha carried them, the last time her mother had carried her as a child. There always had to be a last time. Tabitha hated that, but now she let herself think about it for a second while she nibbled at her candy and Nora mixed chocolate chips into the batter. That dinner had been so, so hard and really the last thing in the world she wanted to do. There was not one tiny ounce of her that wanted to be eating out with her mother. She wanted to be home with the kids and Stuart. She wanted to be reading in bed, or binge-watching *Friday Night Lights*. She did not want to basically carry her frail, wrinkled mother into Sang Kee, the best Chinese restaurant near her mother's apartment in Wynnewood. Of course, the table was up a few steps, so everyone came running to take an arm and carry the walker up, while Tabitha stood behind her mother with her arms outstretched, just in case. Her mother had been wearing a light-blue sweater, with a scarf neatly tied around her neck, and those strange black pants that Tabitha always suspected were really pajama bottoms, even though her mother insisted they were not. They finally were seated at the table, her mother smiling, so happy to be there, and Tabitha being curt, rushed. But her mother had pretended not to notice. She ordered her favorite—moo shu chicken—and she had a drink, a scotch. Had that been her last scotch? The last one of thousands she'd had in her lifetime?

"Can you open the oven for me, dear?" Nora asked, the filled cupcake tin in hand. Tabitha noticed that she had sprinkled sugar on top and made smiley faces with the chocolate chips: two eyes, a nose, and a happy mouth.

"Wow," Tabitha said, leaning in to get the door. She pulled it down and waited for Nora to slide the tin in, then she shut it a little harder than she meant to. She reached for her candy and took a sizeable bite.

"Oh dear, that's a lot," Nora said seriously. "You aren't driving home, are you?"

"No, I walked here." Tabitha continued to play along. "But thank you for your concern."

"Those will be ready in about twenty or twenty-five minutes," Nora said. "Can you keep track of the time?"

"Sure."

"Let's retire to the living room," Nora said, grabbing her piece of candy.

They sat down, and Nora turned her full attention to the caramel, pulling tiny bits off and placing them in her mouth, then closing her eyes. Tabitha watched, taking another nibble of her candy and wondering if thinking and believing something had special powers was enough to give it special powers. Nora seemed completely uninterested in conversation, and Tabitha didn't mind. She was just thinking that the muffins must be close to being ready when she started to feel a little light-headed, and then she was filled with this great feeling, like everything was going to be okay. She put her head back, smiled. *Oh my god,* she thought, *I'm high!*

"Oh good, dear, it must be working," Nora said, surprising her. Maybe Tabitha hadn't thought that. Maybe she had actually said it.

Tabitha wanted to say something nice, like she was sorry she had doubted Nora in the first place. Also, how stupid of her. Of course, she knew edibles were a real thing, she just hadn't had the chance to try any. How hilarious was it that an old lady introduced her to them? She wanted to talk about all of this, but she couldn't find the words. Where were her words? She'd find them eventually. What was important now was to take another small bite of her candy.

Tabitha could sit here all day. There was something magical about this apartment with its funny-candy tin and muffin-making oven. Suddenly, she didn't feel like she had to confess anything. So what if she took a few stuffed peppers? Nobody was eating them anyway. And as for the cinnamon sugar, she'd replace it as soon as she could. It was totally worth it to see Fern's face that morning when she presented the cinnamon toast—sure the bread was old, but once it was toasted you could barely tell. Really, she was doing her best; she didn't have anything to own up to. Everything was great, perfect even.

Tabitha wasn't sure how much time had gone by, but she smelled something. She sniffed and looked around. Nora appeared to be asleep. Tabitha forced herself up and tried to follow the smell, which eventually reminded her of the muffins. She scrambled to find oven mitts and pulled them out just in time. Another few minutes and they would have been all-out burned. But they looked good, like the best muffins she had ever seen. Fern was going to love them. She put them on the top of the stove, turned off the oven. She saw the candy tin, which was still open. She took a caramel and put it in her pocket, for later. She helped herself to a muffin, which was quite hot, but she couldn't get it down fast enough. She looked at her watch. It wasn't even lunchtime yet. She was planning to call the pediatrician today about Fern's leg. She thought she could hear her moaning a little during the night, and putting it off didn't seem right, but now that she thought about it, it seemed a little better this morning. Didn't it? And Fern hadn't complained about it at all that morning. In fact, Tabitha was pretty sure it was going to be completely back to normal soon, if it wasn't already. *You know what,* she said in her head, or at least she thought it was in her head, *I'll wait and see how it is today, and then I'll call.* Or maybe she wouldn't have to call at all. That was a very likely scenario. Everything was going to work itself out. Wow, she felt good. Why did she ever stop smoking pot? It was like she was free. What was she worrying about earlier?

She went back to the living room and sat down, laughing a little, or was she laughing a lot? She wasn't sure. Nora opened her eyes and laughed too. Her face looked so much like Tabitha's mother's, didn't it? Those strong cheekbones that were now hard and prominent, no longer padded and soft, making her look a little stern. All those wrinkles around her eyes. But it was really the neck, or the lack of it. Why did people seem to lose their necks when they got older? They looked like their heads were placed right on their shoulders.

"I have to go now, Nora," Tabitha said. She had to pull herself together.

"Don't forget the muffins, dear," Nora said, her eyes closed again.

"I won't, thank you," Tabitha said. "I'll come back soon."

"Please do, dear," Nora said. "Nobody else will do the marijuana with me, and I don't like doing it by myself."

"Well, I like doing it with you," Tabitha said, feeling only slightly guilty about the extra candy in her pocket.

She went back to the kitchen, found a ziplock bag in a drawer, and piled all the muffins in. Then she grabbed one back out and ate it quickly. It was still warm and gooey and everything she could ever possibly want a muffin to be. She wanted another—would that be her third? But she also wanted to save them for Fern. She zipped the bag shut firmly, went back to the living room.

"I'm leaving now," she said. "Can I tell you something before I go?"

"Sure, dear, anything," Nora said sleepily.

"I'm worried that I might be responsible for the death of two people." There, she said it. It was nagging at her, bringing her down. It was so easy to say things when she was high!

Nora opened her eyes. She didn't look worried or even concerned. She looked amused—no, that wasn't right—she looked interested.

"Oh, dear, I doubt that's the case," she said nicely, barely lifting her head. "But if you come back again, we can talk more about it. I'd like that. I can make more muffins. And maybe we can play some Monopoly."

~

Tabitha's business had been running for a solid five months when it happened. She was already thinking about what she could do to celebrate the six-month anniversary. She was leaning toward a drawing to give away a free meal—the only caveat was that the customer couldn't choose the menu. She would do something crazy, exotic. It would be so much fun.

That night she served Asian beef, and it was good. Her true talent was in the details and the packaging, both of which she knew were making it hard to actually make any money, not to mention stop losing it. They didn't have much savings to begin with, only a little in an untouchable college fund. They had already pulled out the bulk of their savings, with a penalty, when Stuart started his own firm. When she said she felt it was only right that she have a chance to start her business with what was left, Stuart had surprised her and agreed. In the end, she had been so glad she had taken that chance. But she just couldn't figure out how to skimp. Really, she didn't want to skimp, and that night the meal was as high end and delicious as any. She made an amazing braised beef with soy, sesame, and ginger, which she served with a side of wonderful sushi rice, a tower of beautifully washed and crisp butter lettuce leaves, and tiny beef spring rolls, which she fried herself. She put the meal out on her app around four o'clock. The business wasn't totally legal, since she was cooking in her own home and often for more people in a night than was okay without a professional space. Also, she was charging money, which added that other requirement for supervised sanitary conditions. But she wasn't the only one doing it. Shepherd's Pie, her biggest competitor, had been successfully doing it for over a year before she even started. At first, she had people pick up the orders from the lobby, but that was especially difficult and raised all sorts of questions. Once she surpassed ten customers a night, she had to change that, so she hired a delivery guy on a bike—another expense—and bought a big warming bag. She had always been a good baker, baking for local cafés here and there, but she found she loved this even more.

They were the last customers of the night. She'd always remember that. In fact, the order didn't go through on the app—she'd cut off digital orders because she was out of food. But they had called. At first she said no, she was finished for the evening. But they said it was the man's birthday, and this was exactly what he wanted. Also, they wanted to eat good food at home; he didn't want to spend his birthday out at a restaurant. She said okay, she could put together one more order. She took their information, telling them it would be ready in about forty-five minutes, and got to work.

If they had gone the usual route, through the app, it would have prompted all the questions about food allergies and restrictions. She had thought about it so many times. Imagined saying: *Just do it on the app, I'll let it go through.* Would that have made a difference in the end? She just wasn't sure. She hadn't listed the oil as one of the ingredients, somehow that hadn't been done, a huge, unforgiveable mistake on her part, but maybe if they had seen it written out in the allergy section they would have said something. Maybe seeing it would have made her think to ask. What she really wanted, what she wished for more than anything, was to go back to the beginning of the call, and when they said, *"The app isn't working. It says you're sold out, but we wanted to check just to make sure,"* that she had said she was sorry, but it was true, there wasn't any left. She wished she had said emphatically that she was finished for the night. If only she had said that, everything might be different now.

CHAPTER NINE

Levi Brewer didn't really have plans to play *Call of Duty* with Butch on Saturday, despite what he told his mother. She was so easy these days, it was ridiculous. That was the only good thing about his dad being gone—it was easier to get away with stuff. She never would have let him walk alone before. Also, Fern had plans with Sarina—Levi thought they were going to some dumb water park in New Jersey, even though he knew Fern's leg was still bad. What was his mother's deal? She used to have them at the doctor's for a stuffy nose and now with this, she was just ignoring it? She kept taking Fern's word for it that it didn't hurt! Didn't she have eyes? But Levi was okay with the water-park thing, because when Fern was busy his mom was always more eager to let him go somewhere, too. It was like if they were both home, fine, but if there was the chance she could be alone, she'd pretty much do anything to make it happen. At least that's how it felt lately.

So Levi left the apartment and walked through the Square, right to La Colombe, where he went through his usual ritual of looking at the money and the note. But that was only the beginning of his day. He had plans. For the first time, he was going to spend some of the money.

He had already talked to Nancy, and all he had to do was get to the school in Kensington. She was cooking all day and doing inventory, and she was so happy to have the help, she'd said. She did ask if Levi's sister and mom were coming, too. It seemed like she would have liked that, but when he explained that they had plans, she didn't ask any follow-up questions. That was a relief, because he was smart enough to know that it was usually the follow-up questions that got him into trouble.

He pulled out a ten and went to the counter. He'd been there at least five times and had never once ordered a thing. But he thought he'd look older if he had a cup of coffee in his hand.

"One small coffee, black," he said, repeating exactly what he heard his father say so many times. He had no idea what it would taste like but, whatever, he wasn't really planning on drinking it.

"Coming up," a tall guy with a man bun said, taking his ten and giving back seven and change. *That's an expensive cup of coffee,* Levi thought, but he accepted the change and the hot cup and walked out. At first he thought he could order an Uber, he even had an app on his phone that his dad had set up for emergencies. But when he went through it to see if it would work, he was told that the credit card on file was no longer valid. So that was out. A cab would probably cost him at least ten dollars there, ten back, maybe more. He would be almost halfway through his money then. But he wanted to do what his dad wanted, he wanted to be able to tell him about it when he finally came home. So he opted for a bus but had no idea how to find the right one. There were lots of buses on Walnut Street, but those were heading west. He wanted to go north—at least he knew *that.* So he started walking north, thinking he'd eventually see a bus. He carried his coffee out in front of him, pretending to take a sip every now and then.

Tabitha wanted to go to the Fox & Hound for the Michigan–Penn State game, but she couldn't say no to Rachel again, so she put on a cute fall dress, even though all she really wanted to put on was Stuart's rumpled Michigan T-shirt, and she left to meet Rachel at the Dandelion on Eighteenth Street.

"Hi, hi!" Rachel said, as Tabitha moved toward her through the small crowd in the foyer of the English-style pub. There was a fire burning in the fireplace, and suddenly Tabitha felt happy to be there.

"Hi!" Tabitha leaned in to kiss her on the cheek.

"They have our table ready," Rachel said, pointing to a woman holding menus. They followed her up the carpeted stairs and turned left into the dog room which was decorated with photos of different breeds of dogs. They smiled at each other, since it was their favorite room in the restaurant, and took their seats at a comfortable corner table for two.

"They don't usually bring bread at lunch, but I'm going to ask for some," Tabitha said. If she filled up on bread she could get away with ordering something small—soup maybe, or that great butter lettuce salad. Plus, they had some of the best bread and butter she'd ever tasted.

"Sure! I want this to be a celebration," Rachel said. "There's something I want to talk to you about."

Tabitha squinted her eyes the tiniest bit at Rachel, trying to get a sense of what she wanted to talk about, but Rachel just smiled and looked at the menu.

"Can I get you started with some drinks?" a server asked.

"Yes!" Rachel said quickly. "Two glasses of prosecco please."

Tabitha was already calculating the prices.

"Are you ready to order?" the server asked. "Or should I grab your drinks and come back?"

"We're ready," Rachel said. "We'll have the shrimp cocktail, the Welsh rarebit, the butter lettuce salad, the shepherd's pie, and the fish and chips." It was everything they usually ordered, everything Tabitha loved, but she had planned to say she wasn't that hungry today. Now that seemed too conspicuous.

"All great choices," the server said before walking away.

"So," Rachel said, putting her hands on the table and looking right at Tabitha. "First, let me say this is totally my treat. I am going to ask you for something, and even if you say no, I want to take you to lunch. Okay? Agree to that before I tell you about the thing."

Tabitha tried not to look so over-the-top thrilled. "Yes, I agree. Thank you."

"Okay, good," Rachel said. "Oh, you forgot to ask for the bread!"

"That's okay," Tabitha said. "We're getting so much good food."

"Okay," Rachel said, and Tabitha realized she was stalling. She was clearly nervous. She was breathing heavily through her mouth, even though they'd been sitting for a while already. "So, you know Michael and I broke up a little over six months ago. I mean, of course you know that, but I'm just setting the scene. And you know we broke up because he didn't want to take the next step, or the one after that, or any future steps with me at all, which really sucked."

For a minute, Tabitha thought Rachel would cry. It had taken her four months to be able to mention Michael without crying. She watched as Rachel shook her head.

"Again, just setting the scene," she said. "This is not about him."

"Okay, good," Tabitha said, encouragingly.

"And I'm just tired of waiting for the right guy. I'm worried that I'll find someone I like, someone who seems to like me, and then I'll waste a year or two years, and I'll end up right back in this same place, only older."

"No, that won't happen," Tabitha said, reaching across the table and patting Rachel's hand.

"Just hear me out," Rachel said.

The server brought over the prosecco. It was bubbly and delicious looking in its tall, elegant glass.

"Cheers," Tabitha said, holding hers up.

"Oh shoot, I didn't time this right," Rachel said. "I meant to be finished with my speech so we could toast. Oh well, cheers!"

They clinked glasses, and Tabitha took a huge, long sip. Then she stopped herself. She wanted to make it last.

"I'm just going to get to the point," Rachel said, looking down at her lap and fiddling with her napkin. "I want to have a baby, and I'm just going to do it. Or, at least, try to do it. And while I don't think I need a man, although, don't get me wrong, if it all worked out and the right person came along and he didn't mind that I had a baby, I would be very open to that. But that might never happen. And I know I can't do it totally alone, so before I do anything—before I look into a sperm donor and find out about insemination—I wanted to ask you if you would be part of my support system. I would want you to be the baby's godmother, but I would count on you for more than that, if you agree to this. For example, if I was really going crazy and needed a minute or sixty, I would call you and see if I could drop the baby off. If I was sick, I might ask you for help. If the baby was sick and freaking out and I didn't know what to do, I might ask you for help. You get the picture, right? You are such a great mother—you seem to have it so together—and Levi and Fern are such great, great kids. I mean, I've been paying extra attention lately, and you really make them your priority. I mean, if they need you, you don't just skip out and go to yoga class. You are there for them. That's the kind of mother I want to be. I could really learn from you. What do you think? There is nobody I would rather do this with."

The words hung in the air, and if Tabitha weren't so truly dumbstruck, she might have laughed or said that sounded a little like a marriage proposal. But Tabitha had to use her energy to keep her mouth from dropping open and from saying, *Are you crazy? I'm a total mess.*

Rachel leaned in. "I know things aren't great with Stuart," she said quietly. "At least that's what I've been assuming. But that hasn't stopped you from taking amazing care of your kids. Where is Stuart, by the way?"

Again, Tabitha squinted her eyes. Was this a joke? Was this Rachel's way of getting her to confess? *No,* she honestly didn't think so.

"Still on the Upper Peninsula," Tabitha said, "Dealing with that mining strike."

"All right, so you see what I mean?" Rachel said, like she'd just made her point. "You're basically a single mom a lot of the time. We could help each other. I could help you more than I do now. It could be like a partnership."

"Sure," Tabitha said, even though what she wanted to say was, *Can I think about it? Can I figure out where my missing husband is and try to get some cash flow going before I commit to helping take care of a new human being?*

"*Sure,* as in *yes*, as in, you'll do it?"

The server placed the appetizers on the table. Tabitha lifted her fork; she couldn't wait to try that Welsh rarebit with all its mustardy cheese.

"Sure, as in *yes*, I'll do it," Tabitha said, putting down her fork and smiling at Rachel.

"Thank you," Rachel said. "Thank you, thank you, thank you."

When she was almost back at her apartment she checked her phone. No word from the kids. Fern had seemed better that week, so Tabitha had let her Wednesday deadline go by. Thursday was okay, Friday, a little iffy, and then today Fern practically skipped out the door on her way to the water park. The hurting-knee saga just might be behind them. That would be one big relief.

On Facebook, she saw that the football game, which she thought started at noon and would therefore most likely be over, had just started twenty minutes before, at three, so instead of going home, Tabitha walked to the Fox & Hound. Why, she had no idea, except that she didn't want to be alone. She felt either that she was pretending or there by proxy in pretty much everything she did lately. She'd just spent hours pretending with Rachel—that everything was fine, that she was just busy, that her marriage was not so bad, that she had plenty of money, that she had the time to dedicate to Rachel's future baby. And talk about not really belonging someplace! The synagogue, for one, where she had no idea what was going on half the time, and now the Michigan games. It was like she was living Stuart's life, but he wasn't there to see it, appreciate it, or help her get through it in any way. Maybe not with Rachel, but with everything else.

She worried a little about Levi but imagined that he was completely immersed in the land of whatever video game he and Butch were playing. Knowing him, she wouldn't hear from him for hours. She thought about texting him, but decided not to. Maybe she'd get lucky, and Butch's parents would invite him to stay for dinner. Fern was taken care of, at least for the afternoon. Maybe Tabitha could get away with just taking home some of the food from the sports bar and passing it off as a meal, again.

She could see how crowded it was when she walked up. People were everywhere, standing up against the big plate-glass windows, spilling out the door. She knew the Michigan–Penn State game wasn't the only one going on, but she imagined it would draw the biggest crowd. She walked in, pushing by people who were far younger and far drunker than she'd been in years. Suddenly, she was glad it was so crowded. It was easier to hide this way. She thought of the quote from *The Great Gatsby*, the one about there being no privacy at small parties, and she wished she had someone to share that thought with.

As soon as she came around the corner, she was overwhelmed by the sea of maize and blue. She stopped and blinked for a second, the place was eerily quiet, but then the crowd erupted in crazy cheers and then, of course, "The Victors." People were handing around a stack of small papers, each taking one before passing it on. Tabitha took one and read it. It said: "From now on—when Penn State says 'WE ARE'—I want everyone in the room to mouth, definitely not say out loud, the word *shit*. They won't hear it but they will feel it." Tabitha shook her head—these people were nuts. She doubted anyone would actually do it. But she watched as other people took a paper off the pile, read it and nodded or smiled, or, in some cases, nodded *and* smiled.

The head of the alumni association chapter climbed onto the table in the middle of the room. His entire face was painted blue, including his ears. His hair was dyed a strange yellow that Tabitha thought nobody would really call maize, more like mustard. He wore a sparkly maize sweater and had blue gloves on with a big block *M* on each hand. Tabitha wondered if he was okay.

"Wolverines!" he yelled into the crowd. His voice was hoarse. "You are doing an excellent job of keeping the energy up in this room, but I need you to keep it going. We need another touchdown! Can you guys do it?"

"Yes!"

"What did you say?" His voice cracked on the last word, and he put his hand to his throat, then tried again. "What did you say?"

"Yes!"

He pointed his blue-gloved finger into the crowd, moving it slowly from person to person.

"I'm watching you," he said after a few moments had gone by.

It felt like a threat to Tabitha. Who was this guy? How did someone take on that sort of role? She'd been more and more interested lately in how people got to the place they were in life—how people established their normal, whatever that might be? She spotted the food and walked right over to the buffet. The thing was, she wasn't hungry. Available food should never go uneaten, but she'd just eaten a huge lunch with Rachel, which she thoroughly enjoyed. Maybe this was a waste of time. She turned away from the bar and saw an arm moving out of the corner of her eye. She followed it and saw Toby waving wildly at her, smiling. She couldn't believe it, but in all this craziness, he had actually saved her a seat. At least she thought he had. There was an empty seat next to him, decorated the same as last time, and he had his nonwaving hand on it. He pointed to the chair furiously. She couldn't stop herself from smiling.

"Hi!" she said, once she reached him, which was no easy feat. There was barely any space between people. She would hate to have to get out of there in a hurry.

"Thank goodness you're here," he said. "They are like lions, tigers, and—no, they are like Wolverines. I don't think I could have held them off a minute longer. Please, sit, immediately."

"Thank you," she said.

"What took you so long?" he asked.

"Well, I wasn't even necessarily planning to come," she said. "It just sort of worked out."

He looked at her incredulously. "It's the Penn State game," he finally said. "So many local and personal rivalries going on in this room right now. You can't miss that."

"I know, I know," she said. "That's why I came!" She didn't have the energy to say that she got it, she really did, but that this wasn't her thing. It was Stuart's thing, and she was here because they had a good buffet of free food.

Toby turned his attention back to the game. She was glad to not have to talk. They watched in hushed horror as Penn State almost made a touchdown, but at the last second Michigan intercepted the ball and ran it all the way back. She was glad, she really was, but she worried about the colorful guy getting back up on the table. Everyone sang, and they started to pass the chair of the alumni association chapter around rock-concert style. Toby put out his hands to help support him as he came by, but Tabitha stepped back so she wouldn't have to. As soon as the man was safely delivered to other outstretched hands, Toby looked at his phone.

"Shoot," Toby said.

"What?"

"I have to be home in an hour to walk my dog. I just got a text from the dog walker that he couldn't get in; the key didn't work. That's never happened before. She's been alone for, let me think, about three hours. I might have two hours before I have to take her out. She's a good dog, but dogs will be dogs, and she's getting older."

"I didn't know you have a dog," Tabitha said. It was a dumb thing to say—she didn't know much about him at all. "What's her name?"

"Yo-Adrian," he said matter-of-factly.

"You mean her name is Adrian?"

"No, it's Yo-Adrian. Her whole name is Yo-Adrian. I call her Yo-A mostly."

Tabitha shook her head. That was the most clever dog name she'd ever heard. She loved it. She had always been a sucker for *Rocky* references.

"That is so great," she said. "When I was a kid, we had a dog named Buster. We might as well have named him Dog, I guess."

"No, Buster's a great name," Toby said, like he meant it. He reached out and took her hand. It was so startling and unexpected that she literally yanked it away.

"Sorry," he said, as nicely as he'd said everything else. She waited for him to say more, to explain that he thought there was something between them, or that he was getting mixed signals, all the things people usually said when one reached out but the other didn't reciprocate. But he didn't. He just went back to watching the game.

Tabitha felt claustrophobic. She had to get out of there. She checked her phone, hoping a kid would need her, but nobody did. She was just sitting up straighter, getting ready with an excuse, but then Penn State scored, and the group at the other end of the huge bar screamed, "We are—" and everyone in their section mouthed, "Shit." You could almost hear it, though not quite. It was like a ghost whisper.

"So, I'm planning my mother's birthday party, and I could use a little help," Toby said, like they were in the middle of a conversation.

There was no indication that he was embarrassed or had any regret about trying to hold her hand. Had he actually tried to hold it, or had she imagined that? Now she wasn't sure.

"How old is she?"

"She will be eighty years old," he said, proudly. "I have a great idea. Want to hear it?"

"Sure," she said, relaxing again.

"The theme is Uranus."

She must have heard wrong.

"As in, *your anus*?"

"Yes, Uranus."

"Wait, you mean like your butt?"

He smiled a slow smile.

"No, like the planet."

He let it sink in. He had good timing, this guy.

"That's a strange theme," she finally said. "How about a garden party or *Harry Potter*? Did your mother read *Harry Potter*? Even a pirate party might be better. I always love a good pirate party. No, I know, a *Wizard of Oz* party! That was always my mother's favorite. She loved recreating the yellow-brick road."

She tried not to let her entire face change. Toby didn't know anything about her mother. He didn't know about her last few horrible days, he didn't even know that she was dead.

"No, the Uranus party it is!" he said. "I am committed. I've been thinking about this since I learned about the planets in seventh grade. I always hoped she'd live long enough so I could do it."

"Okay, so then I have two questions. How do you think I can help? And why Uranus?"

"Both very good questions," Toby said, brushing a piece of maize confetti off of his leg. "I will give you the answers in the reverse order in which they were asked. Why Uranus? Because it takes a little over eighty years for the planet Uranus to orbit the Sun. From what I understand, that means that Uranus will travel all the way around the Sun once in many peoples' lifetimes. How cool is that? In a perfect world, I might wait until my mother turns eighty-four. I think that might be a more precise number, but this is such a big birthday and well, you never know."

He paused here, and Tabitha nodded.

"Also," Toby continued, "and I have to give you some credit for mentioning this earlier, there is that intriguing idea that *Uranus* sounds like *your anus,* and in my experience, older people are more focused on that body part since so many people have trouble in that area as they get older."

Toby took a breath before continuing, and Tabitha thought she should feel embarrassed—sheepish at the very least—but she didn't. She thought it was a brilliant idea.

"I imagine lots of images of Uranus—with the word written out, so people can say it, and if that leads them to a discussion about their time in the bathroom, then so be it. The way I see it, these people have lived long enough to know what they do and do not want to talk about."

Tabitha smiled.

"So, where do I come in?"

"Well you've already helped me by letting me talk it through," he said, shouting a little over the roar of the crowd. "But I was hoping you could help me with the menu. That's a tricky one. I mean, what sort of food do you serve at a Uranus party?"

"Space food?" Tabitha asked.

"Yes! Space food! I can get some of that freeze-dried ice cream, maybe make a big vat of soup or overcooked pasta or whatever the astronauts bring with them when they travel. It's probably really mushy. Perfect for the guests we'll be receiving."

Tabitha laughed so hard she couldn't stop. She hadn't laughed like this in . . . weeks? Months? When was the last time?

She reached out and brushed another piece of confetti off of Toby's hand. It was warm and soft, and suddenly she had an urge to squeeze it. She let her hand rest on his for a beat longer than seemed normal, then pulled it away.

"Let's get out of here," he said.

"Now? But it's the fourth quarter."

"They're gonna win despite that last touchdown. I just know it," he said. "Come on, I have an idea."

When they got up, Toby gathered his decorations, carefully folding the banners and placing them back in his backpack as two drunk girls, dressed completely in maize, pounced on the chairs, one sitting on Toby's hand before he had a chance to move it. The girl didn't even notice. He pulled his hand out and shook it, smiling, and then they pushed through the crowd and went out into the chilly evening. Tabitha hadn't thought of the kids in a little while, but now she did.

"You know what?" she said, a little out of breath. "Eventually, I have to track down my kids and take care of them. How big a time commitment is this idea of yours?"

"Not too big," he said. "Maybe thirty minutes, tops? I have to get home to Yo-A soon anyway. This is something I do sometimes. It might not work out. Timing is everything, as they say."

"Okay," she said, following him west on Spruce Street—actually toward her apartment—but he didn't know that, so she felt okay about it.

"Where's your daughter this weekend?" she asked.

"With her mom," Toby said, and for a second Tabitha thought he wouldn't say any more. But then, "Things have been pretty rough. She isn't being very nice to me right now—my ex, that is—my daughter is the loveliest human being you have ever met. Well, that I've ever met. You probably feel that way about your own kids. Anyway, I don't blame her, really, at all. Truth be told, there was an incident that sparked our downfall, and it was my fault, so, I guess, I get what I deserve."

Tabitha was beyond curious, but if she asked him to explain, then she'd feel like she owed him an explanation of her own.

"I'm really sorry," she said.

"Yeah, so am I."

At Eighteenth Street he guided her right, and for a second, Tabitha panicked. Did he actually know where she lived? She tried to go over everything they had ever talked about to remember if she had told him. No, she wouldn't do that. She barely knew him. She was happy when he stopped to cross the street toward Rittenhouse Square.

"Where are we going?" she asked.

"Okay, I'll tell you, because I don't want you to be disappointed. We're going to this great coffee place called La Colombe, do you know it? Because at closing time they give away all the baked goods that are left at the end of the day. Now, when I say timing is everything, I mean it, because there might be none left, or there might already be so many people there that we won't be able to grab any. We'll see."

Tabitha couldn't believe it. She had once practically lived at La Colombe. Though, obviously, she hadn't enjoyed one of their luscious cappuccinos in way too long. And free food? Was he kidding? How come she didn't know about that? But the bigger question might be, why did he want to get free food? Did he somehow know she needed it? Did he suspect, since she was always pilfering the buffet at the Fox & Hound? Or did he need free food?

It looked like their timing was perfect because, while the place was still crowded enough, no one seemed particularly interested in the food that had been placed on top of the glass counter. There were cheese croissants, mini challah loaves, whole baguettes. There were chocolate scones and coffee cakes. Her mouth was already watering.

"Take a bag and fill it," he said, pointing to the stack of large, brown-paper bags.

"Okay," she said, grabbing a bag.

They were quiet while they each filled their bags. When they were finished, there were still some pastries left over, but she didn't want to appear too greedy. She wondered if they'd have a picnic in the Square, or if they'd just say good-bye, and each take their loot back to their own homes.

"Now what?" she asked, tucking the stuffed bag under her arm.

"Now we find some homeless people."

~

Levi couldn't believe his eyes. Was that his mother? And who was that man?

He had been sitting at La Colombe for over an hour, trying to pull himself together, still carrying that stupid cup of coffee he had bought that morning. Really, thank goodness he did, because having that in front of him made him feel like he had a right to be there, like he could sit as long as he wanted to. But the place was closing and he had to leave and go somewhere else, probably home, but that was the last place he wanted to go.

Someone had just announced the free food, apparently they actually let people take the things that were left over. And he was going to get up to take some. He wasn't stupid. He wasn't sure exactly what was going on, but he knew they were eating very strangely lately, and there was never really quite enough. Some extra bread sounded really good.

So he was about to get up and take some stuff, when he saw his mother come in. He turned so fast back to his table that he knocked down the cup, which was still almost full, and he hunched over, trying to look as invisible as possible. She was never going to not see him; he knew that. She had eagle eyes. But she barely glanced around, and she and the man stuffed those bags so full and walked out.

The day had been a disaster. He never made it to The Family Meal. It was so hard to find it, and the buses, they were so complicated! He spent all his money trying to get there, and between buses, cabs, and one burger along the way—all fifty of the dollars were gone. He felt so stupid. And dirty. And where the hell was his father? He checked his email one more time, seeing if by chance his father might have written, maybe, finally, today. When there was nothing, he couldn't stand it anymore. He started a new email to his father, using the only email address he had for him. He hadn't wanted to do this, he didn't want to reach out to him and have him not reach back. That was his worst fear. At least now he could tell himself his father didn't know how much he missed him, he didn't know that he was desperate for some word from him. But maybe that's what his father needed to know to get in touch. Maybe his father was so busy that he just didn't realize how important this was.

> Dear Dad,
>
> Where exactly are you and when are you coming back? I wanted you to know that I am working with The Family Meal for my BM project and they seem great. But I do have some questions. Can you call or write back? Soon? And one more thing, I spent your money so can you send more? I didn't spend it on stupid stuff like video games, I spent it trying to get to The Family Meal. I know how much you care about that so please help. Okay? This is hard without you.
>
> Love,
> Levi

He didn't even read through it, like his mother always told him to do. He just pressed "send." When there was no bounce-back notification, nothing saying he was out of the office, or out of the country, or out of his normal life, Levi felt vaguely satisfied. He grabbed the last challah roll and headed home to an empty apartment.

CHAPTER TEN

Tabitha didn't remember ever being wooed by Stuart when they were dating. He was kind and dependable, two qualities her previous boyfriends had not had, qualities that seemed most important in choosing a husband. Also, they were so compatible. They liked to go to bed at the same time, they both wanted to have two children, they agreed to have fish for dinner at least two nights a week. Who cared if he was a little distant, if there were times he seemed to be thinking about things other than what was right in front of him? She was done with the craziness of being so in love with someone that it hurt. That was young love, not married love. She wasn't looking for that anymore. She didn't remember ever thinking about Stuart—*Huh, he's funny,* or *Huh, he's clever,* or *I wonder when I'll see him again,* all thoughts she was surprised to have in relation to Toby. With Stuart, there hadn't been any real surprises, not until recently anyway.

Well, there was that one surprise. The one that now basically informed everything, she guessed. They had already been dating for eight months, they had just gotten engaged two days before, when Stuart said there was something weighing on him, something he had to tell her. She was so trusting. Now that she looked back on it, she couldn't figure out why she wasn't the least bit worried about what he was going to tell her. She imagined it would be something about the wedding—his mother insisting on a certain type of flower or a certain type of cake. Or maybe about where he wanted to live. *Anywhere but the Upper Peninsula of Michigan,* she remembered thinking.

Even though they were engaged, they weren't living together yet. It was late at night, but he said he would be right over. They spent the occasional night together, though that was more and more rare as they got deeper into planning the wedding; they were always so tired, they just wanted to go home and sleep in their own beds. When she opened the door that night he looked pale, she remembered thinking, and she wondered if he wasn't feeling well.

"Sit down," he said.

She did.

"I don't know why I didn't tell you this before. I was going to. And then, well, so much time went by, it seemed hard to find the right way to bring it up. It's like when you recognize someone at say, school or something from last year, but you don't say anything, and eventually more time goes by, and it gets harder and harder to say something. Or if someone has a loss, say a beloved dog dies, and you don't . . ."

"Stuart, I get it. You wish you had told me sooner. What is it?"

"I was almost married before," he said. "I was engaged to someone before you."

"That's okay," Tabitha said, a little confused, wishing he weren't making it such a big deal. Was it a big deal? "Lots of people almost get married to someone before finding the actual right person."

At the time, she had a lot of hope that she was the actual right person for him, and that he was for her. But he hadn't grabbed on to that as a defense. It would have been easy enough to do. He let her statement go by without acknowledging it. *Was that my first moment of doubt?* she wondered. No, not really, that had come later. Looking back though, it should have been.

"Is that everything?" Tabitha finally asked, after what seemed like minutes went by.

"I suppose so," he said.

"Well, okay then. Thank you for telling me."

~

What she didn't know at the time, what he didn't tell her until later, was that the person he had been engaged to marry before her was named Abigail Golding. She was a freshman at the University of Michigan when he was a junior, and they fell in love quickly. After that, they were never apart. He went on to the law school there while she finished her undergraduate education, and then she stayed in Ann Arbor working at the Borders bookstore while he finished his last year of law school. She was from Petoskey, the upper part of the Lower Peninsula, but was happy to move to Marquette on the Upper Peninsula. She had a dream to open a rec center for bored teenagers, where she would encourage literacy. She was going to do incredible things, change lives—that's how Stuart put it anyway. They were to be married at a family friend's house right on Lake Superior in early August. It was all planned; everyone was invited. Five days before the wedding, before any of the guests arrived, she called it off.

That was all Tabitha knew, until the week before Stuart disappeared at least. Stuart could never really talk about it after that rare confessional moment during their engagement. If it ever even almost came up, he would walk out of the room or change the subject. When Tabitha first heard the details, about two years into their marriage, she was shocked on so many levels. What could possibly prompt someone to do that? If Abigail had given him a reason, he never shared it with Tabitha. But the thing that shocked her the most was that the man he described, the person who went to law school and was going to marry Abigail Golding, who sounded like he was fun loving and playful, present and interested, climbing a tree on a dare or staying up all night just to be able to say he did it, didn't remind her at all of the person she married. That person was all business, never straying from the plan. That is, until last summer.

~

Tabitha had managed to hold on to the baguette. They had run into a fair number of homeless people, and each time Toby would kindly ask if they wanted something to eat. He would then hand them some of the baked goods, explaining that the food was clean and untouched. And each time, Tabitha had to look slightly away, because she didn't want to give the food to these people, she wanted to keep it for herself. Finally, Toby seemed satisfied, and she still had the long loaf of bread in her hand. She held it up to him, raising her eyebrows as if to say, *What about this?*

"Keep that one," he said kindly. "They make delicious bread."

At the corner of Walnut and Eighteenth, Toby's phone rang. Tabitha watched as he turned away and said something quietly, then moved a little farther away, leaving Tabitha standing alone. He was back in less than a minute, but the excitement that she was getting used to seeing on his face was gone.

"Are you okay?" she asked.

"Yes, fine," he said quietly. "That was my ex-wife. The good news is that I get to see my daughter. Something came up for my ex, and she asked if I could take her tonight."

Tabitha wanted to ask what the bad news was, but she didn't. She wasn't sure how they were going to end their time together, so she was somewhat relieved that it was ended for them. When they said good-bye, she vaguely waved in the southern direction, indicating that she lived nearby, but she didn't give him any specifics. Toby hesitated for a second.

"See you at the next game?" he asked.

Now she hesitated. *Well, no, not necessarily,* she wanted to say. She glanced at the bread in her hand, then back toward Toby. She took a deep breath.

"Yes, see you there," she said.

Toby grinned at her, and she felt herself grinning back, then laughing. He waved, and as he walked away from her, east on Walnut, she could still hear him chuckling.

Now she headed home but took a slight detour to the house with the window box full of basil. She could make her usual toast tonight. If only she had a tomato. With that, it was sad enough. But bread and basil was even sadder. She was happy to see the plant was as robust as ever. She waited until there was nobody near her and ripped a handful of leaves off. She tried to look like she was comfortable doing it. Maybe it was her house, and she was simply picking her own herbs. It was all a big show, because absolutely nobody seemed to care. She told herself to write this down when she got home.

Where could she get a tomato?

And then she had what had become an outrageous idea. She'd buy one. She stuffed the basil into her purse and zipped it shut. She walked into the small grocery store she used to walk into almost daily, and she pretended for a few minutes that things were like they used to be, when she could walk in and use her debit card for forty dollars or ninety dollars, and it just didn't make a difference. Right away she saw Marlon, her favorite check-out person. She walked over to him.

"Hi! I just wanted to let you know, I got the bread before I came in," she said, holding it up for him to see.

"Oh, okay, no problem," he said. "Where have you been? I haven't seen you."

"I was away for a little while," she said. "I don't know where I was."

She had to keep moving. Seeing Marlon and having him be so kind was not helping her pretend. She felt the burn of tears behind her eyes and faked a sneeze.

"Bless you," he said.

Now she was having trouble holding back the tears. They spilled out and she wiped them away, looking in her purse for a tissue, but she saw the basil and sensed a sob building deep inside her chest.

"Be right back," she said, and walked away toward the produce section. Why did she think this was a good idea? She sensed Marlon's eyes on her. He had seen her in much worse situations. Like the time Fern had just learned to walk, well, really, she had just learned to run, and Tabitha was checking out. She had a huge pile of items on the belt, and Fern got away from her for one second, really, it was one second! And when Tabitha looked up, Fern was outside the store, on the sidewalk! And moving toward Spruce Street. Tabitha screamed and ran, leaving everything. When she got to Fern, she couldn't breathe. Fern was fine. She might never have run into the road: she seemed to sense the division of sidewalk versus street even then. But Tabitha was traumatized. She could have so easily gone back into the store and finished. But she didn't. She just picked Fern up and walked the one block home, leaving milk and cereal and pounds of sliced deli meats on the belt to be put away by someone else. What did they even do with meat that had been sliced for someone but not bought? She didn't go back for a while—weeks—and when she did, nobody said a word.

Then there was the time Levi had to go to the bathroom *so bad*. He was about four, and they could not have made it home. The store had a strict no-bathroom policy, but Tabitha carried Levi in and begged. She was near tears that time, so worried he would have an accident and be afraid to leave the house without a diaper in the future. And they let her, they led her right through the employee-only door to the bathroom, smiling, happy to help. She had seen other desperate people, adults, beg to use the bathroom, and they always said no. They had always been especially nice to her.

Now she stood over the bananas. They offered two choices—organic and not organic. Three months ago, she would have picked the organic, not giving the higher price a second thought. But she knew she couldn't buy bananas and a tomato, and at this point, dinner was the priority. She moved to the tomato bin. She was crying hard now. It was almost impossible to remain quiet, and even more challenging to see. She was trying to act normal. Anyone could be here. She leaned over the tomatoes, hiding her face. They all looked pink. And they were almost two dollars a pound. She chose a tiny red one at the bottom, maybe leftover from a better crop. She took a deep breath and turned. Marlon was standing there.

"Are you okay?" he asked. "You seem upset."

"I'm okay," she tried to say, but it didn't come out that way. It came out all slobbery and hiccuppy.

"Come with me," he said.

She didn't even ask where. She followed him to the back aisle and across the store. They went through the same door she used when she took Levi to the off-limits bathroom. Then they went through one more door into a tiny, but very nice room. She assumed it was the employee lounge.

"Do you want to sit?" Marlon asked, grabbing a cup from the watercooler and filling it up. He handed it to her.

"Thanks," she said, but she continued to stand.

"I've seen it all," he said matter-of-factly. "I've seen fights. I've seen mothers curse at their kids. I've seen kids curse at their mothers. I had one customer who came in after being in jail for nine years. He said he was wrongly accused. He finally got out on new DNA evidence and came right here to get a Tastykake. I've seen it all."

"Yeah, well, my husband disappeared and left me in my really fancy apartment with my two kids but no money, no word, no return date. I don't know what's going on with our cell-phone payments, or our health insurance, or my children's mental health. Fern hasn't been feeling well, and I've been avoiding taking her to the doctor. Oh, and I don't want anyone to know, so I'm pretending everything is fine."

She felt such relief after she said it that she had to sit down.

"Please, don't tell anyone," she said. "I don't know what came over me just then."

"Your secret is safe with me," Marlon said.

"I should go," she said. "I'm just going to get this tomato."

"Okay, I'll check you out. I just want to show you something in the cheese section."

She followed him back out, and they turned right and walked past the milk and yogurt to the cheese. He scanned the shelf for a minute and pulled out a big hunk of cheddar.

"This is good with tomatoes," he said.

"But I can't," she said.

"Come on, I'll check you out," he said.

She followed him back to his lane. She saw he'd put a tented note on the belt saying he would be back in ten minutes. She was touched by that. She watched as he weighed the tomato.

"Thirty-five cents," he said. "The cheddar is on me."

"No, that's too much," she said. "I can't let you pay for that. Please, just charge me."

"Employees get one free item a week. That's my item for the week. Come back next week, after Thursday, and I can give you an Entenmann's marble pound cake."

"Oh, wow," she said, afraid to talk too much because she could feel the tears building again. "Thank you."

"My pleasure."

She spent the short way home thinking of what she could do to repay him. Everything she thought of involved money, so she eventually gave up. As soon as she got inside what she thought was an empty apartment, she pulled out the small notebook and added the basil, then the cheese, and wrote *MARLON* in all caps at the top of the page.

"Hello?" she called out for good measure. It was all quiet, but it didn't feel like she was alone.

Tabitha was already dreaming about the toasted-cheese and tomato sandwich they'd have for dinner, and she was eager for everyone to get home. She walked through the apartment, coming last to Levi's closed door. It was almost always open when he wasn't in it.

"Monkey?" she called.

She thought she heard a response, but it was so quiet she wasn't sure.

"Are you in there?"

"I said, 'Yes.'"

"Oh, I didn't know you were back from Butch's," she said. "Come out. I have a good dinner planned."

"I'm not hungry," he said.

"Can I come in?"

"No."

"Okay, suit yourself," she said before walking away.

Tabitha decided that he'd come out when he smelled the cheese. She took out her phone and called Sarina's mother. She was happy to have all this time to herself, but this was getting ridiculous. She let it ring, but it went to voicemail. So she headed into the kitchen and took her time cutting the bread and slicing the cheese and tomato. The relief she felt after talking to Marlon was slowly dissipating. What was she doing, letting the kids be on their own so much?

The front door swung open, and Tabitha was startled. There was no reason to call up from downstairs, Fern was a resident here of course, but for some reason she expected some warning. Tabitha walked to the foyer with a big smile on her face, ready to greet Sarina's mother or both of her parents, but it was just Fern.

"Hey, Fernie Bernie, how was it?" she asked, walking over to her and kissing the top of her head. She smelled like chlorine.

"It was good," she said sweetly. "Thank you for letting me go."

"They didn't walk you in?"

"No, but they watched me from the car," she said, like that was more than enough.

"Okay," Tabitha said, feeling somewhat out of control, like she was leaving too many details to chance. "I'm making cheddar-and-tomato sandwiches on good bread for dinner. They'll be ready soon."

"No thank you," Fern said. "There was a lot of food at the water park."

"Suit yourself," she said again, but she said it a little nicer to Fern than she did to Levi.

"I'm going to go watch TV," Fern said.

"Okay, sweetie. I'll be in soon."

"Mama?" Fern asked.

"Yes, sweetie?"

She hesitated for a few seconds, looking all around the kitchen. "Forget it," she finally said.

"What is it, Fern?" Tabitha pressed.

"Nothing," Fern said, getting impatient. "Just nothing."

"Well it seemed like you were going to ask *something*."

Fern took a deep breath. "You bug me," she said, before walking toward the living room.

Tabitha watched her stomp through the kitchen, wondering if that was what Fern was going to say in the first place, or if she bugged her because she wouldn't leave her alone. She wasn't sure which would be better—neither really. She wanted to call her back and ask, but decided to let her be.

She stood at the counter thinking she didn't much want a sandwich either right now. That lunch with Rachel was more than she'd had at a single meal in a long time. She wrapped everything up, deciding it would make a great breakfast or lunch tomorrow. Before joining Fern in front of the television, she went into her bedroom and pulled the list out of the drawer. She scanned the items to see if she'd come across any answers. She always hoped she'd see something in a different way. But it all looked the same: a list of mysteries, partly, she knew, because she had been leaving out this next item. She had not wanted to admit it, but it was time, she knew that. It was time to start dealing with it. She grabbed a pen and added item number nine—Stuart's marriage that never was. She looked at it for a minute. That wasn't exactly right. She took a deep breath and crossed it out with her pen. It was a big mess, but that seemed appropriate, given the situation. She tried again, this time writing one simple word next to the item number, one name—*Abigail*.

At the way bottom of the paper she wrote in all caps *HAPPILY EVER AFTER*, then next to it she wrote *NOT* in parenthesis. As she and Stuart walked back down the aisle after they were married, Stuart put his arm around her and leaned in close. He said, "And they lived happily ever after," into her ear. She smiled, she liked that, but when she turned to look at him, she could see something in his eyes. She had the feeling he was trying to convince himself. Did that count as a clue? She decided it did, it all counted, and wrote *item number ten* next to it. She folded the paper back up and went to sit with Fern, who was watching an old DVD. But she couldn't get comfortable. She kept shifting positions. Fern was still in her bathing suit with shorts over the top, even though it felt cold in the apartment.

"I'll be right back," Tabitha said, but she might as well have been talking to the wall, Fern was so absorbed by the show. She put a throw blanket over her, hoping that would rouse her, but Fern just let it settle with no reaction.

Tabitha went back to her bedroom and pulled out the list again. She was so tired of her lists. The other one, the one with the stolen items, was necessary. But this one was doing her no good. First she circled the ninth item—Abigail. It was the most important clue here, it was what had brought them to this place. It was the one she should focus on, the one she had been focusing on at first with Internet searches and random phone calls and no luck; she couldn't get any traction at all. She should try harder, keep looking. She didn't need the list to do it; the list was distracting her. She read through it one more time, then she ripped it up into tiny pieces, took the handful to the toilet, and flushed, glad that if this caused a backup she could just call the maintenance person. At least that wasn't something she had to worry about all by herself.

She let everyone sleep late the next morning, and she truly believed she rested better without that list next to her. Maybe it was less about getting rid of the list and more about beginning to acknowledge the actual problem, but either way it felt like the first step in moving forward. She sat up in bed and pulled a book off the top of her pile. She hadn't read a book for pleasure in a long time. She was just about to open it when her cell phone rang. She looked at the display—it was Sarina's mother.

"Kaye, hi, I was going to call you this morning," Tabitha lied. "I want to thank you so much for yesterday. Fern had such a good time."

There was silence on the other end, and Tabitha thought maybe they'd been disconnected. She pulled the phone away from her ear to check, but saw the seconds were ticking away.

"Kaye?" she said into the phone.

"I'm here," she answered, but there was something cold about her usually warm voice. Didn't Kaye just call her? Tabitha got a weird feeling in her stomach.

"Is everything okay?" Tabitha asked.

"I was going to ask you the same question," Kaye said. "Did Fern say she had fun yesterday?"

"She did," Tabitha said, trying to remember if she actually said she had fun. She didn't say she *didn't* have fun. What wasn't to like about a water park? "It sounded like a good day. She said there was a lot of food." Suddenly Tabitha remembered Fern's tiny outburst after she got home. Had she missed something?

"Well, yeah, there was that," Kaye said slowly, drawing out the words. "But, Tabitha, I'm concerned about Fern, and I'm also concerned about you."

"What? Why?"

"Fern was unable to participate yesterday. She was in a lot of pain."

Kaye let the words sit there.

Tabitha could play dumb. She could ask, *What pain?* But she knew. "Do you mean her knee? And what do you mean she was unable to participate? She was with you all day. Why didn't you call me?"

"She didn't want us to," Kaye said, and there was something about the way she said *us* that bothered Tabitha. Like now Kaye's family was a unit protecting Fern.

"Well, I would have come to get her right away," Tabitha said defensively. "I wasn't doing anything important. I was just waiting for her to come home really."

"Look, we've known each other for a long time," Kaye said, and her voice sounded a little warmer. *Don't be too nice,* Tabitha thought, *or I'll cry. I'll break down like I did in the stupid grocery store yesterday. Be mean, it's easier.* "And I know what a good mother you are. I mean, you really are. But lately, something hasn't seemed right, or at least it hasn't seemed the same. I know Stuart's away, and I can only imagine how hard that is. I hate when Hugo goes away, even for a night or two. It's not that, though. It's that Fern said she's been in pain for a long time and, well, I am just wondering why you haven't done anything about it."

"That's ridiculous," Tabitha said. She felt like a strobe light was blinking at all the ends of her body—her fingers, her toes. How did she let it get to this point? "I've been paying close attention to what's going on with Fern's knee. In fact, we have an appointment tomorrow morning."

"You do?" Kaye said, and Tabitha could hear the relief in her voice. *Screw you!* she wanted to call through the phone. *I don't need you to feel relieved that I'm taking care of my child.* "Fern didn't mention that."

"Well, she didn't know, I guess," Tabitha said. "But thanks for your concern."

"Sure," Kaye said, now the flustered one. "I just want to make sure you guys are okay."

"We're fine," Tabitha said, before hanging up.

Tabitha didn't ask Fern about the water park or about what she told Sarina and her family. She kept things as simple as possible all day Sunday, not asking anything of the kids, basically just sitting around the apartment eating the bread, cheese, and tiny tomato. She didn't even make them do their homework. Her main goal was to let Fern's knee rest.

Monday morning she woke up extra early with the intention of taking Fern to the walk-in hour at the pediatrician's office. It wasn't really meant for Fern's situation—she knew that. It was meant for something that literally came up overnight. But she couldn't stand the thought of calling the triage nurse and waiting around all morning for her to call back while Fern watched more TV. She had an urge to do something *right now*. So she left Levi in the apartment with the instructions to leave in ten minutes and go straight to school, something she had never done before, and she and Fern set out for the pediatrician's office less than four blocks away.

"Fern Brewer," Tabitha said to the smiling receptionist.

"Birth date?"

"May eighth," she said.

"What's the problem?" she asked.

"Her knee is really bothering her. She's having a hard time walking on it. Also, it's hot and looks red in the back."

"How long has this been going on?"

"About two weeks, no, maybe three weeks," Tabitha said, quickly and quietly.

The receptionist looked up from the keyboard. Tabitha waited for her to tell them this was not what walk-in hour was intended for and that they would have to make an appointment and come back. But then the receptionist looked at Fern, and Tabitha hoped she was thinking she should give them a break. She sighed and looked back at her keyboard.

"Any injuries?"

"Not that we're aware of," Tabitha said with relief.

"Any recent illnesses?"

"She had a fever and a stomach bug recently, but I can't imagine this is related to that."

"Okay, you have a twenty-dollar co-pay for today, and I can see you have a previous balance that hasn't been paid yet."

Tabitha handed over her credit card and held her breath.

The receptionist took it and swiped it before handing it back, then pushed a receipt toward Tabitha to sign. She had been charged sixty-eight dollars. She signed the flimsy slip of paper.

"Okay, please take a seat," the receptionist said, not looking up. Tabitha wanted her to look. Not only did she want to be allowed to misuse the walk-in hour but she also wanted the receptionist to not be mad at her.

Fern hobbled over to a seat. Tabitha wondered why her knee suddenly seemed so much worse than it did before. Was it that she was being given permission to let it be bad? Or did she feel she had to prove to the receptionist that they really did have a situation? Tabitha followed her and took the seat next to her, scooping her arm around her.

"Fern?" the nurse called.

"That's us," Tabitha said, trying to smile.

They headed back, and Fern was weighed. Tabitha thought she'd lost a few pounds, but she couldn't remember exactly how much she weighed last time, so she tried not to worry about it. They waited about twenty minutes before the doctor came in. It wasn't their usual person, but she was young and nice and seemed gentle.

"So it just started hurting out of the blue?" the doctor asked Fern.

"Pretty much," she answered, looking the doctor in the eyes, which made Tabitha proud.

"And it feels hot?"

"Very."

"And sensitive when people touch it?"

"Yes."

Tabitha wanted to give Fern a look that said, *Really? Why didn't you tell me any of that?* But she didn't. She knew this was way more on her than it was on Fern. The doctor felt around, then stopped and thought, like she was trying to get an image of the inside of a knee in her mind. She kept checking Fern's knee and stopping and thinking.

"Oh, and the back of her knee looked a little funny to me," Tabitha said.

The doctor gently turned Fern's leg over and studied the smooth backside of her knee. It was definitely red.

"To tell you the truth, I'm totally stumped," the doctor said. "Some of the symptoms point to a possible torn or injured muscle, but other symptoms aren't consistent with that. Since it's been going on so long, and since Fern is clearly in pain, I'm going to send you for some tests."

"But that will take so long, and I hate to put her through that. Do you think there's anything simple we can try? Ice or heat? Which is better in this situation? Or both?"

"Sure, you can try heat if you want, but if there's something going on in there, we should really find out. I'd like to begin with an X-ray, and then we'll take it from there. I'll write you a script, and you should have it done at CHOP." Tabitha nodded her agreement. CHOP was the city's children's hospital and was highly respected throughout the region. "I'd like to have this done in the next week or so, at the latest."

"Okay," she said, waiting while the doctor typed something into the computer.

"Oh, and you can give her Advil," the doctor said.

"Thanks."

~

Tabitha was walking away from school after dropping Fern off when her phone rang. It was Kaye. She thought about not answering, but she had always liked Kaye.

"Hello?"

"Tabitha, I'm so glad to reach you. I feel just awful about yesterday. I am so sorry. Things haven't been so easy around here lately. Hugo is working so much, and, well, he's worried it's all for nothing. He isn't sure he's going to have a job at the end of the month." She lowered her voice when she said the last part.

"Oh, Kaye, I'm so sorry," Tabitha said.

"And I was just in a really bad mood. I mean, I was worried about Fern, but I had intended to call and talk to you nicely. I don't even know what happened."

"Well, we just left the doctor," Tabitha said, glad she had that to offer. "And they have no idea what's causing it. She has to have an X-ray."

"Poor girl," Kaye said. "But at least you'll get to the bottom of it soon."

"Listen, I didn't want to ask Fern about it, but when you said she wasn't able to participate, did she not even go on one slide?"

"She went on one, the one that ends and drops you, like, twenty feet into the pool. She was in so much pain after she hit that I thought I'd have to call you. But she asked me not to, really, she begged me not to. We ended up renting one of those silly cabanas, and she and Hugo sat and read most of the day—and ate."

"Oh," Tabitha said.

"But hey, that's not why I called now, obviously," Kaye said, clearly trying to turn the mood around. "Sarina has this crazy idea. She wants to do something nice for Fern, since she hasn't been feeling well, and since yesterday wasn't as much fun as she had hoped. We were thinking a pizza party—maybe even tonight? Sarina wants to invite you guys, and of course Levi can come, plus the six girls—Meghan, Lucy, Sophie, Eliana, Phoebe, and Grace. I know it is totally last minute, but I have a feeling everyone can make it if you can—and we could surprise Fern if you want to—just for fun. I'd leave that detail up to you. I know it's a school night, but who cares, right? Hugo has to work late tonight, so I would love the company. What do you think?"

"Fern would love that!" Tabitha said, wondering if Kaye somehow knew. Could she? "And yes, let's surprise her. Why not? I'll just tell her we have to stop by your place to pick up a jacket, or something like that. What can we bring? What time should we come?"

"I was thinking around six? And let me send an email right now to the girls' mothers. This will be fun! Maybe we can surprise everyone."

"I love that idea," Tabitha said. "You didn't say what we can bring."

"It's going to be enough work to get Fern here," she said. "Please, just bring yourselves."

CHAPTER ELEVEN

The next morning, Tabitha started a new list. This one was about her mother's last days, possibly other stuff, too, and she wrote at the top: *The Worst Things.*

Number one: The Hug.

When she had hugged her mother a few days before she died, not knowing she was going to die as soon as she did but knowing she probably wasn't going to live too much longer, she realized she hadn't hugged her in weeks. If she were being really honest, it had been longer than that. She added a letter *A* on the next line, like she was writing an outline, and added: *Response*. When she hugged her that day, her mother had clung to her.

Number two: The Morphine.

At number two she stopped. She had intended to list the doses, and the times of the doses, and try to figure out where things went wrong, if they went wrong, but she realized now that she wasn't ready.

Number three:—she wrote—and underlined it three times. Then she starred it. The Sidewalk Sale.

She stopped again. When was that? About three months before her mother died? Or was it four months? They had cleaned out the apartment. Well, Tabitha had, after she had completely lost patience. For months her mother had said okay, she was finally ready to go through everything and throw things away. She was ready to *"lighten her load."* But time and time again, they would spend hours going through clothes or books or jewelry—making piles to either keep, give away, or throw out. They would come to the end, and Tabitha would be ready to actually do something with the piles—throw the appropriate pile in the trash, put the "keep" pile back where it belonged, and take the third pile to give away—whatever that might mean. Each time, though, her mother had said no, let's just put it all back where we found it and do it another time. All that work wasted, afternoons and afternoons of expending so much energy with no progress made.

By the time Tabitha held the sidewalk sale, her mother was much easier to trick. She had always been so sharp, but that had changed over the previous few years. So she set her mother up in her bedroom watching a movie, and she slowly took all the things she could remember from the various "trash" and "give away" piles down to the sidewalk where she displayed them all neatly on a folding table and waited to sell them. Of course, she felt bad about twenty minutes into it, so she brought her mother out, expecting her to be livid and demand they bring every single item back inside. Tabitha had already sold a few things—some books, an old frame, a beautiful basket holding Mardi Gras beads. But she assumed her mother wouldn't know what was already missing.

Her mother approached the sale like she had no idea that these were *her* things on display. She walked around the table Tabitha had set up and looked at the items one by one.

"Oh my," she had said, holding up an elaborately decorated cigar box, full of miniature soaps collected from all over the world. "I had no idea other people did this! And look, they went to Paris and Mexico, too!"

Tabitha had been stunned.

"And look at this Bundt pan with the mermaids! I have one just like it upstairs. I use it to make my famous raspberry Jell-O mold every Christmas. Let's buy it. Then I could make two at a time!"

"Come on, Mom," Tabitha had said. "If you have all this stuff already, you don't need duplicates."

Her mother had nodded and gone back inside to finish the movie. Tabitha knew she should have just taken it all back in: most of it was still there in front of her. What would happen if her mother lived long enough to want to make that Jell-O mold again? But she was so mad! And she was so, so tired of it all. And she knew she was going to be stuck going through it, again. She thought about the soap collection. That would be easy to take back to the apartment and place under the bathroom sink where she had found it. But she didn't. She sold a bunch of items for a dollar each, her mother's beloved beach towels, her soup ladle, her cake plate, her Jell-O mold. When she couldn't stand it anymore, she walked armfuls to various garbage cans in her mother's neighborhood, telling herself hopefully that a homeless person might come across it and be able to use it. The thing was, there were very few homeless people in her mother's neighborhood. There probably weren't any.

Tabitha's phone pinged, and she was glad to be pulled away from that awful day. She looked. It was a reminder to herself that she had set so long ago that said Invitations. She was supposed to be working on the invitations for the bar mitzvah, but she hadn't been able to come to any conclusions about where or how to do it. She couldn't think of a single workable option. Even having it at the synagogue was expensive. She couldn't do it at the apartment with all the burned-out light bulbs and lack of funds for food. She could invite everyone to the sports bar—it would be a game day of some sort. She let herself chuckle a little at that thought. Had she really reached this low point? But was it such a crazy idea? Levi loved sports, tons of people chose a sports theme for their bar mitzvahs. The best part, of course, would be that they could eat the food from the buffet. Tabitha wondered if anyone had ever done that.

She spent some time following up on her last interview with the pest control people. She still hadn't heard from them. She emailed to check in, saying she was still very interested. Then she looked on various job sites and sent her résumé with the hope of setting up two interviews—one with a medical supply company, making home visits to see what people needed and following up the visits to make sure everything was working properly, and one with a tree care company, making appointments for people to have their trees evaluated and trimmed. She added them to her job-prospect list, reaching number nine, which made her think of item number nine on her other list, the one she flushed down the toilet.

She had spent a fair amount of time searching for Abigail on all the usual social-media sites, and she just wasn't there. She took a breath and tried again, typing "Abigail Golding" into the browser. It took a second, and tons of Abigail Goldings came up, she knew them all now, had followed them all to dead ends, but none of them was *the* Abigail Golding. She kept moving, clicking on the next page, going back in time, years and years. Still, there was nothing new. She had spent hours making sure none of these were her. And then, like someone was teasing her or giving her a gift, she spotted an unfamiliar headline—the words *Abigail Golding* and *Michigan* jumped out at her, and she stopped, clicked on the link, and waited. A photo came up of a woman: pretty, dark hair, smiley, standing in front of a building Tabitha recognized from Michigan—was that the student union? Tabitha wasn't sure what it was called. The headline said, "Alumna Gives Back." She checked the date—it was ten years old. She read on about how Abigail Golding, graduate of the University of Michigan in 1992, gave money to a literacy program at the university. It was a tiny, one-paragraph article, which Tabitha read over and over again, leaving her wanting more and also wanting less. It didn't say anything about where she lived or if she had a family. It was basically void of all important information. Still, this was the first picture she had seen of Abigail. It was also the first evidence, beyond Stuart's words, that she was real, that she existed in the world. Tabitha copied the link and sent herself an email, so she could have the information—not much, but something. The only other time she'd come across something worth saving was when an Abigail Golding of Michigan had come up in an old obituary, probably for a great-grandmother. No address, nothing beyond the assumption that Abigail had never been married. Tabitha had found a phone number for the address listed for the deceased. It had turned out to be a nursing home, and the people there were unwilling to answer a single question.

Now Tabitha almost didn't want to use this up too fast, the possibility of grabbing on to something—some thread of where Abigail might be, which would possibly then lead her to where Stuart might be. Even so, she googled the development office at the University of Michigan and called, before she could think too much about it.

"Development office, can I help you?" a young voice said. It was probably a student, Tabitha realized.

"Yes, please, I'm looking for an alum of yours. I'm trying to reach her to see if she wants to partner on a literacy initiative, and I came upon an old article which led me to you. Her name is Abigail Golding?"

Tabitha knew before she got the response, but she had to try.

"Oh, I'm so sorry," the voice said. "But we can't provide any information about our graduates, no matter what the reason is."

"Well, I can tell you she will be very happy to hear from me," Tabitha heard herself saying. The words *on opposite day* ran through her head. It was something she heard Fern say sometimes, and it struck Tabitha as a perfect use of the phrase now.

"I'm so sorry," the person said again. "My hands are tied."

Tabitha wanted to say something snarky like, *Are they, are they really tied? Clearly not, since you answered the phone.* But she didn't. She knew it wouldn't get her anywhere.

"Thank you," Tabitha said, and ended the call.

She sat there for a minute just looking at the computer. She shook her head, trying to move away from this place of searching for something that she couldn't find. She decided to stop looking for now, and instead wrote to Kaye to thank her for the night before—which had been great in every way. Fern had been thrilled and smiled so much; Tabitha realized how little she had been smiling lately. She would have to find ways to make Fern smile more.

She got dressed and made the beds. After that she had nothing to do, and she felt a strong need to get away from her computer. She walked outside, thinking that a walk would do her good, and before she knew it, she was standing in front of Nora's apartment building. She looked up at the window she thought might be Nora's—though it was truly a monster of a building, and she could be off by four or five windows. She didn't see anything, any lights, any movement, but she wouldn't really expect to.

It was as though a rope were pulling her forward as she walked in and moved by the desk to the elevator. She could easily say she just wanted to say hello to Nora if there was someone else there. She went to the second floor, feeling a little excited, like she was finally going to do something to improve her situation. She was going to ask to play Monopoly, and she was going to steal some money. She had to be able to pay for Fern's X-ray if their insurance was defunct. She didn't want Fern to be in pain.

She crossed the hall and knocked. No answer, and there was no sound of movement inside. She knocked again. Her phone rang, startling her. It was Rachel. She felt like she'd been caught in the act, like Rachel could see her. She didn't answer but went back across the hall, this time going down the stairs to the left of the elevator and out into the lobby. She touched Rachel's name on her screen and heard the call go through.

"Sorry," she said casually, as soon as Rachel answered. "I was in the shower."

"I'm so glad you called back!" Rachel said. "I need you. I should have called you sooner, but I didn't want to jinx it. I finally got an appointment with the sperm bank. Will you please come with me to look at possible donors?"

"Sure, are you at the store?"

"Yeah, I'll leave here in about fifteen minutes."

"Okay, I'll be right there."

She walked out, feeling like she'd been saved from something, and the idea of reading profiles to choose a possible father for Rachel's baby sounded exciting. She was happy to do something that had nothing to do with her immediate situation. She walked a block on JFK Boulevard, then headed south to Chestnut. Someone familiar caught her eye. Toby. She didn't want to admit it, but she'd been thinking about him, wondering when she might see him again. Her first instinct was to call and wave, but that passed quickly. He was on the phone, having what looked like a heated conversation. He didn't see her. She ducked her head and crossed the other way, so they wouldn't walk by each other. Across the street, she stopped and watched him walk in the direction she just came from.

She felt an overwhelming sense of regret as soon as she couldn't see him anymore. She'd never be able to find him, unless she was lucky enough to run into him again at another game. She wished they'd exchanged numbers, or email addresses, or some sort of information. She shook her head. What was she thinking? She was married.

As she walked down Eighteenth Street toward Rachel's shop, she saw a man sitting on the sidewalk up against the building. That wasn't unusual, there were a lot of homeless people on the streets of Philadelphia. It was his sign that caught her eye. It read **In Need of A Little Kindness**. She wasn't sure why that got to her more than any other sign someone might hold up—more than the **Anything Helps** sign or the **Please Help Me I Have Kids** sign. The ones she usually walked right by, except on those rare days when she and the kids had nothing to do, and she thought it would be a good lesson to them to notice and acknowledge homeless people. On those days, she'd had them make peanut-butter-and-jelly sandwiches—lots of them—and she put each one in one of her boxed-lunch boxes, along with a napkin, utensils, and a cookie. They would go all around Center City, asking first—*Always ask first,* she would say, *Don't ever assume.* They would hand them all out, and then head home feeling like they had done something nice. Now she didn't have any peanut butter to spare. As she walked by the homeless man, she realized he was so young. He couldn't be more than twenty, maybe twenty-five. He was shirtless. His eyes reminded her of Levi's. She looked at his body and decided he was about the same size as Stuart. She wished she had some extra change or some extra food to give him, but she didn't. She crossed the street and practically ran into Rachel, coming out the door of Di Bruno's.

"What took you so long?" she asked.

"Sorry, one thing after another," Tabitha said, and switched course so she could follow Rachel away from the store and down Chestnut Street, toward a potential sperm donor.

~

That night, after Tabitha spent hours looking through profiles with Rachel, she and the kids had frozen lima beans and the last of the peanut butter on Ritz crackers for dinner. She poured a tiny bit of the vinegar onto the beans and swirled them around. When the kids came in to sit at the table, they looked at the offerings and then looked at her. Fern chose three crackers already smeared with peanut butter and scooped a pile of lima beans onto her plate. She immediately started eating. Levi didn't move.

"This is dinner?" he asked.

"Come on," Tabitha coaxed. "It's surprisingly good."

"Crackers for dinner?" he said, his tone getting harsher.

"You know what?" Tabitha said, trying to keep it light. "I'm doing that thing where you completely clean out the cabinets once a year—clear it all out."

"You mean for Passover?" Levi asked again, now sounding incredulous.

"Well, I'm doing it early," Tabitha said, thinking she better look up the term for what Levi was talking about. What if someone at the synagogue asked her about it, or mentioned it casually? She wanted to be ready. Stuart would know the term. But then, as she always did these days, she realized if Stuart were here to tell her what the word was they wouldn't be eating crackers for dinner.

Levi scowled at her, but he took some and ate. She could hear the crackers being chewed. She took one cracker so she could look busy but waited until they seemed to have their fill before eating the last two crackers and the tiny bit of lima beans that was left. That was it, there was nothing left in the freezer.

After dinner she cleaned up, then saw that the kids were watching TV together, which was unusual.

"I'm running out for about twenty minutes," she said.

"Where are you going?" Levi asked, sounding alarmed.

"Just up the street, I have to drop something off," she said. "I'll be right back."

She grabbed the backpack she packed earlier and headed out, past the night doorman and into the cool city air. She turned right up Eighteenth Street, hoping he would be there. As she crossed Chestnut she saw that he was, sitting with his sign that said **In Need of a Little Kindness**. She might not have peanut butter or supplies for her boxed lunches anymore, but she had kindness.

"Hi," she said as she approached him. He looked up, and it seemed like he was out of it, like he was just going to look through her, but then his eyes adjusted and he looked at her. "I don't have food or money to offer you, but I have two blankets, a warm bathrobe, slippers, a pair of shoes, and some clothes. In here." She handed him the backpack. He hesitated, then he took it from her.

"And these," she said, reaching into her pocket for a handful of Stuart's gold cufflinks. She handed them out to him like she was offering change. He put his hand out and accepted them. At first he looked annoyed.

"They are all real gold," Tabitha said quickly, suddenly aware that people were looking at her. "They're worth something. I'm not sure what, but something. It's worth a try."

He nodded and pushed them into a tattered box that sat next to him.

"Thank you," he said, sounding so normal. Totally normal. She would have thought that he would sound croaky, or not be able to speak at all. But no, he sounded just like anyone else. That bothered her more than anything.

"You're welcome," she said, and then headed home.

~

On what Tabitha now thought of as the terrible night—though again, she still wasn't sure if it was the *most* terrible night, and she still couldn't bring herself to put it on the new list—the call had come around eight forty-five. She had finished early, since she'd had so many orders and had run out of some of the ingredients. She had sold her last meal at around eight to those people who called late, the ones with the birthday, who she'd almost said no to. They had come to pick it up at the front desk. They lived nearby, they said—it would be easier that way and the food would be hotter. It was the customers' picking up and her accepting the payment while standing there in the lobby that always felt especially questionable to her, and that night it had more than ever for some reason. She told herself again and again that she wasn't alone, she was jumping on the bandwagon of a whole new era of food takeout. One of her friends from cooking school had started turning his home into a pop-up restaurant a few times a week. He lived in the Italian Market and made some of the best Italian food she had ever had. There was a waiting list to eat there! People called weeks ahead, and paid a fair amount of money, to have a chance to come to his home to eat his home-cooked offerings. And there were other takeout apps out there. There was Shepherd's Pie, of course, another called Dinner Is Ready, and one called The Kitchen Sink, not to mention the ever-popular Food Truck. Tabitha's was growing, she could feel it. It was much talked about on Facebook and Twitter. She had seen some amazing pictures of her food on Instagram—it looked even better in the pictures than she remembered it looking when she packaged it up. She was starting to worry she wouldn't be able to keep up with the demand.

When the phone rang she almost didn't answer it. Stuart was there with her, he had come home early, at least early for him, and they were talking about Fern's teacher who, Fern had told them, had been falling asleep in class on occasion. They both found it odd and were just deciding if they should go to the head of school to voice their concerns when she heard the ring. She didn't recognize the number, but something made her reach for her phone and take the call. That was one of the moments that distinguished *before* and *after*—before the call things weren't great, they were . . . something else. But after the call they were—what? Always up in the air with the possibility of something truly awful constantly looming out there? That about summed it up.

"Hello?" Tabitha had said.

She heard shuffling, some breathing, she was about to hang up, thinking it was a wrong number or a butt dial.

"Were there any peanuts in that food?" a woman's voice said, clear panic in her voice.

"Who is this?" Tabitha asked, getting a terrible feeling in her chest.

"We read the menu, it didn't say anything about peanuts. Were there any? Any at all?"

Tabitha could hear the unmistakable sounds of a hospital through the phone.

"No," Tabitha said quickly, running through the ingredients in her mind. "None at all."

"Ethan can't breathe," the woman said. "It happened right after we ate. About three minutes after. I had to call an ambulance. I don't know what else it could be. But no peanuts? Are you sure?"

Tabitha thought again. Beef, scallions, ginger, sesame.

"I'm sure," Tabitha said.

"Oh, thank God," the woman said. "Thank you." The call ended.

Tabitha held the phone in her hand. The feeling that she was forgetting something was so strong. As she turned back toward Stuart, putting her phone on the granite counter, she saw it. Right there, next to the stove. Clear as day. Peanut oil, and not particularly refined oil, she knew that, because she preferred the way this one cooked. She liked to use peanut oil, especially for Asian dishes. And it was perfect to fry the spring rolls. It left them light and crispy, without a hint of grease. That was why she was so careful with the app—there was a place to write allergies. It was not optional. It was part of the required field. She did that on purpose. The order wouldn't go through unless someone either filled it out or checked the box that said no allergies. Then she had a program that cross referenced any allergies with the ingredients of the day—and if there was a problem it would alert her and she would cancel the order. But they hadn't used the app. When they called she never even asked them about allergies. Had they told her? She didn't think so. She reached for the peanut oil, then pulled her hand away. She picked up her phone.

"What? What is it?" Stuart asked.

She didn't answer him. She found the most recent number on her phone and called back. It rang and rang. She hung up and tried again. Still, no answer and no voicemail.

"Tabitha, what is it?"

"I have to reach them," she said, finding it hard to breathe herself. She thought of the man, he had been young—what could it have been, his twenty-ninth birthday? His thirtieth? He had just the hint of facial hair, the kind that looked good, that was there on purpose. And his hair was dark and a little long, hanging over his eyes when he paid her. She thought about him not being able to breathe. Where was he now? What was going on? She tried the number again. Still nothing.

"It was about a customer," she said, feeling sick, feeling like she wanted to go back in time and change something, anything, but mostly the peanut oil. "He's allergic to peanuts but I didn't know because he didn't use the app, he just called to place the order. That was someone—his girlfriend, maybe—asking if there were peanuts in the dish. I didn't list it. I realize I didn't list it with the ingredients. He's having an allergic reaction. They're at the hospital, I heard a hospital through the phone. I said no. When she was talking to me I couldn't think of any peanuts. But—" She stopped. Stuart's eyes moved to the peanut oil.

She picked up her phone again and was about to dial when she felt Stuart's hand on her wrist.

"Don't," he said.

"What?"

"You've tried," he said. "And you meant no harm. There are a million things he could be allergic to."

"What? That's crazy. If they know what it is they might—" She stopped midsentence when she saw Stuart bend down to get a plastic bag from under the sink. "What are you doing?"

"What's done is done," Stuart said. "He's getting help."

"I have to tell them," she said.

"You'll lose your business," Stuart said. "Or worse."

It was the *or worse* that got her. Stuart was the lawyer in the family. He knew about the things that could happen even when you didn't mean to commit a crime. She watched as he put the peanut oil into a plastic bag. She couldn't stand it. She let the number ring through again. She had to tell them. The words *There were peanuts, I used peanut oil, I am so sorry, god, I am so sorry* were right there in her mouth, waiting to be said. Stuart gently took the phone out of her hand and ended the call. As it was they were going to see that she had tried to call back. That could be bad, right? *Please let him be okay,* she chanted to herself, *Please let him be okay.*

Stuart held the bag casually, with his hand around the neck of the bottle wrapped in plastic. He kept it at arm's length, just at his hip.

"Come with me," he said.

"Where to?" For a brief second she thought they would go to the hospital. She should *bring* the oil. She knew the oil itself could make a difference in determining his reaction—the more refined the less likely to cause a problem. There were only two logical hospitals someone would go to from the neighborhood, maybe three, possibly four. They could go to each one and track him down, bring answers, somehow fix everything. But really she knew that wasn't what Stuart was doing. They walked to the door, but he didn't even put on his shoes. He left the door slightly ajar, not even calling to the kids to tell them they would be right back. She followed as he walked down the hall to the garbage room, pulled the door open, and dropped the bottle in. They heard it rush through the chute and explode at the bottom.

Tabitha didn't sleep that night, but Stuart was strangely and unusually solicitous toward her. He kept checking in with her, telling her it would all be okay, to never mention it again, to try not to think about it. He wanted her to just keep going as planned, to make the cilantro chicken and rice that she had on the menu for the following day. But she knew she wouldn't. She was pretty sure she would never do it again. Still, she felt like he was looking out for her and protecting her in a way he didn't usually bother to do, not that she usually needed protection. He held her hand the whole night, she knew because she didn't doze off once, and in the morning she felt closer to him than she had in a long time, maybe ever. She felt like they were a team.

Still, the next morning after Stuart left for work, she tried the number one more time. By then she knew it was either okay, the man had survived, or it was the worst possible outcome she could ever imagine. Again, there was no answer. And this time she was glad. She had gone against Stuart and she was sorry, not because she thought it would make him mad or that she felt she had to listen to him, but because she liked the feeling that he was looking out for her, and she wanted him to keep doing it. Why did it take such an awful situation for him to do that? Why couldn't he just do it in their normal life? It was what she craved. What she thought married life was supposed to be. She thought it was what she had always wanted. She never tried the number again.

CHAPTER TWELVE

Fern came home with a note from the gym teacher:

> *Dear Tabitha,*
>
> *Fern needs new gym shoes. She has been having trouble participating lately, and today I took the time to feel her toes. They are practically busting through the top of the shoes. No wonder she can't run. I know parents are so busy these days, and so many things are overlooked or given short shrift. I know you wouldn't want Fern to suffer. Please buy her new shoes soon.*
>
> *Thank you!*
>
> *In Partnership,*
>
> *Melanie*

"Did you read this?" Tabitha asked Fern, who was standing at the island in the kitchen pulling things out of her backpack. Tabitha noticed that even the way she stood had changed lately, since she was favoring her bad knee. She'd call about the X-ray tomorrow.

"No, she just said to give it to you."

Tabitha went back to the top and read through it again. There was so much about the letter that irked her, not just the fact that she was being called out on shirking her parenting duties. Short shrift? Why did she have to talk that way? And why even say she knew she wouldn't want Fern to suffer? Was that something you had to say? And *"In Partnership?" Really?*

Tabitha marched to Levi's room. He wasn't home yet and she just walked in, went right to his closet and sorted through his shoes. Luckily they hadn't spent much time clearing things out lately, so she found three pairs that were clearly too small for him and brought them back to Fern.

"Here, try these," Tabitha said, holding out a pair of ratty navy-blue Nikes that might possibly be in the ballpark of Fern's size.

"Are those Levi's old shoes?" she asked, but it sounded like she was saying, *"Are those shoes made of hot lava?"*

"Yes," Tabitha said, without any more explanation.

"I'm not wearing those," she said.

"Just try them," Tabitha said. "Melanie says your shoes are too small."

"They are," Fern said matter-of-factly.

"Why didn't you tell me?"

Fern looked right at her.

"Because you have enough going on," Fern said. "You don't need to worry about my shoes, too."

"That's not true," Tabitha said. "Your feet are very important. And it's my responsibility to worry about them."

"Can we call Dad?" Fern asked, and Tabitha had to work hard not to gasp.

"Um, sure," Tabitha said, thinking they could call his number, he wouldn't answer, and that would be that. She'd give another speech about how he was busy working, and how the mining unions in the Upper Peninsula of Michigan were suffering, and he was working hard to help with their rights, et cetera. They would go back to pretending that was normal for a while, and eventually Fern would ask again. How was it that they were able to do this—to pretend this was normal? And not for the first time Tabitha thought something awful; she thought: *Thank goodness I don't love him so much that I can't live without him.* Despite her hopes and dreams and her picture of what married life should be like, she thought: *Thank goodness it didn't go that way.* "How about we see if any of these sneakers work, and after that you can call?"

"They're not gonna work," Fern said, but Tabitha knew she would try on the shoes.

Fern sighed heavily as she grabbed the dirty shoes away from Tabitha. They actually smelled pretty bad, though Fern didn't mention that. She sat on the floor, pulling off her current pair and trying on the blue ones. They were much too big. She shook her head in a way that said, *"I knew it."*

"Try these," Tabitha said quickly, handing over a not-quite-as-bad pair of red sneakers with a white Nike mark.

Fern sighed even deeper and put them on. They were too small, which gave Tabitha hope. She handed over the third and final pair, light green with a yellow stripe that Levi barely wore because he thought they were too girly. At the time it was no big deal, they just went shopping for another pair.

Fern looked at them with less disdain than she looked at the other pairs. She put them on, stood up.

"They're okay," Fern said.

Tabitha felt sorry for her. They were good shoes, shoes that looked like they might have actually been bought for her. But now Fern had to swallow her pride, basically say she was wrong. And she was willing to do it. She was such a good girl.

"Tell you what," Tabitha said. "Wear those for a few days and we can see. I'm too lazy to go shopping today, and I don't want Melanie to send another note. You would be doing me a huge favor."

"Okay," Fern said, like it really was okay. "Now can I call Dad?"

It was Tabitha's turn to sigh big.

"Here's my phone," she said to Fern as nonchalantly as she could.

"No," Fern said quickly. "I want to use the regular phone, the house phone."

"Okay," Tabitha said, surprised by her forcefulness. She leaned over and grabbed the phone out of its cradle, pressed the "talk" button and was relieved to hear the dial tone. That was a bill she hadn't thought about in a while, and she hadn't used this phone so she was glad to see it was still working. She handed it to Fern with the dial tone leaking out. Fern looked seriously at the phone, pushed the "off" button, and silenced the dial tone.

"Is our number blocked?" Fern asked.

"You mean does it show up on call waiting?"

"Yeah, can someone tell it's our phone calling?"

"You mean Daddy? Will Daddy know? Yes, he'll know. We had a blocked number for a while but we stopped paying for that service," she said, then, "I think."

"How can I be sure?"

Tabitha was getting a little annoyed. She wanted to say, *Just call already, he isn't going to answer anyway*, but the longer she played along, the longer Fern thought she had the possibility of talking to Stuart. So . . .

"Here, call my cell phone, just dial it: 2-1-5, 5-5-5, 2-3-0-9. Push 'one' first."

Fern hesitated, then she pressed the "talk" button again, then the "one," then the first three numbers. She looked up expectantly.

"Five, five, five; two, three, zero, nine," Tabitha said slowly. There was a pause, and Tabitha's phone began to ring. She looked at the display: Blocked Call it said. *Huh.*

"So I guess we are still paying for that service," Tabitha said. "You have to push 'star-eight-two' to unblock it."

Fern looked around for a piece of paper and a pen, which she found off to the side, and she drew a star and wrote *82*.

"Do you know Daddy's number?" Tabitha asked.

"Yes, I do," Fern said seriously.

They just sat there for a minute.

"Are you going to call?" Tabitha finally said gently. A little hope was okay, but she couldn't stand it anymore, the buildup, the inevitable disappointment.

"I'm going to call from my room," Fern said.

"Why?"

"I just want to," she said. "I'm nine and I can have some privacy. Levi has privacy."

Levi. Shoot. He should be home by now. Okay, okay, she'd let Fern call, there'd be no answer, and then she'd think about Levi.

"Fine," Tabitha said as casually as she could.

Fern hopped down from the high stool, and Tabitha noticed that she put most of her weight on her left leg. Once she steadied herself, she padded through the kitchen and turned left, out of Tabitha's sight. Tabitha counted to twenty before walking as quietly as she could toward the kitchen door. She got there just in time to see Fern go into her room and push her door shut. Tabitha waited another twenty seconds. She found herself calculating how long it would take for Fern to realize he wasn't going to answer, and then how long after that it would take for Fern to get over it. Would it be a matter of minutes? Would it ruin their whole night?

Tabitha crept down the hallway and stood just outside Fern's closed door. She wished she had a glass or something that she could put to the wood to try to conduct sound. Did that even work? She waited. There was no sound at all coming from Fern's room, and she wondered if it was all a farce, if Fern never meant to call but just wanted to evoke Stuart somehow, to let Tabitha know she was thinking about him.

"Daddy?"

Tabitha almost fell against the door.

"Daddy!" She said it like he just emerged from the dead, which he basically did. Tabitha had her hand on the doorknob, she was about to force her way in. But something made her take it back. Her heart was beating so hard, she was surprised Fern couldn't sense it through the door.

"I know, I tried, I really tried," Fern said. She was crying now. Could she be pretending? Had she gone crazy and was imagining talking to Stuart the way a traumatized kid created imaginary friends? There was a long pause.

"Okay. Do you promise?"

More silence.

"I just wanted to ask you about this one . . . oh, okay . . . okay . . . I love you, too."

Tabitha had her hand on the doorknob again. She grasped it and was ready to push it open when Fern talked again.

"But when are you coming home?"

With that, Tabitha was in the room. She was by Fern's side grabbing for the phone. The look on Fern's face was pure terror. Fern held firmly to the phone, took it away from her ear, and without another word pressed the "off" button to end the call. All the while Tabitha pulled at it, fighting her for it. They fell onto their sides on Fern's wall-to-wall bright-yellow carpet.

"Ow!" Fern yelled—howled, really. Tabitha had just gotten the phone away and had it to her ear, frantically pushing the "talk" button.

"Hello? Stuart? Hello?" she screamed into the phone.

"You're on my knee!" Fern screamed.

Tabitha moved over, but would not give up on the phone. She went to recent calls and dialed back the number. It was Stuart's cell, the one she had called over and over again with no answer. No voicemail. It rang and rang.

"Was it really him?" she asked, her teeth gritted. She sounded like a crazy person in a crazy movie. "Did you really talk to him?"

Fern was in a ball now, holding on to her knee.

"Yes," she said quietly. "Why are you so mad? Didn't you want me to?"

Tabitha backed off. Fern had no idea what had been going on. For all she knew Tabitha had been talking to him all this time.

"Yes," Tabitha said, pushing her hair behind her ears and wiping the sweat from her upper lip. "Yes, of course I did."

She turned her back on Fern for a few seconds, then she turned back and hugged her.

"Is your knee okay?"

"It hurts," Fern said.

"I'll call about the X-ray tomorrow," Tabitha said. She meant it.

"Okay," Fern said. "Will that hurt? I was going to ask Daddy."

"No, I promise, an X-ray won't hurt at all," Tabitha said.

Again Tabitha wondered if Fern had become delusional. In fact, she decided that was really the only explanation for this. That was worse than almost any other scenario. It was one thing to have a bad knee, it was another thing completely to be living in an imagined universe. She decided to let it go, she simply couldn't deal with it now.

"Hey, did your brother say anything about what he was doing after school?"

Fern smacked her hand to her forehead.

"I forgot to tell you," she said. "He and Butch were going to the library, the big one. He said he would be home by dinner. Or maybe he said by six. One of those."

Normally Tabitha would be livid that Levi relied on Fern to tell her where he was, and that Fern forgot to share the information, but she let that go, too. Fern could also handle only so much, she knew that.

"Next time tell him to text me, okay?"

"Okay."

"I'll be right back," Tabitha said, hoisting herself up.

"Okay."

As soon as her mother left, Fern took a minute to look at her knee. She pulled up her pant leg and studied it. It hurt way more than she had let on. It felt like people were pushing sharp nails into it—sometimes it felt like the nails were on the inside and sometimes it felt like the nails were on the outside. She was going to tell her father about it, ask him what to do, and ask him especially if it was okay to tell her mother, who seemed to have too much to worry about already, not counting the knee or the too-small shoes, but there was no time. He had to go. That wasn't the first time she tried him, but it was the first time he answered. She hadn't been able to get all the things right before—like making sure the number wasn't blocked and calling from the phone they kept in the kitchen. She knew she needed her mother's help, but she was pretty sure her father would be mad if he knew that her mother knew. Except she wasn't sure how she knew that. What she did know was that her mother was mad, and that seemed worse, since her mother was right here. Fern wanted to make her mother be not mad anymore, but lately she seemed so mad, or like she was always thinking about other things. She didn't seem to care about or do the things she usually did, and that worried Fern, who wanted to think of a way to make her mother happy.

She got up slowly and limped to her bed and sat down. She reached under her mattress and pulled out the tattered, white envelope. The one she found on the morning her father left. She hadn't looked at it in a while. It never changed. It was always the same. But this time when she pulled it out fifty dollars came along with it. She had forgotten about the money. First, she spread out the letter to make sure she had done it the right way, that she hadn't made any mistakes. At least not big ones.

Dear Fern,

I am so proud of you. Everything you're doing, especially in school, is exactly what I hoped you would do. I have to go away for a while, and you're sleeping now, so I don't want to bother you, but I wanted to tell you a few of my ideas. It might be hard to not talk, and I don't know when I'm coming back, so I have a pattern we can do if you need to talk to me. Here's what it is. Call from the home phone—make sure I can tell it's the home phone—and call once, then hang up, call again, then hang up, then let it ring through. That way I'll know it's you calling—because I'm so busy with work I don't want to talk to most other people right now. But don't tell anyone—it will be our secret. I am not telling anyone else this pattern—it is just for us. If you can, try to listen to Mommy, it might be a hard time for her. Also, be nice to Levi if you can. Even though I'll be away, I'll be thinking about you. I already miss you, and I love you every day.

Dad

Yup, she did it pretty much right. The only bad thing was that her mom knew. And right there it said her mother might be having a hard time, so she guessed he did tell her something. She had done the right thing by not telling her mother about how much her knee hurt. Her father would be even more proud of her than he was before he left.

Fern folded the letter again and put it in the envelope. Then she looked at the money. She had an idea. She kept the money out, but put the envelope back under her mattress. She thought about hearing her father's voice. It sounded the same, maybe a little quieter. She felt good after talking to him. She'd worried he might not recognize her voice.

She moved to the edge of the mattress and put her weight down slowly. She could stand it. She got up and put the money in her pocket. Then she went in search of her mom to tell her she wanted to pay for dinner tonight.

CHAPTER THIRTEEN

Michigan was playing Michigan State, and for some reason Tabitha cared. Well, she knew the reason, and his name was Toby, but she pretended she cared about the game. It was the same game she and Stuart had watched at the Fox & Hound the year before. It was a crazy, awful game, with Michigan State winning in the last ten seconds. They had all felt terrible as they left, except for Tabitha, who was sorry for them and the team, but was perfectly fine.

She pulled Stuart's T-shirt out from his side of the bed, smoothed the wrinkles, and put it on with jeans. It was a cold November day, but she didn't want to wear anything else. She went into the living room where the kids were watching *The Princess Bride*. The cable and Netflix were long gone, so now they just watched DVD after DVD. Fern complained at first, which surprised Tabitha, since she thought Levi would be the most bothered. But now they just acted like it was normal. It made Tabitha wonder what else they could easily live without. Lots of things, probably.

"Hey," she said.

"Hey," they said at the same time.

"So, you guys don't mind if I go?"

"No," they said at the same time. Their attention was firmly placed on the television screen and the sword fight taking place there.

"I'll be back with dinner," Tabitha said.

"Please bring those mini burgers," Levi said.

"And the chicken fingers," Fern said.

"Will do," Tabitha said. She pulled her red-plaid jacket out of the closet, then thought better of it and put it back. She scanned the coats and saw one of Stuart's fall fleece coats—navy-blue and perfect.

"Bye," she called.

When she got to the bar, it was as crowded as she had ever seen it. She walked in and looked immediately around for Toby, even though she was going to pretend, even to herself, that she didn't care that much. She spotted the head of the alumni association chapter. He was dressed all in maize from head to toe, including his shoes, but his skin was painted blue, every single bit of it, at least every single bit she could see. When he turned around, she could see that his butt was green—the color of Michigan State. He looked crazed, walking from person to person, giving some sort of directions. The game was scheduled to start in eight minutes. People were milling around. She didn't see Toby.

There were no seats at all, so she went to the wall of windows and sat on the bench that ran the length of the room.

"Hey, Justin!" someone called, and the head of the alumni association turned around. "Go Spartans!"

Justin looked confused, then he saw there was a whole contingent of people in green right next to them. That didn't usually happen. Generally there was some effort made to put two opposing teams as far apart as possible in the big bar, or even better, they met at another bar, but apparently not today. Maybe it had been done on purpose. She could see Justin furrow his brow, like he was thinking who to complain to, then he turned his back on the perceived interloper and climbed up onto a table in the center of the Michigan crowd.

"Wolverines!" he screamed. "I need your attention."

Tabitha was happy to have something to focus on. She felt silly sitting there without anyone to talk to.

"I want to sing one rousing round of 'The Victors,' and after that I have an announcement. Are you with me?"

"Yes!"

"Are you with me?"

"Yes!"

"And I want them to be able to hear us in East Lansing—do you hear me?"

"Yes!"

"One, two, you know what to do!"

Just as everyone started singing "Hail to the Victors," Tabitha saw Toby push his way through the crowd. She was so relieved, it caught her off guard. Sure, she came here to see him, she knew that. But she didn't realize *how much* she wanted to see him, how disappointed she would have been if she hadn't seen him. He was wearing a basic sweatshirt, navy with the word **MICHIGAN** spelled out in maize. The whole fight song went by and she didn't even hear it, she didn't sing along like she usually did, she just watched Toby stop at the beginning of the Michigan section and look around, scanning the crowd. When his eyes settled on her, he smiled. She smiled back.

"Now, I am going to make my announcement," Justin screamed. Both Tabitha and Toby looked at him. Justin turned his back to the crowd, then he took green confetti out of his pocket and scattered it from his green butt. Tabitha thought it looked like unicorn poop. The crowd went crazy. It was a recurring theme here, obviously: the opposing team was always shit—in one way or another. She looked over at Toby, who was laughing. Two minutes to game time. Toby moved toward Tabitha, and she felt all sorts of strange twinges and butterfly effects. She worried her mouth was twitching slightly, and she tried to control it; she didn't want to look like she was having a seizure, or, worse—that she was actually nervous.

"Hi!" he said when he reached her.

"Hi!" She hated the way she sounded—breathless and eager. "Hi!" she said again, more firmly.

He swung his backpack around to his front. He looked at Tabitha and scanned the space around them like he was looking for something. There wasn't a single inch on either side of her.

"I figured it would be crazy crowded today," he said. He unzipped the pack and reached in, pulling out what looked like a folded maize-and-blue umbrella or a scrunched-up hammock. She watched while he unfolded it, and it became a tall, skinny chair with **MICHIGAN** written across the back. He put it down, just to the left of Tabitha, and gestured to it.

"For you, madame," he said.

"Thank you," she said, jumping down off the ridiculously crowded bench. Someone immediately squeezed into the spot she just left. These Michigan people were so spirited. Or maybe it was just some of them. Stuart was a fanatic when it came to Michigan football, but he wasn't fun, he wasn't lighthearted.

Toby turned his attention back to his bag and created another chair, basically out of nothing, which he put as close to her as possible. There was very little room, and Tabitha was sure they were breaking fire code. Toby climbed up onto his chair and adjusted it slightly with tiny hops, so that he faced the big screen. He surprised her by patting her knee gently, as if to say everything was okay. It was a gesture Tabitha's mother used to make when they would get settled somewhere—at the movies, in the car, at a dinner—and it conjured up so many emotions in Tabitha, not to mention the fact that she had not been touched much by an adult for months. She fought back the tears she felt forming in her eyes as they watched the coin toss and the first play of the game.

Immediately, Michigan State was off and running, and the wind was taken out of their small corner of the bar. Justin jumped up and frantically sprinkled maize-and-blue confetti on everyone, possibly under the impression that the green-poop confetti was bad karma. He ran between the chairs and tables with a seemingly endless supply of tiny paper pieces in one hand. Maybe he *was* magical. When he got to Tabitha and Toby, he actually stopped and looked at them, like for some reason they demanded more attention than everyone else, or else maybe he got the sense she didn't belong there, or worse, that their chairs were illegal, but he reached into one of his many pockets with his free hand and pulled out small pieces of maize-and-blue ribbon with tiny red hearts among them, which he gently threw at them for a good twenty or thirty seconds. He just stood there and tossed.

"Just a feeling," he said over his shoulder as he finally walked away and went back to sprinkling heart-free confetti on everyone else.

"What was that about?" Tabitha asked, not sure she liked that but also sort of liking it.

"Sometimes he thinks he spots Michigan couples in the crowd, or should-be couples, I guess. He often gets it wrong." Toby didn't say anything else, and Tabitha felt surprisingly unsatisfied. She had that awful response humans have when they think someone isn't giving them enough, even if they didn't know that they wanted it in the first place. She wanted more—from him.

"How's Yo-Adrian?" she asked.

"Wow, you remembered her name," he said, smiling but not moving his eyes away from the screen. "Nobody ever remembers it."

"Seriously?" she asked. "Because it's a pretty easy name to remember."

"Yeah, well," he said.

"How is she?"

"Oh, she's good. Really good," he said.

"Can I have your number?" she asked, surprising herself. It was always her intention to get his number if she saw him here again, but she had planned to work up to it a little. Ever since she spotted him on the street and realized she had absolutely no way of getting in touch with him other than running into him, she knew she wanted to get it.

"Sure, give me your phone," he said, still smiling.

She unlocked it and went to the contacts, then she handed it over to him. She watched while he typed, then he handed it back. The contact name was Toby T. and there was a number following it. She pushed on it, and a few seconds later his phone rang. He smiled, reaching for it in his backpack and ending the call.

"Now you have mine," she said, feeling her cheeks go red.

"Yes, I do," he said. "And I'm happy to have it."

"What does the *T* stand for?"

"Tarrabay," he said. "Toby Tarrabay."

"No way!" she said. "You had parents who liked the *T-T* sound, too! What are the chances? Growing up I was Tabitha Taylor, or Tabby Taylor."

"Guess what my daughter's name is?"

She was quiet for a second. Somehow, learning his daughter's name seemed like a big step.

"What?" she finally asked.

"Tara Tarrabay."

"That's a beautiful name," she said.

"So, are you still Tabitha Taylor?" he asked.

"No, I changed it, and at first I was glad to, it always seemed so perky. But lately, well, lately I miss it."

Now he looked at her.

"What did you change it to?"

"Brewer," she said. "When I got married."

"I've been meaning to ask you more about your, I don't know, your situation," Toby said, but the crowd was going crazy, and they both turned their heads to the screen in time to watch Michigan score the first touchdown of the game. It took a few minutes to get through the cheering and another round of "The Victors," and Tabitha wasn't sure if she hoped Toby would remember what they were talking about before, or if she hoped he'd forget.

"You don't have to tell me," he continued, when the immediate excitement was over. Tabitha knew she should help him, but she wasn't even sure what her answer was going to be. "I guess what I'm asking is, are you, I'm not sure how to put this, are you happily married?"

Even though he was clearly going to ask something about her marriage, she was not prepared for such a direct question. And she thought the question might be more about what she wasn't than what she was. Was she married? Yes. Happily? That was a whole other story, more complicated than she had even realized until recently.

She was relieved when Michigan intercepted the ball, and it gave her a few seconds to think. He turned back to her, waiting.

"Well," she said, stalling. "That requires much more than a simple yes-or-no answer, but I can tell you that my husband and I have not been living together for a while now, and our lines of communication are very bad, as bad as you can imagine. I guess I'm not ready to talk about it all yet, and I don't even understand a lot of it at this point, so maybe we should just—" The rest of her words were swallowed by the crowd as Michigan scored another touchdown. Toby was on his feet. As the sound died down, Tabitha heard a phone ring. She realized it was Toby's phone, which he had propped on his backpack. She could see the display had a local 215 number but no name.

"Hey, your phone's ringing," she said, pointing.

"Oh, thanks," he said, leaning over to grab it. He looked, then answered quickly.

"Hello?" he said. "Wait, I just need to go outside."

He pointed to the phone as if to say, *"I have to take this, I'll be right back."* She nodded. He pointed to his backpack. She nodded again.

As soon as he was gone, she let out a huge breath, which she didn't even know she had been holding. What the heck was she doing? She had to get out of here. She looked toward the front of the restaurant where the buffet was usually set up, but there wasn't anything there. Maybe they waited until halftime; she didn't know. What she did know was that she wanted to bring the kids a good-enough dinner. Fern had been so sweet the other night, wanting to buy dinner. But Tabitha had told her to save her money, though she did wonder later where the money had come from in the first place. When she asked her, Fern just shrugged it off without an answer, and Tabitha decided to let yet another thing remain unknown.

In a few minutes, Toby was back, looking pale.

"I am so sorry," he said, turning his chair into a tiny ball again and stuffing it in his backpack. "You can keep sitting there, I'll get it from you another time."

"Are you okay?" she asked. "Is your daughter okay?"

"Oh yeah, thanks, she's okay, thank goodness," he said. "It's my mother. She fell, and her aide is taking her to the emergency room. I'm going to meet them there."

"Can I do anything?" she asked. "Please, take the chair."

"No, no, really, I have to get going," he said. "I'm so sorry. I'll call you." When he said this last thing, he lifted up his phone and pointed. She smiled, but then felt bad about smiling if his mother was suffering.

"Okay," she said. "I hope your mother's okay."

Once he was gone, she felt silly sitting in the chair, and she realized she had no idea how to dismantle it. There was still no sign of the buffet, and she started to worry about dinner. The kids were going to be starving when she got home and, worse than that, they were excited about the food. She stood and tried to fold the chair into itself, but it just didn't budge, and she kept knocking into people in the process. She gave up and stood there, feeling stupid and stranded. She shoved her hands into the pockets of the jacket she was wearing and felt a piece of paper. She pulled it out. It was a tiny square of yellow, lined paper that looked like it was torn from a bigger piece. In green pen there was a phone number written out in Stuart's handwriting. It wasn't a local number, but she didn't recognize it. The area code was 906. It looked familiar, but she couldn't place it. She pulled her phone out of her pocket and googled it. Oh, Marquette, Michigan. All that frantic searching for a number, and it was right there in the closet all that time. She stuffed it back into the pocket, lifted the chair like it was a mannequin, and worked hard not to hit anyone as she left the crowded bar. Once she was outside, she tried again to see if there was some secret lever or something that might fold it up, but she couldn't see anything. She thought of texting Toby to ask, or sending a silly picture of her sitting in the chair on the sidewalk, but of course she didn't do it. She imagined him getting it while he was at the ER with his injured mother.

She decided she'd take the chair home, and then they'd figure out what to do for dinner. Maybe Levi would want to keep the chair in his room until she could get it back to Toby.

Thankfully, the chair was light. Tabitha got a few strange looks on her short walk home, but she didn't care too much. Just as she entered her apartment building, her phone rang. It was in her other pocket, the one that didn't have the slip of paper in it, and it seemed so hard to get to. She ignored it and headed to the elevator. It rang again just as the elevator doors closed, but then it stopped. As she got to her door it rang again. She put the chair down and pulled out her phone—it was Levi. She fished her keys out of her pocket and rushed inside, leaving the chair in the hall.

"Hi, you guys, I'm home," she said, jogging toward the living room where she had left them. Levi was standing up, his phone in hand. Fern was sitting on the floor with her back against the couch, her leg straight out, looking panicked.

"What is it?" Tabitha asked. "What happened?"

"We were fine, just watching, but suddenly Fern started crying, and then she stopped, which was worse, and she's been like that," Levi said, pointing.

"Sweetie, what is it?" Tabitha asked, kneeling in front of her. "Is your knee worse?"

"It's burning," she said. "I can't stand it."

Tabitha reached out to touch it and Fern yelped.

"You have to do something," Levi said.

"Come on, let's go," Tabitha said. "We'll go to the hospital."

CHAPTER FOURTEEN

The decision was made, but getting to the hospital was much easier said than done. Fern couldn't walk on her leg, and Tabitha couldn't carry her anymore. She was too big, and anyway, Tabitha was afraid to lift her and bang her knee on something. She knew there was a solution to this, but she didn't know what it was.

"Can you call Dad?" Levi asked, and Tabitha was surprised by the urgency she heard in his voice.

"Yes," Tabitha said. "Sure."

She picked up her phone, found his number, and dialed. If there were any chance in the world he actually answered for Fern, maybe he'd answer for her. Then she remembered that Fern called from the house phone, so she put her cell phone down and dialed his number from their landline. She hadn't told the kids that she had not spoken to Stuart since he'd left, and they never asked, directly. She just made it seem like it was a series of missed calls and bad times. But now she needed him. *911—our daughter can't walk! 911—I can't handle this alone. 911—I've been flirting with a strange man.*

It rang and rang. No answer. No voicemail. Fern continued to whimper. Tabitha hung up the phone and walked over to her.

"Here, can you bend it?" she asked, moving to gently grab her foot.

"Nooo!" Fern screamed.

Tabitha picked up her cell phone again and began to text Holly, the emergency room doctor who was also the mom of Fern's friend. Maybe even she and Holly were friends at this point. She was so helpful when Fern was sick earlier in the year. Tabitha worried about bugging her, but she didn't know what else to do. She needed help, and she needed help from someone who was a professional at giving help. But texting could take too long. She decided to call instead. She would normally text something like, *Hi! This is Tabitha, Fern's mother,* so that she could identify herself right away. Calling was a little harder. She doubted Holly had kept Tabitha's contact information in her phone, so it would just come up as an unidentified number.

"Hello?" Holly answered. Tabitha thought of hanging up for a split second. Then she looked at Fern.

"Holly, hi! It's Tabitha, Fern's mom," she said quickly. "I am so sorry to bother you. Really. But I just wasn't sure where else to turn. Fern has had a bad knee for, well, for a long time. I guess I just kept hoping it would go away. We did see the pediatrician and they ordered tests, which I haven't followed through with yet. But now she is in a lot of pain, tremendous pain, I think, and I was considering an emergency room visit since the doctor's office is closed. I wanted to check in to see if you think that sounds appropriate. And also, we're stuck. I can't move her, but she doesn't seem so bad that she needs an ambulance. I thought you might have an idea about how to transport her."

The other end of the line was quiet, and Tabitha wondered if they'd been disconnected, but then she heard Holly whispering to someone, the sound muffled by a hand over the phone.

"Sorry, I was just checking with Mitch," Holly said, kindly. "I'd be happy to come over and take a look."

Tabitha felt such relief, such appreciation, that she had to work hard not to cry. At the same time, she knew it was too much to ask.

"You guys are right on the Square, right?" Holly said. "I was just heading out to the grocery story, literally right there. Let me come up and just see. No need to make a trip if you don't have to."

"Thank you," Tabitha said, quickly giving her the address. "Thank you so much."

Levi looked at her, Fern was too distracted by her pain to care.

"Holly's coming," Tabitha said, like that was the answer. "She's a doctor."

They waited what seemed like a very long time, when in fact it was only about fifteen minutes. The doorman called up, and Tabitha went to the door to let Holly in. She wanted to hug her, but she was too afraid of doing the wrong thing and pushing her away, or making her regret her decision to come over to help.

"Where is she?" Holly asked cheerfully as she walked through the door. She wore a black-and-red fall dress with heels, and Tabitha wondered if she had pulled her away from a party or an early dinner or something, and that she hadn't been going to the grocery store at all. But she didn't ask.

"Over here," Tabitha said, spotting Toby's chair in the hall. She grabbed it and pulled it inside, tucking it into the corner of the foyer.

She expected Fern to perk up once Holly arrived, but she didn't, which worried her. Holly talked to her, and felt around gently. Then she stepped back and motioned to Tabitha to follow her into the kitchen.

"So, it is really hard for me to tell what's going on inside her knee," Holly said kindly. "I was hoping it would be something more obvious, but without a definite injury that you guys are aware of, and considering the fact that she is in such pain, I think you might as well go get it checked out. An X-ray might tell us a lot."

Tabitha started to cry. She didn't mean to. She meant to be strong. But she kept thinking about how she was going to get Fern out the door, and for some reason that made her feel helpless.

"Okay," Tabitha said. "Thank you. I know you're right."

"Hey, is there anyone here to help you?" Holly asked. The fact that she didn't ask about Stuart made Tabitha think that people might be talking. People must have noticed he hadn't been around at all.

"No, not really," Tabitha said. "But I'll figure it out."

"I can call ahead for you," Holly said. "It might not help too much, but it can't hurt."

Tabitha nodded, she couldn't stop crying.

"Is there . . . something else going on?" Holly asked.

"No . . . yes . . . no," Tabitha said. "I've just put this off so long, I feel terrible. I just kept hoping it would get better and it hasn't and I could have probably avoided this situation."

"We all do that. Did you know that the time Evie broke that bone in her foot we kept telling her it was fine? She had to limp around for two days, and someone had to suggest we get it looked at—and we're both doctors! We all want it to be not so bad, and usually it isn't, but sometimes you do need help."

Tabitha was crying harder now. She wondered if she had ever cried this hard in her entire life. Probably, when she was a baby. That's what it felt like. She didn't want the kids to know. She had to get control. She took deep breaths, but it didn't help.

"I can help you get her there," Holly said. "Let me just call Mitch and make sure he and Evie are okay."

"No! Really! I can do this," Tabitha said. "I think they might actually have a building wheelchair. I don't know why I didn't think of that before. Let me call the doorman."

"Mom!" Levi called from the other room. "What are we doing?"

"We're going," Tabitha called back, but her voice cracked, and it sent her into another bought of crying. Her eyes hurt. To Holly she said, "I am so sorry. I am just really, really sorry."

"Let me go get the wheelchair," Holly offered. Tabitha was tempted to let her, but she didn't want to use up all her goodwill. She might need her again, and more than that, she liked the idea of her being a friend.

"No, really, thank you so much for coming," Tabitha said. "You made me feel . . . not so alone."

"Okay, I'll get going, but please don't hesitate to call if you need me," Holly said. "And please let me know what they say about Fern. I'll call as soon as I leave to let them know you're coming. Call your pediatrician—or at least the on-call number—and let them know, too. The insurance companies sometimes want the okay from the pediatrician. I don't know you that well, but I have a feeling there are things you aren't telling me. I wish I could help more, but if I could just offer you a tiny bit of wisdom that I tell myself over and over again when I'm struggling with something—it's that most things that seem terrible at the time rarely stay terrible. Of course, there are exceptions to that, but I hope in your case it will be true, with Fern's knee and whatever else is going on."

Tabitha took another series of deep breaths and touched Holly on the forearm.

"Thank you," she said. "You have no idea how much I appreciate this."

~

When Holly left, Tabitha called down to the front desk. She was elated, if that was possible at a time like this, when Mort answered. He was filling in because Robert called in sick. Tabitha didn't much like Robert, he never would have done anything extra. But Mort? *Thank goodness for Mort.* Yes, they did have a wheelchair, which he brought up, along with two cherry Blow Pops which he gave to Fern. Tabitha thought for a minute that he had nothing for Levi but he did, a Snickers bar. Just having Mort around perked Fern up a bit; he was her favorite, and she wanted him to wheel her out. He had a cab waiting, and he helped them get in, instructing Tabitha to wait in the car with Fern while Levi ran in for a wheelchair when they arrived. He gave Levi the thumbs-up, as if to say, *"You can handle this, man,"* and Levi gave him the thumbs-up back. They took the short ride over the South Street Bridge. Levi quickly and easily got a wheelchair when they arrived, and the cab driver said the fare had been paid for. Tabitha would have to remember to write Mort on her list when she got home.

The hospital was expecting them, and despite the crowded waiting room, Fern was triaged quickly, and then they were taken back to a small private room. There was a television, two chairs, and they were asked if they needed anything. Tabitha thought of the man at The Family Meal who said that he considered a trip to the emergency room for the sole purpose of getting a meal.

"I wondered," Tabitha began hesitantly. "Are there any snacks or anything I can give to Fern's brother? With all the commotion, he hasn't eaten."

"Sure," the nurse said. "We have turkey sandwiches. Would you like one, too?"

"That would be great," Tabitha said.

"Unfortunately, the little lady will have to hold off until we do some tests," the nurse said.

Tabitha felt bad about that, but accepted the sandwiches, which were in plastic baggies, along with small cans of ginger ale and packets of graham crackers.

"Hey, Levi, do we have to go back to The Family Meal anytime soon?" Tabitha asked. Fern was sitting on the gurney. She had calmed down, but she was clearly still in pain. Tabitha took a quick bite, then dropped her sandwich into her bag.

"I don't want to go anymore," he said. "I don't want to do any of it. I don't want to have a bar mitzvah."

Before Tabitha had a chance to take in what he just said, there was a light knock on the glass door, it slid to the side, and a lady walked in pushing a computer on a stand.

"Good evening," she said. "I'm from registration."

"Hi," Tabitha said to her, but what she wanted to do was turn to Levi and say, *What do you mean?*

"Are you Mom?" the lady asked. The words *No, I'm Pocahontas* ran through Tabitha's mind, but she sighed and said yes.

"I'm sorry you're not feeling good," she said to Fern, and Tabitha immediately felt bad that she was annoyed by this lady. Maybe she could get a job doing this, it must not require any medical expertise. But she would have to do it at a hospital far away, or else she would be sure to run into people she knew.

"Thanks," Fern said sweetly.

"So, what I need from you, Mom, is your insurance card, and I'll need you to sign a few things on the screen."

"Okay," Tabitha said. She dug around in her purse for her insurance card and handed it over, hoping for the best. The lady put it through a scanner of some sort and handed it back. She waited, but there was no discussion about whether it was good or not.

"Now, please read this and sign," the lady said. Tabitha scanned the screen, barely acknowledging what it said, and signed. "And here," the lady said. Tabitha did it again. Really, for all she knew it could have said that if her insurance company didn't pay up that she'd owe the hospital her kids, but she just couldn't focus.

"Thank you," the lady said, pushing the cart out. Before she closed the door she turned back to Fern. "I hope you feel better, honey."

"What do you mean, you don't want to have a bar mitzvah?" Tabitha said, sounding much angrier than she felt. Why did she even care? This was always, always Stuart's thing. But no, it had become their thing—and it was supposed to be Levi's thing. It was still important—with or without Stuart.

"I just don't," he said sulkily.

"But," Tabitha said. But what? *You have to? It's the right thing to do?* Tabitha didn't even know.

They sat in silence. Tabitha was so happy to be the one waiting for a decision to be made, to not be the one in charge, that she didn't mind any of it, except Fern's pain. Finally, a doctor came in who ordered blood work and an X-ray. Levi sat and looked at his phone the whole time, asking for two more sandwiches, and Tabitha was glad. She had thought briefly about leaving him at home—it would have been okay—but he seemed so worked up about Fern, and now he had gotten plenty to eat. When they finally gave Fern pain medication, she perked up considerably. The tests didn't show anything, which was mostly good, because they were able to rule out some of the worst possible things, but bad because they still didn't know what was causing this. They said she could go home and ordered a series of other tests for the week ahead. With the pain medication, Fern was able to walk, though very slowly. They took a cab back to the apartment, which Tabitha paid for with her Visa—this definitely counted as an emergency—and the kids went right to bed. Even though it wasn't actually very late, it felt late. Tabitha sent Holly a text, filling her in and thanking her again. Holly sent back a smiley face.

As Tabitha took off the fleece jacket she'd been wearing all day, she remembered the slip of paper with the phone number on it. She reached into the pocket and pulled it out. The phone number was there, clear as day, but there was nothing else, no name or initials, nothing on the back. She held it in her hand as she hung the coat up in the front closet. She thought Stuart might have been wearing the jacket on the last night he was home. Yes, she was sure of it, because it was an unusually chilly night in August, almost unheard of, and also, she remembered thinking it was on the casual side for work. Her first idea was to add it to the list of clues, she wasn't quite ready to actually explore it. It wasn't until she got to her room and reached for the side table drawer that she remembered she had gotten rid of the list. She pictured it ripped up and soggy at the bottom of the sewer, or stuck to the insides of her pipes. That would be somehow fitting.

Fine, she thought, *I'm just going to call.* She was so tired of not finding answers; she wanted to actually get some. Although she didn't dare hope for much—it could simply lead her to a local law office or maybe the miners' union office. It was Saturday, so unlikely that anyone would answer, anyway. But she needed to try, and this was practically handed to her on a platter. She picked up the house phone so the number would be blocked, just in case, and dialed. It was answered right away.

"Marquette General," a gruff man said.

Tabitha hung up. Once again, she had that terrible feeling that she'd been caught at something. It took her a minute to catch her breath. She called back. The gruff man answered the same way, but sounded even gruffer this time.

"Did you say, 'Marquette General'?" Tabitha asked, trying to disguise her voice, which she knew was ridiculous. "As in, 'Marquette General Hospital'?"

"Yes, ma'am," he said, and suddenly he didn't sound so gruff at all.

She didn't say anything.

"Can I help you?"

"I'm looking for a patient," she said. She didn't want to blow this chance, now that she had finally reached someone. On the spot like that, she could think of only one person to ask for. "His name is Stuart Brewer. I'm not sure where he is. Has he been brought to your hospital?"

"One minute, ma'am," he said. "Let me just check the computer. Did you say 'Brewer,' as in B-r-e-w-e-r?"

"Yes," she said, breathless again. Was he finding something?

"Sorry, ma'am," he said. "There is no patient by the name of Brewer here."

"Oh, okay, thank you," Tabitha said slowly. She didn't want to let him go.

"Is there anything else I can help you with?"

"Can you, um, can you see if he was a patient there at one time?"

The man hesitated. "I can see, yes," he said slowly. "But I'm really only supposed to give out information about current patients."

"My husband has been missing for over two months," she blurted out. She couldn't believe she was saying this. "He left, and he hasn't come home or called. I am at my wit's end. My daughter is sick. My son wants to cancel his bar mitzvah. Please, can you just look?"

She wasn't even sure what she would do with the information. It would be one thing if he were in the hospital now, if he had fallen over a cliff and hit his head while he was looking at the Pictured Rocks, maybe during a romantic hike with Abigail, and been in a coma all this time. But if he had been there and was now gone, that wouldn't really help her much.

"I looked quickly, ma'am," the man said, bringing her back to the phone call. She sensed a slight hesitation in his voice. "And there is no record that a Mr. Stuart Brewer was a patient here at any time in the last two years. That's as far as these records go back—after that we have to check a whole other database."

"Thank you," Tabitha said. "Thank you so much."

"I'm sorry your husband is missing, ma'am," he said, and the words felt so strange to her ears, since she had tried so hard to not let a single other human being know what was going on, except, of course, for Marlon at the grocery store. "Have you tried calling the police?"

"That's my next call," she lied. "Thank you again. Um, can I ask you about another possible patient?"

There was no response, and she worried she had lost him.

"Yes, ma'am," he said after a long pause.

"Is there a patient there named Abigail Golding?"

She heard a click-click-click of computer keys.

"Not at the moment, ma'am," he said in such a way that she *knew*.

"Was she a patient there? At one time?"

"Again, ma'am, I'm not supposed to disclose anything but the current patient list," he said.

"Please?" she said.

"There was a Miss Abigail Golding here. I can see she had numerous hospital stays over the last two years. I count seven. The last one was the third week in September."

"And?" Tabitha prompted. Her heart was beating so fast that it was uncomfortable.

"That is the last stay I have on record."

"And she was discharged?" Tabitha asked. She was finally getting her answer. Stuart was with Abigail, which was really not a surprise, not after everything, not after their fight the night before he left. Hadn't she known it all along?

"No, ma'am," the man said. "She died."

Tabitha had been sitting up straight on the edge of the bed, but now she stood.

"Died?' she said.

"Yes, ma'am," he said. "And since I could lose my job for this, I might as well tell you everything I know. The other name you gave me—your husband's name, I assume—it came up on her visitor list."

"For September?" Tabitha asked, but her voice sounded strangled. "Was he on the list in late August and September?"

"Yes, ma'am," the man said. "And before that. As far as I can tell, he was always on it."

"Always?" Tabitha asked. She could hear another phone ringing.

"Yes, ma'am," he said. "Well, for as long as this record goes back. I'm so sorry, but I have to take this."

"Thank you," Tabitha said, so quietly it was possible he didn't hear her. She thought about calling back to say good-bye again, and to say she hoped he wouldn't lose his job, and to ask if she had heard that right, but she couldn't move.

~

After they had eaten the cherry chicken that August night, Stuart offered to help clean up, something that was so out of their normal way of doing things that Tabitha started to wonder if he was sick. Was he trying to do things for her while he still could? She had said, "No, thank you," and he had gone into his study.

She cleaned up, got the kids to sleep, and went to bed. She was reading a Liane Moriarty book about a woman who had lost her memory and didn't know herself in the present—she thought it was ten years before and that she was newly married and pregnant with her first child, when in fact, she had three children and her marriage was unraveling. Tabitha was thinking about that—what it would be like to go back ten years—who was she then? Who were they as a couple? Levi would have been two, and Fern was just on the way. It was a time when happiness still seemed possible, when she still hoped she would settle in and stop feeling like she was getting into bed with a near stranger each night.

And then Stuart appeared. He had a look on his face that she couldn't identify. Maybe he really was sick, and he was going to tell her. He came and sat next to her, on her side of the bed. He put his hand on her thigh and looked like he was about to say something, and the words that ran through her head were: *I don't want to know.* She still wasn't sure why. So instead of letting him talk, she leaned in and kissed him, and he smelled good. Suddenly she craved him, they had barely touched in weeks. And he responded. For the briefest few moments, she didn't think about anything but his body and their pleasure. When it was over, she leaned back in bed, thinking something had shifted, something good. Maybe he was finally coming around, maybe that's what he had wanted to talk to her about earlier.

Stuart got up to go to the bathroom. He was gone a minute or two when she heard something strange. She got up to see, and Stuart was sitting on the side of their big bathtub with his head in his hands. He was crying.

"What is it?" she asked, going to him. "What's wrong?"

"I can't do this anymore," he said quietly. He didn't even sound like himself.

"Do what?" she asked.

"Stay here," he had said. "Pretend."

She had stiffened then. *Pretend.* For some reason that word got her. It *had* felt like pretending. It had always felt like pretending, mixed with a little hope. But hadn't they just connected? Couldn't that be something to build on?

"What's *pretend*?" she asked, standing over him with her arms crossed. "What? Our marriage? Our family? Our home?"

"I'm so sorry," he said quietly, openly. It occurred to her that he was talking more honestly than he ever did. All the time he was so guarded, like if the wrong words were spoken or the wrong move made, he would fall apart. Always on a straight path, never looking around.

"What are you talking about?" she said. "I don't understand."

"I want to go see her," he had whispered. He was still crying.

"Who?" Tabitha had demanded.

"Abigail," he said. "My . . . my first . . . my first fiancée."

It had occurred to her, even then, to wonder what he was going to say. His first love? His first wife? Was that how he thought of her even though they had never gotten married? It was later that she wondered if he had wanted to say, *"My first true love."* Had Abigail been his only true love?

"That's ridiculous," Tabitha had said, strongly and clearly.

He looked up at her then, surprised. What had he thought? That she would say, *Fine, go, see you*?

"What do you mean?" he asked. He stood then. They were face to face.

"I mean, you're being ridiculous. You're having a midlife crisis," Tabitha said. "You have a family here. Despite whatever happened with you two, you chose to marry me. I am your wife. I have been here for all these years. We have two children who need you. I'm sorry. You chose. You can't go."

He looked at her dumbstruck. She wasn't usually that strong willed.

"I didn't choose," he said weakly. "She chose."

"You chose me," Tabitha said, breathing hard. "I didn't even know about her when I agreed to marry you."

"She's sick," he said. "She's dying."

"I don't care," Tabitha said. "Even more reason to not go, to stay. What would the point be? Then you would lose everything."

"I have to go," Stuart said. "I have to be with her."

"Stuart," Tabitha said, taking his arm, then letting it go; she was shaking and clenched to the point of feeling dizzy. "I won't let you. Do you want to do that to the kids? They'll be devastated. And what about your parents? You know how your parents feel about family. What about our friends? Everyone here? Your colleagues?"

That had made him stop for a minute.

"I am not going to let this all be for nothing," Tabitha hissed. "You owe me."

"Owe you?" Stuart had said like it was the craziest thing he had ever heard.

"You never wanted to marry me, or, at least, I was never, ever your first choice," she said. "That is so clear. You have never done a single thing to make me feel special. I can see it all now. I should have known." Tabitha fought back tears. She did not want to fall apart. She did not want their family to fall apart. "But we got married, and we have a family. Now, act like a grown-up."

At that moment, Levi had wandered into the bathroom. He had been calling them, he said he wasn't feeling well and wanted some Advil.

"I'll be right there," Stuart said.

"See?" Tabitha said, like that proved her point. "Stop acting like a reckless kid. We have two kids already."

"Okay," Stuart had said. "You're right. I'm sorry. I don't know what's come over me tonight. I'm sorry if I hurt you. Let me help Levi. You go to sleep. Maybe a Xanax would do you good. We'll both be clearer eyed in the morning, and we'll talk some more then."

That had already occurred to her. She wanted a Xanax.

"Maybe we can talk when the kids go to school tomorrow," Tabitha said. "We can go out to breakfast. Maybe we can call a marriage counselor." Just the thought of it made Tabitha feel relieved. They weren't permanently broken after all. Perhaps they had needed this breakthrough so that they could fix their marriage.

"Okay," Stuart said, but he was halfway out the door, moving toward Levi. While she waited for him to come back to bed, she fell fast asleep. When she woke up, he was gone.

~

All this time, somewhere in the back of her mind, she had known he was with Abigail. She had no proof, but that's what she thought, what she imagined. But if Abigail had died in September—died? Then where had Stuart been in the months since? Where was Stuart now?

CHAPTER FIFTEEN

"I'm so sorry," the woman at the desk said to Tabitha. "But it looks like there's a hold on your insurance card."

Tabitha didn't even know that could happen, though, of course, she had been waiting for this moment. She and Fern were back at the hospital for the next round of tests.

"Huh, okay, well can you bill me?"

"Sure," the woman said. "But I would call your insurance company right away to get this straightened out."

Ha! Tabitha thought. Like it was something she'd be able to straighten out. *911*—she wanted to text Stuart—*your daughter is at the hospital, again, and we are going to owe hundreds, maybe thousands of dollars that I personally don't have. 911—where are you? I need you.*

They spent much of the day there. Levi was on his own again to get to and from school. In the end, none of the tests showed anything conclusive, though one was going to take a few days to come back. When Fern was on the pain medication, she was pretty much okay, but when it wore off, her knee hurt so much that it seemed to be all she could think about. Tabitha started to panic about so many things. What the heck was wrong with Fern? And what was going to happen if she just kept racking up bills? Could they eventually take the apartment away from her? What else could they do?

Tabitha's phone rang just as they were leaving the office. The doctor was still talking, so she didn't feel she could answer it, but she sneaked a peek. It was Toby. Without realizing it, she let out an audible sigh, and the doctor stopped talking for a minute. He thought she was reacting to something he said.

"Sorry," she said.

"Don't apologize," the doctor said. "This is a lot to take in. We'll be in touch as soon as the last test comes back, and we'll come up with next steps."

"Thank you," Tabitha said, but all she could think of was finding a place where she could call Toby back.

Fern followed her, but slowly. Tabitha was slightly ahead and turned to look at her daughter struggling to keep up. She moved her good leg fast, then sort of swung her bad leg around to meet it, then did it again. She had a look of exertion on her face. Tabitha felt like she was on a seesaw—up one second—*Yay, Toby called!*—and down the next—*My daughter is suffering!*

There was a bench up ahead, and Tabitha walked to it, then sat. She pulled out her phone. Toby didn't leave a message, she just had the notification of a missed call. Should she call back? Would she appear overeager? But before she had to decide, her phone rang again, and it was Toby.

"Hey," she said.

"Hey yourself," he said. "I was just calling back to try to leave a message. I called before, but it didn't go to voicemail."

Tabitha's first thought was that all her systems were breaking down. Her second thought was how glad she was to hear from him.

"How's your mother?" she asked. She wanted to tell him about Fern, but she didn't want to one-up his story, whatever it might be.

"Oh, she's okay," he said. "We worried she broke a bone, but we took her for an X-ray and she didn't. She's just bruised. She's fine. Resting, and she can't get around much, at least for the next few days, but she's fine."

"Oh, good," Tabitha said as Fern joined her on the bench. "I'm glad."

"I'm sorry I ran out on you like that," Toby said. "First things first, though, is my chair okay?"

Tabitha laughed. Fern stood up quickly and motioned for Tabitha to get off the phone. She shook her head and put up one finger, letting her know she just needed a minute.

"No," Fern said loudly. "Get off the phone now!"

"Fern," Tabitha said, putting her hand over the phone. "I just need a second. Then we can go."

Fern grabbed the phone out of Tabitha's hand and threw it on the floor. They both stared at it. Then Fern made a move to stomp on it. Tabitha grabbed her, stopping her, and picked up the phone.

"I'll have to call you back," she said to Toby, not waiting for an answer, not even making sure he was still there, before ending the call.

"What was that all about?" Tabitha asked.

"I'm so tired of you always being on the phone," she whined. "You aren't normal anymore. I'm so tired of it."

Tabitha reached out to calm Fern, but she pulled away, and then she started running, as best she could, down the hall and around the corner, Tabitha thought toward the elevators. Tabitha was aware of people looking at her, and kept her eyes down as she followed Fern's route. She wanted to scream at Fern, but that would just draw more attention. She would really yell when they got outside, when nobody could hear them. She would punish Fern for acting like that. She would make her sorry.

As she rounded the corner, there was a tiny boy, walking, but clearly not developing in the normal way, with an oxygen tube in his nose. His mother, at least it looked like his mother, was right behind him, carrying the oxygen tank. Tabitha could see he was struggling, and the mother was encouraging him to keep going. It took all the anger out of her sails. When she moved past them, she saw Fern, sitting on a bench by the elevators, crying. She didn't look up when Tabitha approached.

"I'm so sorry, Fernie Bernie," Tabitha said. "I am just so sorry."

She sat down and reached for Fern, and this time Fern let her.

Tabitha didn't call Toby back until much later that night, after Fern was asleep.

"Hey," she said. "I'm so sorry about that. Fern was upset. She had a bit of a tantrum, which is so unlike her, but I guess it happens to the best of them."

"It certainly does," Toby said warmly. "Believe me, I know girl tantrums."

"So, where were we?" Tabitha asked, smiling into the phone.

"Well," Toby said. "I was just about to ask you out on a proper date. I'm not even sure if that's okay, we were interrupted when we were talking about what is and isn't okay. I figure we can go out and then talk about it. I promise you I will not get my hopes up."

Again, Tabitha laughed. "Sure," she said. "When?"

"Tomorrow?"

"What time?"

"I have Tara tomorrow night, so I was thinking lunch? My treat, of course."

"That sounds perfect."

~

The next morning she got up and walked out with the kids.

"No way," Levi said. "You can't not walk us and then walk us. It's embarrassing."

Fern just looked at her. She should be driving Fern, really, but with the pain meds she'd been okay. The question was, how long was too long to stay on the pain meds? *911—our daughter needs pain pills to walk! And I'm afraid she's going to become addicted to them.*

"Okay," Tabitha said. "I understand."

The kids nodded once in unison; they clearly expected a fight. Or at least Levi did. Tabitha stood on the sidewalk and watched them go through the Square, the way Fern always wanted to go, and across toward Nineteenth Street and beyond. Once she could see them cross by the library, she walked in the other direction toward Starbucks.

"I'll have an extra large, what do you call that?"

"That would be a 'venti,'" the barista said with a smile.

"A venti latte with whole milk please," she said happily. She had found a gift card in a drawer that morning with *$10* written on it. It was underlined twice, so it must have been true. She just hoped it still had money on it, that it wasn't used but not thrown away.

"It's pretty big," warned the barista.

"I'll take it," Tabitha said, already imagining her first sip of the hot, milky coffee. She hadn't had a latte or cappuccino in months. She considered asking the barista to check the card before he actually put in the order. What would she do if the card didn't work? But she wanted it so much, she was willing to risk it. She heard the steaming of the milk and smelled the espresso.

"That will be four twenty-five," the barista said.

Tabitha handed over the card and looked the other way. *Please let it work, please let it work.* She caught herself mouthing the words as she saw Julie, the head of the parent association at the kids' school, tie up her scruffy dog outside and move toward the door. Tabitha had a second of wondering if she could get out of there before Julie saw her, but no, she was stuck. Plus, at this point, she would do anything to get that latte.

"Here you go," the barista said, handing back the card, and Tabitha was so relieved that she didn't even care about seeing Julie anymore. "You still have over five dollars on that."

"Can I give you a tip from the card?" she asked.

"No, sorry, I can't do that," he said nicely. "No worries. Get me next time."

Tabitha thought about the last of the cuff links she had in the bottom of her purse, but she couldn't do that here, not in front of Julie, not with the explanation it would require.

"Thank you," she said. "Thank you so much."

She moved to the other side of the counter and waited. Julie could find her if she wanted to, or maybe she wouldn't notice her.

"Tabitha?"

"Venti caffé latte?" the person behind the counter called.

"That's me," Tabitha said, before turning toward Julie.

"My, my, that's a lot of coffee," Julie said.

"It is," Tabitha smiled dumbly. "And I'm happy to have it."

"Okay then," Julie said, squinting her eyes a little.

Tabitha put some Sugar In The Raw into her cup, trying not to oversweeten it—all this sugar! Just available for the taking! If Julie weren't there Tabitha would have put some packets into her bag. She stirred, put the lid back on, and took a long first sip of the luscious, creamy drink. She closed her eyes and swallowed. Julie was watching her. She took another sip, this time with her eyes open. Did coffee always taste this good? Tabitha didn't think so. And the truth was, Starbucks hadn't generally been her favorite. Well, it was now.

"So, Tabitha, I've been looking for you at school," Julie said. "I haven't seen you there much."

Tabitha didn't know what the right answer to this was. She knew it was good to give your kids independence, but were they too young to officially be walking to school by themselves? She wasn't sure where Julie's judgment would land on this one. She took another sip of coffee.

"I've been around," she said. "I guess I just keep missing you."

"Well, we have the big fundraiser coming up in early spring, and I wanted to talk to you about being on the committee," Julie said. "You are always so good at that."

Tabitha pictured herself last year, probably around this time, going in and out of stores and restaurants, explaining about the Larchwood School, asking if they would be willing to donate anything. Sometimes they gave gift certificates, other times a shirt or a book. If things kept going as they were, she might be forced to pretend she was asking for the school and really take the items for herself and the kids. That was a good idea, actually. Most of the places would probably remember her from previous years and not think anything of it. Suddenly, she wasn't so sorry she had run into Julie.

"Oh, I would love to," Tabitha said, pausing for another long sip of coffee. "But it just isn't a good time for me."

Normally, Tabitha would feel a need to explain. Today, she really didn't. Julie waited, but Tabitha just drank her coffee.

"I see," Julie said after a long pause. "What exactly . . ."

Before she had a chance to finish, there was a ruckus outside with lots of dogs barking. Tabitha thought Julie might actually ask her what she was busy with, and she sort of wanted her to. She had no intention of telling her anything, but she wondered how deep she'd dare to probe. Did Julie think all mothers' time belonged to her, and if it didn't that they owed her an explanation? Apparently so. But Julie didn't ask anything more, she just left. Walked right out, without saying good-bye or nice to see you. Tabitha watched while she knelt down to check on her dog, then she pulled the leash off the hook and walked away. Tabitha continued to drink her coffee. She felt a little buzzed, which made her think of Nora and the pot candy. That was the last time she had felt this good. And she couldn't remember a time before that, since it had been so long ago. She ended up throwing away the edible from Nora's that she had slipped in her pocket—she was worried one of the kids would find it and think it was just candy. But now she was sorry that she did. She stood in the middle of Starbucks and finished the huge cup, threw it away, and walked out and north on Eighteenth Street.

She knew where she wanted to go. She walked fast but felt like she should be doing more than just walking. She took out her phone, googled the synagogue number, and called. She asked for Rabbi Rosen. It went right to voicemail.

"Hi Rabbi, this is Tabitha Brewer, Levi Brewer's mom," she said quickly. "I, um, I just wanted to call before we get too deep into this. Levi is having second thoughts about his bar mitzvah. I think he might like to postpone. Thanks so much." As soon as she ended the call she regretted it. What would Stuart say? Well Stuart wasn't here to say anything, and the more she thought about it, the better she felt. Now it was out there, and she'd see what happened. Maybe the whole thing would just go away.

As she was about to cross Walnut Street, she saw a man walking about fifteen feet ahead of her with Stuart's build and Stuart's shirt. She crossed before she had the light, and a car stopped short, honking at her. She jogged ahead. As she got closer, she saw the man didn't have Stuart's hair, so it wasn't Stuart. This man was balding a bit in the back, which Stuart wasn't. Maybe he was now. How long did it take to start balding? She jogged a little faster, thinking she'd jog by and turn to look at him, but before she could, he stopped and looked her way. It took her a second to realize it was the homeless man she had given Stuart's clothes to. He was dressed in Stuart's shirt, pants, and shoes, and he looked so *normal.* Was that the same guy? Yes, it definitely was. Tabitha remembered his nose and his eyebrows. He saw her, but there was no recognition. She remembered his sign, saying he needed some kindness. She needed some kindness. If she weren't so worried about running into someone she knew, maybe she'd try holding a sign like that, too, and see what she could get. Or maybe she should drive to another town and try it. As she walked by him she smiled, just to see, and he recognized her and he smiled back and tipped a pretend hat. She moved past him, feeling her caffeine buzz begin to wane ever so slightly. She needed to keep going before she lost it completely.

When she got to Nora's apartment building, she went right in, past the desk and to the elevator. She took it to the second floor, crossed the hall, and slowly opened the door. She felt like she could climb the side of the building or swim across a river. She felt like she could do anything, so she might as well do this.

"Nora," she called into the apartment. "Nora?"

"In here, dear," Nora called back.

Tabitha closed the door behind her and walked to the kitchen, expecting to see Nora there baking muffins, but it was empty. She walked into the living room, and there was Nora with her feet up and a magazine on her lap. When she saw Tabitha she smiled big.

"Well, dear, I was thinking about you," she said. "I'm so glad you came to visit me."

"I'm glad to see you," Tabitha said, taking a seat across from Nora. "Do you want to play Monopoly?"

Tabitha had to slow down. She must sound like she was on speed or something. But Nora didn't seem to notice, or at least she didn't seem to care.

"Why yes, dear," Nora said. "I was just thinking, it is a lovely morning for a game. Can you get it, dear? I've hurt my leg, so I can't walk on it right now. It's over there, on the shelf."

Tabitha thought she could just lift the box and run. Nora would never be able to find her, and with a bad leg she wouldn't even be able to try to come after her. *Oh my god!* Tabitha thought to herself. *What is happening to me?*

"Do you have another game, Nora?" Tabitha asked, thinking she needed some time to think. "Anything else?"

"Only cards, and I love Monopoly," Nora said. "I was hoping someone would play with me today."

"Speaking of which, why are you alone again?" Tabitha asked. "Shouldn't there be someone here with you?"

"You're here with me, dear," Nora said. "You're someone."

"That's true," Tabitha said, letting it go. She walked to the shelf and pulled out the Monopoly box. She walked back to Nora and placed it on the small table in front of her. She'd let Nora open it. She watched as Nora pulled the top off. It took effort, and Tabitha knew she should help, but she felt she should let this play out as much as possible without her direct involvement. Once the lid was off, Tabitha saw all the money. It was there, bright and beautiful. Without a word, Nora got to work setting up the board and giving each of them the right amount of money for their banks. She watched Nora touch the bills. They might as well have been play money for all the respect she was giving them.

"Sit, dear," Nora said, slowly putting her legs down one at a time, so she was at a better angle. As she set the second leg down, she groaned.

"What happened to your leg?" Tabitha asked.

"Oh, silliness!" she said, waving it off. "Pure silliness!"

"You go first, Nora," Tabitha said.

"Don't mind if I do," she said, putting her hands together and rubbing them. She rolled and moved her piece. A clock chimed nine times, and Tabitha couldn't believe it was still so early. She felt like she'd lived a whole day since she had said good-bye to the kids. She had two hours, then she'd go home and change for her lunch with Toby. Maybe she'd get one more coffee on the way.

They took turns for an hour, buying hotels (Nora's favorite thing to do), paying each other, and each spending some time in jail. Tabitha kept thinking, *I'm going to take it now, I'm going to take it now.* But she just couldn't do it. If she pocketed any of the bills, Nora would notice the next time she set up the bank. This was a bad idea.

"Can I use your bathroom, Nora?" Tabitha asked. She had to wrap this up. She wanted to leave, and she needed a moment to pull herself together.

"Of course, dear," Nora said, putting her leg back on the ottoman and sitting back, away from the table, with a sigh. "It's just through there."

Tabitha hadn't been beyond the living room before. She walked down a short hallway and saw a bedroom with a neatly made bed ahead of her and a bathroom on her left. It was bright yellow, and the light was on. She went in and closed the door, even though she didn't really have to go to the bathroom. What she needed was to think. As she moved to the sink to wash her hands, she saw a big glass mason jar full of money. She looked closer. What was going on? There were tens, twenties, one-hundred-dollar bills. So many of them. Why did Nora have all this cash? Was it that she didn't trust banks? She'd heard of that before, but she piled the people who didn't trust banks into a category with the people who thought the landing on the moon was a fake, set up in a television studio somewhere. Nora didn't seem that out of touch. She was really starting to like her, more than she probably should. Tabitha wiped her hands on a yellow towel with an embroidered sun, making sure they were completely dry. She reached into the jar and pulled out a twenty, then a ten. She looked at the bills, they seemed as normal as any bill she had ever seen. She stuffed them back in and just stared at the jar. She turned to leave, just walk away, and she saw a piece of yellow construction paper taped to the back of the door saying: **Take Me** and **Yes, That Means You** and **Money Might Not Grow On Trees, But It Does Grow In Jars.**

What was going on here? This entire thing had to be the most elaborate setup in the history of television. But, she kept asking herself, how did they know she was going to keep coming back? She turned back to the jar. It was a big jar. She bet there were thousands of dollars in that jar. She reached in again and pulled out a twenty, then another one. It didn't even begin to make a dent in the stash.

She thought of Fern, and the medical bills, and how much she wanted to be able to get everything bagels and anything else she wanted while they were trying to figure out what was wrong with her leg. "And please, please don't let that be anything terrible," Tabitha said out loud, startling herself. And, on top of all that, there were signs telling her to take it! But really, she didn't know who those notes were meant for, or if they were even real. Tabitha knew it would be weeks before any of the doctor or hospital bills started trickling in, but she felt them out there, tracking her down, eyeing her, coming her way. She had managed to pay the minimum balance on her credit card each month, the one with her maiden name on it, but that was going to get harder to do.

She'd been gone too long. She had to go back to Nora. She wanted the money. Just a little more. Would Nora really notice if some of it was gone? She couldn't even walk, there was no way she counted it regularly. She reached in and fished around for a fifty and a hundred, then another one of each. She folded the bills and slid them into her pants pocket. She made sure everything looked fine and she walked out, deciding to leave the light on the way she found it, in case that was some kind of trick.

She walked slowly back to the living room, working hard to keep her breath steady. She was all ready to say something like: *Sorry, I had a bit of a stomach ache,* or, *I had way too much coffee this morning,* or possibly, but she wasn't sure she dared, *Nora, why do you have so much money just out for the taking?* when she saw that Nora was asleep, her head against the back of the chair and her leg up on the ottoman. Tabitha walked closer to her. She wasn't sure what to do. Should she wake up Nora? Should she put the game back? Should she leave a note? In the end, she did none of those things. She just walked out quietly, pulling the door closed behind her.

CHAPTER SIXTEEN

Tabitha couldn't believe how much money three hundred and forty dollars felt like in her pocket. She could do anything! She could buy as much coffee as she wanted. She could buy any sandwich, any sweater. She could take herself out to lunch. But she didn't have to take herself out to lunch, since Toby was taking her. In fact, she picked up her pace, because she realized she didn't have that much time. He had sent a text last night asking her to meet him at Square on Square at twelve fifteen—the Chinese restaurant in her neighborhood that served her favorite wonton soup. She loved that he picked such an unassuming, cozy place for their date. She felt giddy! She had money! She had to stop herself from skipping down the street.

She veered slightly out of her way to stop at Spread Bagelry.

"A dozen everything bagels," she said to the young man behind the counter. "And a cream cheese and some salmon, please." She felt like she had walked into Tiffany's to ask for the diamond bracelet in the case. She watched as he gathered her order and rang it up.

"That will be twenty-nine dollars even," he said nonchalantly, like everyone could afford nearly thirty dollars for bagels and toppings. She reached into her pocket and pulled out the small wad, then handed him the two twenties, which he took without any indication that what was happening here was nothing short of miraculous. He handed her the change, and she slipped the one-dollar bill into the tip jar.

"Thanks," he said.

She turned and walked back to Locust, through the Square, and home. She had thirty minutes to change and meet Toby.

When she got to her apartment, her landline was ringing. She was so hyped up from the day so far that she leaned over and answered it, regretting it only after she pushed the "talk" button and said hello.

"Tabitha?" a voice said. "This is Rabbi Rosen."

Despite her good fortune, or whatever she wanted to call it, she felt so far away from that moment when she had called the synagogue. Had she really done that? What she needed was more coffee, so she could remember what she was feeling when she made the call.

"Hi, Rabbi," she said. She'd let him lead the conversation.

"Am I getting you at a bad time?" he asked.

"Well, I have to meet someone soon, but I have a minute."

"Oh good," he said. "Because I got your rather concerning message just now, saying Levi wants to postpone his bar mitzvah? Is this true?"

She took a deep breath.

"Yes, it is true," she said. "I'm sorry I left the message that way, I guess I didn't know how to tell you. Stuart has been away for a long time, and I think it's taken a toll, I think it has definitely taken the wind out of Levi's sails."

"When will Stuart be back?" he asked in a way that made her believe Stuart would one day be back.

"Well," she said, so tired of lying. "That's a good question."

"Tell you what," he said. "Why don't you and Levi come in, and we'll talk? There are so many different ways to do this. We can talk through the options. He's worked so hard already, I would hate to see him throw that away."

“That sounds good,” she said, not sure at all that it really sounded good. “When?”

“I have time tomorrow afternoon. Can we say four thirty?”

“Sure,” she said. “See you then.”

Tabitha ran into her bedroom. She was going to change, maybe into a dress or skirt. She looked at herself in the mirror. She was wearing a maroon sweater and jeans. She liked how she looked, and they weren't going anyplace fancy. She decided not to change, brushed her teeth and hair, and left.

She arrived at the nondescript storefront five minutes early but went in anyway. She was greeted right away.

“I'm meeting someone,” she said. “I'm not sure if we have a reservation. Maybe under Tarrabay or Toby.”

She looked around the restaurant. It was full, and she didn't see Toby. The server nodded and was about to walk away when Toby rushed in, out of breath.

“Sorry, sorry,” he said. “I wanted to beat you here.”

“No problem,” she said, surprised by how happy she was to see him.

He turned to the server. “I called ahead,” he said. “Table for two, please.”

The server looked around the room. There were clearly no tables available downstairs. Tabitha expected him to tell them it would be a wait, but instead he grabbed two menus, with purpose, and walked past them to a staircase behind them. She never liked to sit upstairs here, because it made her feel far away from the action, but Toby didn't seem to mind, and she didn't want to seem difficult, so she followed the server with Toby right behind her. When they got to the top, she saw the room was entirely empty, just as she thought it would be. She didn't want to be isolated—she wanted other people around. But Toby accepted the table the server pointed to, and got right to looking at the menu.

“The dumplings are great here,” he said. “Really, everything is good.”

Tabitha took her seat and looked around, feeling suddenly uncomfortable and wondering if she had made a mistake by jumping into this too fast.

"What do you like?" Toby asked, looking up from the menu with a concerned look in his eye. "Are you okay here?"

"Yes, of course," she said, pulling her chair closer to the table and trying to relax. "I always like it downstairs better."

"Actually, I do, too," he said, which made her relax even more. "But this is okay. I'm just happy to be here with you."

Tabitha smiled. Toby closed his menu.

"We never really finished our talk at the game about what is going on with you, with me, with each of us. I guess we barely started it," he said.

The waiter came over and put two glasses of ice water on the table. "Can I get you anything to drink?"

"Do you like champagne?" Toby asked Tabitha. At first she thought he was joking, but she realized he wasn't.

"Sure," she said.

"Two glasses of champagne, please."

She waited for him to start the conversation again, but he just smiled at her. She liked that he didn't feel he had to talk all the time. Stuart was a professional talker. It was like he could never just be quiet or that the silence might reveal something he didn't want to be revealed. Now she was starting to understand why. But this was nice. She liked this.

When the glasses arrived, he held his up to make a toast. She raised her glass.

"I want to make a toast," he said. "To you—for being someone who makes me want to get to know her better. I haven't met anyone like that in a long time. Wherever the dumplings may take us, I am grateful for that."

"Cheers," she said.

As if the server were waiting behind a curtain for the cue of Toby finishing his toast, he emerged with a full tray and set down the promised dumplings along with chicken skewers, two egg rolls (the old-fashioned kind), scallion pancakes, and shrimp toast. Tabitha was confused, since they hadn't ordered, but she was hungry, and she filled her plate. She thought about mentioning how much she liked the soup here, but decided there was plenty already.

"How did he know what we wanted?" she asked.

"Oh, I ordered a sample menu when I called."

"Then why were you looking at the menu?" she asked.

"I don't know, it gave me something to do?" Toby said. "But please, if there is something you want that you don't see here, order it. I was just taking my best guess."

"No, this all looks great," she said. She smiled again and took another sip of the sparkling wine. It was so sweet it could have been soda, but she didn't mind.

"I'll start," he said, like they had agreed upon something to talk about. But she knew what he meant. "First, I should say, and I think this is important, I wasn't looking to meet someone. Honestly. I was just going to the bar to, well, to root for Michigan, and because I was lonely. The fewer meals I have to have alone the better, right? So . . ." he trailed off.

"That's exactly why I was there, too," Tabitha said. "The food!"

They both laughed. Tabitha could have said more, that she wasn't looking to meet anyone either, but it seemed so ridiculous, so obvious, whether he realized it or not; she just couldn't bring herself to say it.

"That reminds me," she said. "I thought you said you didn't eat meat."

"I said I don't eat a lot of meat," he said. "And that's true. But I do eat some."

"Oh, okay," Tabitha said, reshuffling her vision of him. He wasn't a vegetarian. That was good. She loved meat.

"Okay, so the hard stuff," Toby said. "You know a tiny bit. My wife and I are legally separated and moving toward divorce."

He paused, and Tabitha thought, *Actually I didn't know that.* But instead of saying it, she nodded as if to say, *Go on.*

"I know I mentioned an incident, for which I am responsible. I'm sure that conjures up all kinds of ideas in your mind. I'm willing and open to talking about it, if you want me to."

She did want him to. She was curious. She was also a little scared. It was nice having this . . . *possibility*, before he became a real person. At some point, if you talked to someone long enough, they were bound to become a real person. She wanted to put that off for a little while. Plus, she didn't want to be the one answering the questions.

"You know what," she said. "We don't have to talk about that now. Can we just eat and talk about something else? These dumplings are delicious. How's your mother, by the way?"

"She's okay," he said, cutting an egg roll in half and putting a clump of cabbage that fell onto the table into his mouth. "She's still sore, but I think she's a little better each day. It's those damn home-health aides who are driving me crazy. Half the time they don't show up, the other half of the time, they send strangers. I thought I might have to cancel with you because her morning person didn't come, but she assured me she was okay. I'll go check on her later."

Something strange happened in Tabitha's brain. It was like something was nagging at her, but she couldn't for the life of her figure out what it was. She tried to brush it off and focus on Toby.

"That's hard," Tabitha said, without thinking it through. "Taking care of an older parent." She stopped, realizing what was bothering her. She pictured her mother on the last day. She was hooked up to oxygen, her eyes hadn't opened in days. She was right there! But Tabitha couldn't reach her anymore. She had given up on that days before, weeks before—had it been months before?

"It is hard," he said.

"Tell me about your daughter," Tabitha blurted out, before he had a chance to ask what she knew about taking care of an older parent.

"She's great," he said. "She's ten and in fourth grade."

"No way! So's mine! Well my daughter is nine and in fourth grade."

"And she loves to read and play ultimate frisbee. And, as you know, make crafts, especially confetti!"

"That's all so great."

"What about your kids?"

"My daughter's name is Fern, my son is Levi."

"Good names, I'd say."

"Yeah," she said.

The server came back and cleared the plates. There was still so much food left, and these were just the appetizers.

"Do you want to take it?" she asked Toby.

"No, that's okay," he said. And then, "Do you?"

"Actually, I would love to," she said. "My kids could have it for a snack." *And dinner,* she thought, and then she remembered the money that was still in her pocket. Her plan was to put it in the bank, at least most of it, but she hadn't figured out how to do that. She couldn't put it in their joint account, which had almost no money in it since Stuart's checks stopped being directly deposited, because she had no idea if Stuart was still interested in that account. She thought she'd start a new account, but how hard was that? Would they ask questions since her other account had taken such a downward turn and her credit was pretty much maxed out at this point? There was only a paltry seventy-five dollars in the joint account the last time she checked.

"So, I'm sitting here thinking I don't need to know your story, but I think I do," he said, and he said it so kindly, Tabitha didn't mind. "I'll tell you why. I'm starting to like you. I'm sitting here thinking about kissing you."

"I didn't go to Michigan," Tabitha said—blurted, really. She suddenly felt like their whole relationship was built on a lie. "And I didn't graduate in 1994, so I'm actually older than you think. I went to Trinity, in Hartford." She had an urge to cover her face with her hands, she didn't want to see his reaction. Instead she looked down, so she heard his reaction before she saw it, and it was laughter. Toby laughed.

"What?" she asked, daring to look at him.

"I know that," he said, smiling. "I knew it before you said it, but I let it slide. Actually, that's what caught my attention: you were so clearly trying to blend in. It made you seem mysterious. Also, no Wolverine would ever accidentally wear red to a Michigan event. It just doesn't happen."

"Do you still want to kiss me?" she heard herself saying. She hadn't even thought it through, she just said it.

"As much as I ever did," he said in such a way that she felt it in her stomach. "I just want to be sure that would be okay with you."

"It would be okay with me," Tabitha said, surprising herself. She hadn't kissed anyone in months, obviously, but it was the lack of touch that she couldn't stand. She thought of her mother calling her one day, saying that she couldn't stand to not be touched, and Tabitha said that was silly, that she was touched. She hated that memory. She drank the rest of the champagne in her glass and got up and walked to Toby, who stood up at her movement. Without hesitating, she leaned in for a kiss. She wanted to do it. He paused for less than a second, but she could feel it, and then he was all-in, and they were kissing, and she didn't want to stop. She didn't want to face more questions, sure, but she wanted to keep kissing. She wished they were someplace more private, but they were, thank goodness, in a completely empty room. She didn't want to break their connection to look around to make sure nobody else had been seated up there, she didn't want to ruin the mood or give him a chance to talk, but she knew she couldn't go on kissing him forever. Well, maybe she could. Did it ever feel this way with Stuart? She didn't think so. He was pleasant enough to kiss, and he always, always had nice smelling breath, but she could always stop, she didn't mind stopping.

Toby eased back into his chair and pulled her down onto his lap, continuing to kiss her. At first she tried to not put all her weight on him, then she gave up and let go, sitting on him completely.

"Beef chow fun?" the server asked, making them both jump and pull apart. She hopped off his lap, knocking her thigh into the table, then scooted around to her side. Toby was shaking his head, laughing quietly.

"Yes, we're the beef chow fun," he said, louder than he had to.

The server put the dish on the table and went back into the kitchen. Now they were both laughing. Toby could barely catch his breath, he was leaning back in his chair clutching his stomach. Tabitha started slowly, but his laugh was so pleasant, so happy, it made her laugh harder, until she had to wipe the tears from her eyes.

"Beef chow fun?" Toby said, when he'd finally gotten some control.

The server came again.

"Moo shu chicken?" he asked. They were beyond being polite. Toby just pointed to the table without saying a word.

"Would you like me to roll it?"

"No, no, we can do it," Toby said.

The waiter bowed his head and went back through the curtain.

"So my husband disappeared," Tabitha said.

Toby sucked in his breath.

"He always traveled a lot for business, but one morning, months ago, I woke up and he was gone. There was a note, but it didn't say where he was going. I haven't talked to him since."

"Wow," Toby said. "That's a lot." But as always, he said it kindly.

"Yeah, it is a lot," Tabitha said. "I've tried him. I've called, I've emailed. I just, I don't know how to find him. I . . ." She stopped, deciding she wasn't ready to tell him or anyone about the call to the hospital and the realization that Abigail was dead. Or the possibility that Stuart's connection to Abigail had been ongoing.

"Oh," Toby said.

"I should add that things were not great when he left," she said, because she thought Toby deserved that explanation. "Actually, they were never great. Never. I wanted them to be, and he was kind and polite, but there was always something missing. The night before he left we had . . . words . . . well, a fight, but I never thought he was going to just leave. I thought, stupidly, that we were finally being honest. What we talked about, what he told me, sort of put our entire marriage into perspective, and that was a strange relief somehow. That was partly why it was such a shock when he went away without a trace. That and a few other things. But overall our marriage had been, I'm not sure what the right word is . . . strained? Devoid of passion? I don't know. But I never expected this to happen. I never expected him to leave us and not look back."

Unbelievably, the server traipsed out of the kitchen once again.

"Peking duck?"

Toby and Tabitha looked at each other, first with serious looks, then questioning ones, and then they were all-out laughing. They didn't even try to answer the server or respond to him. He just stood there, holding the lacquered-looking duck out toward them. Finally, Toby moved some things around and pointed to an empty place.

"Would you like me to roll it?"

They were laughing so hard they couldn't talk. Tabitha worried she was spitting a little.

"No, no," Toby said, though he was hard to understand. "We can do it."

"As you wish," the server said and walked away.

"Hey," Tabitha said, when she calmed down a little. "That's from *The Princess Bride*. I like that he said that. I hope he doesn't think we were making fun of him."

"We kind of were," he said.

"Well," she said. "We were making fun of his timing, I guess. I'm sorry about that."

"I'll make it up to him," Toby said. "I'll leave a big tip."

They both looked at the food, but neither reached for any.

"Do you want to pack it up?" Toby finally asked.

"That would be perfect."

CHAPTER SEVENTEEN

Tabitha walked directly home and, as soon as she put all the leftover Chinese food in her empty refrigerator, went right to her computer. She googled, "abandonment," and tons of varying but similar definitions came up, basically describing her life for the last few months. She knew this, and it didn't help. She googled, "legal abandonment," and it was pretty much the same, just with fancier words until she got to the phrase "with the intention of not reclaiming it." *Huh.* That stopped her. There was no question that Stuart had voluntarily left everything—the apartment, his things, his children, her—but did he plan to come back and reclaim it? That was the big question, right? But there must be a limit to how long someone had to wait to see. She was just googling, "abandonment limit," when she got a text. It was from Toby.

You home?
Yes
Can I call you?
Sure

Two seconds later, the phone rang.

"Hi!" she said, clicking the images off her screen. She didn't want to talk to Toby and think about abandonment at the same time. "I was going to call you later. Thanks for lunch. It was really nice."

He was quiet for a few seconds, and she wondered if the call had dropped.

"Yeah," he said, just as she was taking the phone away from her ear to see if it was still live. "It was really nice. That's sort of why I'm calling. I have a crazy idea."

"What is it?"

"Well, I think the first question is, how much time do you have?" he asked.

For some reason, it seemed to her that whatever answer she gave would be important. And while she thought he meant how much time did she have now, before the kids came home, she couldn't help but also think about how much time she had before Stuart came back to *reclaim things* or until enough time would have gone by before she would be free. She wished she'd had just a few more minutes to do more research and figure that out.

"How much time do I have?" she repeated the question back to him. "Do you mean now?"

"Yeah," he said. "I mean now."

She looked at the clock on the wall, but its batteries had died, so it had stopped at seven o'clock, and she knew it was not seven o'clock. She glanced at the clock on the oven. It was just before two thirty. Both kids had clubs after school, so she wouldn't have to get them until five thirty, even later if she pushed it. She could go right at six o'clock, just as the doors were closing for the night, and get them then—*reclaim them*, as the case may be.

"I have about three hours," she said.

"Okay, this might sound crazy, and if it does, please don't let it ruin things, just say—'that is crazy'—okay?"

"Okay," she said, drawing out the word.

"Let's go to a hotel."

"What?" she said, letting out an awkward guffaw, which she wished she could take back. It was the least sexy noise she had ever made. Well, that wasn't true, but it was not an attractive noise. "That's crazy!"

"I told you it was."

"Which hotel?"

"I don't know, the Rittenhouse?"

"No, I can't do that. Someone will see me. Also, do you mean, like, for the night?"

"Okay, so here's my idea," he said, sounding like a little kid. "We take one hour, one hour away from everything, and we pretend it's separate from everything else. I can't stop thinking about you. I want to be with you."

She closed her eyes, because she wanted to be with him. She wanted it so much.

"Well, I can't just walk out of my apartment building, across the Square, and into a hotel room. That just isn't done."

"How about the Kimpton on Seventeenth? There's a restaurant there. Walk into the restaurant like that's where you're going and, if you don't run into anyone, walk through to the lobby and take the elevator to the room. I'll go right now. I'll text you the room number."

"Toby, I can't do this," she said, thinking of Fern and Levi at school. "I just can't."

"You can," Toby said gently. "I think you can."

She didn't say anything.

"How about this? I'll head over there and see if this is even possible. Then I'll text you. What do you say?"

She still didn't say anything.

"We can just sit and talk if you want," he said. "Or, can I come there?"

"Fine, go to the hotel, see what they say."

"I'll text you soon," he said quickly, and hung up. She laughed out loud; he so clearly didn't want her to change her mind. She put her computer into sleep mode, though the information about abandonment might be particularly useful right now, and went into the bathroom. She thought about a shower, then she thought about powder and makeup, then she thought about putting on nicer underwear. In the end, she brushed her teeth and went into the foyer to wait. Her heart was beating so fast it made her feel a little sick. Five minutes went by. Seven minutes went by. Her phone binged. It was Levi.

Drums are canceled, can I just come home?

Before she had a chance to answer another text came through. Room 336 was all it said.

To Levi she texted back Just go to the afterschool program and do homework. I'll be there at the usual time. Normally, she would ask if that was okay or let him negotiate a little, but she waited, and there was no response. All she could do was hope he followed her directions.

She didn't text Toby back. She put on a coat and headed out the door, feeling like everyone in the lobby was looking at her, which was ridiculous, of course. She walked up to Locust and over to Seventeenth, and finally north to the Kimpton. She didn't do as Toby suggested but instead walked right into the small lobby, where she didn't see anyone she knew, but she didn't look too hard, walked to the elevator, and pushed "3." She still thought she might not do this. She might take the elevator back down, or she might get off and walk to the stairs to go down. There were many things she could do that didn't involve a hotel room with a man and a bed. The doors opened, she got out and turned right and there it was—room 336. She did not walk by it. She did not ignore it. She knocked on the door and waited. Toby answered right away. As soon as she saw him, she didn't care about any of it—what people would think, what her legal rights were as an abandoned person, what her kids would think. None of it. She was reminded of that scene in *thirtysomething*, toward the end of the series, when Michael almost had an affair. He was with the other woman, were they in a hotel room? They were so drawn to each other, but they knew it wasn't the right thing, or at least he knew. He wanted this other woman, but he didn't want to cheat on Hope; he knew he didn't want to. It looked like actual work to not touch, to remain separate. Tabitha was so mesmerized by that scene because, while she believed it, she had never felt anything like that, never not been able to resist someone. But now, now she understood.

She followed Toby into the nice room. There was a big king-size bed and he sat on the edge of the crisp white cover, smiling.

"I considered putting on the robe that's in the closet. They have very nice robes here. But I thought I might scare you off."

"Good thinking," she said. She took off her coat and let it drop to the floor. Then stepped out of her shoes. She eased off her pants. He was watching her. "But I doubt you could scare me off at this point." She wanted to say other things, like she meant *this* exact point. Five minutes ago, she was still in danger of being scared off, but not now. She wanted to make sure that he meant what he said, that this hour was apart from everything else, and when did the hour begin and end? But she didn't say any of it.

The next fifty-nine minutes were a sensual blur, and when a tiny alarm went off she wanted to cry.

"Really, you set an alarm?" she said.

"I promised you an hour, that was an hour."

"Can I have another hour?"

"If you can spare it. The room is ours until tomorrow."

"I can't," she said. "I should go. The kids. Are you going to stay?"

"Not without you," he said. "It will be too lonely."

They got dressed quietly. Crazy things ran through her mind. They could meet back here later—or in the middle of the night! But she couldn't, she knew she couldn't.

"Hey," he said. "Can you come back in the morning? After the kids go to school? We could order room service."

"I'll see you here at eight fifteen."

~

Tabitha was shocked to find that Levi didn't mind going to see the rabbi. It was almost like he felt he deserved the punishment of it, or at least that was what Tabitha gathered when he nodded once at being told they had a meeting that afternoon. She told him before he left for school, before she went back to the hotel to meet Toby for another wonderful hour full of sex and room-service pancakes and bacon. But now that they were here, sitting in the rabbi's office, Tabitha could see it was something else.

"I just don't want to do it," Levi said, leaning forward in his chair, his hands on his lap. His voice was clear and strong, not that mumbling sort of response that a young teenager often gave in the presence of authority.

"I hear what you're saying," the rabbi said gently. He leaned back in his chair. "But can you explain to me why, so I can understand it better?"

Levi looked at Tabitha. She had to pull herself back to the moment. She was thinking about Toby and how he focused on her for most of their time that morning, completely undemanding, wanting only to know what made Tabitha feel the best. Her cheeks flushed red now as she nodded toward Levi.

"Well, my dad has been gone for a long time," Levi said. "And I don't know when he's coming back. He always works a lot, and I thought this would be something we could do together. I tried, I really did. I've even started my mitzvah project, the one he suggested, but without him here, I just don't want to do it."

"What about your mom?" the rabbi said, nodding toward Tabitha. "What if she helps you? What if you can do it with her?"

"It's not the same," Levi said, sounding more like a whiny teenager.

"It's not the same," Tabitha agreed, backing him up. "I never had a bat mitzvah—I'm learning as he does it. Stuart had a bar mitzvah. This is something he always wanted for Levi."

"Well, let me ask you the obvious question," Rabbi Rosen said. "What does Stuart have to say about this? Is he willing to have Levi give it all up so he can continue to stay away taking care of business? Might he consider cutting his trip short, or at least making a few trips home here and there to help? We're not that far away from the big day."

Levi looked at Tabitha again and raised his eyebrows. *Yes, yes,* she wanted to say, *These are all very good, obvious questions. I just don't have the answers.*

"Well," she said after a too-long pause. "He is extremely hard to reach."

She did not want to blatantly lie to the rabbi. She thought, at this point, he would see through her and know she was lying. He probably already thought she was nuts and undependable, if rabbis thought things like that.

"Can I give it a try?" Rabbi Rosen asked.

Tabitha wondered if Stuart would answer his cell phone if the rabbi called. She doubted it. She flashed back to the other day and Fern's strange conversation with Stuart, still not at all sure what was going on there.

"Look," Tabitha said, after she ran three other sentences through her mind: *I'll try him again. Let's give him more time. I don't think it will make a difference.* "To be perfectly honest, as far as I can tell, he is unreachable."

It was the first time she'd said anything like that in front of Levi. He didn't even flinch or look up at her. Was this not a surprise to him?

"Well, he must be pretty caught up in whatever he is doing," the rabbi said in his gentle voice. "Here's what I propose. Levi, let me know if this might work for you. You are so close. You know your Torah portion, you've probably already done plenty for your project. Let's keep it simple. Don't even think about a party or celebration if you don't want to. You can do that down the road—when everyone you want to be here is here." He paused, and Tabitha took note that he didn't say, *"When your dad is here."* But he also didn't not say it.

"I'll call you to the Torah, we will do the barest minimum. You don't even have to give your D'var Torah. But once I call you to the bima, and you have read from the Torah, you will officially become a bar mitzvah—anything else you want to do or don't want to do is up to you. And that will be something that can't be taken away from you. Believe me, it isn't easy to get back to this place, learn a whole new Torah portion. Once people let it go, they rarely do it again."

"Fine," Levi said, looking up from his lap. "That sounds okay."

"Great," Rabbi Rosen said. "I'm so glad to hear it. And I'll work with you from here on out. No need to set up appointments with the cantor. Just come to me. We'll keep it very simple."

"Thank you, Rabbi," Tabitha said. It was just dawning on her what this meant. No invitations, no party. It was such good news. But then she looked over at Levi, and he was crying. He didn't even try to hide it. Tabitha leaned toward him at the same time the rabbi did, so she leaned back, hoping he'd have something better and wiser to say than she did.

"I know this is hard," the rabbi said to Levi. "I wish I had more answers for you. But please know, I am here for you if you want to talk or if you need anything. Here is my cell number, call me anytime."

He handed Levi a card, which he took and stuffed into his pocket, sniffling. The tears seemed to be subsiding.

911—I need you. Our son is CRYING—he hasn't cried in front of me since he was eight.

Tabitha put her hand on Levi's knee. She didn't touch him much anymore, she realized. Why did people stop touching each other? She half expected him to brush her away, or to stand up, so her hand would be forced to move. But he just sat there, letting her touch him, and it made her feel so sorry for him, she could barely stand it. Much worse than when his room was neat, so much worse than the time he knocked out his front tooth when he was three, too old to have a pacifier still but did anyway, and the dentist said he couldn't have it anymore, that was it, cold turkey. He had turned in the dentist chair and cried, serious, sad tears, and for a minute, Tabitha thought she might never be mad at him again. She felt that way now, times twenty.

"Monkey," she said gently. "I promise, I'm never going to leave you."

He nodded, sniffed a little, then stood slowly, so her hand was moved but not aggressively; it was a natural falling away. She stood, too. The rabbi stood, then, and reached out to shake Levi's hand but instead hugged him. Tabitha thought this might make him start to cry again, but it didn't.

"Thanks, Rabbi," he said.

"Anytime, Levi," Rabbi Rosen said. Tabitha wondered if she could ask him to come home with them. His presence was so ridiculously soothing.

"Tabitha, please know I'm here if you need anything," he said, turning to her. She felt like she didn't deserve his attention—she wasn't *really* Jewish—but she wanted it.

"Thank you," she said. She wanted to add that she was going to try to sort this out, she would bring Levi's father home for him, but that was all so silly. Obviously, if she could have, she would have.

When Levi was out the door but Tabitha was still inside, she felt the rabbi's gentle hand on her shoulder.

"Is Fern doing okay?" he asked. "With all of this?"

Tabitha shook her head and then nodded, one after the other.

"She seems okay," Tabitha said. "Thanks for asking."

~

"Can you drop me at Butch's?" Levi asked, once they were in the car and the doors were closed. All signs of the tears were gone.

"It's dinnertime, and Fern is . . ."

"Please?"

"Fine," she said, going right instead of left, so she could go to Butch's house.

Ten minutes later, Levi was dropped off and she was alone in the car. She called Rachel.

"Hey, I've been thinking about you," Rachel said in her warm voice.

Tabitha immediately began to cry.

"What's wrong? Are you okay? Are the kids okay?"

Tabitha couldn't get a word out. She worried about Rachel's worrying in the time it was taking her to speak.

"Yes," she finally spit out. "Pretty much."

"Where are you?"

Again, it was a long few seconds before she could talk.

"I . . . just . . . dropped . . . Levi . . . off," she sobbed. "Now . . . I'm . . . going . . . home . . . to . . . Fern."

"I'm just getting off," Rachel said. "Can I meet you at your apartment?"

"No, no," Tabitha said, thinking of the state of the place. There were eleven burned-out light bulbs in the kitchen and only one that still worked. Now, though, now she could start to replace them. She had Nora's money. She pictured herself reaching into that strange jar and pulling out the bills, and her crying reached a whole new level.

"I'm coming whether you want me to or not," Rachel said. "I have some stuff to talk about, too. Are you okay to drive?"

"I think so."

"Have you guys eaten?" Rachel asked, but before Tabitha could answer she added, "I'll bring dinner."

CHAPTER EIGHTEEN

Somehow Tabitha got home, and somehow she found a parking spot. She was walking in toward the apartment when she saw Rachel, and she had to work hard to hold it together until they were in the elevator together.

"I'll talk first," Rachel said, shifting the big bag she was carrying from one hand to the other.

Tabitha waited for her to say she was pregnant. That was the obvious news, though it seemed a little soon. Had she even been inseminated yet? Tabitha was having a hard time keeping track of time. They went up higher and higher: five, six. The door opened, and she still hadn't said anything.

"So, here's the thing," Rachel finally said when they were out of the elevator.

"Stuart's gone," Tabitha said, before Rachel could continue. Then she felt bad. "Wait, sorry, god I've been holding that in for so long. I wanted to tell you but, well, there's a reason I didn't. We are all pretty much falling apart. I just—"

"He's gone?" Rachel asked. "I thought he was sick. I thought maybe, I mean, it didn't make any sense, because if that were true, you would be with him, but I imagined he was sick somewhere, with some awful mystery illness, getting treatment."

"I think that would be better," Tabitha said. "Than this."

Rachel leaned against the beautiful, fully-maintained, recently painted wall in the brightly lit hallway and sank slowly to the carpeted floor. She looked like she was getting ready to settle in for a while. But already Tabitha regretted what she'd said. The threat—*"I'll tell them what you did"*—was now screaming in her head. It was always there, whispering, reminding her. But now it felt like she had unleashed it and there was no holding it back. *"I'll tell them what you did."* Why? She wanted to scream. *Why will you tell them what I did? And more important, what did I do? Which thing? Was it the peanut oil or the morphine? Or both?*

Tabitha could smell the food in the bag. She guessed some kind of stewed chicken in a Marsala sauce with mushrooms and noodles. That was one of the store's specialties. But despite her having eaten so little today, she wasn't hungry. She couldn't imagine putting a piece of chicken on a fork and bringing it to her mouth, chewing. Fern must be hungry, though. Poor Fern, who had been alone for hours now.

"Let's go inside," Tabitha said, leaning over to offer Rachel a hand, which she took. "Besides, I sort of jumped in there. You said you wanted to talk to me about something. What is it?"

~

Levi did not have any intention of going to Butch's house. He just couldn't stand the thought of being with his mother for one more second. Why had he let that happen—to cry in front of her? What was he, like five? He didn't even recognize himself anymore. So when his mother dropped him off just down the block, because there were no spots closer, he was glad. She might stay to make sure he got inside, but she was so distracted these days that he didn't think she would.

He walked as slowly as he could toward the stoop leading up to Butch's perfect house with his perfect family. He hadn't talked to him all day—in fact Butch wasn't even in school today—but he could just imagine them in there, all four of them, playing board games or watching some show together on the nature channel. Probably something about how animals stuck together, or how the male of the species rarely abandoned his young, and when he did, there must be something pretty defective about his offspring. After that, they'd go into their brightly lit kitchen, not a single light bulb would be blown out in there, Levi was sure of it, and they would eat something wonderful that Butch's mother properly shopped for and maybe even spent much of the day preparing. Something like lasagna or brisket. No way, he couldn't stand to see that today. But his mother didn't leave. He could still feel the car behind him, he could hear it. He turned back toward her, just to get a sense of what she was doing, and he could see she was on the phone, and was she crying? Oh man, this couldn't get any worse. He looked ahead again, fairly sure she hadn't seen him. He was just going to have to keep walking, past Butch's house, and if she called him on it, he'd deal with it then.

Butch lived on Mt. Vernon, two houses shy of Twenty-First Street, so if his mother wasn't paying close attention, he might be able to make it look like he was moving toward his house when he was really going around the corner. He held his breath as he passed his false destination, waiting for a honk or to hear his mother call his name, but nothing happened, and then he turned right on Twenty-First Street and was out of sight. He moved fast and made the first right onto the next block, one he didn't know at all, and waited. What he was waiting for, he didn't know. So he decided to keep going on that block, back to Twentieth Street and beyond. At Nineteenth he started walking south toward the Ben Franklin Parkway and home, even though he had no intention of going home. There was the chance his mother would see him. It would be plain old bad luck if she did, but it wasn't impossible. He kept his eyes open for their car, and he walked.

He was just across the parkway, near the main branch of the library, when he saw him. He was facing the other way, but it was him. His hair looked thinner, but that could be from all the stress, or something. He would have an explanation. He always had an explanation. Levi walked faster. He could see his shirt, a shirt he knew so well, mostly blue with red checks, it looked almost purple from a distance. He could see his hands. They looked like the hands he remembered. He couldn't get to him fast enough. He started to run.

"Dad!" he screamed. "Dad! Dad!"

His father didn't turn around, but he didn't go the other way, either, which was what Levi was afraid of. Where had he been this whole time? Had he been this close? He was almost to him, and he could see that the shirt had a big hole in it. The khakis had an ugly brown stain on the butt.

"Dad!" he screamed again, and this time the man turned around. For a second he thought, how could he look so different? Could a person change that much? And then he knew. It wasn't his father at all. He slowed just enough to get a good look, to be sure, before speeding up again. He kept running, right toward Logan Square, where the light for the westbound traffic had just turned green.

~

Inside, Fern was watching television. When Tabitha got closer she could see she was watching *The Walking Dead*, and her first instinct was to yell at her. What was she doing? She shouldn't be watching that! But then she felt so utterly sorry for her that she just sat down next to her and didn't mention the content of the show. She knew Fern had watched all the DVDs they had over and over again, she probably held off on this one for as long as she could. It was a gift Tabitha had bought for Stuart last year. She thought at the time it might be something they could watch together, something that had absolutely nothing to do with their lives, something that might make their own lives seem not so bad. They never watched it. Tabitha could see the clear plastic on the coffee table that Fern had peeled off of the DVD.

"Hey, Fernie Bernie," she said soothingly. "Aunt Rachel is here. She brought dinner."

Fern nodded, her eyes on the screen. A man with a beard was hacking away at a zombie.

"Here, turn that off for now, come eat."

Fern didn't respond. Tabitha sat back to get a better look at her. Her bad leg was stretched out, completely stiff, and her other leg was tucked under her. She looked thin, and there were purplish circles under her eyes. Tabitha was doing a terrible, terrible job of taking care of her.

"Come on, Fern," she coaxed. "Come into the kitchen. You must be starving."

"When this is over."

"How much longer?" Tabitha asked, hoping this was one of the less violent episodes, if there was such a thing.

Fern sighed and pushed a button on the remote to pause it.

"Eleven minutes," Fern said.

"Okay, fine, but come in when it's over," Tabitha said. "Don't start another one."

Again, Fern didn't respond. Tabitha got up and walked back into the kitchen. Rachel had pulled the containers out of the shopping bag and placed them on the granite island. Tabitha was wrong, it wasn't chicken Marsala. It was meatballs and lasagna and some kind of parmesan: chicken or veal or eggplant. It all looked so good. Now she could imagine eating this, chewing, swallowing.

There was literally one light bulb illuminating the big, grand kitchen. Tabitha knew Rachel would normally say something about this, but she didn't now. She pretended to not notice, or that it was normal, something. Tabitha took a seat on one of the stools and let Rachel do all the work, set the table, hunt for napkins that weren't there. Again, she didn't ask.

"Okay, so please tell me what's going on with you," Tabitha said, leaning her chin into her left hand. "I'm so sorry I stole the thunder."

"Yeah, well you did that," she said, but nicely. *Thank goodness for Rachel.* "Okay so here's the thing. And my thing is not as important as your thing, I think, even though an hour ago it seemed very important; it seemed like the most important thing in the world. I can see now, my thing is something that doesn't exist yet, while your thing exists and needs help."

"Wait, I didn't mean we had to be in competition, whose thing is more important," Tabitha said. "I didn't mean that at all. I don't even know what your thing is."

"No, I know that," Rachel said, spooning a little of everything onto Tabitha's plate. "Is Fern coming?"

"In a minute," Tabitha said. "She's finishing a show."

"Okay, well, what I meant was that it sort of helped put my thing in perspective. I am all cleared and ready to be inseminated. I can go into the doctor's office on Monday, and they can shoot the sperm toward an egg, and then I would wait, and it could go one way or another, I don't know which."

"That's so great," Tabitha said, moving off the stool and going to hug Rachel. "Do you want me to come with you?"

"Wait, I'm not done," Rachel said, stopping Tabitha mid-hug. "So, when I think about waiting, and finding out which way it might go—am I pregnant? Am I not pregnant?—I honestly don't know which I would hope for. That's crazy, right? I should know. I should be hoping to achieve pregnancy. That's the goal here."

"Sure," Tabitha said. "That's the goal."

"I don't think I want that," Rachel said slowly. "I don't want to be home alone with a newborn baby. It seemed like such a good idea two months ago. A way to not be alone, a way to have a baby without needing to find the right person to share it with, a way to make my eventual old age seem not so bleak, but now I realize, it might not be for me. If I could jump ahead and have a ten-year-old maybe, or even a seven-year-old, that sounds okay. Busy, but okay. But how does anyone recover from newborn hell all alone? Doesn't that ruin a person? Wouldn't I be doing everything in my power to make myself unattractive to a potential partner? *'Oh hey, sorry I left the spit up out of the picture on the dating site, but you better get used to it,'* or, *'You don't mind waiting while I nurse the baby, do you? It will only take a few hours because the baby is having trouble latching, and after that we can go on our first date.'* I can see it might be right for someone, but I don't think it's right for me. The thing is, now I've started this process. I picked the donor: we have the sperm, and I have imagined this possible being, so now it feels like I'm saying good-bye to something."

At that moment, Fern came into the kitchen. She was limping, but she never mentioned the pain, if there was any, or the limp. Rachel moved toward Fern, giving her a quick hug before piling food onto her plate. Fern didn't even ask what it was, she just ate. Before the women had a chance to get settled and join her, she took her last bite and pushed her plate away.

"Can I go back to watching?"

"Sure," Tabitha said, more because she wanted to continue the conversation with Rachel than because she thought it was okay.

"She seems a little down," Rachel said when Fern had left the room.

"Yeah, as I mentioned, we're all falling apart a little."

"And what's with the limp?"

"We've been to a bunch of doctors, but nobody can figure it out," Tabitha said. "I need to take her for more tests. But wait, I want to keep talking about you. Have you considered storing or freezing the sperm or something? That way you would still have the option, but you could take more time to think about it."

Rachel reached into the bag and pulled out a tomato and a small, perfect bunch of basil. She walked to the sink and washed first the tomato and then the basil leaves, one at a time, with her back to Tabitha.

"Shoot, I forgot to put this out for Fern," Rachel said.

"It's okay, she probably wouldn't have eaten it anyway. But have you? Considered that?"

"I guess, I just don't know," Rachel said slowly. "I mean, I feel like my body is ready, but my brain isn't. Will you come with me on Monday morning to talk to them about this? I don't want to go alone."

"Yes, of course I will," Tabitha said.

Now Rachel turned around and smiled.

"Okay, good," she said. "That makes me feel better."

She pulled a knife off the rack on the wall and slowly sliced the tomato, perfect, round, red slices. Then she rolled the basil leaves into a cylinder and sliced those, sprinkling them on top.

"Hey, I forgot dressing, do you have any?"

Now Tabitha felt exposed, even though she shouldn't have. Her big secret was already out of the bag. Almost anything she said at this point would be okay, it would make sense, considering. But still. She went to the cabinet that used to be full of oils and vinegars and other sauces that were completely used up now. She pulled down the last of the olive oil, followed by the bottle of Zingerman's aged balsamic, the one she'd been saving. She moved the squat bottle this way and that and watched it swoosh around: there was about a tablespoon left. She handed both to Rachel, who poured them out, not knowing that that was the absolute last of it. Just as the last plump, syrupy drops of vinegar fell onto the tomato, the house phone rang. Tabitha thought about ignoring it, but it was so loud, louder than a usual ringing phone, at least that's how it seemed to her in the moment, that she just wanted it to stop.

"Hello?"

"Tabitha, it's Julie, from Larchwood." She sounded out of breath, and it was extremely noisy wherever she was. Tabitha couldn't believe it. Was she really calling *now* to ask for a snack tray or teacher treat?

"Julie," Tabitha started, "I'm so sorry, but we are just sitting down to—"

"I'm with Levi," Julie said, interrupting her. Did she sound upset? With Levi? "He, he's been hit by a bike. I am here with him waiting for the ambulance. It should be here soon. I—"

"What do you mean?" Tabitha said firmly into the phone. "With Levi? Where? He's at Butch's house. Are you sure?"

"I'm very sure," Julie said. She didn't sound like her usual perky, always-asking-for-something self. Tabitha wanted her to go back to that. She wanted her to be calling to ask her to bring something to the next conference day. She'd bring something really great. Anything. Donuts, with a dairy alternative.

Tabitha realized that Rachel had walked over and was standing just beside her but not touching her. She was waiting, but not mouthing, *"What is going on?"* the way people usually did when they wanted to know what was happening on the other end of the phone. Tabitha heard Julie talking soothingly to someone.

"They're on their way," she was saying. "Any second now."

Tabitha listened as hard as she could, but she didn't hear a response.

"What should I do?" she yelled into the phone. "What should I do?"

"I'll stay with him," Julie said, so kindly. "I'll go in the ambulance with him. I'll call again as soon as I know where we're going."

The sound of the siren got loud now. It was right in Tabitha's ear.

"Where are you?" she screamed, but Julie was talking to someone else, and then the call cut off. "Where are you?" she screamed, again to nobody.

Tabitha stood there dumbly with the phone to her ear, waiting for instructions. It took her a second to place herself: in her kitchen, with Rachel by her side, and Fern in the doorway looking scared.

Rachel didn't say anything, she just waited. It must have been very clear that Tabitha had no answers. Finally, Rachel said, "It's Levi?" She took the phone out of Tabitha's hand and pressed the "off" button, then handed it back.

Tabitha nodded, and miraculously, the phone rang again.

"Where are you?" she screamed into the phone.

"About to get in the ambulance," Julie said gently. "They're taking us to Hahnemann. It's the closest hospital. I asked them to take us to CHOP, but they have to go to the closest hospital. I'll stay with him. I'll be right here until you get there."

"Is he okay?" Tabitha screamed. She seemed to have only one way of communicating now. "Is he awake?"

"He just opened his eyes, but—" Julie said. Then, to someone else, "Oh, okay, sorry. I have to hang up. I'll be with him."

"But what?" Tabitha screamed. "But what?"

"Where is he?" Rachel asked gently. "Can you tell me what happened?"

"Hahnemann," Tabitha said. "He was hit by a bike."

Rachel punched something into her phone, then she helped Fern get her shoes and coat.

"Come on," she said.

They went down in the elevator, but it seemed different; it did not seem like the same elevator she was in just an hour before. An Uber was waiting for them. They got in. Rachel talked to the driver. Tabitha knew she should be helping Fern, telling her everything would be okay. But would it be okay? She needed someone to comfort her. She thought of Stuart. Then she thought of Toby. Then she tried not to think.

They were dropped off at the wrong place, the place where ambulances go in, but it was easy to find the right door. Rachel did all the work. She talked to someone, she had Fern sit in a seat in the surprisingly empty waiting room. She took Tabitha into the emergency department.

"Over there, number twenty-one. I'll stay with Fern."

Suddenly she was back to herself, and she was running. There were people all around him, mostly by his head. How many people? Six? Seven? A lot of people. She moved as close as she could. She wanted to grab him and take him back to the moment before whatever happened, happened. She was close now, close enough to see his face. His jaw looked funny, moved somehow. And there was blood, a lot of dried blood. Was it dry? Maybe some of it was still wet. Where did that come from? She thought she could see a line, a clear line up his chin and over his face. She moved back in horror. Did the bike literally run over him? Right over him? She was about to start screaming again when she felt a hand on her shoulder. She turned quickly, ready to be mad at whomever it was. It was Julie. She shooed her away and looked back at Levi. They were giving him oxygen; they seemed concerned about his breathing and she could see why. He seemed to be working hard at it, and his mouth looked so strange. Why did it look so strange? At that moment, his eyes opened and he saw her. He saw her and he reacted to her—it was a combination of relief and fear—what sort of trouble was he in? She was so relieved, so completely relieved, that when Julie nudged her again, she turned to her and obeyed her gentle suggestion that she follow her out of the small curtained room.

"What happened?" Tabitha said, no longer yelling, her voice sounding strange and raspy.

Julie shook her head like she was trying to rid it of an image. Or at least that was what Tabitha thought. She moved away from Julie, back toward Levi. What was she doing here with Julie? She wanted to be with Levi.

"Wait, just give me a quick second," Julie said, sounding like herself, like she might be talking about food trays and nondairy alternatives. And suddenly Tabitha was so grateful to her. What if she hadn't been there? Would they have figured out who Levi was by now? Did he even have any ID on him? Tabitha didn't think so.

"Thank you," Tabitha said. "Thank you for everything you did. How were you even there? How did you know it was Levi?"

"It was his jacket. His bright-red Larchwood jacket with the big lion on the back. It's so familiar, both my kids have that same jacket, so when I saw him running, Tabitha, he was literally running, into the street, I saw him. And I yelled to him to stop, to wait. But he didn't hear me. Or he didn't want to listen. He just kept running. And I could see that the light had turned green and the cars were going to move. And it was really the bus that I was worried about, but, somehow, thank God, the bus driver saw him and swerved to the left, but he must have startled the bike, because the bike came up fast on the bus's right and well, that's what caused the impact." She said the last part quietly, like it was something that shouldn't be said out loud.

Tabitha took a step back to steady herself. It was so hot in here. Why didn't they make it cooler? And did the floor have to be so swirly, and the curtains! Why did they have to have such busy designs on them? Didn't they know dizzy people came in sometimes for help?

Tabitha felt someone grabbing her arm, and then easing her down into a chair, but she took it one step further and kept going, putting her head down on the chair next to her and closing her eyes. She felt alone. Did Julie leave? But then a nurse was there, asking if she was okay, asking if she could hear her. She opened her eyes and nodded.

"Let her sit just a minute," she heard the nurse say. "It's going to be a few minutes before he's ready to be transferred."

"To where?" Tabitha asked, sitting up too fast and then leaning back over and propping her head on her hand. She did not feel well.

"To CHOP," the nurse said. "He is stable enough to be moved now, and they are so much better equipped to treat children."

Thank God, Tabitha thought she said out loud, but then she realized she just thought it. She needed to get herself up, she needed to go be with Levi. She should tell Rachel what was going on. She should see if

Fern was okay. Maybe they could look at her leg while they were here. There was so much to do. Tabitha closed her eyes.

"Hey, sorry to bother you," Julie said, gently putting her hand over Tabitha's hand. "I left my kids with a friend, I have to go get them. Will you be okay? Is there anyone here with you? It's great that he is stable enough to be moved."

Tabitha nodded, but didn't specify what she was nodding about.

"Okay then," she said kindly. "I'm glad . . . well, I'm glad . . . well, I guess I'm glad it wasn't worse."

Tabitha nodded again. It was so noisy in here, but she felt like she could just fade away. No, that was ridiculous. She opened her eyes and pushed herself up so that she occupied only one chair. She waited to see how dizzy she was going to feel, and it wasn't so bad. She stood, walked back to Levi's small curtained-off area. She felt almost afraid of him, like if she didn't get too close then maybe this wouldn't really be him. There were only two people with him now, and his eyes were closed again. He looked the same as before, like something had shifted in his facial bone structure.

His eyes opened, and he looked like he was trying not to cry, then they closed again. Tabitha was next to him in an instant, kneeling on the floor by his face, so close, she could see what she thought was the actual line of a bike tire up Levi's neck and chin, right to his forehead. Tabitha made a noise she didn't recognize, and then she cleared her throat. She wanted to touch him and smell him. She wanted to bury her nose in the top of his head, the way she used to when he was younger, the way he didn't let her anymore, hadn't let her in so long.

She cleared her throat again. "Can I touch him?" she asked the nurse, or maybe it was a doctor, she wasn't sure. A nurse, it was definitely a nurse.

"Gently, and maybe just his hand for now," she said. "Until we determine if anything is broken. The good news is his airway is clear, no damage there, so they'll do more tests and X-rays when you get to CHOP. The ambulance is almost ready to take you over."

Tabitha reached out and touched his hand, barely, but it was warm and soft. He opened his eyes and lifted his head ever so slightly. He opened his mouth, and she expected him to say something, but he didn't. There was nothing, no words, no sound. He let his head fall back onto the pillow and closed his eyes.

"Were you going to say something, Monkey?" she asked him, soothingly, and all the tears came silently to the forefront and spilled out, no fanfare, no warning. She just let them fall. "Monkey?"

"He hasn't said anything yet," the nurse said. "We think there might be a fracture in his jaw, which would make it hard to speak."

Rachel came to the curtain and leaned in like she was about to ask something, but then she saw Levi.

"Oh, Levi! Thank God, thank God, thank God," she said it like he was sitting up and playing cards. Like he was sitting there eating a cheesesteak. Not like he was lying there with a bent and possibly broken jaw and tire marks on his face. It took only a second for Tabitha to realize why—Rachel thought he was in terrible shape. Did she think he was going to die? That thought made Tabitha so mad. Levi wasn't going to die. He was never going to die, not until he was old, really old, like, a hundred years old. Did Rachel think Tabitha was such a bad mother that Levi could die on her watch? Even as she thought it, she knew one thing had nothing to do with the other. Accidents happened all the time, no matter how vigilant a person was. But it made her so mad! She wanted to scream.

"Do you need something?" Tabitha said harshly.

Rachel looked taken aback.

"Sorry, yes, they are asking for the insurance card. Do you have it?"

Yes, she had it, but it wouldn't work.

"Um, no, not with me," Tabitha lied. Now she didn't feel so angry. What would she do without Rachel? "I ran out so fast I didn't even think about it."

"That must happen all the time," Rachel said. "I'll go tell them. I can run to the apartment and get it later."

"We're moving, to CHOP," Tabitha said, like that was the answer to the problem.

"Oh, okay," Rachel said. "But you'll still have to give them your insurance information, I'm sure. I'll tell them what I can, and then if I have to bring it back, or send an image of it through email or whatever, I'll do that."

"Thanks," Tabitha said. "Where's Fern?"

"She's fine," Rachel said. "They gave her graham crackers and some juice. She's playing on my phone."

Tabitha wanted to yell that Fern should not be left alone. She felt something and looked down. Levi had grabbed her hand.

CHAPTER NINETEEN

Eight hours later, they were settled into a room at CHOP. It had been determined that Levi's jaw was not broken, and he had no catastrophic injuries, which was nothing short of a miracle. But they were worried about a concussion, and they wanted to make sure they didn't miss any internal bleeding so he was staying for at least a day or two. Rachel had taken Fern home with the promise of returning first thing in the morning with the completely defunct insurance card, which she would never actually find since it was right there with Tabitha. What in the world was she going to do then?

She glanced at Levi in his bed in this surprisingly nice private room, which she was sure would cost more than the most luxurious hotel in the world. He was asleep, finally, though the bruises were starting. She could see them on his face, but she knew they would run all the way up his body, following the path of the bike. Tabitha asked, and the biker was okay. He was thrown but landed well, they said. He had a badly scraped elbow but nothing more. Apparently he was very worried about Levi at the scene. That was about as far as Tabitha could go in her mind before she had to shut her eyes and try to imagine something else—the two kids sitting on the couch watching television was the image that kept coming back to her, the one that calmed her.

Tabitha tiptoed out of the room. Two nurses talked quietly at the dimly lit desk.

"Can we help you?" one of them asked.

"Yes, I wondered, I'm worried about my daughter at home. Levi is sleeping. Would it be crazy to run home and see her, and then come right back? We don't live far."

"You can go, of course," the nurse said. She was so pretty, with blond hair and a clear, open face. Tabitha decided there was no way that she always worked overnight. Someone who worked overnight regularly couldn't possibly look that fresh and vibrant. "I'll keep an eye out. When should I tell him you'll be back, if he wakes while you're gone?"

"I should be back in an hour, two at the most," she said.

"I bet he'll sleep through," the other nurse said now. "He's had a lot of medication."

"Thank you so much," Tabitha said. "I'll hurry. I just want to give her a hug and let her know Levi is okay."

"I completely understand," the first nurse said. "We'll see you soon."

Tabitha went back to get her purse and gave Levi one last check. He was fast asleep, breathing through his mouth, which still looked misshapen, but she had been assured it would work itself out, though it might need some help. She grabbed her bag and walked out, past the nurse's station and to the elevator. Downstairs, she walked out through the main entrance into the cool night air. It was so dark out. She got a cab right away and gave the address, Nora's address. She had no intention of going home. She never did. Fern and Rachel were fast asleep. They didn't need her right now.

The cab driver grunted an acknowledgment and pulled away from the hospital. She watched the people coming and going, so many people either just beginning to deal with their emergency or safely on the other side. She looked in her purse and pulled out a scrap of paper and a pencil. She had been formulating a new list in her head—what she owed and what she was terrified might be taken from her, what was almost taken. She set the paper on her knee and drew a line down the center making two columns. On the left she listed two things: *my mother, the allergy*. On the right she listed two things: *Fern, Levi*. At the bottom she scrawled: *a life for a life?* How much did she owe? Did it even work that way? And how much did she take? She still wasn't sure. She turned the pencil around in her hand and began to erase everything. It was messy, and the eraser kept getting stuck on the paper, ripping it. When the words had almost disappeared, though, she could still make them out if she looked very hard, she ripped the paper into tiny pieces and kept them in her clenched fist.

She had not thought about actually paying for the cab. She still had the cash from Nora, she never put it in the bank, so she pulled out a twenty and waited for the change, giving a 10 percent tip, then adding two more dollars at the last minute. She got out and walked into the quiet lobby. She thought for sure she'd be stopped now, or probably Nora's door wouldn't be open. It was practically the middle of the night, for heaven's sake. She had not thought through any of these complications. She walked by the desk where a man looked half asleep, maybe two-thirds asleep, if that was possible, definitely more than half. She leaned over to drop her paper pieces into the garbage can next to his desk. She waited as they fluttered down, pushing the last few off her sticky, sweaty palm.

The man cleared his throat.

"I'm going to care for Nora," she said, before he asked. "On the second floor."

He looked at his watch.

"That time already?" he said, then, "It's a little early."

She had no idea what he meant. Early for what?

"It is," she said. "I just got the call."

"All right then," he said. She waited a beat longer but he seemed to be done with her.

She went to the elevator and pushed "2." While she was going up, she brushed one last tiny piece of paper off her shirt, which she let fall to the floor. She got out, walked across the hall, and opened the door. She wondered if Nora was sleeping. It didn't make any sense that she would be in here, defenseless, with the door open. She would talk to someone at some point about this, maybe she'd have to make an anonymous call to Home Comforts, which was so clearly an incompetent company, and just hope someone answered the phone.

The lights were on, but she didn't want to yell out the way she had before. She tiptoed in thinking, *This is crazy!* What was she doing? But if she could just get to the bathroom and get that money . . . Maybe she could do it all without anyone knowing. As she came around the corner into the living room, there was Nora, on the floor, her knees elegantly to the side in a position Tabitha would not have thought her capable, especially with her recently injured leg. Her white hair, which was usually up in a bun, was down around her shoulders. It looked thin and slightly greasy. She had clearly been crying.

"He's gone," Nora said when she saw Tabitha. "He left me."

Oh, Tabitha thought, *this is what I read about that first day in the file.* She knew exactly what was going on here.

"Oh, Nora, I'm so sorry," Tabitha said, joining her on the floor. "Are you alone?"

"We were having a lovely picnic," Nora said. "He wasn't acting right. He wasn't as, I don't know, attentive as usual. I had a terrible feeling in my stomach. I couldn't eat the sandwiches I made."

"Oh, Nora," Tabitha said again. She reached out and patted her hand. As soon as she felt Nora's dry, cracked skin she pulled away. It felt like her mother's hand, at least how her hand had felt at the end. She had thought many times since then that she should have rubbed lotion into her mother's hands. Why didn't she do that? She knew why. She'd barely touched her—hand lotion wasn't even a consideration. The only reason she knew what her hands felt like was because they kept flopping off the bed and hanging, and the nurse asked her over and over to move them back onto the bed, so they wouldn't strain her arms. What was Tabitha going to say—*No, you do it?* But now she wondered what the big deal was. She always could have washed her hands after. She looked around for lotion, maybe she could rub some into Nora's hands.

"I'll be right back," Tabitha said, taking her bag with her. She moved toward the hall bathroom. As she got closer, she heard someone snoring. It was so quiet at first and then louder. She peeked in the bedroom next to Nora's, and there was a woman sitting in a chair, fast asleep. She was wearing scrubs, so Tabitha assumed she was the home-health aide. A lot of good she was doing. She tiptoed into Nora's room, where the bed was messed up: clearly it was slept in. Nora must have gotten herself up and dressed after the aide thought she was fast asleep. Nora could be in New Jersey by now! Tabitha went into the bathroom and closed the door quietly. The jar was still there, but, to make herself feel better, she looked for lotion first. There wasn't any, not on the counter, not in the medicine cabinet. Maybe she would have to buy some and bring it next time.

The money jar was like a magnet, she was so drawn to it. She grabbed and grabbed—taking what she hoped would end up being thousands of dollars. She had to pay for all the medical bills; she kept telling herself, she needed this. She made sure to leave enough that when she spread it out, the jar almost looked full—well, not quite, if you looked closely, but almost. She stuffed it all into her bag and went back to the living room. Nora was still on the floor. She hadn't moved an inch. No wonder she got stiff and couldn't get up after one of these episodes. Tabitha intended to just keep walking, right past Nora and out of the apartment, but Nora was weeping now.

"Miss," she called to Tabitha. "Miss, have you seen a very handsome boy? Tall? He was just here. Oh, I hope he's coming back."

"I'm sure he'll be back, Nora," Tabitha said, still on her feet.

"Miss," Nora said again. "Have you ever been in love?"

Tabitha didn't know the answer to that, so she didn't say anything.

"Miss," Nora said. "Have you ever done anything bad?"

Now she wondered if Nora was playing with her. Could that possibly be the case?

"Because I did something bad," Nora continued, and Tabitha relaxed a little. "I did something very bad."

"Nora," Tabitha said, coming closer, sitting on the floor and putting her now stuffed bag behind her. "You didn't do anything bad. You're good. You're just confused. I did so many bad things. Do you want to hear them?"

"Sure," Nora said, and she sounded like a teenager who was ready for some good gossip.

"Well, I wasn't very nice to my mother when she was dying. She had been sick, and I got used to not touching her, and I never really got back into the habit. But the worst thing is, I think I killed her. I think I gave her too much morphine and cut her life short, not by much, maybe a few days, a week, unless of course she was going to rally and get better, which she had done before. Maybe I cost her months, who knows? I will never know."

Nora nodded but didn't seem to comprehend what Tabitha was saying, which only served to fuel her confession.

"Also, I worry I killed a man. I didn't mean to, but I didn't properly follow my food-allergy protocol one night when I was cooking—I used to have my own business—and his girlfriend called after the meal. She said he couldn't breathe, were there peanuts in the dish? I said no, because I truly believed there weren't. As soon as I hung up, I realized there had been, I had sautéed the beef in peanut oil, and I had fried the spring rolls in it. Some peanut oil can be okay and not cause a reaction, even in very allergic people, but some can, and I would never normally take that chance. I wasn't sure what kind of oil I had used, I think possibly the bad kind. I . . . I could have done more research about that, but I threw it out—*we* threw it out, my husband and I. I tried to call back, I tried to tell them. But I couldn't reach them, and then my husband discouraged me from it, and eventually I stopped trying."

Nora nodded again.

"And I've been stealing," Tabitha said. Now she was crying, and she was too loud; she could wake the aide in the other room. She lowered her voice a little. "I've been stealing from people all over the city, and I've been stealing your money. You make it so easy. Why do you have so much money here? In the Monopoly game and in that jar in the bathroom?"

Nora nodded again. Tabitha was ready to go, she'd told all her secrets, and hopefully nobody was the wiser, since Nora thought that it was over sixty years ago and she was in the park on a picnic. As Tabitha moved to get up, Nora reached out her dry hand. Tabitha stopped and looked at her. Something changed on Nora's face. She looked around, startled. She moved her legs, slowly, and twirled her hair back into a bun, securing it with a rubber band from her wrist.

"Oh, it happened again," Nora said sadly.

"You're okay now," Tabitha said. "Let me help you get to the chair, and then I have to go."

Nora let her grab her under the shoulders, gently—she was so light—and helped to push herself up. Tabitha got her sitting in her chair with her leg up on the ottoman.

"Good night, Nora," Tabitha said, turning to leave, pushing the bag to her other side so Nora wouldn't see it.

"I heard you," Nora said. "I heard what you said about the stealing."

Tabitha stopped but did not turn around.

"Bring me the phone, dear," Nora said. "So I can call the police."

Now Tabitha turned back slowly. She imagined the police storming the apartment, the man at the desk saying, *"Yeah, it seemed too early. I knew something was up."* Tabitha being carted away, so she couldn't get back to Levi in the hospital. She looked up at Nora, thinking she was just going to run. Nora would never be able to find her. And she saw Nora smiling.

"I got you!" Nora said. "It was too easy!"

"Got me?" Tabitha asked, slowly, still ready to run.

"I know about the stealing, dear," Nora said, sounding like her old self. "I put the money there for people to take. I have so much, and so many people need it. I have one aide who can't afford to buy her son a birthday present. He's turning ten. Ten years old! Well, I hope she took some money. I have another who doesn't eat much—she gives all her food to her kids and eats only what's left over. Boy I hope she took some money. And you, well, you looked funny to me. I wasn't sure but, I've been meaning to ask, are you a registered aide? You don't dress like everyone else, and you don't act like them either."

At this, Tabitha relaxed a little. She had the urge to laugh, but she didn't dare.

"There are no banks in heaven dear, or stores for that matter," Nora said. "What am I going to do with it all?"

"Well, I plan to pay you back," Tabitha said. "One day I will, I promise."

"No need," Nora said with a wave. "Take more. Just leave a little for the others. I'll have my son go to the bank and get more cash out this week."

"Does your son know you do this?" Tabitha asked.

"Oh yes," Nora said. "The thing is, people don't want to take money that is handed to them, but some don't want to steal either. That's why I put all the signs on the door. I should add some to the Monopoly board. But I still suspect some of the ones who need it have never taken a dollar. I worry about them. The best I can do is leave it and hope they find it. I'm going to have to come up with a new system."

"I wouldn't normally steal," Tabitha said, because she felt she had to. "I've been . . . I guess the word would be *desperate*, lately."

"We all are sometimes," Nora said.

Tabitha felt she had to get back to Levi. She felt a physical pull.

"And dear?" Nora said.

"Yes?"

"Don't feel guilty. Did you have a good relationship with your mother most of your life?"

"Yes, very good," Tabitha said, surprised that Nora actually heard what she said about her mother.

"That's what's important. Let the rest go. That's what she would want, I'm fairly sure of that."

Tabitha was crying now, with inappropriate spurts of laughter escaping every few seconds.

"And that man, the one with the peanut allergy? Are you sure he died?"

"Oh, no," Tabitha said quickly through her tears. "I'm not. I have no idea actually."

"Well, find out," Nora said. "You might be worrying about something that never happened."

Tabitha nodded. She considered telling her about Levi, but she couldn't confess any more. Plus Nora hadn't even asked her for an excuse about why she took the money.

"I'm going to go now," Tabitha said. "And I have money in my bag, from the jar in the bathroom, lots of it, do you want me to give it back?"

"No, dear," Nora said.

"I'm keeping a record of it," Tabitha said. "I'll pay you back."

Nora waved her off as she moved around to try to get comfortable in the chair. She reached behind her back and pulled out what looked like a bent photo that she had been sitting on, one of those old Polaroid pictures, the kind that come out the bottom of the camera. Tabitha hadn't seen one of those in a long time. Nora worked to unbend it.

"My son threw me a birthday party," Nora said, holding out the photo. "I have one clever son."

Tabitha reached in to take it.

"I should explain," Nora said, but Tabitha was barely listening, something in the picture had caught her eye. "It might seem uncouth to you if I don't. You might be aware that it takes the planet Uranus eighty years to orbit the Sun, or is it the Earth? Well, it takes Uranus eighty years to do something important. And I just turned eighty, so my son thought, well, he thought it would be funny."

Tabitha held the photo close to her face, it was slightly out of focus. There was Nora, all dressed up. She must have had her hair done, it looked elegant and flawless. Behind her was a big sign that said **HAPPY URANUS BIRTHDAY NORA!** She looked even closer, so that the picture was practically touching her face. To Nora's right, a man stood just off to the side. He was wearing a navy sweater with a maize block *M* on the front. It was Toby.

CHAPTER TWENTY

On the way out, Tabitha called the nurse's station.

"Fifth floor, can I help you?" Tabitha thought she recognized the pretty nurse's voice.

"Hi! This is Tabitha Brewer, Levi Brewer's mom." She loved saying that. "I'm on my way back, and I wanted to ask if he's woken up at all?"

"I was just in there, and he is still out," the nurse said. "I have a feeling he's going to sleep for a while."

"Okay," Tabitha said. "I might walk back then, since I probably won't be outside much today."

"Take your time," the nurse said reassuringly. "But be careful. It's still dark out there."

Tabitha had decided to walk home to drop off the money. She couldn't very well take it to the hospital with her and hand it over. She smiled at the doorman, wondering if there had been any talk about what happened to Levi. She didn't want to answer questions now and was relieved when he didn't say anything beyond the usual "morning."

Upstairs, she found Rachel sleeping in Fern's bed with her. She went over and nudged her gently. Rachel jumped, and Tabitha immediately felt bad. She put her finger to her mouth and motioned for Rachel to follow her. Once they were outside in the hall, it took a few seconds for Rachel to gain her balance. Tabitha put her hand out to steady her.

"Is it Levi?" Rachel asked.

"He's okay, the same as when you left him," she said. "I had to do a few things, but I'm going back now."

"You had to do a few things? It's six in the morning. What did you have to do?"

Tabitha reached into her purse and brought out the first pile of money she could grab. She held it up.

"What the hell is that?" Rachel said, too loudly. "Did you rob a bank?"

"Look, I have no money," Tabitha admitted, and it felt surprisingly good. "None. I know you had some hints of that, but it's even worse than you may have thought. You know that insurance card you're supposed to bring over to the hospital today? I've had it the whole time. It doesn't work."

"I have money," Rachel said.

Tabitha sighed. She knew she could have asked Rachel all along. But she also knew she had paid for the sperm donation herself and that she was usually careful with her money, leading Tabitha to believe she didn't have *that* much, at least not an unlimited supply, which is what this would take.

"I'm going to put it in the bank tomorrow," Tabitha said.

"I think you might be in jail tomorrow," Rachel shot back.

"No, no, it isn't like that," Tabitha said. "I got it from a friend. I'll tell you all about it later. For now, I'm going to put it in my closet, in the top drawer. I have to go. I have to be with Levi."

"That must be some friend," Rachel said. "Okay, okay. I'll stay here with Fern. I'll make her pancakes. Should I bring her over?"

"I think so," Tabitha said. "Let's talk in a few hours. Oh, and when you do come, make a big show in front of the nurse about not being able to find the insurance card. Hopefully that will buy me another day at least. I'm going to have to set up some sort of payment plan. And we don't have any pancake mix." She pulled forty dollars out of the pile. "Take her out for pancakes on your way over."

"Thanks," Rachel said, taking the money but giving it a strange look when she took possession of it. "Hey, now might not be the best time to talk about it, but I've made a decision. A real, final decision."

"About what?" Tabitha asked, but she immediately regretted it. "Oh, you did? A final decision? What is it?"

"I'm going to do it," Rachel said. "I'm going to try to get pregnant. Being with your kids, seeing you handle everything yesterday without Stuart here, it made me think I can do it, too. I want to do it."

Tabitha wanted to say all sorts of things, the first being: *Are you crazy?* But then they both turned to look at Fern, who was curled on her side, looking in that moment much younger than she was, and Tabitha understood.

"I'll help you in any way I can," she said.

~

After Tabitha stashed the money and was in a cab heading back to CHOP, she had a thought: Stuart. He didn't know about Levi. If anything would bring him back to Philadelphia and to them, this would be it, right? She decided she'd ask Fern about that call, see if she really spoke to him and had any ideas about how to reach him. She'd say Levi needed him. Fern would do anything for Levi at this point. But as they neared the hospital, another thought crept in. She didn't really want him to come back. She wanted the stability she used to have, sure, and the security of a working insurance card, but she didn't want *him*. She made her own final decision in the back of that cab as they drove over the South Street Bridge. She was going to file for divorce. And with that, a third thought crept in . . . Toby. Sweet Toby. She thought she would never be able to speak to him again, not after what she'd done. Not now that she knew Nora was his mother. And somehow, at that moment, that seemed like the greatest loss of all.

~

Levi ended up spending four days in the hospital. They were strangely peaceful days. Levi didn't talk at all until the third day. The first thing he said was, "I thought I saw Dad." Tabitha was deep into research about her rights and how and when she could officially file for a legal separation and divorce. It was going to be harder than she had thought. Stuart had to be gone for a year before she could claim abandonment, which is what she wanted to do. She was trying to figure out how to start the process without the actual charge of abandonment. It seemed the only other way to do it was to file a complaint for divorce, in which case Stuart would be named as the defendant. It all seemed so complicated and upside down to her. She eased her laptop closed and looked up at Levi.

"What?"

He cleared his throat. His voice was raspy. "When you dropped me at Butch's, I never went. I walked around. I thought I saw Dad ahead of me. I was running toward him, and when I realized it wasn't him, I guess I just kept running."

Tabitha got up and sat on the edge of the bed. He was so bruised now, but he looked so good. He was going to be fine.

"Why did you think it was Dad?"

"It looked like him, from the back," Levi said, clearing his throat again. Tabitha should probably have told him to stop talking. He couldn't not talk for days and then talk so much, but she wanted to hear what he had to say. "And he was wearing his clothes, or at least a shirt that Dad has, and I think his pants."

"Oh my god," Tabitha said, remembering when she thought she had seen Stuart on the street. "I gave some of Dad's clothes to a homeless man. You must have seen him wearing them. I saw him once and thought for a minute it was Dad."

"Why would you do that?" Levi asked, and she could sense he was getting angry. She knew this tone, and she guessed he was about to shut down, which would probably be good for his voice but not for her.

"I don't know," she said. She wanted to take his hand, but that would be a sure way to get him to turn away, so she didn't. "You know, it's been a hard few months. I didn't want to burden you guys with it, but in the end, I probably should have been more open about what was going on. This was not the way to do it. The bottom line is that I was trying to make ends meet, and I ended up taking stuff from people that we needed, so I wanted to give something back. That's why I gave some clothes to the homeless man."

"But where's Dad?" Levi asked in a harsh whisper.

"Shhh," Tabitha said. "You should rest your voice."

Levi narrowed his eyes and raised his eyebrows. Tabitha could hear him saying, *"Fine, but where is he?"* without his actually saying it.

"I don't know where your dad is," Tabitha said. "I haven't known this whole time. I had one idea, but then, well, I found out that that isn't where he is, at least not anymore."

Levi closed his eyes and turned slightly toward the window. *Please don't let him cry, please don't let him cry,* Tabitha chanted to herself. Her phone rang, but she didn't move toward it. It rang three times, harshly, and then it was quiet. A few seconds later, she heard the beep that a voicemail message had been left. Levi opened his eyes and turned to her. He wasn't crying. His eyes were clear.

"I thought so," he said quietly. "I thought that all along."

Tabitha's phone rang again, and again she didn't get it. Fern was in school, hopefully fine. She would deal with her phone in a little while. It was probably Rachel checking in with them.

"Well, I should have told you," Tabitha said.

"Is he coming back?"

"I don't know," Tabitha said. "I just don't know."

"Can I be alone for a little while?" Levi asked.

"Sure," Tabitha said, gathering her purse and phone. "I'll just get some coffee."

She wanted to wait to see if he was sad, or what his reaction would be, but she didn't. She wasn't at all sure she handled that well. She wished she'd taken more time to think it through.

As soon as she got down to the lobby she checked her phone. There were actually five voicemail messages. She panicked as she went to the screen to listen, and realized they were mostly from different people, which was good, at least they weren't all calling about Fern.

Two were from Toby. He kept calling, but she had not called back. She pressed "play" on the message.

"Hey, it's Toby again," the first message said. "Not sure what's going on with you. Did our time at the hotel scare you away? I'm beginning to think you can't take an hour or two out of the real world without it somehow seeping back in. Okay, well, please call me." Hearing his voice made her whole body hurt. If she never spoke to him again, maybe he would never have to know that she stole the money from Nora. Also, he would never have to know she might have killed two people, or that, in the end, she was not a good wife, not that she ever really had the chance to be, but still.

The next message was from a number she didn't recognize.

"What's the scariest thing you've ever seen?" the voice asked, and the first thing she thought was, *My son on a gurney in the emergency room after being hit by a bike.* But she knew the answer this guy was after. It was Mr. Hiffen, from the pest control company. She missed the rest of what he'd said, so she went back to hear it again. "What's the scariest thing you've ever seen? That's right! A rat! And you are going to help us stop people from seeing those. You got the job! The office opens next month. Call me back."

Huh. Her first thought was that she didn't want it; she had to put all her energy into the kids. Her second thought was that she wanted it! It would give her money and more freedom. She'd call him back later to accept the job.

The next call was from Rabbi Rosen saying he heard about Levi and would stop by later that day. Tabitha wondered how he heard. Maybe Rachel called him. The fourth was from the kids' pediatrician.

"Hello, it's Dr. Randall. Please call me back."

And finally, it was Toby again.

"So, I'm thinking it was nice while it lasted, right? It was like a fantasy. But now it's probably over. I am releasing you. Go forth and be happy. Sorry again about the hotel. Not about our time there, that was spectacular, but I'm sorry if that was too much, if that made you not want to do this. Bye."

She looked around for a place to sit. She felt so sad suddenly, that it was almost hard to stand up. She wanted to tell him he was wrong, the hotel was great. Those two hours were the best hours she'd had in so long. She couldn't call him back because she had been stealing from—she could barely bring herself to even think the words, there was no way she could ever speak them out loud—but she forced herself to say the whole sentence in her mind: she had been stealing from his mother! And sneaking in and trespassing when she had no business there. She was a bad person. He was better off without her. She stood again and dialed Dr. Randall. She waited to be put through, she assumed he was calling about Levi.

"Tabitha," he said. "I'm glad to connect with you."

"We're at the hospital," she said. "Levi is doing a little better."

"Levi?"

"Isn't that who you are calling about?"

"No, I'm calling about Fern. All her tests are back. Listen, this is really a diagnosis of exclusion, but I feel comfortable at this point to say she has conversion disorder. It should go away on its own, and I think it was brought on by stress. This can happen when people are under intense amounts of distress. Has that been the case for Fern at all lately? Is there any reason she has been anxious lately?"

"You could say that," Tabitha said, as the relief spread through her body. She was surprised at her relief, because Fern's distress was exactly what she was so afraid of. Clearly, Tabitha couldn't shield her, and Fern had been upset all along. But it wasn't a tumor, and it wasn't some awful disease. It should go away on its own! She wanted to jump up and down. She wanted to hug the doctor walking by. She wanted to celebrate with Fern.

"Thank you so much doctor," she said.

"I'm sorry we don't have a more definitive answer," he said. "But I am sure I'm right about this. I've seen it before."

"I'm so glad you don't have a more definitive answer," Tabitha said. "This is the best thing I could have hoped for."

"I think some therapy might be in order; maybe getting to the root of her stress and giving her some tools to help her deal with it better is the best place to start. And if the pain doesn't resolve itself soon, let's talk about setting up a little physical therapy for her, too. In the meantime, let me know if there's anything more you need," he said, and Tabitha sighed and told him about Levi.

~

Rabbi Rosen came around three, and, as usual, his presence was calming.

"Well, Levi my boy, I am certainly glad to see you," he said, pulling the chair close to his bed. "You don't look nearly as bad as I thought you might. Thank you for calling me."

That explained how he found out, it wasn't Rachel after all. In the farthest reaches of things Tabitha would expect to happen in the world, having Levi call the rabbi would not appear anywhere. She was dumbfounded. She watched as Levi tried to smile, but Tabitha could tell it hurt.

"So, I'm not going to stay long. I just wanted to say hello and see for myself how you're doing," he said. "And to ask you to think about our plan for the bar mitzvah. You can take a little time to decide, but it is less than a month away. I think, given the circumstances, we should keep it as simple as possible. Just what we talked about, maybe on an even smaller scale."

He looked at Tabitha. "Does that sound good?"

She nodded. "Yes," she said. "I think if we do it, we'll just have a small lunch after. I don't think I'm going to invite anyone beyond a few friends."

"Whatever you decide, I fully support you," the rabbi said.

Tabitha listened while they talked about television shows and what Levi would eat when he could eat everything again, and then the rabbi patted Levi gently on the arm and stood up.

"Is there anything I can do for you before I go, Levi?" he asked.

"Not that I can think of," Levi croaked out.

"Take care, both of you," he said, turning to leave.

"Thanks for coming," Levi said. "And I do want to. Have my scaled down bar mitzvah, I mean. I really want to."

Rabbi Rosen turned back toward him.

"Great!" he said. "That's great news. It will be a memorable day. I'm honored to be a part of it."

Tabitha walked Rabbi Rosen to the elevators.

"How are you holding up?" he asked. "Things were rough enough and now this. I am just so glad he is on the mend."

"He'll go home tomorrow, I think," Tabitha said. "Thank you so much for coming."

"Listen," the rabbi said. "I've put some calls out to try to reach Stuart. It might be a futile effort, but I feel it's my duty to see if he needs any guidance, and to touch base about the bar mitzvah. Have you been able to reach him?"

"No," Tabitha said. "I thought for some time he might be with, well, with someone he was going to marry long before he married me. She called it off right before the wedding. We had had some, well, I guess the only way to describe it would be harsh words about that right before he left. But when I finally reached someone about that, the hospital in Northern Michigan actually, that woman had died—in September. So I really have no idea where he could be."

"Wow," Rabbi Rosen said. "That is some heavy stuff. Well, I'll let you know if I have any luck. Is there anything you would like me to not tell him?"

Tabitha was taken aback. She thought of the rabbi more as Stuart's than as hers, so this gesture touched her in a way she didn't expect. She considered his question. Would she not want him to know about Levi's accident? No, he could know. She was so tired of keeping secrets.

"Nothing that I can think of," she said. "But thank you for asking."

~

The following Saturday was the Michigan–Ohio State game, and Tabitha couldn't get it out of her head. Levi had been home for over a week and might even go back to school part time the next week. Fern had been so quiet and understandably clingy. Rachel, who was now waiting to see if she was pregnant, had just left after spending most of the week with them, bringing in their Thanksgiving dinner from Di Bruno's and eating with them. The whole time Tabitha kept thinking *I am so thankful, I am so thankful.* She thought the holiday had more meaning this year than it ever had.

"Hey guys," she said to them now. They were on the couch next to each other, watching a movie that Fern had bought for Levi with some of her money. This was the image of calm that Tabitha had thought of during that awful first night in the hospital. "Do you mind if I run out?"

"No," they said at the same time. Rachel had given everyone lunch before she left, so they weren't hungry. She'd just take a walk and peek in the window. She might not even go inside.

~

Fern wasn't sure if she wanted to do this. She had been thinking about it for so long now. She even tried to come up with a way to do it for Levi in the hospital, but it just wouldn't work without the home phone. She turned to Levi, now that they were finally alone.

"I know a secret way to call Dad," she said.

At first he didn't move. It was like he didn't hear her or something. But then he turned to her slowly, scowling.

"What do you mean?"

"Well," she said, now worried that she shouldn't have mentioned it. Her dad said not to tell anyone, and Levi seemed mad. "When Dad left he wrote me a note. He told me how to call him. I did it once."

"You've known how to reach Dad all this time?" Levi said. "And you didn't tell Mom?"

"Well," Fern said, now even more unsure. "No, I, well, I was afraid to. Dad told me not to—in his note."

"Okay," Levi said, challenging her. "Call him then."

Fern went to get the house phone but then couldn't remember how to unblock the number, or was it not blocked in the first place? She wasn't sure. She put it down on the couch and ran to her room. She came back with a folded piece of paper which she unfolded carefully. She read it, and then lifted the phone, unblocked their number, and dialed. She waited a few seconds then hung up. She did it again and hung up again. Finally, she didn't hang up, she held on and waited.

"Hello darling."

"Daddy?"

"Is that really Dad?" Levi asked, grabbing the phone away from her. Or at least trying to. She held on tight.

"Is that Levi?" Stuart asked. "Fernie, I asked you not to tell anyone about . . ."

"Levi got run over by a bike. He was in the hospital for days, but now he's home," Fern spurted. "And I don't know if you know that his bar mitzvah is coming up. It's soon. I wondered if you plan to miss it."

"Back up a minute, Fern," Stuart said. "Levi got run over by a bike? Is he okay?"

"Yes, I told you he's home," Fern said impatiently. "What I need to know is if you are coming for his bar mitzvah."

"Does your mother know you're calling me?"

"No," Fern said. "She went out. Do you want to speak to Levi?"

Levi reached again for the phone, but Fern held on. There was a long silence.

"Yes," he finally said.

"Dad?" Levi called into the phone. He was crying, which for some reason surprised Fern. She didn't feel like crying. She didn't feel much like anything. She waited. She couldn't hear what her dad was saying now, and she was sorry she had given up the phone and her power. Also, this was ruining the movie that she had bought to cheer up Levi. Maybe she should have waited until it was over. She lifted the remote and pressed the "pause" button.

"Okay," Levi said into the phone, sniffling. "Okay."

He hung up. Fern was so mad—she had wanted to talk again. Now she had lost her chance. There was so much she needed to tell him.

"Well?" Fern asked, pouty and annoyed.

"He's coming for the bar mitzvah," Levi said. "He said he'll be there."

~

Tabitha arrived at the Fox & Hound much too quickly. She wasn't ready, and she didn't have a plan. Before she left she had put on Stuart's Michigan T-shirt, and now she wished she hadn't. With it on, she was clearly coming here, to watch the game. If she didn't have it on, she could say she was walking by and happened to see him through the window, or maybe she could have just stood out there and hoped to run into him. *No,* she told herself, *No more lies.* She couldn't stand all the lies.

She went to the big window facing Spruce Street and tried to appear casual as she looked inside to see who was there. The window was smudged, and it was pretty crowded, so after a few minutes of pretending she wasn't really looking, she stepped closer and put her hand around her face to keep out the glare. She saw the head of the alumni association chapter standing on a chair, talking to everyone. As usual, he was completely covered with Michigan gear and body paint. She wondered if the walls of his home were painted maize and blue. She looked to his left and to his right. She recognized a few people she'd seen there before, including Stuart's friend Henry, the slow talker, but no one else.

"Are you looking for me?"

Tabitha jumped and turned. Toby was standing in front of her.

"I, um, was deciding if I wanted to go in or not," she said. "Did you just walk by and see me here?"

"No, I was inside," he said. "I saw you doing your Peeping Tom impression. I thought I would save you the trouble."

She wanted to say something like what made him think she was there for him? But it just seemed so tiring.

"Thanks," she said.

"Do you want to go inside?"

Now that she was here with him, she didn't know what she wanted. Well, she wanted to reach out and touch his hand, and she wanted to lean in for a kiss, one like the many they had shared at the hotel, but she couldn't do any of those things.

"I don't know," she said. "I'm not sure why I came here."

"Well, are you sure about why you haven't answered or returned any of my calls?" Toby asked, and even with his accusing words, he still sounded kind and gentle. "Because I would love to know."

Tabitha looked around. It seemed it would be hard to talk here, but she wanted to be with him so much that it also seemed worth it. She nodded toward the wall, just below the windows, and she sat down. He followed her. They heard cheering come from inside the bar, so presumably Michigan had scored or done something good, but neither turned to see what had happened.

"There are so many reasons I didn't answer your calls or return them," she said. "First of all, Levi was in the hospital last week, and then he's been home this week. He was hit by a bike. It was the scariest thing in the world. He's much better now." She stopped. Just saying it was hard. While she talked, he reached out and grabbed her knee. Now his hand rested there and he waited.

"Here is the hard part, the part that is going to make you never want to call me again," she said. "I know your mother. This is one of the craziest things I have ever done, I mean that, though I realize you don't know me very well, so you really just have to believe me on that. I went for a job at Home Comforts. It was chaos there, they thought I was an aide and sent me out to your mother's apartment. I wasn't going to go, of course, but the file they gave me said she had problems and couldn't be alone and, this is really why I went, she has the same name as my mother. I mean, what are the chances of that? So, first we just hung out; she made me muffins. But I could see she had a lot of cash. When Fern's knee started acting up, I never even told you about that, but Fern has had knee pain for months now, and we had to see doctor after doctor. I went back and took a little cash—she literally has cash lying around everywhere, I'm not sure if you realize that. But that doesn't make it okay; that isn't what I'm saying. Then the other night, after Levi's accident, I went back again and took a lot. I told her, and she said she didn't mind, that's what it's there for, but I know it isn't right. Who steals from an old lady?"

Tabitha stopped talking. She hadn't meant to say that much, but once she got started she couldn't stop. Now, though, now she readied herself to say good-bye to Toby. She expected he would get up and walk away.

"You're the lady?" Toby asked. "Oh my god, that is truly the craziest thing I have ever heard. I mean, what are the chances? My mother told me about you, but she didn't know your name. I thought she must know it but couldn't remember it. Did you ever tell her?"

"No," Tabitha said. "I mean, I think I said my first name when I went there the first time, but she didn't even seem to acknowledge it. After that, my name never came up."

They sat in silence for a little while. Toby had removed his hand from her knee. People walked by. The crowd inside roared again. Tabitha moved to stand. Toby just watched her but didn't move. He stayed sitting on the dirty sidewalk.

"So, Levi is okay?" Toby asked.

Tabitha nodded. "Yes," she said firmly, deciding a nod wasn't enough to express how important that was.

"And Fern's leg?"

"Also okay," Tabitha said. "Thankfully."

"I'm glad," Toby said.

"Well, now you know," she said. "I'm sorry it didn't work out better—between us, I mean."

"That's it? That's all you have to say? There must be more," Toby said gently.

"There is, so much more," Tabitha said. "I hesitate to tell you this because you are going to think I'm making an excuse, but you know my husband took off, right? Well, some things were paid for—school, the apartment—but so much wasn't. His checks stopped being deposited, the insurance was cut off—I was desperate."

"Yikes," Toby said in such a way that Tabitha thought she really had to get out of there. All this was doing was making her like him more, and there was no scenario in which she could imagine this working out.

"There's even more," Tabitha said solemnly. "But I think I'll leave it at that. At least this way you can remember me with a little fondness. Though probably not."

"What?" he said. "Where are you going?"

"Home, to my kids," she said. "And by the way, our time at the hotel did not push me away. Not one bit. If anything, it is just making all of this so much harder."

"How did you figure it out?" Toby asked. She could tell he was stalling, trying to keep her there.

"What?"

"That Nora is my mother."

"The picture," Tabitha said. "Of the Uranus birthday."

Toby nodded.

"I just want you to know that I'll never do it again," Tabitha said as she backed away. "And one day I will pay it all back—all of it."

"I'm not worried about that now," he said, and she thought he must be as crazy as the rest of them. How could he not be worried about it? "Please, come inside."

She shook her head. At this rate, she was going to end up confessing everything, and then not only would he spend the rest of time thinking she was a thief but also a murderer.

"I can't," she said. "And this really has nothing to do with you. Please know that." She turned and walked quickly away from him, leaving him sitting on the sidewalk.

CHAPTER TWENTY-ONE

Stuart Brewer looked out the window of his Hampton Inn hotel room and wondered what it would be like to start swimming across Lake Superior and never look back. How long would it take him to panic? Would that time ever come, or could he just keep going, to the deepest part of the deepest lake, and fade away?

He knew now that he had been going through the motions, not feeling anything, for years. He was barely present. He worked, had dinner, came home. He did that over and over again for so long. And then a few years ago, he couldn't stand it anymore, and he went searching for Abigail. How was it that he could be two completely different people, one warm and fun loving with Abigail, at least that's what he remembered, and another cold and impersonal with Tabitha? He didn't want to do it anymore.

He thought Tabitha would have called him on it so long before—really, she never truly pushed him on why he chose to start his own firm to work specifically with the miners, or why he had to go to the Upper Peninsula so often. It took a long time, but he finally found her. It was the lucky shirt, he was sure of it. The old Michigan T-shirt she had given him so long ago that he always kept. He started packing it for all his trips, but that day he decided to actually wear it. That was the day he ran into her in Marquette. It was a crazy, crazy moment, when years and years of feeling came to the surface, and he burst. That's what it felt like. He was walking into a coffee shop and she was walking out. It almost seemed like she was going to walk by, away from him, and he gently grabbed her wrist, feeling a jolt the likes of which he hadn't known in years. She had stopped then and smiled at him. He convinced her to go to a park nearby, and that's where she finally told him everything. Suddenly the big mystery of his life was solved. He learned about her cancer, and that the reason she had called off the wedding was because she had been diagnosed just days before with a bad prognosis. She had not wanted that to be their new married life. She didn't want to drag him down into a sick life with a sick house and a sick bed. Those were her words, exactly. Instead, she had decided to set him free. How could she not have known that setting him free, as she called it, was forcing him into a life of unhappiness? How could she not have known that? Eventually she had beaten it, she told him, and she had been in remission for years, but it had come back, and she was in and out of the hospital again. Yes, she told him without his having to ask, she had thought about calling him so many times, but by then he was married with a baby on the way. How many times could she rearrange his life, stop it midstream? She knew that she had made a terrible mistake letting him go; that the years they could have had together would have been worth anything. If she could go back in time, she would make a different choice, but there was no going back.

Even then, even after not talking for years and years, even after marrying another woman and having two children with her, being in Abigail's presence and hearing her voice was the best, most comforting thing he could ever imagine. And the saddest. It made him feel full and empty at the same time. It made him feel like he had everything and nothing in those few minutes they were together. She begged him to forgive her for what she had done, for what she had kept from him, for what she had taken from him, from them. But she had to go to an appointment. He wanted to go with her. *"No,"* she had said, but she was glad to have that all out in the open. She thought that would help somehow.

He created more excuses to go to Michigan, and he always tried to see her. He went to the hospital, where she was on occasion, the only place he knew to find her since she would not give him any more information, and when she was there, she would let him come visit, sit with her, hold her hand. Other times he would go looking, and she wouldn't be there, and he would spend those days hoping to run into her but he never did. There were six months in there when she was not in the hospital at all, which under normal circumstances would be a good thing, but for Stuart it was awful. He hired a private investigator— he was desperate and felt there was only so much time left. That was the beginning of the end of the money, and with the spending and the working less and less, it just drained away.

Abigail was finally found. She was living in a tiny cabin, just miles from the spot they had once called their home, on the shore of Lake Superior. A cabin that didn't have a landline or a proper address. Stuart never would have found her on his own. That was the week before he told Tabitha. He had completely given up on work by then, and once he found Abigail, he had nothing to do except figure out his plan. So he went home early that week, night after night. He knew he had been a disappointing husband, that he had basically allowed Tabitha to buy into something that didn't exist. He had never loved her in that way. But he loved the kids—so much. On that last night, he came home to the most familiar smell. Tabitha had made his mother's cherry chicken. It tasted exactly how he remembered it, the oniony combination of salty and sweet. He realized in that moment, he just couldn't do it anymore.

This was not his home. Abigail had always been his home, and he had spent most of his adult life being homesick.

He wanted to say he was sorry. Tabitha hadn't done anything wrong. But now, at least for the near future, he had to be with Abigail. That night he went to Tabitha to say good-bye. She mistook his kindness and pushed to have sex, which he let happen—he still wasn't sure why—and after, he went to the bathroom. She found him there, crying. She was so confused. What was wrong? She wanted to know. And he told her, he uttered the word that had been rolling around in his mouth for so long by that point—*pretend.* It all felt like pretend. That's when the first hinge snapped in her. He kept going, he told her about Abigail, about how he had always loved her. And Tabitha got the most awful look in her eyes. She knew then that he had never loved her the way she had hoped, the way she thought he might one day, the way she deserved to be loved. What he had wanted to say was, *Is this really a surprise?*

"How could you take so much from me?" she had said to him, or some version of that.

He had been surprised; somehow he had expected her to be more sympathetic. They had fought, and then Levi had come in. Levi needed him. When he got back, she was asleep, and he had time to book a flight, check in on the kids, and write notes to each of them. He wasn't sure what he would find in Michigan—he was so scared. It felt like such an unraveling of everything—of his lifelong love with Abigail, of his home, however much he didn't feel like he belonged there. And he was so mad! How could Tabitha be so harsh? Say the things she had said? So as he finished her note, he scribbled the words that would come to haunt him at the bottom of the page—*"I'll tell them what you did."* He knew Tabitha well enough to know that a small threat would keep her wondering and probably prevent her from telling anyone he was gone. She was always so ready to blame herself for things, it was almost too easy. He knew he was doing something bad, he knew ultimately he was to blame for beginning the possible dismantling of his family, but

Tabitha was far from perfect; she had done some very bad things, too. He wanted to keep things on a somewhat even playing field, until he figured out where he stood, and that seemed like one way to do it.

He had intended to keep paying for everything, to get back to work and let the direct deposit checks be available to Tabitha. When he got to Michigan, however, Abigail seemed fine. He was so surprised. But he was so happy to see her that he didn't question it, and she welcomed him. He settled into her lakeside cabin, each day thinking, *Tomorrow I'll go back.* Or, at the very least, *Tomorrow I'll call the kids.* Or, *Tomorrow I'll call a client.* But he never did any of those things. And he completely stopped working, stopped making money. Two weeks later, she was back in the hospital. She declined rapidly. She died a week later, on the twenty-first of September.

That was when he totally dropped out. He went back to her cabin. He simply existed there, taking walks on occasion, barely showering, fishing every other day. He was just going to let himself go—slowly starve or walk himself into the ground. None of it mattered anymore. He took his cell phone and shoved it under the couch, let it drain completely and didn't give it another thought. He didn't even know where his computer was. It was like he had truly disappeared.

One night, over a month later, he had a dream about Fern. She was walking through a tunnel, calling for him, screaming, and he couldn't get to her. He couldn't answer. That was when he finally realized the magnitude of what he had done to his family, not just these last few months, but always, the whole thing had been built on nothing. But Fern, sweet Fern, he knew from the beginning he had to have her be able to reach him if she needed to. He had given her a way. He had considered giving the same option to Levi, but he knew he would be okay. He was a big boy now. And besides, Levi wouldn't have been able to keep it from Tabitha. Not in a million years.

So Stuart plugged in his phone and let it charge. It wasn't too long after that that Fern called. He could barely stand to hear her voice—he was going to cry, so he rushed her. And then he wished he could get her back. Weeks later, one of Abigail's cousins came by, reclaiming the cabin, and thinking he was a squatter—it was such a mess inside he could see why the woman thought that. There was talk of calling the police, but he said there was no need, he would be out by the next morning. That's when he left the cabin and moved into the Hampton Inn, using the last credit card that he had that was not maxed out or canceled, and charged his phone and sat looking out the window at Lake Superior, wondering if he dared go out there. He could see all his missed calls and texts, but by then they seemed beside the point. And Fern called again, that time with Levi. Stuart hadn't expected to feel what he felt. It was awful, he had let them down, and there was never, ever going to be a way to make it up to them, to take away what he had done. He missed Abigail desperately, and knew he would never stop thinking about the time they lost, the time that was wasted. He was so alone.

Was it worth it? He would have to say it was, despite the absolute hopelessness he felt now. He loved Abigail as much those last few weeks as he ever had. He could never go back to Tabitha, not like that. But he wanted to see the kids, those wonderful kids, and he wanted to see Levi become a bar mitzvah. He picked up the phone and called the airline. He would fly in for the big event. After that, well, then he might just let it all go.

~

When Tabitha got home, the TV was still on. Levi had dozed off and was leaning on Fern's shoulder. Fern was staring straight ahead, like he wasn't even there. Tabitha noticed that the house phone was on the coffee table in front of them.

"Did someone call?" she asked quietly. Levi was still on an assortment of different medications, and they made him tired, so finding him in this state wasn't surprising.

"What? Why?" Fern asked.

"No reason," Tabitha said. "Just that the phone is there, I wondered if it rang."

"Levi was going to order a pizza," Fern said quickly. "Then he remembered that we don't have any money."

"Oh," Tabitha said.

The intercom buzzed, and they both froze, then Tabitha went to it.

"Hi! It's Tabitha." She never knew what to say to the buzzer.

"It's Ron," the doorman said. "You have a guest. A male."

"A male?" Tabitha repeated, dumbly.

"Yes," Ron said.

"Does the male have a name?"

"Oh, let me ask," Ron said, and Tabitha rolled her eyes. She hadn't had a guest other than Rachel or responded to the buzzer in so long, it had thrown them all off. She had the well-formed thought that it would be a relief to not live in this building anymore. As nice as it was, something a little simpler might be even nicer.

Ron was back. "Yes, the male's name is Toby."

Tabitha wondered if Toby could hear the doorman talking. She decided that she didn't care. She also didn't care anymore that there was only that one working light bulb in the kitchen, she hadn't gotten around to replacing the bulbs yet, or that she had absolutely nothing to offer him except for ice water.

"Okay," Tabitha said. "Send him up."

She went to the front door and opened it. She didn't realize how much she wanted this, she didn't let herself even think this was a possibility. But still, maybe he was coming to tell her she was a thief and he wanted nothing to do with her. Or maybe he was coming to take back the money—which technically she could give to him, it was in her room. The elevator dinged and opened. He was the only one in it, and he hesitated for a second before stepping out into the hall.

"How did you find me?" she asked.

"I followed you," he said.

"Oh."

"For some reason, I didn't expect this, though," he said, waving his arms around. "Fancy."

"Yes, well, looks can be deceiving," she said. "Come on in."

He followed her into the dark foyer, where she did not turn on a light because it wouldn't work even if she did. They walked by the living room, where Fern was still watching TV and Levi was still sleeping. Fern had turned as far around as she could without disturbing Levi, but when she saw Toby, a stranger, she just shrugged and faced forward again. Maybe she thought he was a maintenance person or something. Tabitha led Toby into the dark kitchen. She flicked a switch, and the one bulb illuminated. She did not apologize for it. She opened the fridge and made sure he could see how empty it was.

"Do you want some water?" she asked. "It's all we have."

"Look, Tabitha, I didn't come here for a drink," he said. "I want to talk to you."

"I know, what I did is bad," she said. "Believe me, I know it."

"That isn't even what I came here to talk about," he said. "Well it is, but it also isn't. Yes, it's bad that you stole from an old lady, but the honest truth is she left it there for you to steal. You didn't take her wallet, or weasel her PIN number away from her. You took the money she put in front of you. This has been an ongoing battle I have had with her for years. Would I rather she saved the money for herself and eventually give it to Tara? Of course I would. But the truth is, she has plenty, enough to leave a nice amount to Tara and give some away. She thinks everyone is suffering, and she wants to be the one to help. You know how little girls want to be princesses? Well, my mother wants to be a fairy godmother. It is her fantasy, and if she can do it, I guess she should do it. The fact that you became involved, that you went to her apartment under those false pretenses and met her in the first place, well, that's just bizarre. But none of that is why I followed you home."

"Why then?"

"Because you walked away from me," he said. "And I didn't like that at all."

"I'm sorry," she said.

"The bottom line is: I don't care. I don't care about the bad things you did," he stopped.

She thought to herself, *If you only knew.* Then she thought, *No, you should know.*

"Let me tell you about all of them, and you can decide," she said, getting up to check on the kids before continuing. She lowered her voice. "Stealing is not the worst of it, believe me."

He raised his eyebrows. She motioned for him to follow her, back past the living room and the kids and into her bedroom. She was glad she'd made the bed that morning. She let him walk by her and then she closed the door so it was just slightly open. He stood waiting for an instruction of some sort.

"Sit," she said.

He did, on the edge of the bed. She sat next to him.

"You know what?" he said. "If this is going to be a day of confessions, can I go first?"

"You have a confession?" she said. "Sure, you can try to one-up me, but I don't think you're going to win."

"I'm not trying to win," he said. "And I'm not trying to one-up you. My point here is that we all have confessions to make. We've all done things we're sorry we did, things that if we could do over, we might do in a different way. Not a single one of us has a clean record. Not a single one of us is perfect."

"Okay, I'm interested," she said, but really she wanted to sit closer to him, rest her head on his shoulder. Or maybe his lap. His lap would be nice. "What did you do that you want to confess to me?"

"I have to warn you, it's possible that this is going to make you not like me," he said, so seriously that she started to laugh, but she realized he meant it.

"Really?" she said, not laughing anymore. What could he possibly have done? She was a little scared. She didn't want to not like him anymore.

"Here goes," he said. "Remember how I said there was an incident with my wife, and that's why we aren't together anymore? Well, that incident was me having sex with her cousin on a family trip. It is the worst thing I have ever done, and I still can't figure out why I did it. If someone had said to me, even that morning—no, make that an hour before it happened—that I was going to do that, I wouldn't have believed them for one second. I loved my wife. Our marriage was actually pretty good. We still had sex, we loved being Tara's parents. But that night, Tara wasn't feeling well, and Jane took her back to the hotel room. We were all in Cancun, celebrating Jane's dad's seventy-fifth birthday. Can you imagine the scandal? I mean really, and I was not *ever* the one in the middle of a scandal—before that night, that is. Jane's cousin had always been a little off. Maybe *off* isn't the right word. But something. She isn't married. She's used to getting a lot of attention from men. At first, I just thought she was overly friendly. That night, though, we had all been drinking. I drank way too much, I completely lost control of myself. She was so pretty. I hadn't realized how pretty she was until that night. She laughed at everything I said. She stood so close, then she was touching me, then we were alone. It was like she was irresistible, though I know that's no excuse. The thing is, ever since then, I can't put my finger on what was irresistible about her. She should have been fully resistible. I have gone back to that moment so many times, when I went from just being a cousin by marriage to kissing and then being alone in her hotel room and having sex. Jane couldn't find me, she was worried something happened to me. She thought that I drank too much and went swimming, or that someone abducted me. She had her mother sit in our room with Tara, and she went room to room. I had fallen asleep. I was naked. You can probably imagine what happened after that."

Tabitha felt nothing. That wasn't true. She felt everything she felt before, but nothing from his story. No dislike or repulsion. She simply didn't care that much. Or maybe it just seemed so unreal.

"Do you think there's a chance you were drugged?" Tabitha asked practically after a few seconds had gone by. It seemed like the obvious question. "By her or by a bartender?"

Toby hesitated, then he shook his head.

"Drugged or not I did it and I have to own it. Even if I had been drugged, and I have to admit I have considered that, I still did it. It is still something I did."

"Okay," she said. She was quiet for a minute. She didn't want to say that it was nothing, or, at least he didn't kill anyone. She didn't want to make it a competition. "Thank you for telling me."

"Oh, I get it," he said, sitting up. He had slumped over more and more as he talked, like the weight of what he was saying was pushing him down. But now he straightened and shifted on the bed. "You're going to be all polite, and then I'll leave, and that will be it. You'll never answer my calls and you'll never agree to see me again."

"Let me tell you my things, and then we'll see who never agrees to see who again," she said. She felt like she was playing a game. *How Honest Can I Be?* or *What Will It Take to Push You Away, and Can I Do It?* It was like Nora's Monopoly money—it felt real and not real. He sat back now, ready.

"I think I am responsible for my mother's death. She was very sick, she was going to die anyway, but I think I sped it up with morphine," she said. "And I think I may have killed someone I cooked for. I had a business, cooking out of my house, and it was late, I had finished for the night. They called, I agreed. The normal channels were not gone through. He had a peanut allergy but I didn't know, I used peanut oil. I think of him every day. I know he was in great trouble, but I don't know what happened. I never reached anyone."

"I hear a lot of 'thinks' and 'not knowing,'" he said matter-of-factly. "From what you just told me, it is also possible that you aren't responsible for any deaths. Am I hearing that right?"

"Well, I'm pretty sure I am," she said.

"You need all the facts," he said. "If there is anything I've learned, it's that you need all the facts."

"If you're pushing me to get all the facts, why don't you want them for yourself?" she asked.

He looked at her quizzically.

"The possibility of being drugged?" she said.

"No, it's too late for that," he said. "Believe me, it is too late. That fact wouldn't help me now. But your facts, those could help you. Here's a fact: there's a lot of peanut oil that will not cause an allergic reaction. I know, Tara has a peanut allergy. The doctor even said she could have certain oils and not have a problem. We don't do it—I don't dare—but did you know that?"

"I did," she said slowly. "I do. But I don't know exactly what kind of oil it was. I threw it out."

"Maybe it was the kind of oil that was okay," Toby said. Tabitha just shook her head. He got up, tentatively, and Tabitha thought he might be walking out. She didn't know Tara had a peanut allergy. She imagined Toby must have a zero tolerance level for any indiscretion when it came to food allergies. But he closed the door quietly and soundlessly rotated the lock. He turned back to her and raised his eyebrows. She nodded. She felt like this was their good-bye. There was no way in the world he would want to be with her long term now. No way. They had both done terrible things. Even so, she let him kiss her, all the time with her ear out for the kids. They kissed and kissed and eventually she began to cry. He was so kind, so tender. He looked her in the eyes as much as he possibly could. And she looked right back. There was nothing to hide from anymore. He knew it all. He didn't push to do more than kiss, and neither did she.

Eventually she stood and brushed her clothes to get the wrinkles out, not because she wanted to, but because she felt she had pushed it long enough with the kids. He did the same, and together they straightened the bed. She turned the lock and opened the door, tiptoeing out, a little afraid that Fern was going to say she knocked but no one answered, or that she would ask where Tabitha had been. But Fern was sleeping now, too, with her head leaning back against Levi like they were holding each other up. Tabitha looked at Toby, who smiled. He kissed Tabitha on the head, breathing in as he did. She closed her eyes.

"I'll call you," he whispered.

"I need some time," she said. "I have so much to sort through, and the kids need all of me right now. I don't want to drag you into it. I just need time to think."

"Okay," he said. "But I'm still going to call." He leaned in again to kiss her, lingering there. He was going to say something else, she was sure of it, but instead he turned and walked out. She stood there for a few seconds, thinking the house felt so empty, then she lay down on the floor in front of the kids and eventually fell asleep.

~

As promised, Toby called twice a day for the next week, and Tabitha didn't answer or respond; she simply didn't know what to say to him. But she missed him so much it hurt, which was a relief, because she thought she might never feel that way about anyone. She never missed Stuart this much. Did she ever truly miss Stuart? Toby never left a message. He just called and let it ring and then hung up, so the only notification she got was one that said Missed Call, over and over again, and, of course, the pleasure of seeing his name—Toby. On Friday, Toby called and left a message. She saw the phone ring and eventually stop, and that was all she expected, but the notification of Voicemail appeared, and she almost hit her head on the bookshelf, she stood up so fast. She immediately pressed "play"—she couldn't do it fast enough.

"Listen, I know you want time," he said, and he sounded as kind and sweet as ever, not mad or defensive. "But I have a problem, and that problem is named Nora. She misses you. She wants to see you and she doesn't know how to find you. She keeps referring to you as 'that dear girl,' but I know who she means, unless there are a number of strangers waltzing into her apartment, which I guess is possible, but not likely. She seems sadder than I've seen her in a long time. Please call me back. Please come see Nora."

Two requests, not necessarily connected. They could be, or they might not be. Please call me back was one and please come see Nora, the other. She could do one without the other, or she could do both. Today was the first day Levi was back at school for more than a few hours. He was talking more and more comfortably, though his face was so badly bruised, it was hard to look at. It was a deep purple, which was now speckled with a sickening yellow. He was going to see how long he could stand it, and she would pick him up when he called. But it would be just as easy to go from Nora's, really. She was about to go see her, she thought she would, and just deal with whatever she found when she got there, but as she was reaching into her drawer for a bra she touched the money. All of it. The shame she felt was overwhelming. She sat down on the bed. She couldn't go. She wouldn't go. Instead, she gathered the money, every last dollar, and she took it to the bank where she planned to open a new account.

Toby didn't call again. Not Saturday. Not Sunday. On Monday morning, when the kids were in school, Tabitha got dressed. She was supposed to have an orientation with the pest control company later that day, but she had a few hours. The relief she felt about finally making money was huge, and she sang a little while she chose jeans and a pink cashmere sweater. She grabbed her purse and walked out, turning right toward Walnut Street. She didn't let the actual thought of where she was going form in her head. She told herself she would just see where she ended up. But she knew.

When she got to Nora's building, she walked right in and to the elevators. She would feel better if she planned to return the money, but she felt pretty good that she didn't plan to take any more. Maybe, once she started getting a regular paycheck, she would be able to bring some back. If Nora didn't want it, at least she could leave it for someone else who might.

She opened the door slowly.

"Nora?" she called.

Tabitha heard footsteps and waited, surprised, since Nora usually called back. A woman dressed in teddy-bear scrubs came around the corner and down the hall. She looked stern.

"Yes?" she said.

"I'm a friend of Nora's," Tabitha said, realizing how disappointed she was. Did this mean Toby wasn't there?

"She's napping now," the woman said. "It took me a while to get her to relax, and we don't appreciate unannounced guests."

We or you*?* Tabitha wanted to ask. She had a vision of storming by the aide, of waking Nora and asking if she wanted a visitor now. Tabitha looked at the woman. "I'm sorry," she said quietly.

"Can I tell Nora who stopped by?" she said, continuing to talk in a formal tone.

"Tell her it was 'that dear girl,'" she said, stepping back into the hall.

The woman smirked at her, like she thought she was trying to be cute or something. She nodded and waited for Tabitha to be fully out before closing the door without a sound.

~

On the last day that Tabitha and her mother had an actual conversation, Tabitha did hug her. She walked over to her bed and leaned in, feeling the soft, light-purple cashmere of her sweater and thinking: *This feels surprisingly good, why didn't I do this more often?* Of course, she didn't know it would be the last time they would ever speak to each other, or the last time they would ever really touch, at least with any meaning. Tabitha had been mostly sleeping at her mother's apartment for the last few days, though she had hated it. They were all there, on a death watch, though they didn't know how quickly it would come. Even the kids had settled in, sleeping in the guest room, watching television shows endlessly.

On that day, Tabitha had sat on a chair at the end of her mother's bed. Her mother was sitting up, though she wouldn't be for much longer. She looked like a baby, or like a puppet with a big head as Levi had said once, with such strong emotion it had surprised Tabitha.

"I want you to know that I will be okay," Tabitha had said. She had wanted to say those words for a while. She wanted her mother to know. "I have a family. I will be okay." At that moment she'd had no doubt that that would be true.

It was just a few hours later that her mother's breathing became so labored, it was alarming. Should they take her to the hospital? They all wondered. It would have been one more in a long string of recent hospital visits that patched her up just enough to come home and continue to suffer. No, they all agreed. This time they were going to wait it out, see if she could pull through on her own. Really, it had already been decided, weeks before, but it was hard to not at least discuss the possibility again. The aide suggested that Tabitha call her mother's doctor to tell him what was happening. He agreed with their decision and prescribed liquid morphine, to make her comfortable, he had said.

They started giving it to her that night, little drops under her tongue. At first she took it like a little bird, opening her mouth and accepting it. Slowly she became less involved in the process, but she never fought it. It was surprisingly easy to give it to her. They were overly careful at the beginning, not giving her more than the label said, even if she became fitful before it was time for the next dose. Tabitha began to have trouble sleeping. She didn't want to do this anymore, but she felt so bad about feeling that way. She quickly lost track of the last dose, and then the next one. She wasn't sure when they were given, how much they were supposed to be. Had she just given her mother morphine? No, that was hours ago. But then she would give her a little and panic: Had it really been hours, or minutes?

She told herself everything would be better once it was over, and they could finally come together as a family when this wasn't pulling at them anymore. And pretty quickly her mother faded away. Nora couldn't rouse herself out of her stupor anymore when Tabitha called a loud, "Hi!" to her. She had always, always responded to Tabitha before, no matter how sick she was. At that point, though, she didn't react to her at all. She just lay there, and they could hear her breathe, every single breath.

In the end, Tabitha had no idea how much morphine her mother had. And in the end, it didn't matter, because by morning, Nora Michelle Taylor was dead. But it did matter. Tabitha went over it so many times in her head, had she or hadn't she given too much? She would never know.

CHAPTER TWENTY-TWO

On the morning of Levi's bar mitzvah, Tabitha woke up crying. She couldn't grasp on to what she was crying about. A dream? The fact that Stuart wasn't here to see this? The fact that she was so grateful that Levi was here and walking and talking and able to do this? She wasn't sure. Before she got out of bed, her phone rang. She didn't recognize the number.

"Hello?"

"Tabitha, it's Rabbi Rosen, I just wanted to let you know we are so happy about today, and we are here to help you with anything you might need."

Tabitha's tears hadn't really stopped before she answered, and now they flowed freely and heavily.

"Thank you," she managed to get out.

"I can only imagine it's a hard day for you," the rabbi said. "But I think it's also going to be a great day, a magical day, an awesome day, and we are so happy to be a part of it."

"Thank you," she said again, a little stronger this time. "We'll be there in about an hour."

"I'm looking forward to it," the rabbi said.

She got up and intended to go right to the shower, but she walked to Levi's room instead. He was fast asleep and had the same expression on his face he had when he was a baby. Tabitha sat gently next to him but didn't dare touch him, partly because he might be annoyed and partly because he was still sore. He opened his eyes.

"Hi," he said.

"Hi," she said, expecting him to yell and tell her to get out, but he didn't.

"Wow, I'm nervous," he said, sitting up. His bruises were more yellow than purple now, which she knew was a good thing.

"Don't be," Tabitha said. "It will be mostly just us, then lunch at Di Bruno's after—Aunt Rachel has that all set up. It will be a nice day."

Levi nodded. She got up and left him to get ready. As she headed to her shower she saw Fern, walking around her room in circles. She hadn't even realized she was awake.

"What's up, Fernie Bernie?" Tabitha asked.

"My leg feels better," she said. "But I just want to make sure."

"That is amazing news," Tabitha said. "Just in time for the big day."

"Yeah," Fern said. "Just in time."

~

Stuart Brewer woke up in a hotel room, and the first thing he did was look out the window, expecting to see Lake Superior. He never slept with his blinds closed anymore; he felt too hemmed in. But he didn't see Lake Superior, he saw the Delaware River. He sat up and cleared his throat. He had about an hour to get there, and he still hadn't figured out how he was going to do it. Should he call first? Just show up? Throw himself into the river and never go at all? He showered and dressed, went down for a cab, the whole time his hand was on his phone in his pocket, but he did not pull it out.

"Rodeph Shalom," he said to the cab driver.

He looked out the window as the cab took him north and eventually west. The cab stopped in front. The renovation, which was underway when Stuart left, was now complete. It almost looked like an entirely different place, at least from this angle. This moment, this event, was the only thing he had on his calendar—at all, for the rest of his life. Without Abigail out there somewhere—and since she had died, he realized that he'd always been aware that she was out there somewhere—he felt completely ungrounded. He swiped his last, barely working credit card and got out. He was going to see so many people he knew. He had no idea what Tabitha had been saying these past months. And none of it compared to what it would be like to face her.

He walked around the new grand entrance to the older one, which was grand enough for him. By doing that he avoided a lot of people, though as far as he could tell he didn't recognize any of them. For a brief moment he thought he might have the wrong day. He walked in and grabbed a program, saw he had the right day, then went to sit in the back with a yarmulke on and his head down.

They came in, and all he wanted to do was run to them, but he didn't; he stayed seated, pretending to be completely immersed in a prayer book. They sat in the front row. The seats filled in, but he noticed there was no additional family here, none of Levi's friends. Oh, he saw Butch off to the side, but that was it. The music started, and Levi was up there. He had grown, and Stuart could see there was something wrong with his face. It was discolored. He was glad to know about the bike accident or he would have really worried. Suddenly, Levi was saying something in Hebrew—this was it, and Stuart had the urge to slow it down. What was he going to do after this? But Levi saw him. He clearly saw him, and he stopped saying whatever he was saying. Now faces turned to see what Levi saw. Some looked right past him, but Tabitha noticed him. Her face completely changed when she spotted him. It was almost like all the muscles in her cheeks clenched up and twitched. Then she turned back toward the front of the sanctuary, toward Levi. She sat so straight that she looked uncomfortable. Levi stumbled, then used the yad to find his place. He kept going; his words were beautiful. His voice became stronger and stronger.

He came! Levi couldn't believe he came! He felt this might be his only chance to show his father what he could do. He had worked so hard for this, for this exact purpose. To prove to his father that he was worth sticking around for, worth being proud of, worth claiming as his son. He stood up straighter, held the yad as Rabbi Rosen had instructed him to do, and he read perfectly from the Torah, his inflections just right. He never wanted it to end. What would happen when it was over? Would his father disappear again? No, don't think about that. Focus. Read.

Fern couldn't stop looking at him. He looked the same, well, almost the same, but she felt uncomfortable, like he might not reach out and accept her into his arms the way he always did, or the way he used to. But she wanted to show him her leg was better! She couldn't wait to show him! And then something gloomy came into her mind. He never even knew her leg was bad, so he wouldn't care that it was better. How could she have lived through something so important, something so hard, completely without him?

Levi stumbled over his Hebrew words. He cleared his throat and started again. Fern turned her attention back to her brother.

Tabitha waited. It was ruined for her, but she did not want to ruin it for Levi. She sat, feeling like something was sticking through her middle, like she had been pierced, and she waited. She smiled when she joined the procession walking the Torah around the sanctuary, something they had practiced, and Stuart had enough sense to not join in. They all had enough sense to avoid his row. He just stood and watched. It was like she knew him and she didn't know him. When it was finally over and everyone crowded around Levi, Tabitha walked toward Stuart. She pointed toward the closest exit, and he followed her into a stairwell. She didn't plan to stay long—she didn't want Levi to notice she was gone—but she saw no other choice. To let him come and to not call him on any of it would be like letting him get away with something, and she couldn't do that.

She turned to Stuart, who was now sitting at the bottom of the stairs, his face in his hands. She hated him. There was just no other way to describe what she was feeling. She took a chance on him, and now she knew she had wasted her life. He never deserved her trust, and her love, and her hope.

"I don't even know where to start," she said, keeping her voice down and pacing. A few weeks ago, before the accident, this would have gone a different way, but now, now that Levi was okay, all of this mattered so much less. But still . . .

"Are you going to make me ask the questions?" Tabitha said. "Really?"

He didn't say anything. She felt that she could hear the seconds tick away; she wanted to be with Levi. She heard Levi laugh, and she relaxed slightly—he wasn't looking for her yet.

"Why are you here? Why did you come?"

"I was always going to come," Stuart said, more to his hands than to her. "What I wasn't going to do was stay away so long. When I left, I knew it would be some time, but I didn't know how long."

Ten questions were trying to get out of her mouth at the same time, and all she wanted to do was go back to Levi. She heard him laugh again.

"You know what? I don't want to do this now," she said. "I don't want to miss any of this."

"I have questions, too," he said dumbly.

"I want you to leave, but I can't do that to Levi. We will go back in, you will tell him he did a great job and that you're proud of him. You are not welcome at our celebration today. I want to meet you tomorrow at noon at Starbucks to talk this through. You can tell Levi you will celebrate in your own way if you want to, or not. That is up to you."

Stuart nodded, and she expected him to dispute something or fight for something she hadn't given him. Instead, he stood and reached for the door, pulling it open, and Levi's voice spilled toward them. Stuart stepped back and let Tabitha go first, then they both walked toward their son.

~

Tabitha entered Starbucks half expecting that Stuart wouldn't come. She never specified which Starbucks, though she hoped he would know she meant the one a block away from their apartment, that was always *their* Starbucks. She had no idea what he did after the ceremony yesterday or where he slept. She didn't try to call him or email him, not that she would have gotten through, but she was aware of how done she was with him. She did hope to get some answers, though, and would be disappointed if she didn't get the chance. Mostly, she wanted to have a chance to tell him how horrible what he did was, not just to her, that was bad enough, but to the kids. She hoped she'd be able to keep it together. She knew how hard it was to get through to him sometimes. Well, most of the time. Somewhere, deep down, she also knew she was not entirely innocent in everything that transpired between them. She walked in and ordered a latte, paid, stuffed a big tip into the jar, and sat at the long table toward the back. She faced south, so she couldn't see her building, but she knew it was there. The kids were happy and safe inside.

"Hello," he said, startling her. She didn't see him walk in.

"Hi," she said, standing, but immediately regretted it, because it seemed like the normal thing to do, and this was anything but normal. She sat back down. He looked around and chose the seat across from her. She was glad. She didn't want him to sit next to her. He looked pasty and he had circles under his eyes.

"So after all that, you went to Abigail?" she asked first, because even if that wasn't where he had been recently, it seemed that was where he had set out to go.

"Yes," he said quietly.

"Why the threat?" she spit out—she just couldn't wait, couldn't take the time to build up to it. He looked at her, surprised, that wasn't what he thought the next question would be. "The threat! At the bottom of the note!"

"Yes," he said slowly, sitting up a little straighter. "I know. I wrote that at the last minute. I was terrified. I was also surprised you had been so forceful that night. I don't know what I expected. I think I always thought if I was ever completely honest, if I ever laid it all on the line, you would understand, or, at least I would have a clear way out. But that didn't happen, and I was scared, and mad. I just wrote it. It was the last thing I did before leaving the house. I guess, if I really had to say, I wanted you to remember that you had done some bad things, too, Tabitha, that you weren't perfect either."

"It was awful," Tabitha said. "Possibly the worst part of your leaving."

"Well, I think that is very telling then," Stuart said, sounding a bit more like himself. Tabitha felt a need to take back control of the situation.

"So, you went to see Abigail, and then she died," she said, not exactly cruelly, but not kindly.

"How did you know that?" he asked.

"The better question would be, 'What have you been doing since then?'"

"Nothing," Stuart said. "Basically, staying away from society. I completely fell apart. I haven't worked. I haven't done anything."

"That sounds luxurious," Tabitha said coldly.

"Not really," Stuart mumbled.

"Well, I would have liked to do that, too," Tabitha said. "Just drop out. But I couldn't. Because I had kids to take care of."

She took a sip of her latte, but it didn't taste good anymore.

"Well, thank you for that," he said. "I am so sorry, for everything. So sorry that she was always pulling at me somehow, even when I didn't realize it. When I had the chance, this last chance, I just couldn't pass it up. I had to be with her and try to give her what I could."

"Interesting that you say that," Tabitha said. "Because I have reason to believe this was not your first visit to see her. I have reason to believe this was ongoing."

He just looked at her.

"Was it?"

"Well, to answer what I think you are really asking, which is: was I unfaithful before, the answer is no, if you are thinking of it in a physical way," he said honestly. "But yes, it's true that about two years ago I found her. I ran into her, but I was always looking for her, long before that. And she let me see her, in the hospital, that was it, but nothing else happened then, the times I visited her in the hospital, that is. Not until this time."

Tabitha didn't know what to think or feel. She didn't know if that was a relief or not. She just dropped it all into the same pot—her failed marriage.

"You were so dishonest with me, Stuart, from day one," she said. "You were never available to me, never."

"I wanted to be," he said. "But she was always out there."

"She stole from me," Tabitha said.

"No, she didn't, she stole from me," Stuart said.

"The way I see it, the things she took were meant for me, at least given the choices you made. For example, your love," Tabitha said unkindly.

He nodded.

"Our money?"

He nodded slower this time.

"Our kids' happiness?"

He didn't nod.

"My sanity?"

He looked away.

"I want a divorce," she said, too loudly for a crowded place like Starbucks.

He didn't meet her eye but he nodded.

"I want to sell the apartment."

Another nod.

"I want the kids to go to public school next year."

"Yes, to all of that, if you think that's best for them. All I want at this point is to be a part of the kids' lives, on your terms," he said quickly. "That's really all I want."

She wanted to scream at him. How dare he ask her for anything? He was never Tabitha's for the taking! Why did he ever pretend he was? Why did he ever let her think he could love her fully, when he was always going to love someone else more? She wanted to spit at him, to kick him in the shin. She wasted so much of her life on him—so much. But then, the image of Levi crying in the rabbi's office flashed into her mind followed by the memory of Fern walking in curious circles yesterday, making sure her leg was feeling better. And she knew she wouldn't change a thing, even if she could go back in time, even if she could be transported to the moment she first set eyes on Stuart. She wouldn't change a thing if it meant not having Levi and Fern. She felt her body relax, which surprised her. She tucked her right leg behind her left leg, not that she was ever really going to kick him, not here at Starbucks anyway.

"Please," he said. "I did so many bad things. But please, don't cut me out of the kids' lives. I know it's a lot to ask considering . . . what I did. I never meant to hurt them, as strange as this sounds, this was never about them. I want to be their father. I want to be a part of their daily lives."

She hadn't realized how much she was hoping for that, despite everything. It was one thing for her to feel abandoned by him, she would get over it, but it was another thing entirely to have Levi and Fern feel abandoned by him.

"So, I'll set that all in motion, okay?" Tabitha asked. "The divorce, the sale of the apartment, finding them a new school, everything I mentioned."

"Okay," he said slowly. "But what about the kids? Please, Tabitha, I don't want to leave here until we talk about that, until we come to some agreement."

She took a deep breath. She could make him wait, she could hold that over his head while she got everything else set up, just in case they disagreed, but did she even have grounds to keep him from seeing them? And how would that help anything at this point? It would only further hurt the children.

"Fine," she said.

"Can I take them out to dinner tonight?" he said, sitting forward on his chair. "I am desperate to be with them."

She still needed to know some things. She wasn't ready to have this conversation be over, either.

"Let me think about it," she said. "But first, I have to know, what was the threat about? What would you have told people I did? What, specifically, were you referring to?"

He sat back in his chair and pulled his jacket over his lap.

"I was crazed," he said, like that explained it. "I hadn't thought it through."

"I don't buy that," she said. "Clearly you were referring to something."

"Do you remember those last few days when your mother was sick, and we took turns sitting with her? I was so unhappy then. I tried to hide it, and I felt I owed it to you to do all I could to make things okay between us. So when your mother was so sick and so demanding, I didn't think you could take it anymore—it had already gone on for so long. That's when we started talking about the morphine. You were so tired, so out of it. And I wasn't positive, because we never talked about it, but I was fairly sure you had lost track of how much your mother had had. I could see the panic in your eyes, I saw you reading and rereading those labels over and over. But I was the one who gave her too much. When you weren't looking, when you were with the kids or taking a quick rest those last two days, I slipped her more and more morphine. I had heard stories of people lingering for weeks and sometimes months. She wasn't really living anymore, she wasn't happy. I felt, and still feel, it was a kindness. I thought maybe if she died, the pressure would ease a little and we could be happier together. We could go back to our apartment and try to enjoy our lives. But that wasn't the case, that was never going to be the case."

Tabitha felt herself relax even more, though for a brief moment she wondered if she should be even angrier with him for doing that. How dare he? But really, despite everything, he was now giving her gift after gift.

"Oh, okay," she managed to say. "I wasn't sure which *thing* you were referring to. I thought maybe the peanut oil."

"The peanut oil?" he asked, like it was the last thing he would be referring to. She couldn't believe it. "No, not the peanut oil. We don't even know what happened with that. Are you still thinking about it?"

"Forget it," she said.

"Well," he said, gathering his jacket like he was thinking of getting up soon. "Thank you for letting me sit with you and talk about these things. I feel like I've been to a confessional."

She took a good look at him, and the truth was, he did look a little lighter.

"Okay, you can take the kids out tonight," she said quickly, before she changed her mind. But as soon as she'd said it, she did change her mind.

"Terrific," he said, just as she was about to take back her offer. She could see his eyes brighten with sudden tears that he didn't wipe away. "That is terrific."

"Look, honestly, I'm not sure about this," she said. "I don't want to make this easy for you."

Stuart nodded, letting a tear that welled up in his left eye fall down his cheek before he wiped it away. She thought he knew exactly what he was doing, which made her angry all over again, but then she thought of the kids.

"If you ever, ever hurt those kids, or disappoint them, or disappear again, or not show up when they are expecting you, I will stop letting you see them," she said. She knew his next line would be something about how he's the lawyer, at least that might have been his next line before, but right away she could see that he wouldn't say that today.

He just nodded again.

"I'll have them in the lobby at seven," she said. "We can sit there and tell them what's going on before you take them out, okay? We have to start to be honest with them. They deserve to know."

"I agree," he said.

She felt herself softening toward him, but only for a moment. She had already given him the best thing—time with the kids. She was still so angry—for all of it—but she was so grateful about the morphine. As completely awful as it was that Stuart had used her confusion about it against her, at least she didn't have to live with the guilt anymore. She watched as Stuart got up. He hesitated for a second, this was the time he would lean in for a kiss or a hug, and the physical realization that that would never happen again, that they would probably never touch again, had a palpable presence. She still didn't know where he was staying or what he would do now. She did know that she would start the divorce process the next day. She threw out her latte and bought a Starbucks gift card. She shouldn't be using Nora's money, but she reminded herself that she would soon have money from her share of the sale of the apartment and health insurance through her new job—something they were surprisingly generous about. She didn't even care anymore if she ran into someone she knew in her new office.

She crossed Eighteenth Street to the small grocery store and was happy to see Marlon at his usual check-out lane. He didn't have a customer at the moment, so she entered his line. He raised his eyebrows as if to say, *"Where is your stuff?"* She handed him the gift card—her first official payback effort.

"Thank you for helping me that day," she said. "You will never know how much it means to me."

"Oh, thank you," he said, smiling big. He blushed a little and looked down. "You didn't have to do that."

"It is my pleasure," she said, before waving and walking out. If she did that once a week for a year, she would have paid everyone back and then some. Next, she would do something for Julie, though she would be a hard one to repay. She'd have to think about that. Tonight she would make a new list of all the people she wanted to thank—of course Holly would be on the list, and the rabbi. And one day, when she had more control of her finances and maybe even had some to spare, though she wasn't sure when that day would come, she would do something to repay Nora. That would be a very good day.

As Tabitha entered her lobby her phone pinged. She looked at it and saw she had missed two calls from Rachel, but there was a text.

I have good news! it said, with the emoticon of a baby face. Tabitha looked up, she wanted to tell someone, she wanted to be with Rachel. She would see if she was free for lunch. Today, Tabitha would treat her. She would recreate the lunch they had at the Dandelion, minus the champagne and plus the kids—present and future. And then she decided this day, the one right here, was a very good day.

~

As soon as the kids were out the door with Stuart for dinner, Tabitha walked to the corner of the lobby and called Toby. The discussion with Stuart and the kids had gone surprisingly well, they were just so happy to know the truth, she realized. And now she wanted more than anything to speak to Toby. She thought he might not answer—she would deserve that—but he did, on the first ring. Or at least someone did. The phone was answered, but nothing was said.

"I need help," she said, hoping she was speaking to Toby. "I need your help."

"Well, that's a coincidence," he said. "Because I could use some help myself."

As soon as she heard his voice she knew she wanted to be with him more than she had ever wanted to be with anyone.

"I'll help you," she said. "What can I do?"

"For starters, you can agree to see me," he said.

Tabitha laughed.

"That's easy," she said.

"And you can spend another hour at a hotel with me someday," he said.

"Easy again," she said, smiling so big she thought she must have looked like a clown.

"What can I do for you?" he asked.

"Well, you can start by coming over," she said.

"Done."

"And I need you to call someone for me," she said, not smiling anymore. "I have to find out what happened to my customer. The one with the allergy who ate the peanut oil."

"I will gladly make that call," Toby said. "And I hope what we find out is good news. If it isn't, I will be there for you. I will always be there for you."

"When can you get here?" she asked. She thought she'd run upstairs and change, maybe shower. She'd blow-dry her hair. There was a long pause, and she wondered if he was reconsidering. And suddenly there he was, walking into the building holding his cell phone to his ear.

"Have you just been waiting out there all this time?" she asked, confused. "Were you stalking me?"

"Let's just say I've spent a lot of time at the Fox & Hound lately, hoping you would show up."

"I'm so sorry," she said, ending the call and talking directly to him. "I just needed some time to think and work things out, and I think I have, or at least I have begun to."

"I am so glad to hear that," he said.

They went upstairs together, and without a word, Tabitha dug out her file. She went right to the number she had as a contact for the couple. She handed it to Toby. She did not want to change her mind. He took it and dialed, slowly, then let it ring.

A man answered, Tabitha could hear his deep voice. She held her breath.

"I'm looking for Ethan, is he there?"

"That's me," the voice said. Tabitha could hear it through the phone. She eased herself to the ground.

"I'm calling from the Food Allergy Association to see if you would be willing to take an important survey," Toby said.

"Sure," she could hear Ethan say on the other side of the call.

"So, this is the right Ethan, the one with the peanut allergy?"

"That's me," he boomed again. "Hey, how did you get my name?"

"There's a data bank," Toby said in his own kind tone. Nobody would ever doubt him.

"Oh sure," Ethan said. "Now?"

"Hang up," Tabitha whispered giddily.

Toby pointed to the phone as if to say, *"Are you sure?"*

She nodded her head enthusiastically.

"We're just lining up participants now," Toby said. "I'll have someone call you to set up a good time."

"Sounds good," Ethan said.

"Thank you so much," Toby said, and ended the call. He eased to the floor next to her. She didn't say anything for a full thirty seconds, and she could see Toby was looking at her, ready to explain what just transpired, as if she needed it to be explained to her. She felt so much building up, a sigh, tears, laughter. It all came out at the same time, and as they sat there, mostly laughing, Tabitha could feel her worry and fear slipping away. She hadn't quite realized how much that had weighed.

"Now, I need help," he said seriously.

"I thought I already helped you. I let you come over, didn't I?" she said, teasing, not wanting to give in to his apparent mood shift yet. She still wanted to be here, focusing on this monumental discovery. She had that feeling she got when she carried one of the kids' backpacks that was so ridiculously heavy that she had no idea how they didn't bend over backward when it was on them, and then they took it from her for the last block, and she felt propelled forward by the sudden lightness. But Toby had given this to her, so she would try to give him what he needed.

"Okay, okay," she said now. "What can I do to help you?"

"I don't know exactly," he said. "I have to figure out a way to live with myself after what I did to Jane. I need to do that so I can honestly and openly move on—with you. Telling you was helpful, but how can I make it better? How can I pay my penance?"

Tabitha thought again about her question of whether unsolicited drugs played a part. But she could see that he and Jane were long past that at this point. What he was really talking about now was making amends for the havoc it all caused.

"Have you talked to her? Have you said you were sorry?" Even as Tabitha said these words, she wondered if they were the right ones. Apologizing was one thing, opening the door to mending their marriage was another. Though she was pretty sure that wouldn't happen.

"I have," he said. "And she is happy now. She just got engaged. I just found out a few days ago. I am really, really happy for her."

"Wow, that's something," Tabitha said. "That's a big something. But I do have this idea, which is to do something nice for someone once a week, or maybe even once a day for an entire year. I don't mean my kids, or you, or Rachel, because I always want to do nice things for you guys, of course, but I mean the people I took from, stole from really, and the people who helped me, and also people I don't know, strangers who need help."

Toby didn't say anything, and she thought he must be thinking she was even more of a crackpot than he realized, thinking that if she went out and sprinkled glitter around, things would magically be okay.

"I want to start now," he said, surprising her. "What can I do?"

"Really?" she said, sitting up. "I don't know. We could go out into the Square, and you can do something for a homeless person, maybe. You've already started to do that, now that I think about it, by giving away the bread, so that counts for something. I would say we could go out there now and offer a few sandwiches, but I still haven't gone shopping, and I have absolutely no food in the house."

"I do," he said, pointing toward his bag. "I've got a bunch of things from the buffet at the bar—I know how much you like that. Tacos, chicken wings, you name it. The spread isn't quite what it was, now that football season is morphing into basketball season, but it still looked good."

She smiled. That was classic Toby, as good as naming his dog Yo-Adrian. How lucky was she that she was going to get to be an official part of it all?

He jumped up and held out his hand to her. She let him pull her to standing.

"Are you game?" he asked.

"It was my idea, wasn't it?"

They put on jackets and he grabbed his bag. He was quiet in the elevator, and when they got out in the lobby, he stopped.

"This is silly, right?" he said. "Giving a homeless person tacos and wings is not going to take away the fact that I slept with my ex-wife's cousin and ruined our family unit for my daughter. It is not going to fix the fact that I took an oath that was meant to last a lifetime, but in a matter of minutes I hacked it all to hell. Nothing is going to take that away."

"No, of course not, nothing is going to take that away, but I have this idea now that we take and we give, right? And it isn't always to the same people. Sometimes you take from one but give to another. So, you did some bad things, one really bad thing. I did some bad things, though, I am so happy to say, I did not do as many bad things as I thought I did—though still plenty. If we try to even that out with good, that is something. Really, that's all we can do."

Toby smiled. He put his arm around her as they walked out into the frigid night air. Tabitha wondered if the kids were having a good dinner with Stuart. She hoped so. She hoped he would come back to Philadelphia and be a part of their regular lives. It sounded to her like that was his plan. She hoped she would be able to find a small apartment, keep her new job, be with Toby. Across the street she stopped and leaned into him. He leaned back.

"Dare I say: 'And they lived happily ever after'?" Toby said jokingly, his lips on the top of her head. She could feel them move as he talked.

"No!" she said, pulling back. "Don't ever say that!"

"Why not?"

"Nobody lives completely happily ever after—haven't you realized that by now? The pressure is too great. I don't want that pressure. How about: 'And they were not perfect, and they had many things to atone for, but they had a lot of fun and could eventually afford light bulbs and everything bagels.'"

He nodded and pulled her back toward him.

"I can live with that," he said. "Now let me go start this long process of canceling out the bad with a little good. I wish I had brought blankets for someone. It is so cold out here."

"Next time," Tabitha said. "We'll do that next time."

ACKNOWLEDGMENTS

Thank you to my wonderful agent, Uwe Stender. We've been working together for over eleven years now, and he continues to support and amaze me all the time. Thank you also to everyone else at TriadaUS—there is no better agency to have behind me.

Thank you to my thoughtful and smart editor, Jodi Warshaw at Lake Union Publishing. This is our third book together, and I couldn't ask for a better guide and advocate. Thank you to developmental editor Jenna Free for working so hard to make sure Tabitha's story was told in the right way, and never, ever, pushing me to move away from what I believed that should be. Thank you to Marlene Kelly, Amazon's marketing director, for working to capture the essence of *Not Perfect*, and to Nicole Pomeroy, Amazon's production manager, for doing so much to keep the book on track. Thank you to designer Emily Mahon for a fabulous cover. Thank you to Ginger Everhart, who copyedited the book with spectacular care, and Caroline Sibila, who proofread it with a kind heart and a sharp eye for detail. Thank you to Gabriella Dumpit, Amazon's author relations manager, for continuing to work her magic behind the scenes. To Dennelle Catlett and Kathleen Carter Zrelak, thank you for working so hard to get the word out about my novels—I love working with both of you.

Thank you to Jennifer Weiner, Meghan Burnett, Melissa Jensen, Petula Dvorak, Kathleen Woodberry, Jane Greer, Andrea Cipriani Mecchi, and everyone who has supported me along the way. I would also like to thank Cynthia Mollen for her insight into some of the medical details in the book (if I made any mistakes, they are mine). Thank you to Nina Pritzker Cohen for always wanting to talk about my books in depth. Thank you to Meg Mitchell Moore for her kindness and enthusiasm. And thank you to Melissa DePino—I miss her when I'm writing solo, but she is always there for me to bounce an idea off of or to give me great feedback. I can't wait to write the next one with her.

Finally, and most important, thank you to my family, especially my husband, Craig, and my children, Alice and Arthur. They fill our house with love and inspire me in everything I do.

ABOUT THE AUTHOR

Photo © 2016 Andrea Cipriani Mecchi

Elizabeth LaBan is the author of *The Tragedy Paper*, which has been translated into eleven languages; *The Grandparents Handbook*, which has been translated into seven languages; *The Restaurant Critic's Wife*; and *Pretty Little World*. She lives in Philadelphia with her restaurant-critic husband and two children.